They Started Walking
to Their House When,

without warning, a barrage balloon, punctured
by pieces of shrapnel, came hurtling from the
sky. Kitty was terrified to see that shining,
hissing monster rushing headlong at them
down the street, its sides heaving, its steel
cables trailing over the rooftops and scraping
off tiles that flew in all directions. Bill flung
his arms around Kitty and pulled her down
against a brick wall. As they crouched there,
Kitty wept and shivered with fright.

"Oh, take me home, Bill," she wailed.

He picked her up like a child and carried her
across the road to the house. Once home, he
placed her in an armchair, wrapped a blanket
around her and made her a cup of tea. But
still she shivered. She could not stop herself;
it was convulsive shuddering that shook her
frame. Then, as Bill went to fill a hot-water
bottle, the pain came. It was a hot, searing
pain which coursed fiercely through her body.
"Oh, dear God," she cried, "it's the baby, it's
coming too soon!"

Books by Lena Kennedy

Kitty
Maggie

Published by POCKET BOOKS

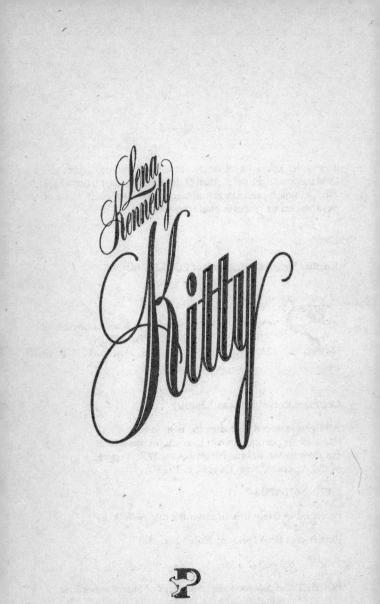

Lena Kennedy

Kitty

PUBLISHED BY POCKET BOOKS NEW YORK

This novel is a work of fiction. Names, characters, places and incidents are either the product of the author's imagination or are used fictitiously, and any resemblance to actual persons, living or dead, events or locales is entirely coincidental.

Another *Original* publication of POCKET BOOKS

POCKET BOOKS, a Simon & Schuster division of
GULF & WESTERN CORPORATION
1230 Avenue of the Americas, New York, N.Y. 10020

ISBN: 0-671-42558-7

Published in Great Britain under the title *Nelly Kelly*

First Pocket Books printing November, 1981

10 9 8 7 6 5 4 3 2 1

POCKET and colophon are trademarks of Simon & Schuster.

Printed in the U.S.A.

*In fond memory of
Cornelius Erin Kennedy,
my late father*

Contents

Kitty

CHAPTER ONE
Kitty

The children stood in two long lines before her. Her
name was Miss Victoria. She was an unmarried, middle-aged lady. Her name was reminiscent of a certain
English queen, as was her appearance with the high,
stiff lace collar clasped tightly around her scraggy neck.
Her steel-gray eyes looked down sternly over the tops
of the pince-nez; a thick blanket of propriety kept out
all signs of human emotion.

This was their last day at school. In the large, bleak
hall the boys stood in one line, the girls in another.
Some were tall and gangly, having outgrown their
strength from lack of vitamins; some were small and
scrawny, having ceased to grow for precisely the same
reason. All were poorly dressed. The girls wore ragged
pinafores and faded dresses, the boys patched trousers
and old jerseys. They were all just fourteen and ready
to leave school and disappear into a chaotic, depressed
world. They had spent most of their time in these cold
marble portals of the County Council school, and today
was crucial, as they were to receive a precious testimo-

1

nial from the headmistress. That piece of paper was very important in those years of poverty. It meant survival. It could determine whether you got a good job or remained unemployed.

First came the pep talk. They must, Miss Victoria instructed them, above all things be clean, punctual, very tidy and obedient to their employers. With this lesson in mind, each one had to step forward in turn.

There was no one to wish them well, no congratulations, no fond farewells. Life went on in the rest of the school as usual. The drone of children's voices from the nearby classrooms wafted across the hall as lessons were learned, as they always were, by rote.

"Step forward first, John Hill." Miss Victoria's voice rang out sharply. A skinny, tousle-haired boy took a step toward her. "Let's see, now," the headmistress continued. "We must not forget you're unintelligent. Let's say you're good with your hands."

She scribbled this down on the report, which she then held out in front of her. The boy blushed scarlet. Grasping the paper, he turned and shuffled out of the door, into the world outside.

Everyone was dealt with in this way. Once all the boys had been attended to one by one, Miss Victoria turned to the girls.

"Anything particular you would like to do, Mary?"

Mary was a large, blowsy girl with a grubby face. She already had a child at home—reported to be by her own father. She giggled. "Dunno. Up the factory, I think."

Miss Victoria sighed. "Strong-willed girl," Miss Victoria said out loud as she wrote down Mary's report.

One by one she ticked them off until she came to a thin little girl whose gangly legs emerging from under her faded pinafore made her look taller than she was. "I want to write," Kitty announced loudly, sticking out her chin determinedly.

Miss Victoria looked quite taken aback. What insolence, she thought. This motherless child had hardly ever come to school, and here she was saying she wanted to write. "Well," she answered sarcastically, "you'll have to learn to type. Your handwriting is atrocious."

She wrote down Kitty's report. "Unpunctual and needs discipline." Then, with a twinge of conscience, she added: "Might do well in connection with books."

The next day, Kitty and Mary wandered through the narrow back streets on their way to the city in search of a job in a clothing factory. Mary swung her fat hips from side to side, complaining loudly about her sister, who had refused to recommend her for a job at the match factory where she worked. But Kitty just looked straight ahead and hardly listened to her friend. She was worried about Bobby, her small brother, who had fallen on his arm that morning. She knew she should have taken him to the hospital, but she had been so anxious to get a job she had not. It had only just stopped raining, and the pavements were wet and shiny. Kitty's feet were cold. She had forgotten to put new cardboard in the soles of her shoes, and water seeped in, soaking her stockings and chilling her toes.

The girls had walked a long way before they finally came to the right address. They climbed a steep, smelly flight of steps to the factory and entered the small office. Mr. Fox, the boss, had a bald, shiny head and bulbous, red-veined eyes. As Kitty and Mary came in, he looked up from his desk. Kitty clenched her hands nervously.

Mr. Fox surveyed the pretty girl in front of him. She hardly looks fourteen, he thought. "What's yer name?" he shouted.

"Katherine," she murmured softly, "but I'm called Kitty."

"Right," he said, "I'll call yer Kitty then."

Sweat dropped from his broad forehead as he squinted at Kitty's precious testimonial. "Books?" he roared. "Won't get much bleeding time to read books here. I'll put yer on pulling bastings. Eight bob a week, time-and-a-half overtime.

"Now, what about the other bugger?"

Kitty's smile lit up her face. She had a job.

Without bothering to look at Mary's testimonial, Mr. Fox shouted out: "Harry, some kids to 'elp yer." A small wiry man came into the office and took the girls off to sit in the busy workroom on a low wooden bench next to an enormous old-fashioned lift. Icy gusts of wind constantly blew up the lift shaft, making Kitty's limbs numb with cold as she sat pulling out the basting stitches from huge gray woolen overcoats. The coats were so weighty it took both Kitty and Mary to lift one off the pile.

Mary sat with her legs wide apart. A musty smell came from her as she used plenty of swear words to tell the surrounding male population what she thought of them. The cutter and tailor stood nearby snipping material with large shears. They made joking comments about the girls and encouraged Mary all the more.

Kitty was self-conscious and embarrassed. The pile of coats grew and spread out all around her. "Get a move on, Kitty," said Mr. Fox whenever he passed.

As fast as they could Kitty's thin little fingers picked and pulled at the strong white basting cotton amid the whirr of the sewing machines, the babble of conversation and the harassment of those waiting for her work. Kitty's life in the sweatshop had begun.

The long piercing wail of the hooter cut across the dull humming of the sewing machines. It was six o'clock on the dot. With a clatter everyone downed tools and started rushing for the exit.

Kitty was still sitting on her bench. There was a buzzing in her ears even though the machines had stopped their chugging. Over the long day she had got used to the noise, but now she was suddenly aware of it again.

She looked for Mary in the crowd of workers but could not see her. She got up with stiff legs, and her back ached as she started her way down the flight of stairs with everyone else.

It was all confusion on those steps as she got caught up in the homeward rush. Boys tore past jumping two at a time; fat women carrying large handbags waddled down more slowly. Kitty was pushed and shoved. Everyone had a desperate urge to get out into the cold air. It had been so hot in the building.

Kitty pondered on the finality of it all. These people did precisely the same thing every day. She felt trapped and had a dull ache inside her. Her sticklike legs ached, too. She felt as though she had been walking about all day rather than sitting down.

Suddenly she felt a hefty blow in her side as Mary pushed past her. "Going home on the tram," yelled Mary as she ran down the steps. "Scrounged a penny off some fella up there." Her wide shape disappeared from view.

At last Kitty reached the bottom of the stairs. It was nearly dark outside. She stood there in the night, watching the trams trundle past. Inside, passengers were fighting tooth and nail for spaces. Kitty had no money for a tram and would have to walk home, but she was not sure of the direction.

After a moment of indecision she began to walk back the way she had come with Mary that morning. She flinched nervously as she passed the dim street corners where the unemployed men loafed. None had jobs and many had no home.

Trying to ignore the shifty characters, Kitty relived the first day at work in her mind. She could still hear the guttural voice of the guv'nor and taste the bland bread and margarine they had all eaten at midday, perched high at the tables.

There was no use complaining; at least she had got a job. But the thought of returning to it the next day made her heart sink.

She was glad when she finally reached her own little street with its row of gray-brick terraced dwellings. It was in the heart of the East End, in Hoxton. It was a working-class area, and the houses were small and cramped. Most of the families living in them were so large there was no room inside for the kids to play, so their mothers would push them outside whenever they could.

The kids were still out in the road, playing in the light of the streetlamps. One mob chased another in a hectic game of tag; little girls played hopscotch in chalk squares. They yelled and screeched and fought with each other. The noise was almost deafening, but Kitty found it a refreshing sound after the dull humming of the sweatshop.

At the end of the street was Kitty's home. It was different from the other slum houses, which looked right onto the road, for there was a cobbled entrance that led to a dark yard where several carts were tipped up. Their shafts loomed balefully through the gloom.

A coster's barrow obstructed Kitty's path as she picked her way through the yard. She wove around it to find the familiar doorway that led up a flight of uncarpeted wooden stairs to the rooms where her family lived. Once inside, she sighed with relief. She was so scared of the yard when night came. Every single day of her life, she dreaded going through that dark yard. Often an urchin would be hiding in the shadows to jump out at her yelling: "Yah, yah, I'm the bogeyman!" And Kitty would nearly jump out of her skin. They were only small hooligans, so why she let them bother her she never knew. But she was always afraid when she entered Daly's Yard, as it was known in the street. Not that it belonged to her family; they had never owned much. They only rented the rooms over the stables for three shillings a week. That was all they were worth, Kitty was quite sure, and even that was not paid regularly.

Kitty's confidence returned as she climbed the stairway. Her heart no longer raced as it had. Reaching the top, she undid the wooden catch on the gate to the landing. It was strange how that homemade gate affected her. It was like a gateway to safety. Once she had opened it and was onto the landing she felt secure. Dad had made the gate from an old orange crate. It had originally been built to prevent the baby falling down the stairs, but there was no need for it now. The baby had died, and that same year her mother had also died of pneumonia.

The big front living room was cold and empty. Kitty's brother and sister were probably still playing in the street. Maybe Bobby's arm had got better, she thought optimistically. Dad had not arrived home yet. She knew she had to hurry to build a fire and get the kettle boiling. Dad would be cold and tired, too, when he came in.

She removed her coat and set about making a fire. Once it was blazing, she swept the hearth. Dad liked to see a tidy hearth. Then she put the heavy iron kettle on to boil.

In a bowl of cold water she washed the potatoes and placed them in a saucepan by the kettle. Dad loved spuds boiled in their jackets. Next, Kitty poked into the wire-covered "safe" that hung on the wall outside the door. In the days before refrigerators this contraption kept food cool. She was pleased to find a bit of marge. Perhaps Dad would bring in some bread and sausages —then they would have a real feast.

She crouched beside the fire, her thin face worried and anxious, her wispy chestnut hair hanging over her face in an untidy array. Her dark green eyes became misty as she thought about that lovely character who was within her during quiet moments.

Her name was Nelly Kelly, and she had fair cork-screw curls and always wore a pretty dress. Kitty now had her away at boarding school with a whole wardrobe —a real gymslip, plimsolls, navy knickers, the lot. The rest of the dormitory was admiring her party dress and she had just returned, all suntanned, from a holiday abroad.

Sitting silent and still, Kitty could see Nelly having a good time with the rest of the girls in that big boarding school that Bessie Bunter attended. Yes, that funny fat girl who was always in the comics that Kitty read was there, too.

Kitty's daydream was suddenly shattered by the noisy arrival of Noni and Bobby, her sister and brother. Little Bobby looked pinched and pale, and he had a big woolen scarf wound around his arm.

"Bobby's arm don't 'alf 'urt 'im," Noni declared. "Mrs. Brown said yer ought to take 'im up Slope. Disgraceful, she says it is, a little boy going about crying all day."

Kitty gently unwound the scarf from Bobby's arm. It looked twisted and swollen. The boy's long lashes dripped with tears. "I want me mum," he whimpered.

A lump came to Kitty's throat. "Stop sniveling!" she shouted impatiently. "I'll take you up the Slope."

Giving Noni instructions to mind the spuds, and without even a cup of tea inside her, Kitty took Bobby by the hand and started off for the casualty department of the Metropolitan Hospital. It was quite a way down the main road, and Bobby whined all the time.

The casualty department was called the Slope because the entranceway ran at a steep angle so that the stretcher bearers could run quickly down it.

Once they were there, Kitty and Bobby sat in a long line with all the other casualties—a motley crowd of emergency cases of cuts and bruises and broken bones. They all sat miserably waiting their turn, many periodically wincing or moaning with pain.

Bobby looked paler and sicker than ever, and his arm had turned a blue color and was very swollen. When they finally reached the door of the surgery, he began to vomit.

One nurse ran out with an enamel dish while another dashed to get a mop.

"Who is in charge of this child?" roared the sister. Kitty stood up. "I am," she said. Now the doctor had arrived. "Great Scot!" he cried. "This child has a broken arm. Why wasn't he brought here before now?"

Kitty's lips trembled and tears sprang into her dark eyes. "I had to go to work," she murmured.

"Oh, dear," muttered the doctor, wiping his brow as he stared down at the young girl. "Where are your parents to let a little lad suffer all day?"

"My mother is dead," said Kitty, "and Dad's not home from work yet."

The doctor looked bewildered, but then his voice became kinder. "Take this girl up to the canteen with you," he said to one of the nurses. "Get her something to eat and I'll fix up this boy."

It was half-past ten when they left the hospital. Bobby now had his arm in plaster and looked much more cheerful than before. They had both been given hot Bovril and biscuits in the staff canteen and been fussed over by the nurses there.

"It's nice in the hospital," announced Bobby as he trotted beside Kitty's weary legs. But Kitty did not answer. She was so tired that all she wanted to do was get home and go to sleep; otherwise she would never get up in time for work in the morning.

CHAPTER TWO
The Blouse

After a few weeks the terrors of the sweatshop were not so great for Kitty. She became quite used to most of the other workers there, and she didn't mind the cheekiness of the cutting-room boys who whistled and chanted little ditties about her: "Kitty Daly, with a hole in her sock, a hole in her shoe." Kitty would hurriedly pull down the tattered skirt of her dress to hide the ladders in her stockings and run nervously past them, pretending not to hear the last line—"Kitty was the prettiest girl down our alley."

Flirtation and vanity were still very new to her, and anyway, it was the dirty old rats that concerned her most. She did feel a certain amount of pity for them, for she was a great animal lover, but all the same, these huge gray creatures that crept up the lift and darted through the factory terrified her. The women leaped up onto the benches, shrieking loudly and holding up their skirts, while the men chased the rodents with shears. When the rat catcher was called, he placed huge trails of evil-smelling jelly around the lift. Then the rats would get stuck on it and lie there dying all day. Sometimes there would be a female, and its babies would come out and lie beside their mother. The smell was always disgusting, but no matter how hard she tried, Kitty could not get her mind off the baby rats who now had no mother. She would stare anxiously at them until she got a thump from the nearest worker.

"Get on with the bastings, Kitty. We're working; never mind about the bleeding rats."

But that sour, rank smell would stay under her nose even when she left work and walked home.

Her companion at night on the long trek home was a faded-looking woman in her late thirties named Lilly. She was a charge hand and had taken poor little Kitty, as she referred to her, under her wing. She was of a very nervous temperament, and having someone to walk home with at night was a Godsend for her. She had been crossed in love, and Kitty was subjected to the lengthy tale of her unhappy love life, hearing a fairly long installment every night. But Kitty didn't mind. She found it strangely stimulating, like reading a romantic novel. Most of Lilly's friends were sick of her tale, having heard it many times, but to Kitty it was all new, and she showed great interest. This really pleased Lilly, who wore gloves and hand-knitted jerseys and pleated skirts. She had a kind of genteel air about her, but she never had any time off work, for she had to support her aged mother. Kitty looked forward to those long walks through the cold winding streets listening to her new friend. She would say good night to Lilly at the corner of the street, for Lilly lived in a more middle-class district a little further on.

"I'll get you taken off bastings, Kitty," Lilly said one day, "seeing as you are so nervous of the rats."

Thus Lilly's support got Kitty put on "specials." This seemed like a big jump up, but in fact she was just an errand girl and chased about all over the factory looking for certain garments whose production had to be speeded up. There was also a good bit of profit

attached to this job, as Kitty soon discovered. At
lunchtime she was in charge of bringing in the food
from the shops. She would go around with a list and the
other workers ordered what they fancied. It was mainly
a pen'orth of chips, for that was the cheapest, but
sometimes it was hot pies and saveloys and fishy kosher
foods that the Jewish tailors enjoyed.

Each day from quarter to twelve to quarter past,
Kitty would wait in the warm atmosphere of the
fish-and-chips shop, watching the chipman shovel up
the long golden potatoes into paper bags. Fat Mary
would often come with her and the two young girls
would treat themselves to a pen'orth to share—for
there was always the odd half-penny left over, and
sometimes two or three. Then often on Fridays, when
the wage packets were opened, the men would throw a
sixpence in her direction. "Treat yourself, Kitty," they
would say.

While still sewing, the men would hold up their heads
and swallow whole raw-looking fishes. They looked like
the sea lions Kitty had seen on a visit to the zoo. Kosher
food seemed very strange and smelly.

After they had finished eating they threw the wrap-
pers and remains of the food on the floor for a
stupid-looking boy to sweep up with a large broom.
Kitty became wise to the job and copped all the odd
pennies and tanners, spending them on chips and
chocolate bars for herself. She was not hungry anymore.

The other workers relied on her, too; she had a good
head on her, they knew. "If you ask Kitty to take a
message, she always gets it right," they would say. "Not
more than two pints of piss high," said one uncouth
fellow, "but she's all there, our Kitty."

Often there was a very important task for Kitty to
attend to, like popping around to Kate Ward's old mum
with a shilling to buy milk. Kate was a short, robust
little woman with an endless number of children. She
was kind and humorous, and pressed trouser seams all

day with a big flatiron. On Fridays when the pay
envelopes came around, Kate sang popular songs, and
all the rest of the factory workers would join in.

"Kitty, darling," Kate would say, "take this around
to me mum, and don't say nothing to no one."

Full of importance, Kitty would nip down the road
and hand the coin wrapped up in a piece of newspaper
to the bedraggled old woman who sat on the doorstep
nursing Kate's latest baby.

So in some ways Kitty's was a special job, and it
suited her. She loved listening to people talk about
their lives, and in this job she saw more and heard more
of what went on around her than anyone else in the
factory. It all fed her lively imagination.

Kitty had started work in the same old black dress
that she had worn for her mother's funeral. It was long
and hung around her legs unevenly since she had lost
the tie-belt. The dress did not get washed very often,
but black did not show the dirt anyway.

But one day Kitty arrived at work in a white blouse
and black skirt. It was the same old black dress, but it
had been turned into a skirt and washed, ironed and
shortened. The blouse had cost three shillings and
elevenpence from Levi's, the local shop. It was snow
white with a Peter Pan collar and three pearly buttons
down the front.

Kitty was so proud of that blouse. She had looked at
it in Levi's window for a long time before she got up
enough courage to ask the price. Now that she was
earning, she had two shillings pocket money each week.
She had agreed with Dad that out of the eight shillings
she earned she would give up six for her keep. He said
he would buy the other children some strong boots for
school with the money, and Kitty was perfectly happy
with her cut.

When she asked the price of the blouse, Mrs. Levi
had replied: "It's three shillings and elevenpence, dear,
and a good bargain."

Kitty's face dropped in disappointment. "Sorry," she said, "I haven't got enough money on me."

"How much have you got?" asked Mrs. Levi, anxious not to lose customers.

"Two shillings, that's all," replied Kitty unhappily.

"I'll tell yer what I'll do with yer," gabbled Mrs. Levi. "Pay two bob of it, and I'll save it for you. Then next time you come in, you get it with another two bob and a penny change."

A smile lit up Kitty's pale, worried face. "Can I do that?" she asked.

"Of course you can, darling," said the old lady kindly. "And you're gonna look real nice in that white blouse. Gonna be a pretty girl when yer growed a bit."

Feeling very excited, Kitty handed over her two shillings. Then she kept her secret safe for a week. The next weekend she paid off the rest of the money to Mrs. Levi, collected the blouse and rushed home ecstatic. She washed her black dress, cut it into a skirt and put elastic in the waist.

On Monday morning, beaming with pleasure, she went off to work as excited as a young deb at her first ball. When she reached the factory she took off her shabby coat and walked leisurely through the workroom, displaying all her new finery.

"Christ!" yelled the cutter. "Just look at our Kitty!"

"My, my, very nice," said the forelady.

All through that day, Kitty wallowed in the pleasure of being admired. At lunchtime Kate handed her an apron. "Put on my old pinny," she said. "You don't want to mess up your nice new blouse with those greasy old chips."

Kitty was completely spoiled that day. Everyone made a fuss of her. It was something that had never happened to her before. The warmth that came from being loved and admired at that grimy old sweatshop passed through Kitty like rays from the sun. In all her short life she had experienced only nagging misery and worry—over the housework, or over the kids whenever her mother had been ill and her Dad so careworn. The unhappiness that had built up inside her like a huge canker was now slowly beginning to disappear. Her cheeks filled out and she developed a saucy grin that made two dimples form on each side of her mouth. She even hummed tunes as she trotted up and down the stairs from eight in the morning until the end of the day.

At home, however, things had gone from bad to worse. Noni did not have the slightest idea about keeping the place clean or caring for Bobby. She loved her little brother and was always taking him to play the endless street games that he liked. But she was placid and plump and never cared how untidy either she or the home was.

After her mother had died and while she was still at school, Kitty had done all the cooking and most of the shopping. The family's staple diet was pease pudding and faggots from the cookshop. But now that Kitty was working, Noni was supposed to organize the meals during the week, and she was always too busy playing after school to remember. She and Bobby snatched meals at the pie shop of pie and a bowl of green liquor made from the eel water and colored with parsley. Luckily, in spite of its appearance, it was quite nourishing, and a ha'p'orth of liquor was often the staple diet for most of the kids in the street.

Another of Kitty's previous errands had been humping fourteen pounds of coal home every other day from the woman down the road. Now it was Noni's duty to get the coal, but very often she forgot, being too busy playing hopscotch or tag in the street. So as well as the food cupboard and the outside "safe," the coal cellar at home was nearly always empty.

Since Noni hardly ever prepared the meals, Dad began to spend more and more time in the local in the evenings. Kitty began to dread returning from work to that cold, untidy, lonely room with the litter on the table and the old fireless grate. During the week she would often eat only bread and margarine when she got home, as she had no energy to prepare a meal herself.

On Saturdays Kitty would valiantly try to clean up the week's accumulation of mess. She swept the floor and dusted the battered furniture. She wiped the table and then prepared for the weekly baths and wash. After placing the old tin tub in front of the fire, she filled it with water that she had carried in buckets from the end of the yard and heated on top of the stove. First Bobby was dumped in and thoroughly washed as he squealed and yelled like a stuck pig. Then in went Noni, who blew bubbles with the soap and larked about so much that Kitty always got frustrated and cross with her.

Finally it was Kitty's turn. She would wash herself thoughtfully and carefully and then sit by the fire to dry off.

When she was dressed again, Kitty would collect more water and do some washing—vests, socks and shirts—and then hang it about the fireplace where it dried in no time.

On weekends Kitty would prepare the meals, so the family got more nourishment then than they did during the week. On Saturday evenings, with sheets of newspapers as a tablecloth, they would all sit down to a slap-up meal of pigs' trotters, boiled spuds and cabbage. Sometimes they had skate, if the fishmonger had some going cheap.

Kitty was happy then, when the family ate together in front of a blazing fire. It reminded her of when her mother had been alive. After the meal they would eat oranges Dad had bought from the market stall and sweet nougat from the blind man who came into the pub at lunchtime.

Dad liked the kids to be in bed early on Saturday nights so that they would be up bright and early for Mass the next morning. Noni and Bobby did not mind; they would sit up in bed enjoying the goodies Dad had brought them and fooling around.

Once the younger kids had settled down and Dad had retired to the pub, Kitty would get out her books and comics and cuddle up in the old armchair in front of the fire. Of late she had tired of Bessie Bunter and the girls of St. Cliffe House and was finding more stimulation from boys' comics—*Gem*, and *Magnet*—for her heroine, Nelly Kelly, was now becoming a bit of a tomboy. In her imagination Kitty had recently taken Nelly to a cricket match and, after reading *Treasure Island*, on a long sea voyage.

When Dad returned home after the pub had shut, he always found little Kitty looking exhausted with dark shadows under her eyes, still sitting in the chair and reading, her legs pulled up, her bony knees hugged tight against her small breasts. "Come on, gel," Dad would say gently. "Time for bed."

His young daughter would look up at him, smiling, still completely immersed in her dream world. She was a good girl, his Kitty, thought Dad, but he was never quite sure how much of her attention was elsewhere. Since his beautiful wife had died so tragically, Kitty had coped well—despite her age. She was like a second mother to the youngsters and she did a good job keeping house—much better than Noni. But there were times when her mind seemed so far away, so distant.

"You're a foine gel, Kitty, but odd," he would say as he kissed her good night.

And still Kitty's eyes seemed not to focus on him before she turned to watch the dying embers in the grate.

CHAPTER THREE
A Political Problem

Sunday was always an important day. Dad rose very early and gave the kids cups of tea in bed. Then Kitty had to get Noni and Bobby clean for ten o'clock Mass.

Noni dressed in a clean frock and a straw hat bound with a green ribbon. Kitty always had to insure that Noni's knickers were pulled up tight and secured with a safety pin. But however carefully she fastened them, by the end of the day Noni invariably had her bloomers at half-mast, as Dad would remark. Somehow one part of them would be hanging down; either the elastic had gone from one leg so that the material swung to and fro over Noni's chubby knee, or the top elastic had gone so the child would frantically try to pull them up with awkward twists of her body, as though she had St. Vitus' dance.

Bobby would look smart with his dark curls all brushed down and wearing a blue serge suit—worn only on Sundays. And Kitty would see that both had their boots laced up tidily. All set, Dad would proudly lead the younger ones down the market street to the Catholic church.

Since she had been working, Kitty had not been able to go to Mass with the rest of the family. She had too much to do at home. She would go later, sometimes catching the last minutes of the service while sitting in one of the pews at the back; sometimes meeting the others as they came out of the church; and other times just waiting quietly on the step outside the pub while Dad had his after-Mass drink inside.

Kitty liked the church, but she could not abide the long Mass. The unintelligible drone of the Latin tongue annoyed her. Never having attended a Catholic school, she could not understand the words. She would kneel and rise with the congregation, never knowing why. But she always looked in wonder at the beautiful circular window above the altar. It really thrilled her. It was made up of purple and gold stained glass and depicted lots of kneeling saints and flying angels. While the Host was being offered up to God and a holy silence reigned throughout the church, Kitty would be concentrating on the window, wondering what the saints and angels were doing. The tinkling of the Communion bell would lift her spirits and she would imagine she had wings and was floating over the heads of the congregation.

On her tardy way to church Kitty would often see a girl who lived in the same street. Her name was Flossie Brown. She came from a family of thirteen children, and Kitty used to wonder how they all managed to squeeze into their two-room house and scullery.

Mr. Brown, the father of those thirteen children, was seldom home. He worked long hours as a French polisher in the furniture trade, and he liked to have a drink in the pub on his way home in the evenings. When he did eventually arrive back at his house, there was rarely a place for him to sit down because there were so many children. He was a tiny man, soft-spoken and humorous. When the house was particularly crowded with his own children and their friends, he often clambered up onto the stone copper in the corner of the scullery and, with chin on his hands and elbows on his knees, he would try to sleep amid the clamor of all the young ones sitting and playing on the floor.

All the members of Flossie Brown's family were always very clean, and every day their back yard displayed long lines of snow-white washing flapping in the wind. Mrs. Brown was a large rosy-cheeked country woman who spent most evenings in her front room ironing. She would heat the flatiron and spit on it vigorously as she pressed all the small trousers and shirts and dresses so that each of her children could go to school neat and clean.

Whenever Kitty saw Flossie Brown scurrying off down the road on a Sunday, she always wondered where the other girl could be going. She would walk along behind her trying to think where it might be—not the Oarsmen's Mission, not the Sally Army. Where could she be bound for?

One Sunday Kitty's curiosity got the better of her. Gathering up her courage, she caught up with Flossie. "Where are you going?" she asked timidly.

Flossie was about the same age as Kitty, but plump and fair and adult in her ways. "To the barves," she replied primly. "I go regular, every Sunday."

"Why can't you wash yourself at home?" quizzed Kitty.

Flossie's mouth dropped open in surprise. "You must have a barf," she said. "You smell if you don't have a barf."

"Can I come with you?" Kitty asked. All thoughts about getting to Mass had disappeared. The idea of doing something different for a change was very exciting to Kitty.

"Well, you're supposed to take your own soap and towel," said Flossie. "But if you've got tuppence you can hire them. Also, you'll need another tuppence to get in," she informed Kitty in a businesslike manner.

Kitty hesitated for a second. She had a threepenny bit which was meant for the church plate and a few pennies in her coat. She would take a chance, she decided, and go to these barves that Flossie seemed to enjoy so much.

They soon came to a large, grim-looking Victorian building whose green-and-white tiled corridors echoed coldly as the two girls walked down them. Flossie bossily guided Kitty through the turnstile. An irritated-looking woman glared at them from a small window. "First or second?" she snapped.

"Second class," Flossie replied.

The woman handed Flossie a ticket, and then Kitty.

"My friend," said Flossie haughtily, "wants soap and a towel."

Kitty handed over the extra tuppence and was given a hard white linen towel and a small square of green soap. Her heart pounded. Her knees felt weak with the excitement of it all.

The two girls sat silently on a long wooden bench. Other people who sat in front of them would now and then get up and disappear into another room from which came lots of noise and clouds of steam. Then a gruff voice roared: "Next!"

"Now, Kitty," said Flossie, jumping to her feet, "don't forget what number you're in, and then we can make sure we come out together."

Kitty nodded anxiously as Flossie disappeared from sight.

"Next!"

It was Kitty's turn. She got up and advanced slowly into what looked like a marble cell in the middle of which was a huge deep bath. Steaming water rushed from a pipe, pouring into the bath at a terrific rate.

"Come on!" snapped a stout woman with a purple face. The sleeves of her overall were rolled up to the elbow. "Get in! Don't dawdle. And don't lock the door—you kids lark about too much. Get it over, gel."

She closed the door and left the terrified Kitty alone with all that water.

Bravely, Kitty undressed and tentatively dipped her big toe in the water. It was very hot.

Suddenly Flossie's voice came from over the walls of the cell. "What number are you, Kitty?"

"No. 5," said Kitty, looking up at the number on the door.

"Good, I'm next door, No. 6," returned Flossie. Her voice had a comforting effect on Kitty.

"I can't get in it, it's too hot," she called back timidly.

"Call out for more cold, you silly cow," cried Flossie. "Like this." In a loud voice she yelled: "More hot for No. 6! Now you call out for cold, Kitty."

Kitty's thin voice tinkled up over her cell door. "Will you put more cold water in No. 5, please."

Flossie roared with laughter, but it had worked, for the attendant's voice growled: "Say when," as a great volume of cold water shot out of the pipe into Kitty's bath.

"When!" cried Kitty, having at last mastered the problems involved in having a bath.

Soon she was immersed in the steaming water. All around her she could hear intimate conversations going on between the other people in the cells, and much singing of popular songs.

She splashed the hot water over her skinny limbs and lifted one leg high in the air to see the effect. Why, her skin looked a different color! She suddenly felt so relaxed. She lay back and rested her head against the side of the bath. For the first time ever, Kitty experienced the satisfaction of a good, hot, luxurious soak.

Every Sunday from then on, Kitty went to the barves instead of going to Mass. She had to keep it a dark secret from Noni, who was a terrible telltale and would cause trouble if she could. Dad would be upset about Kitty missing church altogether, and Noni knew that.

Back at home there were still plenty of domestic

upheavals. Noni refused to take any responsibility or
help Kitty out very much, so Kitty had to cope on her
own. It was hard not having a mother to depend on or
to confide in, but at least she had her friends at the
sweatshop.

After being worn every day for two weeks, Kitty's
lovely white blouse had become a little grubby. Kate
Ward said in a motherly fashion: "Wash it out tonight.
Get some warm soapsuds to soak it in. Put it on a
hanger to dry overnight and then wear your old jumper
in to work tomorrow. Bring the blouse, and I'll iron it
nicely for you."

That evening Kitty washed the blouse carefully and
hung it up as Kate had advised. But the next morning
she woke up late and rushed off to work, forgetting to
take the blouse with her.

"Never mind," said Kate. "Bring it tomorrow."

But when Kitty returned home at dusk, she found
Noni dressed in the beautiful white blouse, playing tag
up and down the street with a mob of kids.

Kitty was overcome with rage. She dashed at her
sister and tried to pull the precious garment off her. But
Noni was sturdy and fought back violently until the
blouse was in ribbons.

"Ow, leave me alone!" howled Noni, struggling
under Kitty's grip.

"You spiteful cow, Kitty," yelled a neighbor. "Leave
your little sister alone!"

Before Dad had reached the entrance to Daly's Yard
that night, he was informed of the scrap by the nosy
neighbors in the street.

"Dearie me," he said later to his two daughters,
"little birds in their nests don't fight, and so brothers
and sisters must love and respect each other."

The girls stood before him, red-eyed and ashamed,
scratched and bruised from their battle.

"Now both say you're sorry," Dad said. "And Kitty,
I'll see you get a new blouse."

Kitty and Noni never got on well together. Noni

always seemed to resent the position of authority that
Kitty had inherited on their mother's death, and Kitty
was also probably a little too bossy and heavy-handed
with her younger sister. Little Bobby, on the other
hand, was a favorite with everyone. The only boy, he
was the apple of Dad's eye, but, although he was the
baby, he was never spoiled enough to ruin his good-
natured ways. It upset Bobby to see his sisters fighting,
and he frequently distracted their attention while they
were brawling just to make them stop. He was a good
boy, everyone agreed.

Dad never did buy Kitty a new blouse, for he spent
all his money too quickly being overgenerous with the
hangers-on at the pub. Dad had a regular job as a
navvy and had never had a day out of work since he had
come over from Ireland, as he would proudly announce. But he was one of very few who did have work
during the Depression. He was also rather fond of beer
and the gee gees that took most of his wages, but he
always made sure his family had food—even if their
diet was sparse and plain. It was more than what most
of the children in the street got.

Immediately after school there was usually a general
exodus of local children down to Daddy Burt's Mission,
where they were given free food.

"Going up to Truss," they would shout as they
dashed out of the school entrance, "Truss" being short
for one of Father Burt's Trusthouses. Father Burt was a
great philanthropist who did much good work in that
poor area of London.

Kitty had been to the Truss only once in her life
during the school holidays. She had taken Noni and
Bobby with her—they all wanted to see what it was
like—and they had queued for an hour outside the
doors. They stood their ground against all the rough
children who fought and swore and persecuted the
more timid ones.

When the doors opened there was a great rush,
everyone pushing and shoving to get seats on the low

benches by the long wooden tables. Once they were all settled, a prayer was said.

The very hungry children waited expectantly for the meal to arrive. Kitty watched one girl of about twelve in charge of four or five brothers and sisters, and some of the families seemed to be made up of sixteen or even seventeen ragged little children.

Finally a man came along and placed a tin plate containing pie and potatoes and a slosh of brown gravy in front of each child. At the word "Go," the kids scoffed down the food like pigs at a trough. Those who finished first larked about, shouting loudly, pinching the others' food and throwing around spoons and plates.

Kitty was horrified by the sight, and she never went back again.

Recently Kitty had begun to take quite a pride in her appearance. After her weekly baths her skin felt fresh and clean. She set her soft chestnut hair with clips, put a small kiss-curl stuck down with sugar water on her forehead and wore a round slide that she had bought at Woolworth's. Although she was very slim, her breasts had grown and her hips filled out to form a pleasing figure. Kitty did not own many clothes but she always made sure that the ones she did have were clean and tidy.

The boys on the corner gave her wolf whistles when she walked past, but Kitty ignored them and strode on. No low-life was going to influence her, she decided, not like poor Mary, who was now expecting another baby and had got the sack from the sweatshop because of it.

It was about this time that she made friends with Kunner. The name was Yiddish for Anna, but everyone called her Kunner in such an expressive way that it sounded like a rude word. This was probably because she was generally disliked by her workmates. She was classed as a "sweater" because she was greedy for work, always on the look out for an extra penny.

Kunner was an odd-looking woman in her thirties who sat on a high stool, with her head down and her shoulders rounded as she worked. She had short legs that were always crossed and high insteps that bulged out under the straps of her surprisingly smart shoes. She always wore red—a red high-necked jumper and either a red pleated skirt or a tight straight skirt that showed up her fat bottom and bandy legs. She wore silk stockings with seams down the back, and before leaving each night she spent a lot of time making sure they were straight.

Kunner rarely had any conversation with the workers around her, except to argue about the price of the work. But to Kitty she was always gracious. She offered her matzos spread with white butter, which Kitty found strange but very appetizing.

Kunner's task was to line the handmade waistcoats. She was a fine needlewoman and expert at her job.

At that time unions were frowned upon by many workers, as well as by the bosses. The defeat of the general strike had left its mark, so anyone who had a steady job would hang on to it at all costs. But the tailors' union was growing in strength among the foreign tailors. Many of the Jews from the East End had strict socialist principles, having been students of Marx and influenced by the Russian Revolution. Kunner was one of these, and her unpopularity was due partly to this fact as well as her argumentative nature. She shrewdly noticed that Kitty was a bright little girl and soon set about using her.

"Kitty, my dear, do us a favor," she said one day. "When you go down to the basement, ask Mick for his union dues. Do it quietly and don't tell anyone, and on Friday I'll give you a tanner. When he gives you his threepence, put it in this little box and keep it in your apron pocket."

So Kitty collected the union dues first from Mick and then gradually from the others who were recruited by

Kunner. It had to be done secretly, as the union was forbidden in the factory. Kunner managed to recruit many more men than women, for the women were rather suspicious of such goings-on.

In a small notebook, Kitty kept an accurate record of all the money she collected.

"You little wonder, Kitty," Kunner would say as she gave her a tanner every Friday.

During the lunchbreaks Kitty would sit with Kunner and talk about socialism with her. She was curious about other people and different ways of thinking, and she wanted to find out all about this movement that gave equal rights to rich and poor. Kunner loved to educate her little disciple and surreptitiously gave her Communist pamphlets to read.

Kate Ward noticed their friendship and took Kitty aside one day. "Don't get too thick with Kunner, Kitty," Kate said.

"Why not?" demanded Kitty, annoyed at Kate's interference.

"Well, she's political," said Kate, "and you don't know what she might get you into."

This advice only made Kitty all the more interested in Kunner and her secret goings-on. So when Kunner asked her to go with her to a meeting on Friday, Kitty was pleased to say yes.

After work they set out for the meeting place—a room off a dark alley behind the church at Bethnal Green.

Kitty found the evening very enjoyable. A lot of people made speeches from the platform, and during the interval everyone was served buns and a cup of tea. She liked the atmosphere because it was so free and easy, and even though she didn't understand much of the talk, she found it very stimulating. She also liked the buns.

Kitty decided then that she would go every Friday. Before long she had absorbed the socialist doctrine and was often getting into heated arguments about it with her workmates at the factory.

Kitty had been working in the sweatshop for nearly a year, and Noni was now almost fourteen and about to leave school and start work in a box factory down the street.

Since there would be no one at home to look after Bobby when he returned home from school, it was agreed that he would be cared for by Nan—Kitty's late mother's stepmother—thus taking a lot of responsibility from Kitty and giving Nan a small subsidy and Dad more time in the pub. They would all miss Bobby, but he wouldn't be far from home.

Nan lived only a few streets away from Daly's Yard. Her stepdaughter's sad death had upset her, and she did her best to give the family extra treats; but she was very poor and getting on a bit, as well as having her own family to look after.

Kitty was very fond of Nan. If anyone had ever shown her any real affection as a child, it had been Nan. When things had got really bad at home, the girl would escape around to Nan's to find her sitting on the doorstep if the weather was fine. Nan's thick curly hair would be piled on top of her head, her dark gypsylike eyes twinkling in amusement at the antics of the street population.

"Come here, darling," Nan would say as she embraced Kitty. "Just look at what fools they make of themselves." Nan would point to two ridiculous women arguing over their children.

Nan did not belong to the East End. She came from an old French-Canadian family and had come to London in service. In her youth she had been very beautiful, with dark skin and black hair, and her vivid personality easily won the heart of the strong wild Irishman who became her husband.

But he was gone now, and she sat reading the books

she had collected throughout her life and watching the world go by.

On the doorstep, Kitty would snuggle close to Nan and listen to her fascinating tales of her childhood in the wilds of Canada. When Kitty visited Nan her heart was uplifted and her imagination was well catered to.

She always recalled that warm day when Nan was not there on the doorstep when she arrived. The front door was shut tight. Kitty's heart thumped as she peered down the grating into the basement kitchen. A strange sight met her eyes. Three well-dressed women sat around the table while Nan, dressed in a bright shawl, laid cards out in front of them.

Kitty was terrified, and she crouched outside for about ten minutes until the grand ladies had left. She dashed into the house.

"Nan! Nan, are you all right?" she cried.

"Sure, darling, what's the matter?" Nan said, comforting her.

"I saw all those ladies playing cards," gasped Kitty.

Nan pulled Kitty onto her lap and held her tight. "Nothing to worry about, darling," she said. "Just some extra pocket money from those ladies. They come from the house where I used to be in service. I tell their fortunes every now and then. It's something I inherited. Perhaps I'll teach you one day."

The warm love that Nan gave Kitty was very much appreciated, and Kitty received an education from her that no school could ever have provided. And now Kitty knew that Bobby would be better off being looked after by Nan rather than being allowed to run wild in the streets after school.

Kitty's original income had increased to twelve shillings a week, and with the odd tanner she made with her willing ways, she boosted her pocket money quite a bit.

She began to buy new things to wear, as well as badly needed items for the home. One of her first investments was a new coat from the tallyman.

The tallyman was a very slick, smooth-faced gentleman called Mr. Mac. He always wore a bowler hat and rode around the streets on a bicycle with his ledger book under his arm. He would knock on a door discreetly and usually had to wait for some time before a small child appeared.

"Me mum says she ain't in," the child would announce.

"I know she's in!" the tallyman would holler. "Tell her to give me a few bob off the bill if she's short."

The child would disappear and a harassed woman would come to the door and haggle on the doorstep with Mr. Mac, who would refuse to budge until he had been paid.

Kitty often watched these dramas from afar, wondering what Mr. Mac carried in the big suitcase strapped to his bike. No tallyman ever knocked at the Dalys' door, for Dad would roar like a lion: "I'll have no bloodsucking fellow at my door! Be off!"

Kitty noticed that Flossie Brown always had a good coat or dress, and she asked her, on one of their Sunday visits to the baths, how she could afford them.

"Don't be daft, Kitty. How can you get good clothes if you don't pay for them weekly? The fellas won't look at you unless you're a bit smart," Flossie informed Kitty authoritatively.

Flossie was short and very dumpy, and Kitty did not think she looked so great. All the same, she did often admire the things Flossie wore—in particular, her best Sunday coat with a fur collar.

Flossie decided to take Kitty in hand. "Tell you what, Kitty, I'll tell old Mac to knock at our door. Don't matter as long as you give the money to me mum regular."

So Kitty got her coat. It was identical to Flossie's, except that it was the rusty color of brick rather than a Conservative blue. But both had little fur collars—coney, according to Mac, but even Kitty knew that for that price it was just rabbit.

She was so proud of that coat! She waved her hair and put the kiss-curl on her forehead and walked proudly through the market showing it off.

She did not wear the coat to work, but she wore it to the meetings with Kunner.

"That's right, Kitty," said Kunner, admiring the coat, "keep yourself well togged. It goes a long way."

Kunner always carried a book with her and often spent the lunchtime reading. She belonged to the Foyles Book Club and received a copy of the current best-selling novel every month for the price of two shillings.

"Don't make them dirty, and I'll lend them to you," she said to Kitty.

So Kitty moved into the world of great literature, and Nelly Kelly faded from her mind as she wallowed in the new excitement of fiction and politics. In between books, Kunner continued to feed her with Communist literature.

On her way home from work Kitty's mind was never quiet. She would struggle with ideas about equality for rich and poor and how it would be achieved. Only by revolution, she was sure. She had just seen a film in which the freed people of the land marched with the aristocrats' heads on sticks. She was certain that she would be marching and singing as they did when the revolution came, and probably Mr. Fox's head would be on a stick.

When Kitty was sixteen, the Party members were very keen that she sign up with them now that she was old enough. Kitty was quite eager to do so.

"Yer father'll slaughter yer, Kitty," Kate Ward warned. "Told yer not to get mixed up with that cranky red cow."

But Kitty still enjoyed the Friday evening meetings at the Party headquarters. It was really the social life that she liked the best. On one special occasion they held a dance, but Kitty did not enjoy that. She sat glued beside Kunner, who also refused to dance, watching

the other girls having a lot of fun and wishing fervently
that she knew how to dance, too. But she wanted to be
able to dance properly, close up to some nice young
man, stretching her legs out backward, gliding across
the floor—not the Irish jigs and reels that Dad had
taught her.

At the end all the comrades stood up together,
clenched fists raised, singing the "Red Flag." But Kitty
was lost in another world, dreaming of herself gliding
smoothly over the polished dance floor in the arms of a
handsome escort.

Kitty was confused by the political meetings. She
liked the warmth and community spirit of the Party, but
she still wasn't sure of their ideas. She loved the history
of the kings and queens of England, the colorful clothes
they wore and the victorious battles they fought. But
these folk did not believe in such stuff, so she kept quiet
about her interest.

The other Party members liked Kitty. Her voice was
clear and precise, and she was often asked to stand on
the platform and read the literature out loud. She gave
encouragement to the other youngsters, and at weekends she stood around the open meetings selling the
Daily Worker. They all agreed that little Kitty was a
great worker and a good comrade.

Unfortunately it all had to end. The Party thought up
a scheme to send some young members to Russia for a
holiday on a student exchange, paid for from the funds.
Popular Kitty was immediately elected as a delegate to
go, and the organizers wrote to her father asking for his
permission.

When the letter arrived on the Saturday a week later,
all hell broke loose. Dad went wild, got dead drunk and
smashed up the little furniture they had left.

"Is this the sort of company you've been keeping all
this time, Katherine Daly?" he roared. He stamped
and shouted and raised hell, but Kitty stood her ground
even though she hated to upset Dad.

It was only when he started yelling that he was going

to find Kunner and give her what for that Kitty got scared. She rushed out of the house and went down to find the parish priest, Father Blake, who was understanding and kind. He suggested that she should keep herself occupied on Friday evenings by coming to church meetings.

Kitty had no intention of going around the church in a long blue cape and a white cap, but she did compromise.

"Right!" she announced. "I'll give up me bloody job!"

CHAPTER FOUR

The Tweeny

Kitty was determined to leave her job rather than annoy Dad. She had never for a moment considered the consequences of her going to those Friday evening meetings.

Luckily Dad was kind about it all, once he had got over the shock of his Catholic daughter mixing with the Communists.

"It's time we got straightened up here," he said, looking around at the shambles of what had once been quite a comfortable home. The long leather sofa at the back of the room was a sorry sight. Bobby had used it so often as a horse in his wild games of Buffalo Bill that now the springs sagged down to the floor and bunches of horsehair protruded obscenely through the worn leather. The lace curtains that Kitty's mother had been so proud of—a wedding present—now hung down in tatters and had turned a musty yellow. They covered windows that were so dirty that it was impossible to see through them. There had once been geraniums and marigolds growing outside in a window box, but these had been so neglected they had lost all hope and died.

This was indeed a home without a mother.

"There's more work around at the moment," said Dad, when Kitty told him she was going to leave her job. "I'll do some overtime, and Noni's bringing in a few shillings. 'Tis better you stay at home, Kitty, and look after the place. I can't abide seeing you mixed up with them heathens." To his mind that meant anyone who was not a Roman Catholic.

On Monday morning Kitty confronted an astounded boss.

"Please, Mr. Fox, can I have my cards?" she asked quietly.

Mr. Fox looked puzzled. For the last eighteen months Kitty had truly become one of the firm, darting here and there, knowing her job well and doing it cheerfully.

"What cards?" he asked, scratching his bald pate.

"I intend to leave, Mr. Fox," said Kitty firmly.

"Leave me, Kitty, my love? Don't kid me, it ain't April Fool's Day yet." He walked off quickly. But she darted in front of him.

"I'm giving a week's notice," she announced.

Mr. Fox looked at her, grinning as though it were some kind of joke.

Kate Ward was very upset when Kitty told her of her decision. "You know, Kitty, it's not easy to get another job. Why do you think I slave here day after day?"

Kitty looked at Kate's faded face and her long tangled hair hanging down her back. Her hands had large swollen veins from continually lugging the heavy pressing iron back and forth.

"Well, I won't be missing much," Kitty remarked breezily.

Kate looked hurt. "Everyone has been so good to you here, Kitty, so don't get cocky, my love."

"Me dad wants me to stay at home and look after the house," said Kitty with a certain amount of self-importance.

"Oh, dear," said Kate. "Has he come into some money, or just laying off the booze?"

Kitty tossed back her hair. "Mind your own business, Kate Ward," she retorted cheekily.

"Saucy young cow," Kate shouted at her as Kitty walked away. "Well, I know why you're leaving . . . it's that bleeding Communist party and that red cow Kunner. I warned yer not to get mixed up with them. Now get on with it!"

From across the room Kunner muttered threats in Yiddish at Kate, who ignored her and said to Kitty, "Please yerself, it's a free country."

On Friday Kitty haughtily departed from the sweatshop. As she climbed down the steep flight of stairs for the last time, she did feel a slight pang of remorse. Although the work had always been hard, she had made some good friends there—people who had been very kind to her and looked after her. Poor old Kate Ward, in particular, had been loyal to her. Kitty did feel a little sadness that she would never see any of them again, but then she shrugged it off. How nice it will be not to have to get up early for work on Monday morning, she thought gleefully.

Staying at home all day was not at all how Kitty had imagined it would be. It was hard work. First she gave the house a good cleanup. Down on her knees, she scrubbed the plain wooden floorboards with a big stiff brush. The rusty nails sticking up from the old wood tore her hands while the soda water made them very sore. She wiped down the grimy walls with soap and water and scraped the soot off the kettle and pots with some metal gauze. She dusted and swept and washed and repaired. When she had finished, the place looked a little more clean and tidy.

After several days she was at last satisfied with her efforts, and she went off to join the local free library. There she found books to take home with her, and she spent the afternoon huddled in the old armchair reading until Bobby came home from school. Now that Kitty was at home, Bobby had returned from Nan's.

When she had been at school, history had seemed so dull, even though Kitty had been fascinated by royalty. But now, when she read about it in the library books, it all came alive for her and she loved it. As she cooked the evening meal her mind buzzed with the antics of the great historical characters she had been reading about. But even they could not make up for the fact that life for Kitty had become desperately tedious. She felt confined and bored. The quiet isolation of home was a sharp contrast to the warm chatter and clatter of the sweatshop she had left behind. Kitty missed the friendship of her old workmates and now, after spending so many hours alone talking to no one, she lost much of the vitality and sparkle she had displayed when she had gone out to work each day.

The urge for companionship soon got the better of her. After several weeks of housekeeping, Kitty decided that she missed her pocket money and was fed up with staying at home all day. Dad had noticed how listless his eldest daughter had become since she had left her job, and he wanted her to be happy, so he did not object when she announced her intentions to him one day. Soon, with Dad's blessing, Kitty was off to the city to find another job.

She had seen one particular job advertised in the evening paper. The advertisement read: "Clean young woman required for olde tyme coffee shoppe situated at Burnhill Row. Good wages. Food and uniform."

To Kitty this sounded very interesting, and she set off to try her luck. She was very excited at the prospect of getting a new job, and hummed happily to herself as she walked through the busy London streets. She found the right address and pushed open the heavy wooden door. A bell rang at the back of the shop. Kitty stood for several minutes waiting for someone to appear.

The coffee shop was a big old-fashioned place and very dark inside. There were low oak beams across the ceiling and well-scrubbed pine tables surrounded by high-backed pine chairs. Gleaming horse brasses hung down the walls on leather straps, and an enormous pair of bellows rested by the large fireplace. Kitty was enthralled; it seemed so historic. She could just imagine King Henry VIII drinking mead in a place like this.

Her daydream was suddenly interrupted by the appearance of a tall girl in a uniform. "I'm here about the job," Kitty said as politely as she could. The girl smiled and led her into the kitchen to meet the boss.

Mr. King was very tubby, and he interviewed Kitty while slicing a huge lump of beef with a long sharp knife. Every now and then he wiped his hands on the large white apron wrapped around his fat belly.

"Well, well," he said, frowning down at Kitty. "You're a bit tiny. Have you been in the trade before?"

"No," replied Kitty, "I was in tailoring."

"It's hard work," Mr. King informed her. "But if you want to train, I'll make you a tweeny. You'll get a good meal and two pounds a week."

Kitty's heart nearly missed a beat. By the time she left the sweatshop her wages there had averaged fifteen shillings a week.

"You can start at eight o'clock on Monday," went on Mr. King. "That all right?"

"Oh, yes," said Kitty, nodding eagerly.

She walked home in a dream. Two pounds! What riches—just think what you can do with two pounds every week, she thought.

On Monday morning, complete in coffee-shop uniform, Kitty became a tweeny. Her outfit consisted of a pink cotton dress with very full sleeves and was a little too large for her. The dress was covered with a large, frilly white apron, and on the top of her head she wore a stiffly starched mop cap.

There had been much debate among the two older girls who dressed her.

"Blimey, ain't you a sprat. Never mind, you might grow into it," one girl said.

"It's hard work," the other said. "You'll never be able to carry those heavy trays."

But Kitty felt very smart and was not put off.

From eight in the morning until six o'clock every evening, Kitty trotted up and down the long dark passage carrying heavily loaded trays. Her main task was to put the food onto the plates and carry it on a tray from the kitchen to the dining room, put the tray on a stand for the waitresses and then return with the empties.

The two tall and nimble waitresses served the food at the tables to very genteel-looking customers from the surrounding banks and city offices.

The early morning was not too bad. Kitty cleaned the silver and laid the tables for lunch. Well-dressed city gents came in for morning coffee, and then there were the hectic lunches. There was the frantic rushing and shouting that went on in the kitchen and the bossy waitresses thrusting pieces of paper at her and shouting: "One roast beef and cabbage; two roast lamb, one cabbage, one peas."

Kitty frequently got the orders all mixed up; the beef would get the peas and both the lambs would get the cabbage.

After the lunch had been cleared away, the tables had to be prepared for dinner. Kitty was pleased to find that, being underage, she was not allowed to work late, so she did not have to cope with the dinner as well. Nevertheless, at the end of each day her legs and arms ached. And when she emerged from the dark rooms into the light of day, her head swam.

Despite the terrible hard work, Kitty persevered through that first week; the thought of those two-pound wages kept her going. But on Friday, she was bitterly disappointed to find that ten shillings had been deducted. She only received thirty shillings. Mr. King had stopped so much for her food and uniform, and even more for two coffee cups that she had accidentally broken.

Luckily, there was not much housework to do back home because Noni, for once, was helping out a bit and Bobby had been dispatched to Nan's again. It was just as well, because Kitty was much too weary to do anything at home after working all day and getting back after eight each night.

Her only real consolation was the good lunch and suppers she got while she was at work. The cook felt sorry for this thin, pale child and piled her plate high. "Eat it up, Kitty," she would say. "And have some nice pudding after."

Kitty had never tasted such appetizing food before and tucked in with relish. She liked the cook, who was a jolly, fat woman with a kindly red face.

Mr. King was very proud of his business and talked a lot about it. "This place is of great historical interest," he said. "Folks come here from all over the world."

Kitty stared at the poky, low-ceilinged room in amazement. Since she had been working there, the coffee shop's aura of history had faded for her.

"See that fireplace?" Mr. King went on, waving the carving knife. "That, my dear, is five hundred years old."

Kitty looked at the large open fireplace and was unimpressed.

"The Lord Mayor of London once owned this coffee shop," said Mr. King. "He built that fireplace, and you know, me girl, his descendants come from all over to eat here. Once a year we have a founders' dinner, and it's coming up next week. You'll have to get your finger out, me girl, because we'll be entertaining some very rich people."

To Kitty this last piece of information was very interesting. In some of the novels she read, poor serving wenches would often meet rich men and end up being duchesses. It would have to be thought out very carefully, she decided. And she would get a good look at these folk who never had to work and just lived for the pleasures of life.

On the great day, the coffee shop was closed to ordinary customers. While the grand dinner was being prepared, Mr. King shouted and hollered at everyone, and the waitresses quarreled with the cook. Shortly before midday, the staff all lined up to await the wealthy guests.

Mr. King looked very spruce. He had removed his apron and put away his carving knife. He wore a jacket and stuck a red carnation in his buttonhole. The waitresses wore their best uniforms and had been told many times how to behave—to say, "Yes, sir" to the men and drop little curtsies to the ladies. In her kitchen, the overworked cook was red-faced and disgruntled.

"Yes, sir, please, sir, three bags full, sir," she muttered. "They don't even know what a nice piece of pastry is, so I don't know why I bother."

Then came the big moment. As the guests arrived, Kitty respectfully took their coats to hang up. Then she retired out of sight to her position between the dining room and the kitchen. Her bright eyes watched the arrival of a tall, mournful-looking woman in a long fur coat, and two languid, very bored boys who accompanied her. Then came two fat men who puffed cigars and talked very loudly, slapping each other on the shoulder. Well, she thought, if this is high society, she did not think much of it.

The very last guest to arrive, however, was a young man, tall and fair and in his twenties. He wore an open-necked shirt and a blazer. He apologized to Mr. King for being late, muttering something about tennis.

Kitty recognized him as the Prince Charming in all her romantic novels. She could already see herself living with him in his castle. Suddenly her dreaming was interrupted.

"Hurry up, Kitty!" the waitresses shouted from the kitchen.

The guests seemed to be performing some sort of ceremony, gathered around the fireplace, holding their wine glasses in the air.

Kitty wanted to linger more to watch and listen, but her duty had to be done. So back and forth with plates and glasses, bowls and jugs she rushed, between kitchen and dining room. The meal went on for hours, and it seemed like an age before the guests had eaten their fill.

At last Kitty had a chance to pause. She was in the passageway, standing on one leg trying to rest the other and snatching glimpses of the beautiful rich youth, when a waitress suddenly dashed out of the dining room and a big fuss started in the kitchen.

"They want English Cheddar," the girl announced.

"But I've bloomin' well got them some fancy French cheese," said Mr. King indignantly.

"They say they don't want any smelly Froggy cheese. They say this is an English occasion and they want English cheese."

"Kitty!" called Mr. King irritably. "For Christ sake, run over to the dairy and get that English Cheddar he's got there."

Quite surprised, Kitty dashed off out into the street and crossed the road to the Welsh dairy.

"Mr. King wants an English Cheddar," she gasped.

"What, the whole cheese?" the shopkeeper asked, looking astonished.

"Quick!" said Kitty desperately. "There's no time, he's waiting."

The shopkeeper whisked up the huge round cheese and put it into Kitty's arms. Her knees almost gave way; the cheese must have weighed at least twelve pounds. She struggled back to the coffee shop hugging the cheese to her breast. As she came through the dark passage she missed three steps and went down with a resounding crash. The cheese fell from her arms as she tried to save herself and rolled into the dining room straight into the famous fireplace.

Kitty could hear roars of laughter as the young boys went to retrieve the cheese. She sat up on the floor, looking dismally at her scratched bare knees poking through her stockings. All the wind had been knocked out of her.

Then a gentle hand lifted her up and sat her on the steps. A white handkerchief was placed in her hands to dab her grazed knee. She looked up to see two merry blue eyes laughing at her. It was the beautiful guest, saying: "I say, did you hurt yourself?"

Mr. King suddenly came rushing through from the kitchen to take Kitty back to work. He gave his apologies to his posh customers, but they did not seem to care; they were on their fourth bottle of Mamsey wine, and very merry on it, too.

Kitty, still shaken, sat down on a stool in the kitchen.

"Rest awhile," said the cook kindly, "and then you can clear the tables."

"It was a bloody silly thing to do," shouted Mr. King, "running about with that big cheese when I only wanted a couple of pounds of it."

But Kitty was still too dazed to be bothered by his rage.

She rested for a few minutes and then went back to the dining room to clear the dishes. The young man said: "How are you? Does it still hurt?" He lifted Kitty's skirt to look at her knee. The other guests roared with laughter. Kitty did not mind. She was thrilled by all this attention.

As the guests started to leave, the youth lingered. "What about a date?" he stuttered drunkenly. "What time tomorrow?" He spoke loudly for the benefit of his friends.

"Six o'clock," answered Kitty, astonished.

For the rest of the day, all Kitty could think about was that she had actually got a date. She had often heard the waitresses talking about their dates, but so far it had never happened to her. And now this good-looking, rich young man had asked her out.

At home in bed that night she lay sleepless, wondering what she should wear, how she should behave. She would have to be careful to speak nicely—she began to despise the flat Cockney intonation in her voice. This was no corner boy; he was a real gentleman. If he was going to court her, she had to make sure she acted in a very ladylike manner. He would probably want to hold an intellectual conversation, she thought, and she would be able to discuss the most recent contemporary novel she had read.

She decided to wear her best coat with the fur collar, a skirt and her new woolen jumper. It was bottle-green and matched her eyes. She was quite sure it suited her.

When morning finally came, Kitty rose early and made preparations before going to work. She pushed waves into her glossy hair and gave an extra twist to the kiss curl on her forehead. Noni tumbled out of bed while Kitty was doing herself up.

"Blimey," said Noni, "have you got a date?"

"Maybe I have," replied Kitty grandly.

"Don't believe yer," said Noni.

"He's a very nice young man, and very rich," retorted Kitty.

But Noni was not impressed. "Serve yer right if he murders yer," she retorted. Noni was obsessed with the idea of people being murdered.

Kitty ignored her sister and set off for work.

Having spent so much time getting ready for her date, she arrived an hour late at the coffee shop.

"What bloody time do you call this?" yelled Mr. King.

"Sorry," lied Kitty, "but my knee hurt."

Mr. King looked down at her in bewilderment. "She's got to go," he muttered to the cook.

"Oh, give the kid a chance, it's all new to her," the cook defended Kitty.

That day Kitty worked well and willingly, and the atmosphere in the coffee shop was quite congenial.

At ten minutes to six, she stared up at the clock and then at the pile of teacups that she still had to wash up and stack neatly in the cupboard before she left. Frantically she hurried through the nasty job, missing some and leaving others to dry. It was unusual for her to skip her chores, but tonight she had to rush.

At ten past six she hurried out into the street, hobbling on the high heels she had slipped into as she left the coffee shop. Her young man was nowhere to be seen. She must have missed him. She should have been on time, she thought, how terrible.

But then a few yards down the road she spotted the tall figure. He was wearing a pin-stripe suit and a natty bowler hat. No wonder she hadn't recognized him.

She dashed up to him and grasped his arm.

"Sorry I'm late," she gasped.

He stopped and stared at her incredulously, for he had forgotten his date. It was a total coincidence that he just happened to be on the way home from his city office. But suddenly the penny dropped. "Why, it's little Kitty from the coffee shop. How are you?"

He spoke so softly and pleasantly that Kitty was thrilled.

The man seemed to hesitate and looked puzzled by the way she clung to his arm.

"Where are you taking me?" Kitty asked coyly. He looked thoughtfully across the road to Burnhill Fields and the old churchyard. There was a footpath through it they would walk along.

"Let's go for a walk," he said brightly.

They crossed the road and he guided Kitty down the lonely path.

Kitty tried to act like the heroine in one of the novels she had read. She hoped her eyes looked misty as she gazed up at her young man. She blinked and simpered and pronounced her aitches very carefully. She tried desperately to talk about books, but he seemed quite uninterested in them. He was looking around for the right sort of spot.

"Of course you know," Kitty said in her new posh voice, "John Bunyan is buried here."

"Is he?" said the youth. "Jolly good luck to him then." He steered Kitty to a grassy spot behind a large gravestone.

Kitty stepped out in her uncomfortable shoes, chatting naively as she went with him.

"Come closer, my Kitty, my love." He sighed and put his arm around her. Kitty went limp and pathetic and allowed him to kiss her. He bent her backward, and with his free hand he pulled at her knickers.

They were special knickers—the latest fashion—called French knickers. When Kitty had treated herself to them she had felt very extravagant because they cost so much—five shillings and sixpence at the market stall. They were pale yellow silk, and, instead of being held up with elastic, they were fastened by a small button at the side. They had very wide legs and were inclined to be drafty. But Kitty loved to feel the cool silk against her skin instead of the old fleece-lined bloomers she usually wore.

Now this fine young man, her first admirer, tugged so hard at the silk material that the button popped off. The lovely knickers fell to the ground.

With one hand, Kitty tried to hang on to them and pull them up again. With the other she swung her handbag and brought it crashing down on the man's head, knocking off his bowler hat so that it spun off over the gravestone.

Pulling herself free, Kitty ran as though the devil were after her, still hanging on to her yellow knickers. The young man lay on the ground roaring with laughter.

When Kitty reached the main road she stood still to catch her breath. Looking around to check that no one was looking, she stepped quickly out of her knickers and put them in her handbag. She jumped on a tram to take her back to the slum district.

On the tram she thought that she had better not go up the stairs in case anyone saw that she had no knickers on. She sat downstairs and a little smile lit up her face as she thought that she was like Noni—with her drawers at half mast.

Well, she thought, she had learned the hard way, but it would not happen again.

... ...
... ...
... ...
... ...
... ...
... ...
... ...
... ...

CHAPTER FIVE

Bebe

The day after her unfortunate date was Saturday. Although she normally worked on Saturdays, this time it was her turn among the girls to have a day off. So she did not return to work until Monday morning.

She was due for another shock, for when she arrived the cook was looking very worried. "The boss wants you in his office, Kitty," she said in a serious tone.

Kitty had never been in Mr. King's office except on very special occasions, and she wondered what was up. She knocked on the door and entered, and stood there bright and smiling in front of Mr. King.

Mr. King looked stern but embarrassed. He handed her an envelope. "Here are your cards, Kitty, and wages due to you—instead of a week's notice."

"Am I getting the sack, Mr. King? What for?" exclaimed Kitty in dismay.

"I'm sorry, ducks, I can't afford you," muttered Mr. King, turning his head away. "You are a willing and pleasant enough little girl, but not big or responsible enough for a job like this."

Tears flooded into Kitty's eyes. She had been so sure of her capabilities.

"It took me all Saturday morning to get those cups into shape," Mr. King went on. "You can't do things like that in catering, Kitty. I should go back to tailoring, if I was you."

Kitty's pride suddenly surged up inside her. How dare he be patronizing to her like that! She tossed up her head and declared in true Cockney: "You know what you can do with this bleedin' job? Stick it up yer arse."

She turned around and walked out of the office, slamming the door as she went.

Kitty marched down the street gritting her teeth with rage. Mr. King can keep his bloody job, she thought, sticking her nose up in the air. She had been shocked to be sacked like that; she had not been prepared for it at all. Now she had to think again about what she should do. She carefully summed up the situation. She decided that she could put up with staying at home again for awhile if she had just a little pocket money to keep her going, but she could not survive otherwise. She had been paying her unemployment stamps ever since she had started working, so she was entitled to sign on the dole. And that, she decided, was exactly what she would do.

It was a long way to the labor exchange from the city. She walked through endless, dirty slum streets, and by the time she finally got there, her feet were sore and she was exhausted and disgruntled.

As she walked up the street, fighting against a bitter wind, she saw a terrible sight that repelled her. A huge queue had formed outside the labor exchange—desperate-looking men stood with their collars turned up over their ears, their hands in empty pockets, dejected looks on their faces. They had unshaven chins, blue with the cold, and their expressions were gaunt from hunger. Their toes stuck out of their scuffed boots, the heels so worn that they slumped sideways.

Kitty was horrified, but her heart felt even heavier when she saw another queue moving slowly along by the other side of the building—this one made up of women. Some were old, some young, some middle-aged. Some were dressed fairly neatly while others were ragged and dirty. But all bore the same anxious expression on their faces. All were wondering if they would get a job or whether the six shillings dole money would feed them and their families for another week.

Looking closer, Kitty noticed that many were young women whose boyfriends had probably gone down in the war and who had got left on the shelf afterward because of the shortage of men.

The older women were wide-hipped and poorly dressed. Most of them spent their days trying to squeeze enough out of their husbands' wages to feed their huge families. They did not mind what they did or how hard they had to work as long as they were paid for it. Some of them looked askance at Kitty. She was so very young—not yet eighteen. It was not hard to get work at that age because the employers could pay lower rates. Once someone reached eighteen then out they often went, for a school-leaver to take up the job.

Kitty took a second to decide what to do, but then she joined the end of the queue.

Suddenly, out of the blue, Kitty saw Bebe waddling toward her. Kitty knew Bebe quite well, for she lived around the corner of her street. Her family was Jewish and her father owned a small upholstering business in a tumbledown shop. He was a tired-looking man, and Kitty remembered him sitting in the shop and holding a long needle as he sewed up the upholstery on all sorts of furniture.

The only thing that Bebe and Kitty had in common was the fact that they had both lost their mothers in the same week. Apart from the occasional acknowledgment, they seldom talked when they saw each other in the street. Kitty would often see Bebe's big form filling the doorway of the shop as she waited for someone to pass so she could gossip with them. And now, wearing a lurid-colored scarf on her head with a gushing smile on her face, Bebe stood behind Kitty in the queue.

"Hello, Kitty," she cried affably.

"Hello," replied Kitty, staring at her with curiosity. "I thought you didn't go out to work."

"No, I don't usually, but I'm so bloody fed up with that shop. No one comes in anymore and it's become a real dead hole. So I'm going to get a job at the tin bashers—me mate works there, so I've come to take out employment cards. Why don't you come there as well?" Bebe asked generously.

Kitty was surprised at the offer, but she thought it sounded like a good idea and she accepted.

The two girls stood for hours in the queue among the miserable hopefuls, and finally Bebe managed to get her cards. Then they both went off to Yankey's, the local factory that made tin boxes.

Kitty was astonished by the dreadful noise of the tin bashers factory. Hundreds of tins rattled down a long conveyer belt. A huge crane swung overhead picking up objects, and numerous women with turbans on their heads worked enormous presses that came down every other second with a tremendous thud. The women shouted and screeched at each other; to Kitty it was like some sort of madhouse.

All she wanted to do was turn about and run; her nerves felt twisted like metallic wires, so great was the impact of the noise on the high-strung Kitty.

Bebe waved cheerily to her friend and poked Kitty in the back. "Wait here. We got to see the forelady," she informed her in a fierce whisper.

Soon a husky lady arrived, wide of hip and wearing a flowered overall. She beckoned to them. "Sit down," she said sharply, indicating the small office in which there were a desk and two chairs.

"You can both read and write, I hope," she said flatly.

"Oh, yes," said Bebe, with a wide grin. But Kitty was

speechless. The din was not quite so bad inside the office, but it had left her with a strange, vacant feeling.

"Fill in the form," ordered the forelady. Name and address and previous job was all that was required.

In a big schoolgirl scrawl Bebe filled in her particulars, but Kitty sat tensely in her chair, pen in hand. She could never work in this place, she thought; all that noise would kill her.

Impatiently, the forelady said, "Well, get on with it," and with trembling hands Kitty filled in the form. Every time there was a particularly loud crash outside in the workshop, Kitty nearly jumped out of her skin.

The forelady snatched the forms away from them and went busily off in another direction. "I'll let you know if you're suitable," she said as she went.

The girls got up to go, but as they went out someone called Bebe back. A few minutes later she returned, her face all wreathed in smiles. "Guess what," she said. "I got the job. I start next week."

"Sorry," the forelady said, coming to the door, "but your friend's nerves are too bad. We can't employ her."

Kitty felt suddenly very inadequate. A lousy job like that and she could not get it.

"I didn't know you suffered with your nerves," commented Bebe as they left the noise behind.

"I don't," replied Kitty, "but I'd never work in that bedlam."

"What's a bedlam?" asked Bebe, her mouth open wide in astonishment.

"It's the madhouse," returned Kitty.

"Oh, go on," cried Bebe, "you don't 'alf make me laugh."

It was quite obvious that Bebe did not understand Kitty's attitude, but, nevertheless, a firm friendship was immediately formed between them. Kitty was invited home to Bebe's for a cup of coffee, and in her crowded back room behind the shop, Bebe made some Camp coffee and cut cheese sandwiches.

Bebe was delighted at having obtained a job. "Don't know what the old man's going to say," she confided in Kitty, "but still, who cares? He's always drunk lately and don't do much work in the shop, so I can't see any reason why I should hang about here all day."

Kitty agreed.

"I'll have to keep it dark from me brother Rafe. He's off on tour with the band, won't be back for a few weeks. I'm really looking forward to it. It's a pity you never got the job, Kitty."

So the two girls became pals and exchanged confidences. Kitty had told Bebe the reason she lost the last job, and also about the fiasco of her first date with the rich young man who removed her knickers. Bebe giggled so much she nearly choked.

"Oh, Kitty, you kill me!" she gasped. "Talk about sounding yer haitches and dropping yer drawers."

In a way Kitty could see the humor of the situation.

"I'll take you on the prowl up the Parade at the weekend, Kitty," Bebe promised. "Meet a lot of blokes up there, and don't be a ninny. They will all be after something, but you have to keep them guessing."

Kitty began to see sense in Bebe's technique regarding the fellas, and decided she would go with her out on the prowl, as Bebe put it.

At the weekend Bebe frizzed up Kitty's hair with a pair of waving tongs. They were huge iron curlers that Bebe stuck into the open fire until they were red hot. Then she tried them out on newspaper until they were exactly the right heat. Bebe persistently pulled Kitty's hair as she used the tortuous instrument until Kitty thought she was in danger of being scalped. By the end of the operation the room stank of burning hair and Kitty's locks stuck out like a dishmop.

"Great! You look smashing!" Bebe cried, ignoring Kitty's look of dismay. "Now, how about a nice bit of makeup?"

She rouged Kitty's pale cheeks and put thick scarlet

lipstick on her lips. "Gotta make a nice bow shape,"
Bebe said, as she carefully smeared the lipstick on the
skin above Kitty's top lip as well. "It's good and
attractive."

Kitty caught a glimpse of herself in the mirror and
was astonished by the finished product; she felt completely unrecognizable, even to herself.

Finally, they went out together, arms linked, mincing
down the main road. The general idea was to parade up
and down on the look out for an admirer. Nothing
happened the first time out, and Kitty was not impressed. But Bebe reassured her that it would take a
little time.

One weekend after Bebe had fixed up Kitty's appearance, they left the house in high spirits. Bebe wore a
tight red dress, and Kitty a green one. Both had their
hair bobbed and frizzed, and they wore long dangling
clip earrings. Bebe had lent Kitty a pair on the condition that she didn't lose them. The two brilliant, heavy
glass peardrops spun around on the end of their little
chains, and Kitty loved to toss her head to feel them
swing against her neck.

Together they took the turning that led into Mon-
keys' Parade. This particular stretch of road was so
called because all the local young folk walked up and
down it constantly, first on one side and then the other.
Homes were small, so the best place to display any
finery was outside in the street.

Bebe and Kitty strutted out like two exotic birds.
Kitty was really not sure if she liked the way she
looked, but she reckoned that if this meant being as
smart as a working girl determined to be, she would
have to put up with it.

Bebe kept casting sidelong glances at the boys, who
took one look at her wide waist and boisterous manner
and walked straight on. Nevertheless, Bebe persevered
and continued to march up and down, but Kitty was
getting very bored and wanted to go home. She was

disillusioned; it still wasn't as much fun as Bebe had promised it would be.

Suddenly she saw an old woman, a neighbor who was always nosing out of her front door. The woman looked at Kitty with astonishment. "Christ, Kitty Daly! If your mother saw you she'd turn in her grave. What a flash cow you turned out to be."

Kitty flushed under her rouge, but Bebe came to her aid. "Nosy old cow!" she hollered.

The café was the last port of call. The idea was that the girls would be taken there by the boys who had picked them up. It was on the corner of the main road, just before the road dwindled off into the back streets. It was the main rendezvous for the youths of the district. Bicycles and motorbikes were always parked outside and loud music from the gramophone blared out into the street. It was well lighted, and inside there were marble-topped tables and piles of grubby bottles of condiments. The whole place stank of chips.

The café was run by a middle-aged Italian couple. The wife served behind the counter and the husband did the cooking. She was tall and very regal-looking. Her black hair was piled high on her head, and she wore gold earrings in her ears and a gold crucifix about her neck. She always wore a tight black dress. Kitty recognized her immediately. She had often seen her at Mass when she was younger.

"Well, yer have to buy yerself a cup of coffee," Bebe said bossily to Kitty. "Have you got enough?"

"I've got sixpence," replied Kitty.

"That's enough," said Bebe knowledgeably. "Give it to me and I'll pay."

Bebe bustled Kitty to the back of the café and sat her down at a table where there were several laughing girls and boys. Bebe seemed to know them. "This is me mate," she said to them, referring to Kitty. They all nodded and said hello as Kitty sat down, dumbstruck in the presence of these loud-voiced strangers.

Then Mario, the proprietor's son, came to sit with them. "You want to buy some dance tickets?" he asked.

"How much?" demanded Bebe.

"One and sixpence. Pay me Friday," Mario said.

"Where's the dance?" asked Bebe.

"At the church hall. How many do you want?"

"Two," said Bebe. "Me mate'll come, too."

Mario looked critically at Kitty.

"I can't dance," Kitty whispered timidly into Bebe's ear.

"She says she can't dance!" laughed Bebe loudly. All the other youths stared at Kitty. She was so embarrassed that she wanted to hide under the table.

Mario looked into her eyes. "You can't dance? Well, it's time someone taught you," he said. "Come outside with me." He took Kitty by the hand and led her out onto the pavement. The other young people all came out to watch, giggling and nudging each other as they formed a circle around the couple.

Kitty was nervous, but Mario grasped her firmly and walked her around. "Come on, step backward and open your legs." He pushed his knee between her legs. It was a good sensation to glide over the pavement like this. Kitty picked up the steps very quickly. She was ecstatic. For so many years she had yearned to dance.

"You'll soon pick it up," said Mario. "You have natural grace. Not like your fat friend; she dances as though she's got a kipper between her legs."

Everyone except Bebe roared with laughter at his joke.

"Cheeky bleedin' sod," she declared.

But Kitty was thrilled to be the belle of the pavement ball.

The next Saturday was the first of many hectic nights for Kitty. She arrived at the church hall arrayed in an enormous purple dress that had belonged to one of Bebe's aunts. It had a stiff bustline, a very full quilted skirt and was embossed with silver beads. She had borrowed it from Bebe, who was very proud of her collection of dance dresses—most of which had come from various relatives who had worn them for weddings and bar mitzvahs and then disposed of them.

Bebe had thrust Kitty into this massive gown, sewn up the straps to shorten it and hitched up the underskirt with safety pins.

"I look like a bundle of washing," Kitty had complained.

"Don't be daft," said Bebe, "you look all right. It's because you're so skinny that you feel like that. It's a very expensive dress—it belonged to our Aunt Sadie. She only wore it once."

Soon Kitty stopped resisting and accepted everything Bebe ordered her to do. Her thin neck stuck up above the stiff purple bodice. There was quite a gap between Kitty and the dress; looking down, her small breasts could be seen looking completely lost in the deep neckline.

Once more came the frizzy hairdo and the layers of makeup until Kitty felt like Cinderella going to the ball.

"I just hope," she said, "that I don't turn into a pumpkin at midnight."

Bebe looked quite extraordinary in a fuchsia-colored dress—all loops, frills and fringes. Her face was made up even more than Kitty's. Kitty thought she looked like a ghoul, but she did not say anything.

At the church hall, Bebe grasped Kitty tightly about the waist and propelled her rapidly around the dance floor. Kitty was hardly able to breathe. Bebe had one arm around her shoulder and she smelled so sweaty that Kitty was quite relieved when Mario came up and asked her to dance with him.

How different it was to dance with Mario, to twist and twirl gracefully as one person. It was sheer pleasure.

"You'll soon be a great little dancer," Mario said.

"Maybe I'll take you out somewhere nice." He stared thoughtfully at her and then suddenly started in horror. "Jesus Christ! Where did you get that frock?"

Kitty blushed and looked down at the floor. "I borrowed it from Bebe," she answered quietly.

Mario sniffed. "I thought as much. Well, when I take you out, you won't wear that, will you?"

Kitty's evening was spoiled. She rushed to a corner to hide. Bebe, who had been drinking brown ale at the bar, came back onto the floor and, with various partners, thundered about the room like a huge wagon for the rest of the evening.

"You've gotta let yerself go, Kitty," Bebe nagged on the way home. "It's no good sitting in the bleedin' corner all night. You'll never have a good time like that."

Kitty was not sure about church hall dances, but she certainly wanted to be a good dancer. She had spent the evening watching the other dancing couples, trying to see how they moved so well, and for the next few days she practiced at home while she did the housework.

She was still unemployed, and after cleaning the house she spent most afternoons reading all the books she got out of the library. But it was soon obvious that she had to get another job. Her dole money was hardly sufficient to help the family finances, and Noni was not earning very much at the box factory. It was not only their general shortage of money that Kitty was worried about; she still owed one and sixpence for the dance ticket and had no means of paying it.

One Wednesday Dad came home rather sheepishly and said, "Try to borrow some money from old Charlie Nelson. There's no money for the children's dinner."

Dad had obviously just lost most of his wages on the horses. Kitty was very disturbed at the sudden feeling of being absolutely broke, with no money until Friday when Dad could get his wages. But she did as her father asked and went to visit Charlie Nelson.

Charlie lived in the house opposite and was quite a character. He was the most financially comfortable person in the whole street—he always had a bob or two to spare—but he was also the ugliest. He was huge, both in height and width, and his skin was muddy-colored and pockmarked. His eyes stared out beadily and his lips were like two rolls of blubber. He had a loud, coarse Cockney voice, but he was a fine honest man with a heart of gold.

During the day he cared for the horses downstairs in the stable underneath where the Dalys lived. It was his love for animals that earned him Kitty's respect. He brushed the horses' coats until they shone like glass, nursed them when they were sick and was always available to discuss their merits with Kitty. He would hitch them up with clean harness and sparkling horse brasses and send them out on their long day's work.

When he was not grooming the horses, Charlie worked by day and most of the night as the local knocker-up. He went around very early in the morning knocking on the windows with a long pole to waken the early risers. The working men who had to make an early start all relied on Charlie to tap on their windows every morning with a cheerful gruff cry of: "Wakey, wakey!"

Also, if anyone needed a loan in the week it was Charlie who would always give it. He had a great fondness for Kitty's father, and now he lent Kitty ten bob without any ill grace.

She bought some food and cooked the evening meal, telling herself that she had to get herself another job and earn a proper wage, what with poor Dad having such a hard time feeding them all.

The next Monday, promptly at eight o'clock, Kitty went to apply for a job in another sweatshop. This one was in a poor district, in Nile Street. She was accepted and was to train as a machinist. After that she would work at piece rates—paid for every article produced.

CHAPTER SIX

A New Sweatshop

Kitty's new job was indeed in a sweatshop. At United Tailoring she had to work harder than she had ever worked before, and for less money.

Her small fingers folded the material and pushed it endlessly through the electric sewing machine. She was one in a long line of faceless women who counted each garment made and noted it down in a little red book.

Kitty's task was to make the backs of the men's waistcoats. Waistcoats were very much in fashion—a suit was not a suit unless it was worn with an elaborately buttoned waistcoat with a silk back that had a little strap with a buckle across it. With the incessant humming noise in her ears and a glaring light just over her head, Kitty spent eight hours each day working. Her face grew very pale, and as the roses left her cheeks she resorted to makeup. Now she was never seen without her rouged cheeks and a scarlet slash across her mouth. She seldom grinned or even smiled and had none of the charisma that had made her so popular with Mr. Fox in her first job. Her eyes were rimmed with black pencil and stared out of her head like an owl's.

Kitty no longer chattered naively as she used to or even pretended to be posh. She had a different act: she was a flapper.

Bebe had said to her recently, "I'm going to get my hair Eton-cropped. What about you, Kitty?"

Always influenced by her fat friend, Kitty soon came to work looking like a shorn lamb. Her hair was cut short and two big round gilt loops hung from her ears.

The women at United Tailoring were of quite a different caliber from those Kitty had worked with in the past.

"Oh, me Gawd!" cried one when she spotted Kitty arriving. "What the bleedin' hell's she got up to now?"

Kitty ignored all the comments that were made throughout that day.

"Bloody lesby," said one, "she looks like a boy."

"Flash little cow," said another.

Kitty rather enjoyed this notoriety. Having just been a cog in a huge wheel, her latent exhibitionism was brought out by the new haircut. She perked up and felt quite merry.

Bebe also had an Eton crop and it suited her better than it did Kitty. She had black shiny hair that now lay flat and smooth around her round white face and somehow made her look more compact.

But Kitty really needed her soft curly hair to frame her small face, and the haircut had removed the last vestige of charm from her appearance—and all just to be in fashion.

Kitty and Bebe continued to parade up and down the high road looking for boys, but still without much luck. There was no longer even Mario, their champion and dancing partner, for he now resided in Wormwood Scrubs, and Kitty felt slightly responsible for him being there.

After her first dancing lesson outside the café that Saturday evening, and a couple of Saturday-night hops

at the church hall, Mario had said: "Okay, Kitty, you
can dance very well now. I'll take you to the Saloon
Ball and we'll enter some contests."

Kitty still borrowed dresses for her dancing evenings
from Bebe. None fitted or suited her small figure—
though she never again wore that monstrosity she had
worn on the first occasion. But just before the dancing
contest Mario pushed a newspaper parcel in Kitty's
direction when she was sitting in the café. "Don't open
it until you get home," he whispered.

Bebe was very curious. "What is it, Kitty? Funny,
him giving you a present. You ain't let him do anything,
'ave you?"

"Oh, don't be silly," Kitty said, blushing with annoyance. "He's not interested in me that way."

"Tell me what bleedin' bloke ain't!" Bebe guffawed
loudly as the two girls left the café.

The minute they got home Kitty hastily untied the
parcel. Inside was a beautiful dress. It was a tangerine
color, long and cut into panels that flared out at the
bottom. There was just one shoulder strap, and this was
made up of an inch-wide strip of diamanté.

"I don't think it'll fit you," declared Bebe, holding
the dress up and measuring it against her own fat waist.

"Well, it certainly won't fit you," said Kitty, snatching back the dress and stepping out of her skirt and
blouse to try it on.

The dress fitted Kitty as though it had been made for
her. The long tapering panels and the gleaming material smoothed her figure, giving it grace and beauty. This,
indeed, was an expensive dress.

"Must have cost a bomb," muttered Bebe. "Wonder
where he got it."

But Kitty did not care; she just twisted and twirled in
that lovely frock.

In the smooth arms of Mario, Kitty glided across the
floor at the Saloon Ball. The couple knocked out all the
other contestants until they gained two first prizes—one
in a waltz and another in a tango.

This modern ballroom was a bus ride from Kitty's district. One whole side of the hall was a mirror, so as they danced they could see their own reflections. How Kitty loved to watch herself slide gracefully over the floor, the folds of her gown twirling out and Mario, unsmiling, head held high, partnering her as if she were a queen. As long as Kitty knew the steps and followed him in unison, he was content.

Mario was not always a good-tempered boy, and he was a hard taskmaster. He made Kitty practice outside the café some nights. He would dictate steps to her and guide her over the rough pavement. Dancing was his life, and often he would snap and snarl at Bebe, who wanted to dance with him. "I like dancing to be a pleasure," he would announce, "not hard work."

Often when it was time to leave the dance hall he would say, "Got your bus fare, Kitty? I'm not coming home, got a bit of business to see to."

Kitty did not mind, but Bebe, who always came to the Saloon Ball and played gooseberry, would complain all the way home. "Some bleeding boyfriend. Can't even see you home."

But Kitty was dreaming of the sight of herself in the mirror and did not answer.

Then one weekend Mario disappeared. He was not at the café or even at the church hall. The Saturday hop was not the same without him. "Where's Mario?" Kitty asked his very red-eyed mother.

"Mario bad boy, Mario gone," the Italian woman said, weeping. Then she dashed into a back room of the café in a flood of tears.

"What's up with her?" demanded Bebe.

"He's been nicked," a lad said. "Didn't you see it in the paper?"

The girls looked amazed. "Why, what did he do?" asked Bebe.

"Picked up in Harringay, soliciting," the boy went on.

"Oh, no," said Bebe, "I don't believe it."

"Mean to say you didn't suss him?" continued the
lad. "And that's not all. Coppers found out he's been
pinching stuff from that posh store he worked at. Got
six months, he did."

Bebe's mouth gaped wide open. "Oh, poor sod!" she
exclaimed. "Come on, Kitty." She hustled the rather
puzzled Kitty outside.

"What's soliciting?" asked Kitty.

"Don't kid me. You don't know?" said Bebe.

Kitty shook her head.

"He was a nancy boy. Funny. Well, I often did think
he was a bit of a pansy, Kitty. I bet he even nicked that
frock for you."

It was Kitty's turn to be surprised. A large lump
came into her throat. Oh, poor boy, she thought, shut
away in the dark for such a long time.

"You can't wear that dress any more, Kitty," said
Bebe jubilantly.

"Why not?" demanded Kitty.

"Because if you do they can book you for receiving."

Kitty was very disappointed, but she was too afraid
of getting caught to protest.

The next day the dress was bundled into a paper
parcel with several old dance dresses of Bebe's. Bebe
determinedly wrapped it up in brown paper and tied it
tight with string. Kitty stood by dismally as she caught a
last glimpse of the beautiful silk folds of her first
evening dress. Then off Bebe marched with the parcel
under her arm and disappeared into the dim regions of
Long and Doughtey's, the pawnbrokers. After a few
minutes she came out with a big grin on her face. "Got
five bob," she said, "and no one's going to find it in
there. Come on, Kitty, we've got half a crown each.
Let's go up to the Hoxton cinema."

There was a Broadway melody at this cinema, and it
would have been most enjoyable but for the pestering
of two louts who sat at the back telling filthy jokes and
trying to wedge their way in between the two girls.
Their advances were aggressively resisted by Bebe, and

Kitty was not sorry when the evening was over. She went home and put her head down on the grubby old army blankets on the bed she shared with Noni and wept for poor Mario. But most of all she wept for that lovely tangerine-colored dance dress.

After a while the café changed hands. Mario's parents went home to Italy and the new owner did not encourage the young folk, so a new dive had to be found. Bebe soon arranged Friday night trips to Mrs. G. She insisted on being called Mrs. G., though her real name was Gonsky. She was a very colorful Jewish woman with white hair and a black silk dress, pearl beads, a big cameo on her ample bosom and a very natty display of good rings on her white, well-cared-for hands. She lived at Stamford Hill in a big house and was Bebe's brother Rafe's future mother-in-law. Rafe was engaged to Fay, her daughter, a very smart young lady who had her own hairdressing salon. The color of Fay's hair was always changing; one day it would be red, another, blonde and another, mauve.

"You can have a good nosh at Mrs. G.'s on Friday night," said Bebe. "Come with me and make out you're Yiddish."

In Mrs. G.'s big drawing room there were many well-washed, highly perfumed men, women and young folk—even small kids. Everyone talked at once and at the end, a long table was laden with food. There was more food than Kitty had ever seen before—piles of sandwiches, bowls of soup, pickles and salads and things she didn't recognize. First they had to sit politely and talk with all those large women, who asked Bebe loudly, "How are you, Rebecca? Is your father well?"

Kitty was really surprised. Rebecca? What a name to go to bed with. "Who's your friend? Is she Jewish?" the ladies asked Bebe.

Each time this happened, Bebe changed the conversation. She nudged Kitty with her fat elbow. "Don't answer!" she hissed.

Then a bearded man placed a hat on his head and

candles were lit and prayers were said. Finally everyone dived into the food. It all seemed quaint, but Kitty enjoyed it—especially the food. And the ceremony reminded her of church.

At about nine o'clock Bebe would make her apologies. "Got to get home. My dad's not too well." Then off they would go with a piece of pie or cake wrapped carefully in a serviette by the hostess for Bebe to take home to her dad.

Once outside, Bebe would immediately pick up speed. "Come on, Kitty," she'd say, "we can just get to the Elephant in time for a drink. How much you got?" They would scrape enough money together for two light ales and go off to the pub in Dalston where all the lads were.

It was always hot in the pub, and very smoky. An old man thumped out tunes on a piano, and everyone joined in the singing.

"Sip it," Bebe would whisper. "Make this drink last in case you don't get treated."

They would stand sipping their distasteful drinks— Kitty could not abide beer—until someone asked them to have a drink. Then they would ask for port wine, which made them giggle, and they did not feel quite so awkward.

There were many lads they conned for a port wine, or sometimes two. Afterward the boys would trail home with the girls, hanging on to their arms, determined to get their money's worth. There had been long thin pimply ones, big hefty bullying ones, gentle, sweet, courteous ones—a long succession of escorts who all got the same treatment.

"We'll ditch them," Bebe would mutter under her breath to Kitty, "at the corner. Stay near me." It was safety in numbers and it was essential for them to hang on to their virginity. And by hook or by crook they accomplished it. They were often chased down the road by the lads and once Bebe even received a good punch on the nose. But Kitty was never quite so forward as her friend and managed to keep out of trouble. She would always promise to meet the boys the next night, and they would ask her not to bring "that fat lump" with her.

Sometimes Kitty was drawn toward these boys, but Bebe would say, "Sod 'em! They're only after one thing, and you can't get away with it the second time, Kitty."

Kitty took her advice, and the long line of ditched boyfriends stretched from Dalston to South End.

CHAPTER SEVEN

Tilly

As time passed, Kitty began to get quite skilled at matching the waistcoat backs. Her little red book was full of numbers that were counted up in the midweek and wages assessed by the amount of work done. Each week she earned a little more, which gave her the incentive to go on and earn still more, but this did not make her very popular with the rest of the girls. So Kitty made few friends at work, but she did have one—Tilly.

All her life Kitty felt for the underdog. She would defend anyone tooth and nail if she thought they were being victimized. Poor Tilly had a dreadful affliction—bad skin that was dull and greasy and erupted constantly into large, yellow-headed pimples that left holes in the skin when they disappeared. Kitty would stare fascinated at them, and poor Tilly would hang her head in embarrassment, pulling her straggly brown hair around her cheeks to hide her face.

Tilly sat right at the end of the long line of machines, with quite a few spaces between her and the other workers. At ten o'clock they were all allowed a ten-minute break, and a cup of tea was brought around by a woman with a trolley. The power was switched off and everyone would gather into little groups and gossip. But Tilly always sat alone at the end drinking her tea, her face turned away from the rest of the workers. In her dreamy way Kitty studied her, but one day she took her cup of tea up to the end of the line and sat with Tilly. Tilly gave Kitty a sweet smile and nervously pulled her hair about her face.

"Why do you sit up here by yourself?" asked Kitty.

"It's them," replied Tilly, indicating the other workers.

"What do you mean?" asked Kitty.

"The rest of the girls. They complain. Won't sit with me because of me spots." Tears welled up in her blue eyes.

"Goodness," cried Kitty. "Whyever not? Spots aren't catching, are they?"

"No," Tilly said, shaking her head. "But I've always had them. I'm under the hospital. They said they might go when I get married."

But Kitty was shocked. "How dreadful. Do you mean that they force you to sit up here alone? Why do you put up with it?"

"I'm used to it," said Tilly.

"Well, from now on I'll sit with you if you don't mind," said Kitty. "That will show that common lot what I think of them."

From that moment on Tilly was Kitty's slave. She would bring her homemade cake and little gifts from home. Kitty became very fond of Tilly, but she did think her a terrible mixer, for she would repeat word for word everything she heard in the cloakroom or lavatory to Kitty.

One Saturday they worked overtime. Kitty liked overtime; money had become an obsession with her. It was not to save but to spend very liberally on herself,

her family and friends. But the Friday night before had
been Passover, and she had had a particularly large
nosh-up with Bebe at Mrs. G.'s. Then they had gone to
the pub and drunk three port wines. The next morning,
doing overtime at work, Kitty had a terrific hangover
and was sick. She had dashed out to the toilet to vomit
and returned very pale. At lunch Tilly was full of
gossip. "I wanna tell you something, Kitty," she whispered.

Feeling decidedly irritable from her headache, Kitty
listened. With a great performance Tilly held her hand
over her mouth and muttered: "Guess what I heard
Sylvia say out in the toilet."

"What?" sighed Kitty.

"She said she thinks you've clicked, and she ain't
surprised, neither."

Kitty stared suspiciously at her. So far sex was an
unknown thing to Kitty. The kisses and cuddling and
tussles with the lads were all that her sex life comprised.

"Ain't she got a cheek!" declared Tilly, goading
Kitty and getting ready for battle.

"What does she mean?" demanded Kitty, casting
malevolent glances down the line at Sylvia, who was big
and husky with a long nose and tangled curly hair. Kitty
had never liked her.

"Oh, you know," cried Tilly. "She heard you being
sick, so she thinks you copped it."

"Copped it? Clicked?" Kitty repeated the words in
bewilderment.

"Got in the family way, silly cow," declared Tilly,
disappointed that her news had not had the immediate
effect she had wanted.

"She said what?" shouted Kitty. She jumped up and
marched down the line of women. She took hold of
Sylvia's untidy mop and banged her head violently
against her machine. Soon the place was in an uproar.
Sylvia got up and mowed tiny Kitty down onto the
floor, punching and kicking her while Kitty held on to
her hair and dug her long nails into Sylvia's face. The

other women shouted and screamed as the fighting pair rolled over and over among all the cottons and cuttings that littered the floor. The tailors threw huge bundles of work at them, uttering lewd cries, but Kitty and Sylvia fought on, neither of them gaining much ground.

Suddenly Joe Snider, the foreman, came running in. Without much ceremony, using boot and fist, he thrust them apart.

"Get out! get out!" he yelled. "I'll have no bleeding fights in here."

Once more Kitty was in the doghouse, but bravely she faced the scorn of the workers and the anger of the foreman.

"No one's going to take my character away," she declared. "You can have your rotten old job." She proceeded to put on her coat.

Now Mr. Bloomfield was the real boss, but he always skulked in his cubicle when there was any trouble and let bully-boy Joe Snider sort it out. But this time, when Sylvia claimed the sympathy of the rest of the girls, old Mr. Bloomfield, who had been watching from a distance, called: "Bring Kitty in here."

Dusty and disheveled, Kitty faced her boss. His thick pebble glasses made his kindly eyes look huge and his red nose, purple cheeks and hot breath indicated a bad heart. That was why Mr. Bloomfield avoided trouble.

"Now, now, Kitty, my dear, what's the matter?"

"She took my character away," declared Kitty. "I'm not having that."

Mr. Bloomfield half-smiled. "Now, now, we must not have that. But you're a good worker, Kitty. What about making it up, and I'll keep you on?"

"I don't care," said Kitty. "Never liked that Sylvia."

"Well, now, how would you like to stay in the office with me?" asked Mr. Bloomfield. There was something about this girl; she was like a small, irate puppy hanging onto a bone.

"No, no, Solly," cried Joe Snider, who was listening to his boss. "She's a cow. She'll drive you crazy."

"We'll chance it," said Mr. Bloomfield. "Get yer things, Kitty. I'll show you what I want you to do."

"Will I get the same wages?" demanded Kitty.

"Yes, dear," said Mr. Bloomfield, "and like this you will be in a good position. I trust yer, dear, got a lot of go in yer. I need a girl in here."

Once more Kitty fell on her feet and blossomed as she became the boss's girl. She examined the work when it was finished, and Mr. Bloomfield explained to Kitty how to book it and send it out, teaching her how to pass the work and how to turn back bad work to the machinists, who really got to dislike her as a result. Tilly, however, still stuck to her loyally. Apart from Mr. Bloomfield, Tilly was Kitty's only friend at work.

All her life Kitty remembered decrepit old Solomon Bloomfield, and he was fond of her. While he sat dozing in the chair in his cubicle, Kitty was always there, bright and alert and ready and willing to please him. He had lost his only son in an accident and still his wife pined. The little office where he worked was his retreat and Kitty brightened it up for him no end. She made him laugh with her stories and her sprightly approach to life.

"You marry a nice Yiddisher boy, Kitty, and go into business," he would say. "Make a fortune, you will."

"I'm not going to get married," Kitty would tell him. "If it wasn't for my dad I'd start traveling all over the world, because I want to write a book."

Solly would chuckle. "Believe me, Kitty, you will do it if you say so," he declared.

Tilly still hung on to Kitty. "I play the piano," she confessed to Kitty one day. "I get invited to parties, but I won't go unless someone stands near me. I don't like them to see my face."

Kitty was slightly incredulous. A piano? No one had a piano unless they were rich. But on being invited to Tilly's house Kitty was due for a surprise. Although Tilly lived in a run-down district called the Nile, her home was bright and clean and comfortable. It was a tall three-story house, and a host of relations lived on the various floors. There was a big front room, and in it stood a brand new shiny piano. Kitty could not believe her eyes. When Tilly sat down on the piano stool and her small hands moved lightly over the keys, lovely music rang out. Kitty was really astounded. All the ragtime songs and all the popular dance tunes—Tilly could play every one.

"Well, where's the music sheets?" Kitty asked.

"I play by ear; I don't need music," replied Tilly.

From then on, Kitty spent many happy evenings at Tilly's house, the two of them singing merrily at the piano. Soon Kitty had introduced Bebe to Tilly, and the three of them became fast friends. They all went along together to the Saturday night parties that Tilly was invited to because of her musical abilities. Sometimes it was a wedding or a twenty-first party, often it was just a dinky-do; but always Kitty stuck close to Tilly as she played the piano so that her poor friend would not have to turn around, so ashamed was she of her sickly, damaged skin. Kitty was always a hit on these occasions. She would stand by the piano wiggling and waggling her hips and rolling her eyes as she sang loudly in a plaintive, out-of-tune voice. Her songs went down very well, especially when the party had got underway and most of the guests were drunk.

Between the ages of seventeen and eighteen, Kitty's life was good. Her hair grew a bit longer and she had it nicely permed. She also had a little more clothes sense, for Tilly was a neat, smart dresser and had her clothes made by a dressmaker to whom she introduced Kitty.

Tilly left the sweatshop to work in another factory, leaving Kitty with no friends at work. But Kitty did not care. She had the protection of old Solly Bloomfield, and she did not like the other girls, anyway.

At home there were great improvements. Everyone had their own thing going now. Noni still had her job at the box factory, and even Bobby had started work as a

bellboy in a hotel. Dad frequently put on his best suit
and disappeared to another part of town. Kitty did not
know where he went, but she did not worry. The fact
that he was courting never occurred to her, particularly
as he would often remark: "I'll never put a stepmother
over my children. I promised that to my wife on her
deathbed."

It was Noni, of course, who was always poking her
nose into everything, who told Kitty of the big blond
lady who owned an eel pie shop. "Got a lot of money,"
declared Noni. "Wants our dad to marry her."

Kitty sniffed. "I'll believe it when I see it. He told me
he would never marry again."

"Well," blustered Noni, "don't say I didn't warn
yer." She was obviously hoping that the blond would
push Kitty from her position as housekeeper.

Dad never mentioned his friend, and, as he promised, nothing ever came of it, but he seemed a happier
man and drank much less nowadays.

CHAPTER EIGHT
A Hard Life

Of late, the out-of-work population had dwindled because as soon as a lad landed in trouble with the police, he disappeared into the army—usually in India. Lots of lads now belonged to the Terrys, a part-time army that gave them free uniforms and kept them occupied with drills twice a week.

That another war was brewing did not concern anyone, least of all Kitty, whose main ambition in life was to be a smart dresser. She spent all her wages on clothes to achieve that aim.

One recent piece of excitement in Kitty's life had been the wedding of Bebe's brother. As planned, Rafe married Fay Gonsky, and Kitty, as Bebe's friend, was invited to the big Jewish wedding. It was held in a posh restaurant. All the guests, young and old, danced a kind of ritual dance going around and around, around and around. It was great fun, and after that there was a terrific nosh-up. Kitty and Bebe had a wonderful time, and they were both happy that Bebe was at last free from her brother's wrath when she stayed out late at night.

In the past Rafe had been the bane of Bebe's life. Every time he heard her coming back home late, he gave her a terrific whack as she came in. If he failed to do it at night, he would get up early the next morning and hit her then.

Now that Rafe was no longer around to chastise Bebe, the girls started going to late-night parties dressed to kill. Bebe never seemed successful at catching a beau, but that did not stop her looking.

Often, when coming back late through the lonely dark streets, they would pass the local boys who, on hot summer nights, still lounged around at the street corners. There was a certain spot where the road narrowed and an old shop had been converted into some sort of political meeting place. Men and boys, dressed in black shirts and leather jackets, often stood outside, even when the lights had gone out. There were lurid posters in the window, but to Kitty there was little or no interest in the place. But for some reason, to Bebe it was an evil place. She would creep furtively past, and at the slightest movement from those boys she would yell: "Quick, Kitty, run! They're coming after us!" Then she would scoot off down the road on her fat legs, shouting, "Poppa, Rafe!" at the top of her voice as she neared her house.

Kitty would follow more slowly behind, wondering what on earth had scared Bebe so. "I see no reason why I should run past them," she told Bebe after one of her rapid flights. "Let them start," she muttered as she swung her heavy handbag in the air threateningly. "I'll give them what for."

"Oh, Gawd help yer if they catches up with yer," gasped Bebe. But Kitty was not bothered.

One night, quite late, it happened. As the two girls walked home after another party, the boys spread out in a line across the road, facing them. Realizing that she could not scoot past them in her normal fashion, Bebe began to panic.

"Don't worry," Kitty said soothingly, "it's only a lot of old corner boys."

But Bebe stood quivering like a huge blancmange, mouth agape.

"Get out of the way." cried Kitty at the boys, brandishing her handbag, but they closed ranks even more and hemmed the girls against the brick wall. Bebe started screeching and yelling at the top of her voice. That made them leer even more.

One boy stood apart from the others and did not seem very interested. Kitty recognized him immediately. He was a pale, thin boy who had been in her class at school. His name was Tommy Wright. Now he looked at the irate Kitty, turned to his mate and said quietly, "I'd leave her alone, that's Kitty Daly—her old man'll slaughter you."

The boys hesitated for a second, looking at one another, but suddenly they parted, letting Kitty and Bebe through. As Bebe tried to dash past, one of them pushed her violently and said roughly, "Fuck off, Jew girl."

Bebe fell hard against the wall, grazing her hand. Kitty was startled by the boy's aggression but more horrified by the look of terror on Bebe's face. Then, as she ran to help her friend, Tommy Wright came over, too, and said, "They won't hurt you, they're only having a lark." Bebe was speechless with fright and Kitty with rage as she watched the other boys sniggering, proud of their behavior.

"I'll walk with you," Tommy offered, leaving his gang.

When they all reached Bebe's shop, she said, "Come on in and have some coffee. I'm that scared, and Poppa is over at Rafe's."

The three of them sat up very late, drinking coffee and chattering. Despite his rough companions, Tommy

seemed a nice, polite boy. Kitty was amazed at how
well he and Bebe seemed to get on together; Bebe was
so big and Tommy so small and thin. But he was a very
pretty boy with soft pale skin, golden hair and limpid
blue eyes. And most charming of all was the skin
underneath those eyes, which crinkled underneath
when he smiled.

After that first meeting, Tommy was often to be
found in Bebe's house. On most occasions he would
wait until he saw Kitty and Bebe coming down the road
and then join them. The three quickly became fast
friends.

After a time, Kitty would often say tactfully, "I must
go. Dad'll be looking for me." And she would leave,
giving Tommy and Bebe time alone together.

So began a sweet friendship that lasted through the
summer. Bebe stopped going to the Saturday night
parties, so Kitty went alone with Tilly. By autumn, it
was clear that Tommy and Bebe were lovers, particularly since Bebe would tell Kitty all about it in great detail.
Kitty thought it was all a dreadful bore and truly missed
the Friday night nosh-ups at the Gonskys' and the
weddings and bar mitzvahs that she and Bebe had
previously gate-crashed together. But the loud, colorful
Bebe had settled down.

Despite the loss of her friend's companionship, Kitty
was happy. Her job with old Solly Bloomfield was still
enjoyable; she remained his favorite girl and received
good wages.

One day she decided she was tired of all the late-
night parties and started staying home in the evenings
to catch up on her reading. After she had devoured
most of the enjoyable but terrible love and romance
magazines—trash written specially for working-class
girls—she began to find them boring and started reading the classics. Rejoining the free library, she read her
way through all the modern novels, then the Brontë
sisters, Jane Austen, and on to *War and Peace,* most of
Dickens and some terrible blood-thirsty tales from the

world war. Then one day she got hold of a banned copy of *Mein Kampf* written by a German man named Hitler.

Solly Bloomfield saw her spending her lunchtimes engrossed in this book and said to her, "Kitty, dear, you should not be allowed to read that rubbish."

"Why not?" demanded Kitty. "How will I know what's going on if I don't read about it?"

"Oy, yoy," muttered Solly sadly, "you might be right." He shrugged. "But I hear such things, sometimes I can't believe what's happening."

"Well, it is," said Kitty.

"My life, Kitty," said Solly, "it's a pity they don't have women prime ministers. You would certainly fill the part." It was Kitty's turn to shrug before returning to her book.

Soon after that, as Kitty was washing her hair one night, Bebe turned up to visit her. This was most unusual, as Kitty had never encouraged her friends to come to her home because it was so bare and poor and always untidy. She was very conscious of this and normally kept visitors on the doorstep. But that evening Bebe looked so different and forlorn that Kitty, who had gone to the door downstairs with a towel wrapped about her head, immediately relented. Bebe held one hand over her mouth and Kitty, seeing how distressed her pal was, said rather nervously, "Oh, I suppose you'd better come up."

They slowly climbed the bare stairs into the untidy kitchen, where Kitty said, "Whatever's wrong, you look as if you've seen a ghost."

Suddenly Bebe started to weep and pulled out a handkerchief to mop her lip. Kitty, horrified, noticed that it was swollen and bloody.

"Who did that?" she asked.

"Rafe," Bebe sobbed. "He bashed me up because I told me poppa that I want to marry Tommy Wright."

Immediately Kitty was all sympathy, indignant that a man should dare lay hands on a woman. She put an arm around her friend. "Well, why not, Bebe? You're turned nineteen, nearly twenty, some girls get married much younger."

"It's not me age," replied Bebe tearfully. "It's because of the religion."

"You mean you being a Jewess?" said Kitty. "But is that so important?" She could never understand why religion was so often the basis for hatred and hostility in the world. To her, everyone was fundamentally the same, whatever their creed or religion.

"It's not important to me," sobbed Bebe. "I never kept it up, not since Mum died. And I love Tommy," she wailed, "and anyway, Kitty, that's not all . . . I'm in the family way." Tears poured down her round cheeks.

"Oh, dear," cried Kitty, "what a foolish thing to do!" She recalled all the worldly advice Bebe had given her about boys in the past. But what good had any of that done Bebe herself?

"Well it's done," said Bebe defiantly, looking Kitty straight in the eye. "And Tommy wants to stick by me."

"But he's out of work, isn't he?" said Kitty.

"So what?" replied Bebe. "I've got savings, and it won't hurt the old man to part up with a bit. I don't think Poppa minds that we want to get married. It's that bloody Rafe—he thinks the Gonskys will find out. He says that it would be a terrible disgrace as far as they're concerned."

"Well," said Kitty, "I suppose all old folks are like that. I expect my dad will probably want me to marry a Roman Catholic, but personally, I don't care," she said nonchalantly, rubbing her head with the towel. "Well, then, what you got is love on the dole, like that novel I just read," she giggled.

"Oh, Kitty, don't laugh," said Bebe dismally. "You don't know what the Jews are like. I might run away with Tommy if we can find somewhere to live." There was not much more to be said after that, so Bebe left.

Kitty was not surprised to hear that her headstrong

pal kept to her word and within a week had gone off with Tommy. They did not go far away—just upstairs in his mother's house, in a small back room.

Bebe's brother went down and beat on the door, to no avail, and when her father got drunk he chased her up the street. But still Bebe defied them and finally, when they realized she was pregnant, they gave in and stopped harassing her.

A month later, Tommy and Bebe had a civil wedding at the Shoreditch Town Hall. They rented two rooms of their own in the street next to Kitty's, and Bebe proceeded to decorate them and turn them into a comfortable little love nest. But as far as her family was concerned, she was written off. Rafe and Fay and Mrs. G. had nothing more to do with her, and her father only talked to her grudgingly.

When Kitty's father heard about all this, he commented, "'Tis a pity, a foine gel like that might have married well with her own kind and wanted for nought."

"Well, she's in love, and happy," replied Kitty, jumping in to the defense of her pal.

"For how long?" Dad asked. "All of the Wrights are consumptive, and that's something you can't fight."

Kitty remembered how almost every year there had been a funeral at the Wrights' house—how little white coffins had been carried out and the family had dwindled. The father had sat outside the house in an old chair coughing and wheezing; it had been dreadful to listen to him.

Now there was only the faded old mother and one small sister left in the sad little house where they lived. Kitty felt very unhappy just thinking about it. Why did this illness affect so many young folk? Why was there no cure for tuberculosis? She wanted to know.

In the library Kitty looked up the disease in the medical books. After many hours of reading, she decided that fresh air and plenty of milk and butter were essential for strong healthy lungs. But most of the

time the poor people of the East End had condensed
milk from a tin, and margarine—never butter, it was
too expensive.

As Kitty walked home from the library she began to
worry in case her own family could become infected.
She lay awake at night looking at the damp patches on
the ceiling and the way the paper peeled off the walls.
Sometimes, when it rained, the small window in the
roof leaked so that water dripped down onto the bed.
When this happened, Kitty would get up and put an old
mackintosh over herself and Noni. She realized how
terrible their living conditions were. Something had to
be done; she would try to persuade Dad to move,
maybe to another district where there were some trees
and perhaps a garden to sit in. Everyone in the family
was working—surely they could afford it now.

When Kitty approached her father about moving, he
adamantly refused to agree with her. "'Tis a foine
cheap place, not poky, and with plenty of fresh air," he
insisted.

"But it's damp," said Kitty, "and we might all get
TB."

"Nonsense, nonsense!" Dad cried. "Why, 'tis those
poky old dwellings that harbor the germs. All them
children down the street have gone off with the fever.
Now, you never had no fever, and no hospital treat-
ments."

As they quarreled, Dad got drunk and aggressive,
until Kitty knew that there was no point in pushing the
issue further. If her father was to be so stubborn there
was nothing she could do about it.

The argument with her father depressed her, and she
was to be saddened more by the news that Bebe's baby
was stillborn. As her dear friend later wept on Kitty's
shoulder, Kitty's fear of TB turned to anger. Why did
folks have to live like this? she asked herself. Surely
there was some way to escape. She was quite sure that
even if she could not budge her family, somehow she
was going to get out of this dreary existence. No

out-of-work oaf would ruin her life; that she had much to do before she died was one thing she was very confident of.

As these thoughts troubled her, she began to scribble compulsively in a large notebook. She wrote of the underprivileged—those who had nothing—and others who had it all, of social injustice and evils. Her handwriting was so bad that no one else would have been able to decipher it, but that did not matter; the scribbling proved to be great release for her emotions. Once her writing was finished, she put the notebook away in a suitcase under the bed and forgot about it. She felt relieved and free of tensions, just as if she had confided her troubles to someone.

Having recovered from her tragic pregnancy, Bebe returned to her job at Yankeys, the tin bashers. She was surprisingly cheerful plodding back and forth to work. She seldom dressed well these days; she was too busy cooking and looking after her Tommy Wright, who was still out of work.

Kitty did not see much of Bebe nowadays. In the evenings she usually went out with Tilly, who was now hired to play the piano regularly in the local pub. Kitty bought a long cigarette holder and puffed out clouds of smoke in what she thought was a sensuous manner. She was well supplied with fags by the admiring boys in the pub. The Saturday night entertainment was generally put on by the locals themselves and Kitty was quite surprised at how many of them could give a good performance by singing, dancing or doing a good variety turn. One girl, in particular, sang in a very vibrant way. She chose slightly bawdy songs that were extremely popular, so everyone joined in the chorus. As the evening wore on everyone sang every song they knew, ending with old war-time favorites they sang riotously before having a final, hectic knees-up. When the pub shut there was always someone having a bit of a do at home, and Tilly was commandeered to go along and play the piano in their parlor. Owning a piano—

always bought on the hire purchase—had suddenly
become fashionable, even if it meant going hungry all
week, and even if no member of the family was the
slightest bit musical.

Kitty really longed to have a cozy parlor with a piano
in it, but she knew that unless she had a home of her
own it would never be possible. Dad had a moral
aversion to things paid for on the weekly. "They are all
thieves and robbers taking the working man on," he
would insist.

There were some Saturday nights when Kitty would
look around at the red, flushed, drunken faces and
listen to the raucous voices and watch the fights in the
back yards where one youth would challenge another,
so that coats were discarded and sleeves rolled up as
they indulged in a duel of fisticuffs—usually over some
girl. Kitty's eyes would be sore from the smoke and her
mascara would run down her cheeks. Her voice would
be hoarse from singing, and her legs aching from
dancing. In this pensive moment, Kitty would suddenly
feel a horror at what she saw and heard. Is this what
living is all about? she would think. Surely there was
some other way to live, but how, where and when did
one find it?

On Sunday mornings she would lie in bed with a
heavy hangover and listen to Dad complaining of her
wicked ways as he hustled the others off to Mass. Kitty
was seldom in a good enough condition to rise early for
Mass nowadays. Her conscience would prick her, because she genuinely wanted to sit in the peaceful
church, see the flowers on the altar and sense the
swimming feeling the smell of the incense gave her. But
for some unearthly reason she could never get herself
out of bed; no power on earth could get her out in time.
She would lie there thinking how long a lifetime was,
how long before one got old, ugly and wrinkled and yet
still trudged off to work, like the charwomen she saw
who would go back and forth through the streets every
day of the week.

No, it was not possible for her to live like that, she decided. She would probably die young like her mother. Poor Mummy, she had been a lady, and the poverty had defeated her. It was better in these circumstances never to marry. It was the little children who suffered, those left behind. Death for the dying was nice, kind and peaceful; one only went into a deep sleep.

In the middle of this reflection Kitty would become depressed and spend the rest of the day in a state of deep melancholia, so she was always happy to get back to work on Monday morning, back to the company and affection of old Solly Bloomfield.

Before long, Bebe managed to get her Tommy a job at the tin bashers. He was hired as a laborer and often had to move the heavy trolleys loaded with tin boxes. Despite the loss of the baby, they were very happy, particularly now that they were both working. Their little love nest looked comfortable in spite of Bebe's elaborate ideas—ideas that involved huge paper flowers, gilt mirrors, red plush tablecloths and some quite good furniture that she had come into on the recent death of her poppa. It was all just a little overcrowded, but Bebe was proud of her home and was always taking someone home to tea.

If she was at a loose end on Saturday night, Kitty would arrive at Bebe's for some beer and a chat. Bebe would tell her of her plans to save up and buy a big house and let out rooms. She was so ambitious and full of new ideas, all of which seemed a trifle daring to Kitty. Tommy still looked as strong as ever, but sometimes he had a bad cough. He never had much to say and stayed in the background while Bebe nattered cheerfully to her friends. He always made everyone welcome.

One day a disaster happened that marred Bebe's dreams. As Tommy picked up a heavy box at work, he suddenly collapsed and fell to the ground as blood spurted from his mouth. A lung had collapsed. He was rushed to the local infirmary where he stayed for awhile. Bebe spent many weeks going back and forth to the hospital visiting him each day with fruit and flowers, her face white and drawn with anxiety. It was a terrible period, and Kitty comforted her disaster-prone friend as best she could.

Then suddenly there was hope. The doctors told Bebe that Tommy could possibly be cured if he went away to a sanitarium in the heart of the country. It would be a long treatment, but he was still young, they said, and there were new methods of combating this pernicious disease.

Bebe's reaction was mixed. She was happy that Tommy had a chance of surviving, but was afraid of being far away from him.

"Oh, Kitty, how will I live without him?" she cried mournfully.

Kitty held Bebe's hand comfortingly, but, strangely enough, she felt cold and hard inside. "Well, Bebe," she remarked, "we all have to get by against tremendous odds. That's the process of living, I suppose."

Poor Bebe was dismayed. She did not understand Kitty's cryptic remark. Her jaw dropped and tears came to her eyes. "You don't know what it's like to love someone, Kitty. If you did you would have more feeling."

"I never meant to hurt you," protested Kitty. "It was just life in general I was thinking about."

But Bebe was offended and did not understand. After that she asked Tilly to go with her to visit Tommy on Sundays instead of Kitty. Although Kitty was hurt by Bebe's rejection of her, she was also a little relieved that she did not have to go to the hospital anymore. Being among all those germs she had read about was an experience that really bothered her.

Now Kitty spent more time on her own in the evenings and at weekends. After work she would put on her newest dress and, with her hair all in waves and kiss-curls, she would stand idly at the street door watching the children playing in the street, her eyes on the boy over the road in the yard next to the greengrocer's.

This boy had always lived there, but he never mixed with the rest of the kids. Kitty knew that he was called Tim. He went to a posh school, to which he wore a smart gray blazer with a red badge on it and a small flat cap.

Kitty would watch him with interest. They had to be about the same age, she thought, but he still went to school and she had been working nearly four years.

Tim had recently acquired a motorbike, and without his school uniform—dressed in a roll-neck sweater and a pair of long gray flannels—he looked quite normal. His hair was bright red, his face a mass of freckles. He was always fiddling around with his bike in that yard after school, and he always completely ignored Kitty. Apart from the bike and his pals, he showed no interest in anything that went on around him.

Kitty was very curious. She would spend hours staring over at him in the hope of discovering something about him. Then one evening a group of boys with motorbikes came to call on Tim. They sat on their bikes in the street, revving the engines proudly. Kitty was very excited. She smiled sweetly at one of them—a tall, good-looking boy—who returned her smile and asked her politely, "Want a ride?" He grinned broadly as he spoke.

A shiver of excitement ran down Kitty's spine. She had never ridden pillion before. She walked boldly over the road and swung her slim leg over the bike behind the boy. "Now hold on tight," he said. "Put your arms around my waist."

Kitty did as he told her and held on. What a nice comfortable feeling it was to cuddle up close to this clean-looking youth, whose name, he told her, was Bill Ross.

And off they went. Up and down they rode the street and then along the main road. The wind whistled past her, blowing out her careful hairdo. But Kitty did not care; it was such a complete thrill.

After that occasion, whenever he visited his chum Tim, Bill would come over the road for a chat with Kitty Daly. Then they usually rode off to Epping Forest together. In Kitty's opinion, Bill was such a clean, polite boy, with good white teeth and a fresh complexion. He always wore a stiff white collar that was never grubby. He would wind a long, hand-knitted scarf twice around his neck, saying, "Must not get me collar dirty. Have to wear a white collar for the office—the old man's fussy about that."

Bill was quite different from Kitty's usual escorts; he was courteous and undemanding, and, being interested only in motorbikes, he never seemed to want to kiss and cuddle, no matter how much Kitty waggled her hips or flickered her mascara-thick eyelashes. Flirtatious antics never had any effect on him. But all the same, he seemed to like Kitty and began to call regularly for her. When the gang came to her street in the evenings to pick up their red-headed pal, Bill would wait patiently for her to emerge from the house wearing a blue beret on her head and an old black mackintosh over her pretty dress. They all set off on long rides to a pub in Epping where the bike boys gathered. The other boys picked up girls there to take home with them, but Bill always brought Kitty, now his regular date.

Kitty loved the freedom of riding through the night, crouching close to Bill, sheltered from the wind. She was never frightened; the faster they went, the more she loved it. Bill rarely said much; he never praised Kitty, and never made any important comments. The most he did was to pat the highly polished saddle of his bike and say proudly, "The old girl went like a bomb tonight, didn't she, Kitty?"

Kitty would coyly agree, but she always felt a deep sense of disappointment that the bike got more attention than she did. When she mentioned her feelings to the other boys, all they said was, "Old Bill is a wizard with bikes. His bike is the oldest, but it is also the fastest because he's got it tuned up so well."

In fact, Bill was the mechanic of the gang. He was always the one to be called on whenever any of his pals' bikes went wrong. So Kitty spent many hours sitting by the roadside while Bill repaired these machines. She did not mind too much, for she enjoyed just being with him. For some strange reason they never argued or quarreled, and Kitty often wondered if she was in love with him. She did not feel romantic like she thought she should, the way it was described in novels, but if Bill was ever late for a date or did not come at all, she felt desolate.

To please Bill, Kitty had changed her way of living in every respect. She had her hair cut short again, but this time it was permanently waved in a boyish style. Kitty thought it looked nice and was very pleased. She bought long mannish pants, which made riding the bike easier, and a heavy pullover to keep out the wind when they tore along the roads at top speed.

Tommy Wright had been away in the sanitarium for months, and Bebe and Tilly had become very thick. In the evenings, Bebe joined Tilly at the bar and Tilly, who loved squabbles, sided with Bebe against Kitty. Finally, as young girls are wont to do, they decided they were no longer friends with Kitty at all and refused to speak to her. As Kitty and Bill rode by on the motorbike, the two of them would stand and stare.

"Silly cow, she'll break her bleeding neck one day," Bebe would mutter.

"I heard that those motorbike fellas make you walk home if you don't give in," whispered Tilly cattily. Tilly was the everlasting stirrer.

Kitty did not care about any of this. She had found a new life and she loved every bit of it—the smell of the fresh air as they rode out of London, the wide open spaces, the green grass and deep dark forests.

Every Sunday, they toured the byways around London and rode deep into Essex and Kent. At midday

they would stop for the picnic sandwiches that Kitty
had packed for them. They always went alone, for Bill
no longer wanted to compete against his pals in their
speedy road races because he had been stopped by the
police one night for exceeding the speed limit. He was
ashamed at having to go to court and being fined ten
bob and terrified in case his mother found out about it.

Kitty, who had lived all her life within a criminal
fraternity, could not understand what all the fuss was
about. In the street where she lived, boys regularly
went off to jail. In fact, most of the parties she attended
had been jail parties—going-in parties and coming-out
parties—and everyone always had a good time at them.

Now, for the first time, she got some inkling of
middle-class attitudes. They seemed to include a desire
for something that had nothing to do with being posh,
for Bill was also really working class. Whatever they
were, they created some kind of barrier which made
her feel uncomfortable. She was very aware of the fact
that Bill had never invited her to visit his home, even
though he had become almost like a member of her
own family. But because he never mentioned it she
never broached the subject with him.

Everybody liked Bill. Dad would often pass through
the yard and be amused to see the youth fiddling with
his precious bike while little Kitty gave him all the
chit-chat. In his polite Irish manner Dad would raise his
hat and say, "Good evening to you, son."

"Good evening to you, sir," Bill would reply respectfully.

The first time that happened Kitty giggled. "No need
to call him sir," she said. "It's only our dad."

"All the more reason," said Bill, looking down at her
with his serious blue eyes.

Somehow Kitty thought she had been snubbed.

At that point Bill had never been inside Kitty's home
because, in her usual fashion, she had not invited him.
But one day Dad did. It was raining one evening when

Dad passed Bill in the street. He stopped and shook his head at the sight of the bedraggled boy. "Go into the house, laddie, it's wet out here," he said.

Kitty was at home making a pot of tea when, much to her embarrassment, Bill entered her untidy house. He did not glance at the squalor. He just hung up his coat on the door and quietly sat down to join in a card game with Noni and Bobby. Later, Dad asked Bill about his bike and Bill answered all his questions politely and clearly. But throughout, Kitty felt extremely uncomfortable.

When it was time for Bill to go home, Kitty saw him to the door. "I'm sorry about tonight, Bill. It was such a bore stopping in," she said.

Bill's white teeth glinted in the half-dark. "That's where you make a mistake, Kitty. I like stopping in. Can I come in tomorrow?"

Astonished, Kitty snuggled close to him. As they held each other tight she felt a rush of warmth flow through her. Bill kissed her gently on the lips and affectionately ruffled her hair. With her head against his chest, Kitty smiled. She did love him, she thought.

After that, Bill came courting regularly and, to Dad's delight, bore gifts of food. The first time he brought a big jar full of broken eggs and a large packet of bacon rashers.

Kitty cooked supper for them all—a huge feast of fried eggs and bacon with fried bread and many cups of tea. After the meal, they all played cards, told stories and laughed continuously. There had been so little laughter in the home since Kitty's mother had died, but now Bill's presence began to change things.

"Don't worry about buying butter, bacon and cheese," he said. "I'll bring them. I can get them from work."

Kitty stared at him aghast. "Oh, you don't nick all that food, do you?" They were all precious luxury items that they could normally not buy.

Bill began to laugh heartily. "No, I work for Van Jurgen's, the food distributors, and we're allowed to take home a certain amount of food that would be wasted anyway."

Kitty burst out laughing, too, as she breathed a deep sigh of relief; she had been having vivid memories of Mario and her first dance dress.

CHAPTER NINE

Settling Down

Sundays in Kitty's neighborhood were normally noisy and full of life. The alleyways were filled with children playing endless games of hopscotch and marbles. Knowing that everyone was home, the tradesmen came—the rag-and-bone man with his old horse and cart, the muffin man carrying his goods on his head and the ice-cream man crying as he came: "Hokey, pokey, a penny a lump." And there was so much to buy from the barrows: winkles, shrimps, cockles, jellied eels, watercress and pig trotters. From early morning until late at night the energetic cries of the street folk penetrated the rickety doors and cracked windows of the dwellings, bringing life to the depressed back streets of London.

On this particular Sunday, however, Kitty had just got out of bed and stood listening. Dad, Noni and Bobby were all at Mass, so Kitty was alone in the house. It was silent in the street outside; something strange was happening. Kitty pulled on her clothes and went to the window. Down below she saw little knots of women standing close together talking among themselves in low voices. There were no children playing, and even the tradesmen were absent. The air seemed still and melancholy. Kitty had a creepy feeling inside her as she went out to investigate.

At the end of the street was a small blind alley known as Hobbs Place. Only four small houses stood down there, shut away from the sunlight because they were completely overshadowed by the huge factory beside them. It was here that Mary lived—big, blowsy Mary who had started work at that first sweat-shop with Kitty the day after they had both left school.

Kitty lost all touch with Mary after she had been sacked from the tailor's because she was expecting another baby. Mary's first unwanted child was then not yet two years old. Everyone had been shocked, but the scandal was soon forgotten and Mary had her second baby at home. They all lived in Mary's mother's house, No. 2 Hobbs Place. The mother was a big, tough-looking woman who went out charring and whose husband was doing time for trying to assault a young girl in the park. East End folk never bore grudges about anything. In this case they just said stoically: "Poor sod, the boys will give him hell in the nick—those sexual offenders always get it."

Only a few weeks before this particular Sunday, Kitty had met Mary, who was pushing her two babies in the pram. Mary had looked Kitty up and down, noting the clothes she was wearing. "Cor blimey, don't you fancy yerself," she said tartly. Kitty was shocked and for some reason embarrassed. She blushed. But then, staring Mary in the eye, and with an edge to her voice, she said: "Well, perhaps if you washed more frequently someone might fancy you, Mary. Then you might even get a father for your two kids."

At this Mary swore heartily at Kitty, shaking her fat fist. "Bash yer up, I will, Kitty Daly. Piss orf down yer own street."

Kitty had taken the hint.

But now Kitty had occasion to regret her own spiteful words. During the night a gas main in Hobbs Place had leaked. All the families in those four houses had been affected by the escaping gas. For most of them, it did not prove fatal because much of the gas had collected in the downstairs rooms while they slept upstairs. But in No. 2 it was different. For reasons of economy the family had lodgers upstairs, so Mary, her mother and babies slept below in the front room. They were all dead: poor, ignorant Mary, her mother and the two little unwanted babies.

The police had roped off Hobbs Place, and that was where everyone had gathered to have a look. As Kitty pushed her way through the crowd, a big van drew up to take the bodies to the mortuary.

Kitty watched the plain wooden coffins being carried out one by one, and she wondered what harm Mary or any of them had ever done to deserve a fate like that. And she wept for the little family along with everyone else.

As she walked back home, Kitty recalled her last conversation with Mary. She felt so guilty that she knew she could not tell anyone, but it nagged at her mind all day.

In the afternoon Bill came over to visit. "What, no smile today, Kitty?" he said, noticing her long face. "What's wrong?"

After much coaxing from Bill, Kitty finally told him about the tragedy down the street, and then said softly, "I wish I had been more kind to her."

Bill moved up close and put his arm around her shoulder. As he looked down at Kitty, his eyes were sincere. "Try not to worry," he said. "It happens to everyone when someone dies. There's always something you feel you should have said or something you did not do."

Bill's wise words helped to assuage Kitty's guilt. She

snuggled close to him. He always managed to console her; he always knew exactly what to say.

Kitty was beginning to calm down a little and become less wild in her ways. Her figure had filled out, and, although her face still had a doll-like expression, it no longer looked wan. Under Bill's influence she began to use less makeup, and with her small oval face and soft curling hair she was attractive to look at.

For Christmas Bill had taken Kitty down to the city and bought her a coat and dress of his choice, so Kitty looked neat and smart and was very pleased with herself.

Bill had really become part of the household. The rest of the family depended on him to sort out their various problems, from the crossword puzzles that went on every night to arguments on politics, and even the choice of music. Bill was very tactful and always managed to choose the middle ground and appease everyone.

There was one particular incident that made Kitty very impressed by Bill's diplomacy. Dad had lately taken to wearing a natty black bowler hat on weekends. With that on his head, a flower in his buttonhole and his suit well pressed, he would go off courting and leave all the young ones to their own devices. On his way home he would first visit the barber's, then the pub, so that by five o'clock on Saturdays he was always well boozed. On this afternoon, as Bill repaired a pal's motorbike in Daly's Yard, watched by Kitty and Noni, a small irate man came dashing up waving Dad's new bowler hat. His English was not at all good and he gesticulated a lot, but he managed to get the youngsters to understand that Dad had gone off with the wrong hat from the hatstand in the barber's shop.

Noni dashed off to the pub and looked in to see a florid-faced Dad propped up against the counter. Perched on top of his large red head was a bowler hat that was ridiculously small for him. She ran back to the yard where Kitty and Bill were still trying to pacify the excited foreign man. "Yes, he's got it," Noni gasped, panting for breath, "but he ain't 'alf drunk. I'm not going to get it orf him."

Kitty led the furious man over the road to the pub and tried to push him in to face Dad. But he indignantly managed to tell them, with many more gesticulations, that he was a strict teetotaler and never went into such places. Kitty realized that there was no point in trying to persuade him, so she went into the pub herself to explain to her father.

"Got the wrong hat, Dad," she told him.

With bleary eyes, the man looked down at his daughter. He took off the hat, turned it round in his hands to inspect it and put it back on his head.

"No, gel," he said quietly, "it's me own old hat." And with that he turned back to finish his pint.

Kitty did not know what to do. Even she did not dare to remove the hat surreptitiously while Dad was in the pub. She went outside again where the man was waving Dad's hat in the air and jabbering frantically about how he had now missed his train. Kitty looked at Bill in desperation and shrugged her shoulders. She was at a loss for words.

Coolly, Bill wiped his oily hands on a piece of old rag, took the bowler hat from the flailing arms of the little man and marched into the pub. Dad welcomed him drunkenly and turned to the bar to order them both a drink. While Dad had his back to him, Bill quickly swapped the hat in his hand with the hat on Dad's head. Dad was too drunk to notice a thing. Thus Bill had saved the day again.

Bill was so much at home with the Dalys that he even spent Christmas Day at their house. He arrived in the late morning carrying a turkey—a present from his boss. He had been at the Van Jurgen Christmas party and had many drinks inside him, so the turkey was battered and muddy by the time he arrived.

Kitty cleaned the turkey as best she could and took it

to the bakehouse to be cooked. Most of the houses in the street only had coal fires, and the few gas cookers that did exist were small and unreliable. So it was the custom for weekend joints of meat and Christmas poultry to be cooked in the local bakehouse. For the first time ever, Kitty joined the long line of fowl carriers waiting to carry home the Christmas dinner roasted, brown and appetizing. Other years the Dalys had just had to make do with a sniff of other people's Christmas fare as it was carried home from the bakehouse, as did the rest of the poor who had no dinner. Christmas had always been a nightmare for Kitty in the past as she tried to provide a few luxuries and cope with her father's heavy drinking bouts. Now, as in so many other things, Bill's presence had changed everything, and they had the happiest Christmas ever.

After they had eaten and opened the small number of presents that had been rustled up with a few pennies, and after the revelry had died down a little, Kitty and Bill cuddled up together in the old armchair. "What about your own parents, Bill?" Kitty asked him gently. "What are they doing for Christmas?"

A tiny muscle twitched in the side of Bill's cheek. "Mother has gone to my brother's," he said. "We lost Dad last year. Didn't you know?" He looked down at the floor as he spoke.

Kitty shook her head. "No," she said, "because you never mentioned it."

Bill said no more. The conversation seemed to make him sad, and Kitty did not want to push him. So Bill's home life remained a puzzle to Kitty.

After the holidays Bill suddenly began to visit less. He talked about having nights off and rarely appeared at weekends anymore. Kitty became worried; she was at a loose end when Bill did not come round, for she had begun to depend on him. She would watch and wait by the window or stand in the doorway trying to ignore the sarcastic comments from Noni, who was jealous of Kitty's friendship with the good-looking Bill.

"Ain't turned up again, then?" Noni would say. "Got fed up with yer, Kitty?"

Kitty tried not to show that she cared, but she was bitchy and spiteful to Bill when he did arrive. She never confronted him directly about his absences and he never offered any excuses. So a barrier began to build up between them, and Kitty, having no one to confide in, felt very cut off.

One evening, when it was clear that Bill was not going to arrive, Kitty went out for a walk. She wandered through the streets thinking about Bill. She just could not understand why he had suddenly changed like that. She wondered what she could have done to make him less keen on her and thought about what she could do to win back his complete attention.

As she turned a corner, Kitty realized that she was in her Nan's old street. Tears came to her eyes and she bit her lip as she remembered her dear grandmother, who had died the previous year. At the time she had been too involved with Bill to be very grieved by Nan's death, but now Kitty was painfully aware of her loneliness.

Her Aunt Frances now lived in Nan's house. Aunt Frances was Kitty's stepaunt, and Kitty rarely visited her because, although she thought her kind and affectionate, she found her very naive. But she knocked on the door of the house, drawn by a family bond.

Aunt Frances opened the door and was delighted to see her young niece. She bustled her into the front parlor while she made a pot of tea. The house seemed empty without Nan's flamboyant personality, but Kitty felt secure and warm.

"Where's this nice young man I hear so much about, Kitty?" asked Aunt Frances as she handed Kitty her tea. Kitty looked up at her aunt's kind face and burst into tears. "Oh, Auntie," she sobbed, "he doesn't want me anymore. He's trying to get rid of me."

Aunt Frances put down her cup of tea and took the girl in her big arms. "Now, come on, tell me, what is it?" she asked coaxingly. She held Kitty tight as she listened to the long tale of woe.

After Kitty had blurted out her sad story, Aunt Frances was silent for a minute or two. Then she coughed and said slowly, "Well, I may be wrong, dear, but I'll bet he hasn't been to see you so much because he's got some domestic troubles of his own. What about his mother? She may be very possessive, you know."

After her talk with Aunt Frances, Kitty felt much better. It had not occurred to her that something or someone other than she was the reason for Bill's strange behavior. She became convinced that there was something wrong at Bill's house.

The next time Bill did not arrive when he was supposed to, Kitty plucked up all her courage and marched round to his home up in Islington. Bill had always been secretive about his address, but she knew it because she spotted it on a piece of paper that fell out of his trouser pocket one day and had memorized it.

Kitty would never forget the first time she saw the tall gloomy Victorian house standing in a long winding row of terraced houses. There were stone steps going up to the front door and another set of steps going down to the basement. Neat lace curtains hung in the window, and there was a huge iron knocker on a blue front door that was securely closed. It was very different from the houses in the street where Kitty lived, with their one room up and one room down and front doors always open onto a street teeming with kids.

Kitty's heart was thumping as she timidly lifted the door knocker. She let the knocker go and could hear the noise echo loudly inside the house as if the building were empty. After waiting for at least five minutes, Kitty heard some shuffling sounds from within. Then the door opened very slightly. She could see that it was very dark inside. A head poked around the door. It was a woman in black. She had red-rimmed eyes and a nose so pink it looked as if she had a bad cold. "Who do you want, dear?" she said in a husky voice.

"Is Bill in?" asked Kitty, trying not to sound nervous.

"No, dear," the woman whispered. "He's not home from work yet." With that she closed the door again.

Kitty was nonplussed. She did not know what to make of the woman. She was also extremely disappointed that Bill was not home from work. She stood on the steps for a couple of minutes, and then, just as she was about to leave, she heard the familiar chug-chug of a motorbike. It was, of course, Bill.

Bill was astonished to see Kitty, but he also seemed very pleased. "Hullo, Kitty, how did you find your way here?"

"Well, I did and I'm here," said Kitty defiantly. "And you're late home; thought you finished at six."

Bill smiled and shifted in his seat. "Well, I'll let you into a secret, Kitty. I've got a spare-time job at the film studio. Work in the darkroom to earn some extra cash."

"Whatever for?" demanded Kitty, knitting her brow.

"I'm saving up for something," said Bill very secretively. "Did you knock?" he asked, indicating the door.

Kitty nodded.

"So you saw Mum?" A sad expression came into his blue eyes.

She nodded again but made no comment.

"Mum's been like that ever since me dad died. I can't do anything with her: she just sits in the dark crying," Bill explained miserably.

"Well, she's not going to get over it if you leave her all alone," said Kitty sharply. "Is that why you never asked me around to your house?"

Bill put an arm about her. "I'm sorry, Kitty, I was hoping she would get better. I've been staying home more lately. I'm tired when I come home after doing that extra job. I'm so tired that I don't always feel like coming round," he told her.

"I should think not," declared Kitty. "One job is enough for anyone."

They stood on the step looking at each other. Then Bill asked hesitatingly, "Would you like to come in?"

"I expect to come in," declared Kitty.

Bill grinned, as he always did when Kitty asserted herself. He opened the door and took her hand as he led her through a gloomy passage.

Kitty was most impressed by the huge, high-ceilinged rooms filled with beautiful, old-fashioned furniture. She had never seen such nice things. There were many vases, glass bowls, velvet-framed photographs and a lovely large mirror—but all covered with dust and cobwebs.

With his cap Bill dusted off a chair so that Kitty could sit down. It was a very elaborately carved chair with a plush upholstered seat. He lit the gas light and said, "Excuse the mess, Kitty, but Mum isn't up to doing the cleaning, and we seldom use the sitting room now, anyway."

"But it's lovely, Bill," gasped Kitty. "Look at those mirrors and that beautiful sideboard."

"My dad made most of the furniture," said Bill. "He was a cabinetmaker."

"Will your mum come and see me," asked Kitty, suddenly aware of being a guest, "or shall I go and see her?"

"I warn you, Kitty, she might not be friendly," said Bill. "Come downstairs anyway and I'll make a cup of tea."

Climbing down a dark staircase, they came to a large kitchen the likes of which Kitty had never seen. It was as neglected as the room she had just left, but well equipped with saucepans and a china-laden dresser. Kitty suddenly noticed Bill's mum huddled over a dwindling fire. The room was very cold, and the old woman constantly wiped her nose on a black-bordered handkerchief. Kitty sat down on a wooden chair.

"This is Kitty, Mum," said Bill.

There was complete silence as the red-eyed woman turned her head to scrutinize her son's friend.

Kitty jumped to her feet. "Don't you feel cold?" she asked. "It's chilly in here." Picking up an old cardigan, she put it around the woman's shoulders. Bill's mother's lips moved, as if to smile. "Blimey, Bill," Kitty said, "make up the fire and I'll do the tea."

The fire sputtered into life just as Kitty poured the tea. She gave the first cup to Bill's mum, and then made some toast. They all sat around the now glowing-bright fire, Bill and Kitty chatting and Mum actually beginning to look a little happier.

As it grew late, Kitty rose to go home, saying, "Good night, Mum. Shall I come again?" She held out her hand.

"Oh, yes, darling," Mum whispered, and held Kitty's hand tight.

Because it was so late, Bill walked Kitty home. Kitty nagged him incessantly. "Soppy sod, why didn't you tell me? There you were hanging about our house when your mum was all alone. Isn't that just like a man?" She tut-tutted in dismay.

"Well, Kitty, it became a bit embarrassing. She and Dad were very close. They never mixed with anyone, and then he died so suddenly."

"Well, it must have broken her heart, poor woman," declared Kitty. "Why, I had to look after my dad when Mum died, so you've got to help your mum," she rebuked him sternly.

"But how, Kitty? You tell me," pleaded Bill.

"Well, first we take her out somewhere—to the pictures, maybe," suggested Kitty.

"Don't think she'll go," muttered Bill. "She's never been to the pictures."

"There's always a first time," said Kitty firmly.

From that day Kitty went twice a week to Bill's. They tidied the house, took Mum to the park and then on to the pictures. It was a joy to see the woman come to life again. Slowly but surely she began to smile. She tidied herself up, wore old-fashioned but very good dresses and curled her hair. She laughed at Kitty's wisecracks and even confided in her about her own young days and how she had courted her much-loved Albert.

Bill was so grateful. "You've done wonders for Mum, Kitty, I just can't tell you how much I appreciate it. Honestly, I thought she'd end up in a madhouse."

"It's enough to drive anyone mad, living in that bloody great house all alone," replied Kitty.

Spring came around, and Kitty and Bill were fast companions again. Now that she knew where he was in the evenings, Kitty did not miss him quite so much. One evening as they walked over to Kitty's house, hand in hand, Bill suddenly stopped and placed his hands on Kitty's shoulders. "I've been saving up to buy you a ring," he announced.

Kitty stared at him, her eyes shining bright with delight. "Oh, darling, darling," she cried impulsively, throwing her arms around his neck.

Bill laughed loudly. "Blimey, Kitty, don't strangle me. I'm getting the ring on Saturday. You can come with me."

At the weekend the excited young couple went to Bravington's, the jewelers at Kings Cross. They stared at all the beautiful rings through the window.

"How much can you afford, Bill?" Kitty asked.

"About fourteen quid," said Bill.

"Well, I'll have that one," said Kitty, pointing at a small cluster of diamonds. "It's only ten guineas, so we can have enough over to celebrate."

When Bill put the little ring on Kitty's finger she almost fainted with delight. She danced all the way home; she was so happy and excited to be loved and wanted and wearing a real diamond ring.

It was May 6, 1936, the King's and Queen's Jubilee Year. All the streets were decorated with flags, and there were street parties everywhere. When they got back to Kitty's street, a piano had been pushed outside and everyone was singing and dancing around it. The celebrations went on for the rest of the day, throughout the night and on into the early hours of the morning. Kitty's engagement gave the neighbors even more reason to sing, and Kitty showed off her diamond ring so that everyone could congratulate them.

For several weeks, Kitty's engagement was the talk of the neighborhood, as all such events were. But the special status Kitty enjoyed was nearly marred by Flossie Brown, the girl who had introduced Kitty to the barves many years before.

Recently, the Brown family had become quite affluent because four of the children now went out to work. In her usual homemaking way, Mrs. Brown had not only got a piano in the parlor but also a three-piece suite. Whether or not it had all been paid for yet was of no concern, and Flossie liked to show off her mum's parlor. She allowed the other children in the street to peep through the window into that tiny room. Everyone would gasp appreciatively at the sight of the square of brightly colored lino, a minute settee, two small armchairs and the polished wood piano. There was not much room to sit there, but that did not matter because most of the activities in that family went on in the back scullery.

Kitty had always liked going into Flossie's house. The Brown family seemed to have such fun together, and she was still on very good terms with Flossie. She had even introduced her to one of Bill's pals because Flossie hardly ever left the street or had the opportunity for meeting any boyfriends. But suddenly, in no time at all, it seemed, two weeks after Kitty had got engaged, Flossie had organized her own engagement to Bill's friend and ran around showing off a five-stone ring that made Kitty's own look very cheap.

"I don't understand," said Kitty dolefully to Bill. "We've been courting quite awhile now, and anyway, your pal is out of work."

Bill smiled when he heard her saying this. "Don't

you worry, Kitty. I did two jobs and went without my midday meal to help save up for your ring. Flossie's is on hire purchase and she's paying for it herself."

"Is she?" Kitty giggled, suddenly feeling like a queen in her own right again. "I didn't mean to be discontented, Bill. My ring is lovely; I'll wear it all my life." And Bill kissed her softly on the lips.

Kitty was very glad that Dad gave his immediate blessing to the engagement. To her surprise, he did not seem to mind one bit that Bill was a Protestant. He liked Bill too much to care.

She lost no time in showing off her ring to the girls at work. She allowed them all to examine it and try it on, feeling smug and happy at her choice of husband.

"Settling down now, Kitty?" one asked.

"Certainly," replied Kitty. "I've no time for these girls who don't play the game." She cast dark glances in the direction of her old enemy Sylvia who, although also engaged, still knocked it off with another boy-friend.

"Slice off a cut loaf ain't missed, Kitty," jibed the cutters when they heard that.

Kitty cast them a haughty glance, waving her hands in the air so that the small diamond chips sparkled. "Some of you married men would be better off if you went straight home at nights," she remarked acidly.

"Tell me the old, old story," the cutters sang, as they leaped up to dance and cavort about the workshop until Joe, the foreman, came dashing up. "What's going on? Is it a wedding or something?" he asked sarcastically.

"No," the cutters cried, "but our Kitty Daly's got herself engaged."

"Bleeding time she settled down," muttered Joe. "Might not be so high and mighty when she gets a bit of the other."

Kitty was really shocked at what Joe and the cutters had said. By the time she got home and told Bill about their comments, she was quite indignant. "I hate that lot," she said, angrily pacing around the room. "I've a good mind not to go in tomorrow. In fact, I think I'll look for another job."

"Don't be hasty, Kitty," said Bill, trying to calm her down. "Those cutters were only having fun, and we all get a bit of ribbing at work from time to time."

But Kitty's mind was made up. She knew she would be sad about leaving Solly Bloomfield, but she was damned if she was going to put up with the cutters' remarks. With her usual determination she went off to the city the next morning to apply for another post.

This time it was no grimy sweatshop; it was the tall, well-preserved building of the Canada Manufacturing Company, where they made ladies' coats and gowns. The machinery was imported from America and set up in a very modern way with a conveyor belt and machines on each side. Each worker did a certain part of the garment and became very skilled at it. The clothes would have bits added as they traveled along the belt until they emerged at the end complete.

To Kitty, all this seemed like a living miracle—the clean benches, the shining machines, the huge uncluttered room. It all had a curious kind of beauty.

"We will train you," the manageress, Mrs. Green, informed her, "but if after a month you can't keep up with the track, we won't be able to keep you. Can you machine?"

"Yes," said Kitty, "but I've been working as a passer for the last year."

"Well, that will come later if you learn quickly. We need lots of examiners; the garment is thoroughly checked at intervals, and we like to promote girls from the track."

When Kitty gave her home address, Mrs. Green pursed her lips slightly. "Hoxton?" she said. "We haven't got anyone from Hoxton. We like to employ fairly good-class girls."

Kitty looked at her in dismay. She could not believe

she was going to lose a super job like this just because she lived in that run-down slum district.

But she did not have to worry, for Mrs. Green relented. She gave Kitty a weak smile. "You look nice and clean and seem very bright," she said. "I'll start you on Monday."

Kitty was thrilled. She was to get ten bob more on her wages and two weeks' holiday with pay. It was unbelievable.

"We'll start saving up," she told Bill that evening.

"As you wish, Kitty," he said.

At first Kitty found her new work situation a little irksome. No one was allowed to chat; all thoughts had to be concentrated on the long track, for if anyone got behind, the next girl could not work. The coats were turned out by the thousand, and the women and girls worked with their heads down continuously, ceasing only once every hour for a two-minute break.

Mrs. Green was a tyrant and reduced to tears any girl who dared cross her. But she had no problems with Kitty, who learned very quickly and was soon able to complete her part of the coat in perfect time. In some ways Kitty was content, but she found the work very boring.

The girls she worked with were a very mixed group from all parts of London. Since she had lost the comradeship of Bebe and Tilly, Kitty had not really bothered with girlfriends, but making friends here was unavoidable because everyone was so friendly and helpful. At lunchtimes they all went together to eat in the firm's big canteen. Kitty made quite a few new friends. They were happy, carefree and good-looking young ladies who took Kitty under their wings when she first came. They dressed nicely and did not swear. Kitty admired them and set about copying their appearances. She started by using only colorless varnish on her nails; she went to the hairdresser's every two weeks and wore nicely fitted blouses and skirts. Bill was particularly pleased because he liked her to look neat and tidy.

Kitty still visited Bill's mother twice a week. The two of them had become good friends.

"This house is so big and gloomy, Kitty," said Bill's mother one evening. "When you get married to Bill, why don't you take the flat upstairs?"

"We don't want to get married yet," said Kitty, "not till we've saved up enough to buy our own home. I want a really nice home because it's something I never had; we don't mind waiting."

When she recounted this conversation to Bill, he agreed that his mother needed company, but he was also adamant about wanting to buy a house of their own when they married.

They discussed the current situation further. "I would like to leave this street," said Kitty. "I'm really fed up with Hoxton."

"I have an idea," said Bill. "Why don't you ask your dad if he wants a flat, Kitty? There are four rooms upstairs in our house, and they're never used. And now that Bobby sleeps most nights at his hotel, the rest of you would have plenty of room."

"Do you think your mother would mind us all moving in?" asked Kitty.

"No. You know she likes you and finds the house very depressing. And I'm sure she'll like your dad," said Bill.

"Right," said Kitty. "I'll tackle Dad."

Dad was a little awkward about it at first. "Not much sense moving to a worse place," he said stubbornly.

"You haven't seen it," persisted Kitty. "It's four big rooms and it's cheap."

Finally, after weeks of argument and much to her surprise, Kitty managed to get Dad to agree to move. But he did not make matters easy for everyone else. First there was a big fight about the furniture.

"Dad," declared Kitty, "we can't take that buggy old stuff to Bill's mum's house."

"Why not indeed?" demanded Dad. "'Tis foine old furniture; they don't make good pieces the likes of that these days."

"Nevertheless," continued Kitty, "it's all eaten up with bugs by now, so we'll leave it behind."

"It's a foine thing I'm doing, off to that posh place and never a chair to sit on," said Dad.

"Also the bed," said Kitty. "You definitely can't take that bed."

"Be Jesus, I'll not go then," said Dad, and he went off into a tirade about how that was his marriage bed and his children had been born in it and his wife had died in it. No, he said, Kitty was asking too much. With that he dashed off to the pub, leaving Kitty to dissolve into tears on Bill's shoulder. Bill was always careful to stay out of these arguments.

Around this time Kitty got her holiday pay—two whole weeks' wages in advance. It was exactly £9 10s. She had only been working in that job for six months, and she was thrilled. "If you don't mind, Bill, I'm going to put most of this into buying new things to move with."

"That's a good idea," he said. "Why don't you get something on the hire purchase—a bed, table and chairs—and spend the rest on curtains. I might be able to help; Mum's got several bits I think I can scrounge."

So the two conspirators, with a little help from Noni, managed to get Dad well boozed. Then they took him to the shop to see the new furniture. Not a mention was made of the hire purchase. They picked out a bed for Dad, a put-u-up for Kitty and Noni, a dining table and four chairs and a large roll of lino. The whole lot cost thirty pounds. Kitty paid the five-pounds deposit from her holiday money, and while Bill kept Dad's attention, she signed the hire-purchase agreement with Dad's signature. The rest of Kitty's holiday money disap-

peared on paint and various odds and ends for the flat,
so her wedding day was pushed back a little further.

The Saturday of the move arrived. It was to be a day
of frustration and excitement.

Dad had said a vigorous goodbye to all his pub pals
the evening before, so that by Saturday morning he was
like a bear with a sore behind. Everything that Kitty
tried to throw out would suddenly reappear, and Dad
kept rushing off to the pub for another drink. An
additional complication was that Dad had insisted on
moving everything with a horse and cart instead of a
motor van. At midday a big horse-drawn vehicle driven
by a bandylegged old man appeared outside the house.
The local kids lined up to watch, and heads popped out
of windows to see what was going on.

Kitty was going spare as she tried to organize everything. Noni and Bobby had both disappeared to see
their friends, and Dad was being more trouble than he
was worth. He was determined to take the old round
table which had always stood in the center of the front
room. It was battered and worn and the kids had
scribbled all over it with crayons. Despite Kitty's
protests Dad was insistent. He would not move without
it, he said. They tried in vain to get the table down the
stairs—it was much too wide. Finally they decided that
it would have to be lowered out of the window on a
rope.

A drunken Dad hung precariously out of the window
holding the table on the end of a long rope, while the
driver, who was also well boozed and shaky on his feet,
waved his arms around and tried to catch it with his
hands. The table swung dangerously from side to side
and he missed it each time. The kids in the street
laughed uproariously. "Try again, guv'nor," they
shrieked.

Kitty watched this, blushing with shame. She wanted
to run off, but she was afraid that Dad was going to fall
out of the window at any minute. Suddenly the table

caught the driver on the side of the head, knocking him down with a thump. As Dad tried to lean further out to see if his pal was all right, the rope slipped and the table crashed onto the man on the ground.

Dad rushed down the stairs, swearing and muttering. "Me table, me old table, it's destroyed," he shouted.

Much to Kitty's annoyance, the table had survived the crash. Luckily the bandylegged driver was not hurt, just dazed, and certainly dazed enough to need a wee dram in the pub to steady his nerves.

Kitty had had enough. As she watched the men stagger to the pub she could feel tears of frustration and despair rising in her eyes. "Oh," she sobbed, "please, Bill, come and get me."

Just at that moment Bill came down the street. He looked in amusement at the huge cart with the few pathetic bundles inside it, and the well-splintered table lying in the yard. When he saw Kitty's face he could guess much of what had happened.

"Oh, Bill," Kitty wept, throwing herself into his arms, "I'm so glad you came. Let's get away from here; I can't stand another minute of it."

The young couple took the bus up to Islington. Bill managed to cheer up Kitty, who now had a smile back on her face. Halfway there the slow bus was passed by a huge cart drawn by two highly excited horses. Both Dad and his pal, the driver, were perched lopsidedly on the driver's seat, swearing loudly at each other every time the cart lurched. Dad spotted Kitty and Bill on the bus and waved his hat, cowboy style, in greeting as the driver whipped up the nags and they rushed past.

Kitty closed her eyes, hoping that no one recognized them. She was leaving all that behind her, she hoped.

CHAPTER TEN

A New Home

After the Dalys had moved in, the house in Islington
became a brighter place. During the week Bobby lived
in at the hotel where he worked. At the weekends he
would come to the house, and there was always a
gramophone playing loudly as friends arrived for im-
promptu parties and people ran up and down the
uncarpeted wooden stairs chattering in loud voices.

Despite the sudden new liveliness, the whole house
had a kind of sad, genteel air as if it bewailed the good
old days. Kitty felt this very strongly however hard she
tried not to.

"I suppose I should be very happy here after the
slum I was used to," Kitty said to Bill, "but I'm so
conscious of the atmosphere. I can't get that unhappy
sensation out of my mind."

Bill seemed to understand what she meant. "We
were always a very quiet family," he said. "I expect
that's why I was always out. You see, my dad was ill for
a number of years and we got used to making as little
noise as possible."

"It's strange how an atmosphere can remain in a house, even when there's no cause for it anymore."

"Well, your dad seems reasonably happy here, Kitty. It's a surprise to me after all the fuss he made about leaving Hoxton," said Bill.

"God knows what your mother thinks about that noisy crew up there," said Kitty.

"Oh, it's good for her. She loves to go up and sit talking to your dad."

Dad had been a little sorry for Bill's mother when they first met. "Be Jesus," he had said, "you know that poor soul has never been inside a public house?"

"She's not missed much," commented Kitty.

Before long, Dad had insisted on taking Mum to the local. He filled her up with beer and brandy until she was tottery. When they arrived home she was very giggly and had evidently enjoyed herself. After that she wanted to go with Dad whenever he went out and would stand waiting for him in the hall, all ready in her old-fashioned coat and blue felt hat. Dad went along with this for awhile, but he soon got fed up and began to creep out of the house to dodge her.

For a while Mum became all weepy again, but then she attached herself to Noni, who persuaded the old lady to try another habit—smoking—which she readily took to. She would sit in the kitchen with Noni, helping with the vegetables, puffing away at a cigarette and having the occasional cough.

Being lazy, Noni let Mum get on with the washing-up and various other jobs that Kitty would normally have whisked away from her. The sight of the old lady slowly drying the dishes almost drove Kitty mad. But Mum and Noni got on very well together, and the girl encouraged Mum to bitch about Kitty with her. Kitty was hurt, but she knew that this was stimulating and good for Mum, so she tried not to mind too much.

Kitty still liked her work at the Canada Company and had some very good pals there. She went every day of the week from eight until six. Bill worked extremely

hard, too, from very early in the morning until eight
o'clock at night. At the end of each week they put their
wages together to save up for their wedding, and on
Saturdays they walked about the market looking for
little pieces of china or linen for Kitty's bottom drawer.
She was extremely happy and content.

Slowly the Islington house began to change again as
the wedding preparations began. Kitty and Bill were
determined to build a nest of their own, even if they
could not yet buy a house. They began to redecorate
the two rooms on the middle floor after Mum had been
moved down to the basement and Dad up to the top
floor.

They painted the woodwork a bright primrose yellow
and had cream wallpaper with silver ferns on it. It all
looked so pretty. The rooms were big and spacious—so
unlike those in Hoxton. The ceilings were high, and the
windows large and wide. The fireplaces were very
elaborate and carved in white marble.

When the work was all finished, Kitty was very
proud. She had forgotten about the melancholic atmosphere she felt before. The date for the wedding was
fixed, and the furniture bought and put into position. "I
don't want nothing on the never-never for us," Bill had
said. "We'll buy what we need as we get enough
money."

In April they got married in the Catholic Church.
Kitty wore a long white dress that the girls at work had
designed and made for her. Kitty's workmates were as
excited about her wedding as she was. They borrowed
new designs from the sample room and made her a nice
suit to go away in.

On her wedding morning Kitty had to go to early
morning Mass. Since Bill was not a Catholic there was
to be no Communion service, but it was Kitty's duty to
take Communion before she was wed. When she
returned to the house it was only eight o'clock in the
morning, and she noticed that the doorsteps were
filthy. She was feeling so nervous that she decided to

clean them quickly. She got a bucket, got down on her knees and began to scrub the steps while Noni and Bobby, who had begun to celebrate the night before, slept soundly upstairs.

"Tell your sister I wish her luck," the next-door neighbor called cheerily as she walked by.

"I'll tell her," said the blushing bride, scrubbing harder.

It went off well in the end—the ceremony and the reception, which was held upstairs in Dad's apartment. There was a nice wedding cake and lots of drink and sandwiches. The whiskey flowed as the Irish all got together, and when the arguments started, Bill pulled Kitty aside. "Get ready, Kitty," he said. "We'll hop off before they start to fight."

With confetti in their hair, Mr. and Mrs. Ross slipped quietly off to Brighton, where they found a boarding-house for one night. They went out, had several beers in a pub and walked along the promenade before returning to their room at the boardinghouse.

As they got ready for bed, Kitty suddenly felt nervous. She put on her carefully chosen honeymoon nightdress, thinking of all the passionate wedding nights she had read about in those love novels. She had clung to her virginity all this time, and now she was about to lose it. She had kept it for this very occasion, for this very man. She and Bill knew each other's bodies, they had done enough cuddling during their courtship, but the act of love itself was a mystery to both of them.

She slipped under the covers beside Bill. His soft, clean skin smelled sweet as he put his arms around her and kissed her. She could tell that he was nervous, too, and she buried her head in his chest.

That first night of love was a disappointment to Kitty. She was surprised to find it rather ungainly and passion-less, unlike what she had been expecting. But she consoled herself by recalling how many people said the wedding night was never the best, and she was happy, finally, to fall soundly asleep feeling safe and secure in Bill's strong arms.

The following Monday, Kitty and Bill were both back at work. From then on they followed a settled pattern of living. For Kitty, it was very difficult. Her domestic life became even more burdensome, as she got no help from Noni with the cleaning and cooking. Noni seemed to believe that now that Kitty was married, the housework should be entirely her responsibility. Kitty went to work every day, cooked for all the family in the evening and did the cleaning and washing at the weekends. Her energy was drained. After six weeks she had begun to look pale and tired; nothing like the normally bright, energetic girl she had been.

Bill was worried. "Perhaps you ought to give up work, Kitty," he said one evening when she was looking exhausted.

"Don't be daft, we can't afford it," Kitty replied.

"What I dearly would like to do is buy us a house of our own as soon as possible," said Bill. "They're building some nice little houses not far out that have a bathroom and electric light. It would be nice, wouldn't it?"

"Oh, then I'd have a baby," said Kitty, brightening up, "and really stay home in the house all day."

"You will, darling, just be patient. We'll save as hard as we can, and I'm sure that if I can get the deposit together my boss will help me get a mortgage."

"What's that?" she asked. She'd never heard the word before.

Bill explained. "You can borrow money and they will build you a brand-new house, and then you pay it back in so many years, sometimes twenty."

"It's a long time," said Kitty doubtfully.

"No, it's not, darling, not when you have a lifetime before you," said Bill reassuringly.

With a house of their own to look forward to, Kitty

managed to cope with her unappreciative family as best she could.

It was the beginning of 1938 when Bill and Kitty began to plan to buy a modern house of their own. They rode out on the bus to Leabridge to look at a new housing estate that was springing up there. Many East Enders were moving to Leabridge, for it was not too far out of town and still on the bus route to the city. The Jewish business people found it very convenient, so a fair-sized Jewish community had grown up out there, too.

The houses were smart and had all the modern facilities. Each had a good-sized garden and a little gate, a bathroom and kitchenette and two bay windows. Kitty thought they were quite delightful and, as Bill remarked, at seven-fifty they were a bargain. They put down fifty pounds as a deposit on it and then were ready to wait about six months for the house to be built.

They kept the purchase of the house a dark secret from the family and saved like mad to get another hundred pounds deposit. That year there was a lot of talk about war with Germany, but then it all seemed to die down.

"I'm pleased, Kitty," said Bill. "Because if there had been a war we might not have got our new house."

"Whyever not?" she asked.

"Well, one reason is that they would stop building, I expect, and another is that I would be called up into the army."

"Well, it's all blown over, so we might as well get on with it," said Kitty.

Bill's boss did arrange a mortgage for them, and they were to move into the house in early spring. Until then they went over to Leabridge every Sunday afternoon to watch the progress on the house. So far no one else shared their secret. It was thrilling, and Kitty never had any doubts about leaving the flat in Islington. The rooms were nice and comfortable, but she did get so exhausted by the family battles that went on in the house, and she looked forward to escaping from them to a place of her own.

When the first siren of the war went off everyone was caught off guard. That Sunday morning the whole family had listened to the solemn speech of the wireless announcing that Britain was now at war with Germany. Kitty was preparing the lunch upstairs in Dad's kitchen while Mum peeled the potatoes. Suddenly a weird sound split the air. It was the warning siren.

Bill dashed upstairs into the kitchen. "Come on, Kitty," he yelled, "come down to the basement; there's going to be an air raid! Come on, Mum." He helped the old lady to her feet and led her slowly down the stairs. Before they had even reached the ground floor, they heard the all-clear signal. It had been a false alarm.

That evening Bill looked worried. "Kitty," he said, "this might hold up our new house."

"Oh, no!" Kitty cried in disappointment.

"Also, I've been thinking that if I go into the army, I can't leave you with two old folk to care for. See how slow Mum is? Why, you'd never get her to the shelter in time."

"I'm not worried," Kitty replied. "But our little house—what are we going to do?"

"I've just thought of a plan to keep it," said Bill. "Let's hurry up and move in next year and take Dad and Noni and Bobby with us. In that way I'll be sure you have company, and it will also help pay for the mortgage."

"But what about your mum?" asked Kitty, excited by this idea but concerned for the old lady.

"London won't be safe for her. She'll have to give up this place and live in the country with my brother."

"She might not like that," said Kitty.

"I'm afraid she'll have to put up with it," Bill replied. "If the war gets bad, she'll have no choice."

Kitty felt sorry for Mum, but she was not going to argue. All she cared about at that point was the little house in Leabridge.

Bill managed to convince Dad it was safer for them to live in Leabridge than Islington and, after making a terrible scene, Mum was packed off to the country. So once more the family moved, but this time it was in a van and organized in an orderly fashion by Bill.

Once all the furniture was in position at No. 8 Billington Road, Kitty looked around the front room proudly. At last she and Bill had their own home. Suddenly she looked alarmed. Where were the cats? Up in Islington, Kitty had gathered a trio of stray cats. One was a large tom who was striped like a tiger and exuded a strong smell. He was called Smithy Boy because he had attached himself to Bill's Mum and ruled her with what they all called a paw of iron. If Mum did not feed him on time, he helped himself to food, and generally he did what he liked. Kitty also had two young female cats. These were both white, though one had a black spot on her back. Kitty had taken them in after finding them abandoned on the street. She adored her cats, and she found that they gave her much comfort when family squabbles got on top of her. Bill had promised to bring them along while Kitty went on ahead to get straightened up at the new house. Now everyone had arrived, but no cats.

"Where are the cats?" demanded Kitty, looking first at Bill and then the driver of the van.

"Blimey, lady," said the young lad, "can't spend all day chasing a bloody cat."

"Bill," Kitty cried, ignoring the insensitive remark, "where are the cats?"

"I couldn't find them, Kitty. I think they may have been frightened by the upheaval in the house and run away—you know what Smithy Boy's like. They'll find another home," he said, hoping to be rid of the odor of the old tomcat forever.

He was not prepared for Kitty's reaction. She put on

her coat and burst into a flood of tears. "Oh, how can you be so cruel? Those poor little things will starve. I'm going back to get them myself," she sobbed.

"Don't be silly, Kitty, we've got enough to do, and how will you manage the cats on a bus?"

But Kitty stormed, screamed and stamped her feet until finally, with a worried expression, Bill gave the young driver two pounds to go and round up the cats and bring them back.

The boy was back in an hour lugging a sack over his shoulder, flushed and exhausted but quite triumphant. "Got 'em," he announced, tipping out three stunned and indignant animals onto the floor.

"Oh, you cruel beast!" screamed Kitty in horror. "Fancy putting them in a sack, poor little darlings." She fussed over the young cats while old Smithy Boy flew onto the windowsill with what could have been a scowl on his face.

"Blimey, guv'nor, I'm off," said the young chap. "You'd think she'd be a bit bleeding grateful—I chased them bloody cats everywhere. . . ."

Bill just smiled.

Soon Smithy Boy had established himself among the other cats in the new neighborhood. He went out on a thieving patrol every night and managed to give both of Kitty's young cats a set of kittens each.

Kitty's family soon settled down in the street of bright modern houses and young, pink-blossomed cherry trees. The green field nearby gave them a good sense of space. The house had a tiny hall and cosy rooms, all of which were newly decorated and smelled of paint. It all thrilled Kitty, especially the bathroom.

Dad, however, was not so impressed by the bath. He never once got into it, and he insisted that he only wash some of himself each day, claiming that this was a much healthier way of going about things. "Look, see how clean I am," he would say, showing a leg, "white as when the midwife washed me."

The excitement of moving to the new house was so

great that even though there was a war on, no one in the family was worried. Kitty decided that she could afford to give up work, and now she stayed at home and made cushion covers and curtains in her spare time, while Dad dug in the garden, planting cabbages and carrots. Then, one day in the spring, Kitty realized that her greatest dreams had come true—she was pregnant.

Bill was pleased but rather anxious. "It don't seem much of a world to bring a little one into. This war doesn't look like ending as quickly as we all thought it would."

"Oh, don't be such a killjoy," said Kitty. "What difference can it make to us what goes on over there?"

"It will, Kitty; mark my word, it will," said Bill.

But Kitty went her merry way without a care in the world. She loved nothing more than going out into the garden to pick Dad's ripe vegetables to eat for Sunday lunch. Oh, how great it all was, she thought, when she remembered Daly's Yard with all the horse manure piled up in it. "Oh, darling little baby," she would murmur, patting her stomach, "life is going to be so good to you."

In June everyone was depressed about Dunkirk. The British army had been almost chased into the sea by the Germans. "But now it's all right," Dad said. "We're fighting back and sure to win. Why let a silly thing like a war bother you and spoil your plans for the future?" he said comfortingly.

The hotels had all closed and Bobby had volunteered for the army. Noni was making uniforms in her factory, while Kitty stayed at home and caught up with her reading and sewed little things for her baby.

In August, Bill got his calling-up papers. He was concerned but also optimistic. "My boss says he might be able to get me deferred because I'm working on food, which is essential."

Kitty hoped that he was right: she had so much confidence in her Bill.

There had been bad news from Bill's brother, who wrote to say that Mum had got very tiresome and his wife was finding it difficult to cope with her.

"Poor old lady," said Dad, on hearing this. "She'll not stay in this world long," he added gloomily. Kitty felt guilty, but she had so much to contend with that she chose to ignore the letter.

CHAPTER ELEVEN
The Blitz

In September the Blitz began. Bobby was now away in the army, and Noni, much to Kitty's relief, had married a regular soldier and was living in army quarters. Kitty spent those strange, creepy evenings alone, waiting for the wail of the warning siren, hurrying up with the dinner and praying that Bill would get home before the bombs started dropping. The sirens would sound and then she would hear the heavy drone of enemy bombers as she made a hasty dash to the shelter, worrying whether she had turned off the gas or put Bill's dinner in the oven.

The air raid shelter was in the factory across the road, deep down underground. Once inside, Kitty would sit, still as a statue, anxiously waiting for her man to arrive safely.

Dad was now working outside London, so quite often he was unable to get a train and did not get home at all. All communications would stop once the warning sirens had sent their unhappy sound wailing in and out of London's chimney pots. Dad was quite unperturbed by such interruptions; he simply made his way to the nearest pub and later slept in the railway station, waking early and going back to work as though little had happened. Kitty often wished she was like her father—so calm and serene, so brave, allowing nothing to stop him continuing his own way of life. She found that she was always tense and nervous, overwhelmed by anxiety as she prayed that the night would not be too long. How she hated that stuffy shelter where people lay in all sorts of grotesque positions. The women sat in a row, knitting needles clicking, tongues wagging. No one admitted that they were afraid, and they did not seem at all concerned with what went on outside. The small talk of the day seemed to be all that mattered.

When Bill came back from work he would eat his dinner at home and then join Kitty in the shelter, carrying over a mattress and some blankets. Each family had its own little space, and Kitty would snuggle up close to Bill's warm back. She was quite unable to sleep in these circumstances, but Bill snored lustily. He worked very hard and needed his sleep. So Kitty spent those sleepless nights awake, feeling the child kicking in her womb and wondering how much longer she could endure all this. She would listen to the whining screams of the bombs as they rained down and shiver at the uncanny silence which was broken suddenly by an explosion—the sickening thud of a direct hit nearby. Every time that happened, Kitty desperately wanted to get up and dash out of her dark prison, but she knew she couldn't.

Kitty was now seven months pregnant and, because of wartime conditions, was receiving little medical attention. She ate poorly and hardly got any sleep. In such circumstances she began to look sickly and pale.

From September into November the German bombers made their raids on London, night after night, week after week. Most of the schoolchildren had been evacuated to the country, but so far there was no government scheme for expectant mothers.

"You must be prepared to stay in London until three weeks before the baby is born," Kitty was told at the prenatal clinic. "Then we'll send a conveyance to transport you to our maternity hospital out of town."

Kitty had gone to the clinic for her first medical. She had been excited at the prospect of talking about this wonderful event that was happening to her, for she was sad that she had no mother of her own to confide in. She was afraid that she might unknowingly do something that would harm her precious babe. But the prenatal examination had been cold and clinical. The staff at the clinic were tired and overworked, with no time to allay the fears of a first-time mother.

"No need to come again," the nurse said. "Everything is all right, gel, but of course contact us if you feel ill any time."

Kitty went home feeling numb with worry. Later, she told Bill of her fears. He was as comforting as possible. "Don't worry, darling," he said, "everyone's afraid at first. It's quite natural."

Bill's words, however kind, could not put Kitty at ease. What she was frightened of was, she felt, so vague, anyway—the fact that she was not sure of what was going to happen to her.

"I expect I'll be called up soon," Bill added quietly, concerned for his wife. "I only hope I can be with you until our baby is born. I want you to promise that you won't return to London until the war is over.

"When's that likely to be?" Kitty asked dolefully.

"Well, some say it can't last," replied Bill optimistically. "I've heard that they must negotiate for peace soon."

"Then the Germans will win," Kitty said bitterly. "Is that what you want?"

"No, of course not!" he answered with spirit. "We'll never give in, but they can't afford to keep the bombardment going. Bombs cost money, but the Yanks at least have got plenty of dough."

Kitty shrugged; she was not convinced.

On November 5th, the raids lasted all day. The bombs dropped ceaselessly like rain. Kitty sat without Bill in the shelter feeling sick and faint with hunger. She was near the end of her tether.

That evening, after the all-clear, everyone surfaced from the shelter. Outside the sky was as red as blood, as the tall buildings in the center of town burned fiercely.

Kitty was sick with worry. Why hadn't Bill got home yet? Where was Dad? The baby, which was usually so active inside her, seemed to lie still in her womb, and her body ached all over.

The sirens went off again, and back to the shelter went Kitty and her neighbors. Kitty wondered if she could really stand it anymore.

A few hours later Bill arrived, looking very tired after walking home through the blitzed streets. He lay down wearily beside her. Kitty began to find the damp atmosphere of the shelter overpowering, and the strong smell of disinfectant added to her discomfort. She lay awake all night, tossing and turing restlessly. At dawn she poked Bill in the ribs. "I'm going home," she said irritably. "I've got to get out of here; I can't stand it any longer."

"Now, Kitty," Bill warned sleepily, "don't be hasty. It's not yet daylight, and the bombers might come back."

"Please take me home, Bill, or I'll go alone," she cried.

"As you wish," he replied.

An early dawn light suffused the smoky sky; an eerie silence pervaded the air as they emerged from the shelter. They started walking to their house when, without warning, a barrage balloon, punctured by pieces of shrapnel, came hurtling from the sky. Kitty was terrified to see that shining, hissing monster rushing headlong at them down the street, its sides heaving, its steel cables trailing over the roof tops and scraping off tiles that flew in all directions. Bill flung his arms around Kitty and pulled her down against a brick wall. As they crouched there, Kitty wept and shivered with fright.

"Don't worry, Kitty, it's only a barrage balloon come down." Bill tried hard to console her.

"Oh, take me home, Bill," she wailed.

He picked her up like a child and carried her across the road to the house. Once home he placed her in an armchair, wrapped a blanket around her and made her a cup of tea. But still she shivered. She could not stop herself; it was convulsive shuddering that shook her frame. Then, as Bill went to fill a hot-water bottle, the pain came. It was a hot, searing pain that coursed fiercely through her body. "Oh, dear God," she cried, "it's the baby, it's coming too soon!"

Seeing what was happening, Bill dashed back to the shelter to get a neighbor to stay with Kitty while he routed out the doctor. But it was too late.

"You're going to lose this child," the doctor told Kitty dispassionately. He had been working all night and looked exhausted. "I can attend to you here or you can go to hospital, though I warn you, it's chaotic up there."

This was the last devastating blow for Kitty. "I'll go to hospital," she said defiantly. "At least there they might try to save my baby."

"Can't see the point," the doctor replied wearily. "It's your first child, and there's plenty of time for more. But please yourself, I'm too busy to argue with you."

All the way to hospital in the ambulance Bill held Kitty's hand. "Don't worry, Kitty, perhaps it'll be better if we have a baby when the war's over."

Kitty was nearly hysterical from the pain. "I want to keep my baby," she cried. "The war has only just started . . . and what will I do? How will I get by without your baby? Please, God, let this little life live," she prayed.

But it was all in vain. After many hours of pain, Kitty

gave birth to a stillborn child. It had been lying in the wrong position and was already dead inside her.

"Was it a boy?" she asked the nurse through her sobs.

"Aye, and could have been a bonny one," the nurse replied. "But never mind, this is no world to bring a little one into."

Kitty's conscience nagged at her constantly. She should have known. Why had she not talked with some other woman? She had been too eaten up with domestic cares, taking care of Bill and Dad. Yes, it was her fault she had lost the child. Deep dark despair overwhelmed her. She had run out of tears, but she wept silently inside.

When Kitty returned home from the hospital, there were flowers and messages of condolence from the neighbors. It all seemed very remote to her, as if it were happening to someone else.

Bill had finally been called up, and Kitty saw him off to camp. Her lips were still wet with his kisses as she watched the train pull out. She tried to smile as she waved to him, but inside her there was only hatred—seething white-hot hatred for everyone and everything. She was no longer warm, loyal, little Kitty Daly, full of love and hope and ambition. Instead, she was very bitter at the injustice of what had happened to her. She had never asked a lot from life; she had always done her best to help others. In fact, she had devoted all her time and energy to the family—and now this was her reward.

The night that Bill left for camp, even the little house in Billington Road lost its appeal for her. A direct hit on the factory opposite blasted all the houses in the street. Fortunately, most of the residents were in the deep shelter, so no one was hurt, not even Kitty, who had vowed never to go down into that miserable shelter again.

She had been in the kitchen baking a meat pie for supper while Dad, who was home early for a change, slept in his usual spot in the armchair in the dining room. There had been no air-raid warning, but just before dark the bombers swept over London again, dropping bombs in a long line. No one had been working in the factory, but all the houses took the blast. It was as if a great wind swept through the house. Just as Kitty was bending down to put the neatly made pie into the oven, she toppled forward, knocking her head against the cooker. The pie shot across the kitchen floor and scattered in pieces. Kitty was too shocked to know what had happened. She yelled, shouted, jumped and screamed in temper at the fate of her pie.

Dad dashed in, also shouting, but seeing that the pie was the only casualty, he began to laugh. Calmly, he went to the front door and looked out into the street, still puffing his old clay pipe.

"Ah, factory's copped it," he announced. He started to chuckle. "Old Abie lost his roof." He loved to have a go at the Jewish neighbors.

In the morning, however, the chuckle died in Dad's throat when he discovered that he also had no roof.

That evening, as soon as it got dark, Kitty said, "I can't stick indoors one more night waiting to be blown up, Dad. Come on, let's go out and have a drink."

"Right away, gel," Dad said, delighted to have his daughter as a drinking companion.

Together, father and daughter went to the local, where they drank beer and whiskey. Much later they came home, arm in arm, walking carefully through the blacked-out streets. Dad shone his small torch on the ground to light their way. The air raids and the ruined houses were far away as Kitty happily climbed up the stairs to bed. That night she slept better than she had for months.

After that, the evening visit to the pub became a welcome and regular daily event. After a dreary day cooking and doing the housework, Kitty would go with Dad to sit in the pub and drink. Sometimes, during a heavy raid, the bottles of spirits bounced off the shelves while the landlord and his wife scuttled down to the cellar after clearing the cash till of money, which they put into a canvas bag to take with them. This always made Dad laugh. "Get them up, me boyo, 'afore ye go down under," he would chuckle. "Never mind the money—there's no pockets in a shroud, can't take it with you." He would wink at Kitty and her pale face always creased into a pretty smile as she sat drinking herself stupid.

When Kitty staggered into bed after these evenings, everything spun before her eyes. But she was not worried; she knew she would sleep through the blitz again that night.

By Christmas this strange twilight existence had begun to take its toll. Kitty felt ill every morning and could never be bothered to dress. She just hung about all day in her dressing gown. The daytime raids had eased up a bit since the new spitfire squadron had been formed. The squadron sped out each day over the weald of Essex to intercept the German bombers before they reached the east shore. Everyone listened to the radio each day for news of the number of German bombers brought down. Such news gave them heart, and many more people started coming into the local in the evenings with renewed confidence in the strength of the British Forces.

Some of the new customers were what Dad called grass widows. These were girls whose husbands were away at war, so Kitty was one, too. But Kitty's mouth always tightened with disapproval when she watched the other young women chatting up the servicemen. When she told Dad what she thought about this, he just shrugged his shoulders. "Well, the cat's away, mice will play. What else can they do?" he said.

"I think it's terrible," commented Kitty. "Their men are away fighting for them. At least they could play a straight game."

"Well, it takes all kinds to make a world, Kitty," replied Dad. "That you have to find out."

Kitty just sat very sullenly watching the others have a good time—the old folk singing songs at the piano, the young folk dancing together, boys on leave with their mums and dads, young wives with husbands on that last furlough before being drafted overseas. The whole atmosphere was fraught with excitement; this could be their last moment together.

The other grass widows were a lively bunch. They came in together with scarves wound about their heads, wearing navy blue slacks and colored jumpers. They would laugh and chatter and the men in the pub bought them drinks. When Dad got very tiddly he would also get up and dance with them, while Kitty sat glued to her seat with a sneering expression on her face.

One night a red-headed girl came over to her and said, "Why the hell you sit there all night with that old fella for? You ain't such a bad-looking girl, you know."

"I beg your pardon," replied Kitty icily, "but that old fella, as you call him, happens to be my father."

"Oh, dear, sorry I splashed," cackled the girl and walked away.

Another girl came to sit next to Kitty, whose face by now was red with rage. "Don't let Bertha upset you. She don't mean it," she said.

"I couldn't care less," said Kitty.

This did not deter the girl. "Is your husband overseas? All ours are," she said.

"No, he's still in England," replied Kitty, suddenly softening to this pretty, dark-haired girl.

"Might as well have a good time," the girl said. "It only comes down harder when it comes if you stay at home worrying."

Kitty thought her words made a lot of sense.

Kitty was sad when Bill wrote to say he would not get any leave until after Christmas, when he finished his training. He also said that his mother had recently died at his brother's. Kitty drowned her sorrows in the pub and did not worry too much. Perhaps she was rather unfeeling about Bill's mum, she thought, but there was so little she could do about anything like that these days. She found it fun nowadays to forget her troubles dancing jigs with the Irish boys. She began to enjoy life again and felt calm and rested. After Christmas she looked more relaxed and happier than she had for a long time. "Do you mind, Dad," she said, "if I get a job?"

"Great, gel," he said, pleased that she was taking his advice.

"Live for each day, gel, there's not much else to do."

Kitt's first wartime job was in the tobacconist shop of Maxi Dootins. He was a Jewish man who had volunteered for the fire service and needed someone to continue running the business. In the back of the shop was a barber, and the customers popped in for a quick shave or haircut, stopping to buy a cigar or some cigarettes on the way and having a chat with Kitty.

She loved this job; it was interesting and exciting. She kept the shop clean and bright and made sure she looked nice herself. She would wear a white blouse with a black bow at the neck and a navy blue skirt. Her rich chestnut hair and olive green eyes had quite an appeal for the gentlemen customers. Many a middle-aged and well-dressed businessman would ask, "What about coming out for a meal tonight, Kitty?"

"I'm a married woman," Kitty would reply tartly.

Sometimes a young, lonely soldier on leave would hang about in the shop and say, "I'll take you home, Kitty."

"I'll take my bloody self home," was always Kitty's retort.

Danny the barber always roared with laughter whenever he heard her snapping at the men. "She's a vixen," he would say to his customers. "I wonder how long she'll be able to keep on refusing." And they would lay bets on it. But Kitty was determined to wait for her Bill, and she ticked off the days on the calendar as she waited for him to arrive on his first week's leave.

Then one cold February morning, Bill appeared grinning on the doorstep. He was loaded up like a camel, with huge packs on his back, a kitbag and a rifle. He looked remarkably fit. His hair was cut short and his face had filled out.

Kitty stared at him for a second and then fell into his arms. "Bill, oh, Bill, you're home," she wept. His strong arms held her as he kissed her. Kitty's knees went weak. The anxieties of the past few months were forgotten. Her Bill was back, and she felt warm and secure.

Kitty had saved up all her meat rations for this occasion, so she cooked steaks in the kitchen while Bill told Dad all about his army training. As they ate their luxurious meal, Bill talked about life at the army camp, his pals and his adventures. Kitty listened and felt jealous. Bill belonged to her; who were all these people he was talking of? How she hated them! How dare he be so happy and so self-satisfied when she had been so lonely?

Bill had accepted the army way of life, as he did most things, with stoicism. He enjoyed the open-air existence and even the hardships. His strong, even-tempered personality had won him many friends and privileges. But Kitty could not understand; she felt pushed out, rejected, and there was a deep hurt inside her.

In bed that first night she wanted Bill to love her passionately, not to stop, to tell her how he had missed her and say how very difficult it had been to live without her. But Bill had had too many beers with Dad, and it was early morning before he realized he was in bed with Kitty. Then it was calm, affectionate lovemaking—nothing like what she had longed for all these long lonely months. But she was happy enough.

"I do hope I fall for another baby," she said afterward.

"I hope not, Kitty," said Bill, "I don't want to leave you with extra responsibilities. Soon I'll be sent overseas."

Kitty wept into her pillow. Bill did not understand why she cried. He did not understand that she did not mind his leaving but needed someone to need her. Bill clearly was too absorbed in army life to think about her very much at the moment. But she desperately wanted a part of him, his child. Life would be intolerable without someone to care for.

The last weekend of Bill's leave, Noni came up to stay with her soldier husband, Danny. He was a very nice lad in a tiptop regiment—the 21st Hussars. He lived and breathed army, having been in it since he was fourteen when he had been a drummer boy.

They had a wonderful family party. The men got drunk and the women cooked and waited on them, and they all laughed a lot together. Since Noni had married, Kitty found that they got on together better than before. Neither was so hostile to the other.

The last Monday finally came, and Bill had to go back to camp. "Don't come to the station, Kitty," he said. "Say goodbye here, it's better that way."

They said their goodbyes on the doorstep, and Kitty then watched his tall form go off down the road and around the corner. He made a very smart soldier, she knew, but at the same time she still felt hurt that he liked being in the army so much. Warm, likable Bill, whom everyone relied on, was having some fun of his own. A strange sensation came over her, a feeling that perhaps Bill had gone out of her life forever.

Kitty returned to work reluctantly that week, feeling that there was just a long, lonely uninteresting road ahead of her and nothing to break the monotony of it. The weather had turned very cold, so she had to use the dreadful oilstove in the shop to keep warm. It smoked all the time, letting out quick puffs of filthy clouds which made Kitty cough. While it was burning she avoided going near it as much as possible because it also emitted sudden strange noises which made her jump. Kitty had always managed to cope with such gadgets before, but she could never master this old stove that was so erratic and played up all day.

One afternoon Maxi Dootins, her boss, arrived wearing his fireman's outfit with the brass hat, brass buttons and a chopper in the belt. He marched into the shop like a pompous little bantam cock. "How's business?" he asked Kitty.

"Fine," she replied, smiling at the display of his uniform. Just as she was pulling up a chair for him to sit on, the old stove started to belch smoke and rattle like mad.

"What have you done to my stove?" Maxi hollered in rage. "You have burned me wick! Can't get another wick, it is wartime." He waved his arms in indignation and went over to look at the monster stove. He opened the door to see what was happening and a cloud of smoke covered him as the stove let out a huge belch. Kitty nearly split her sides from laughter as she watched this ridiculous man choking and trying to dust the soot off his uniform. Maxi saw no reason to laugh at all, and once he had recovered his composure he gave Kitty her cards. "Me wick, me wick, can't get another wick, it's wartime," he cried repeatedly.

"Blimey," said Danny the barber when she said goodbye. "What yer done to the guv'nor's wick, Kitty?"

In some ways Kitty felt relieved that she was once more out of a job. Although she had enjoyed working in the tobacconist shop, she was a little fed up with the lecherous remarks of the barber's customers. Since Bill's first visit she had been feeling restless and dissatisfied with her life. She felt she was looking for something but did not know what it was.

That night in the pub, Kitty celebrated. She treated
Dad and all the grass widows to drinks and gleefully
told them the tale of the stove and the guv'nor's wick.
She suddenly felt closer to the grass widows than ever
before and chatted and laughed with them.

"Come over and work in the factory with us," said
the red-headed Bertha.

"It's not too bad," said Joy, the dark-haired girl who
had been nice to her. "It's very light work."

"There's a very good-looking foreman," said Irene
with a secret smile.

So Kitty joined the grass widows.

Before the war, the factory where they all worked
had made wireless sets, but now it produced the small
radios that went into the Air Force planes. Like the last
factory Kitty had worked in, this one had a track and a
long line of workers.

From the beginning Kitty found the work quite easy.
Her job was to wire up and solder a certain part of the
radio set before it went on to the next worker. It was
quick and uninteresting, but there was plenty going on
all around her. There was no discipline as there had
been in the other factory. The women talked to their
neighbors, sang, swore and even quarreled, but as long
as they went on working no one was bothered.

The workers were women from a mixed class. There
were very posh ones doing their bit for the cause, war
widows who needed the money and all girls whose
husbands were away in the service. The pay was good
and they worked five and a half days a week. Anyone
who took time off was fined. The foreman touched
bosoms and bottoms but no one worried, no one cared.
Some girls used four-letter words like conversation
pieces. Others were a little more reserved, but sex was
always openly discussed and bawdy stories were passed
around. All this amazed Kitty, and she listened to
scraps of conversation with great interest. "Had it three
times in the churchyard last night," one pretty girl

announced loudly. "I thought there was butterflies floating about, but it were red-hot shrapnel. We was having it in the middle of an air raid."

Laughter rang up and down the track as the story was passed from one to another. Kitty sat quietly. She was actually a little disgusted. She had grown up in a low-class district, the slums of Hoxton, but she had never heard such outspoken comments on sexual behavior. She was puzzled by the casual attitudes of the well-spoken girls, in particular, who smoked incessantly and dressed sloppily in men's shirts and trousers, their hair pulled back in untidy pony tails. The East End girls seemed to care much more about their appearance, and much effort was put into having a nice hairdo and a good dress. But the majority of these girls were lively, generous and happy-go-lucky, so Kitty began to enjoy the atmosphere. After a time, she even occasionally used a timid four-letter word herself.

Every night after work Kitty went to the local with the grass widows, Bertha, Joy and Irene. She often met Dad there, and, after a good time, the two of them would go home together to supper.

"Leave the old boy at home, Kitty," her new friends suggested one day, "and come up West with us on Saturday nights."

Kitty felt badly in need of some fun and agreed readily. Soon the trip uptown was a regular event in her life.

The preparations for the Saturday nights out were very serious and carefully carried out. At the factory, the girls made hair curlers from wire flex cut from the finished radio sets. Every Saturday morning every girl would sit with lots of red and blue bits of wire in her hair, which they covered with scarves. Then slowly, toward evening, the scarves came off, the wires were taken out and there emerged magnificent heads of curls.

After work, Kitty and her pals bathed and dressed at Kitty's house because she lived closest to the factory.

The masses of curls were combed out and arranged, and the whole house smelled of makeup and cheap perfume as they all got ready for the Saturday night binge.

As always, Kitty loved to dress up and look nice. She wore cute little hats on the top of her curls—now, on advice from her friends, lightened by peroxide—choker necklaces, expansive skirts and frilly petticoats. She took care of her hands, wore a good bra and her waist was neat and trim. But she was still very small and, compared with her friends, she looked so young.

"I don't know how you do it, Kitty," the big robust Bertha remarked, "but you look about seventeen."

Kitty did not take this as a compliment. She longed to look sophisticated and tried very hard to do so, wearing dangling earrings and ridiculously high-heeled sandals in which she could only totter.

At last they would all be ready. As they bustled out of the front door Bertha would always joke, "Here we are, ready to go. All colors—black, red, blond and now Kitty between hearth rug and doormat. Oh, well, they pays their money and takes their choice."

Laughing joyfully, they would set off to catch the bus to the West End, where they went straight to the Palais de Danse. There they sat in a row, but never for long, because plenty of young men soon came over to ask them all to dance.

The brightly lighted hall was way down under the ground, so it was safe and popular. Life continued within its walls as though there were no war on the outside. The only reminder was the number of uniformed young men from all over the world: the British Allies—Dutch, Norwegian, the Free French and of course, the Americans, who introduced to the Palais a new kind of dance, the jitterbug. Kitty had a great time. She twisted and twirled on her stiletto heels, wide skirts swinging out to expose all those frilly petticoats. After a few Saturday night sessions, Kitty could jitterbug with the best of them.

Sometimes the girls "clicked" with some boys. This meant getting themselves escorts. Kitty knew the drill —she had been well trained by Bebe in her early youth. When this happened, the couples all went off together through the blacked-out streets, singing and fooling about. Then there was usually a session of heavy petting, but that was as far as the girls would go before they fled off down the road, high heels clicking, taffeta skirts rustling, leaving the lads stiff, miserable and frustrated.

"They'll try," said Bertha, "but you can't give in to them. We're not bloody whores."

CHAPTER TWELVE

Blind Date

In the early summer Bill came home on another leave. Again, Kitty was very happy to see him, but she still felt that he was holding himself aloof, as though much of his heart were in the army instead of with her. It made her unhappy, but she hid her feelings from him.

Bill was very surprised at the change in her appearance. "Don't bleach your hair, Kitty," he said. "It has such a pretty natural color."

"Why not?" Kitty demanded petulantly, annoyed at his criticism. "Got to keep in the fashion, and blondes are the vogue."

"Not with me they're not," Bill replied.

It was so good to cuddle up in bed with Bill once more. Kitty had guilty feelings about all the good times she had been having. Still, none of the boyfriends or the petting had meant a thing; she was still Bill's wife and had not let him down. Did he suspect, she wondered, that she was not quite the good little girl she had promised to be?

"I'm glad your nerves are better, Kitty," Bill said. "I

141

won't worry so much about you. This is probably my
last leave before we go overseas."

This news did not sink in as it might have. Kitty was
more anxious for his lovemaking that night. She had
yearned for it for so long. Her eagerness made Bill
rather embarrassed, she sensed. Afterwards she said,
"Oh, I do hope I have another baby."

Bill turned to look very seriously at her. His steady
blue eyes looked concerned. "I hope you don't, Kitty,"
he said, stroking her hair. "I don't want to leave you to
fend for yourself and a child."

"Oh, Bill, don't be like that," she protested. "I'd
cope. I've got Dad, and at least then I'd have something to stay at home for, something to make up for the
little child we lost before." But Bill was not convinced.

When it was time for Bill to leave again, he looked
down at his little Kitty. "I'll be back, darling, so try not
to worry. Take care of yourself and Dad and our little
house." With that he kissed her, turned on his heel and
marched off down the street.

It had been too much for Kitty. She cried every night
for a week and prayed that she was pregnant. But now
she knew she would not have the precious baby that she
so longed for. To forget her misery, she worked even
harder than usual, silent and depressed. She also began
to write in her notebook again. Most nights when she
was in bed she would keep a journal of her thoughts
and fears and plans. Her scribbling became an important escape for her—almost as important as the evenings in the pubs or the Saturday night outings. It gave
her something to focus on and helped her keep a grip
on life when she felt really desperate and alone.

Bertha's husband had also come back on leave at the
same time as Bill. "It was nice having a bit of the
other," Bertha said, "but now what am I to do?"

"Don't be crude," Kitty snapped. "Bill and I, we can
get by without all that."

"You're joking," said Bertha. "I go out with lots of

blokes, but I always waited for George because I fancied him. But for two years? I ain't so sure I can wait that long."

Later that week Irene came in to work with her face all bruised. Her eyes were red from weeping. She told them that her husband, who was in the Air Force, had come home unexpectedly and caught her in bed with the foreman. Kitty was shocked.

"Don't tell me you didn't know about them," mocked Bertha. "Why, Kitty, it was pretty obvious, wasn't it?"

It had never even occurred to Kitty. Ah, well, she thought, one certainly lives and learns.

Soon afterward, Irene left the factory to go and live with her mother, and then Bertha decided she wanted to leave London and got herself transferred to an airplane factory down in Dorset. Finally, the little group of grass widows broke up completely when Joy took a job on the buses.

Kitty really missed her pals and for awhile went back to the local and the company of Dad, who was like a steady old oak tree. In spite of his drinking habits, he was always reliable and cheerful. He was a rock of strength to Kitty.

"I'd like to be like you, Dad. You take everything in your stride," Kitty told him one evening.

"I've had my shares of sorrow, gel," Dad replied quietly, "but now I live only for each day as it comes by. Don't always expect happiness; it's better to give it out than just receive it."

This worldly wisdom was no compensation for her. She had received only one letter from Bill since he had left. Most of that had been blotted out by the censor, so she had no idea where he was. But from what she could see of his letter, he seemed very depressed. Kitty wrote every day to him, as she promised she would, but Bill was on the high seas and not receiving any mail. He was not her man anymore; he belonged only to the army.

That thought made Kitty feel strangely remote and unfeeling.

One day Noni suddenly returned to Billington Road. Danny had not yet gone abroad, but Noni had grown tired of the army camp. Dad loved all his children, but seemed to have a soft spot for his younger daughter, possibly because she was most like him. While Kitty had a good head, could conquer many obstacles and was very reliable, Noni was casual, careless and humorous. Her happy approach to life suited Dad, and now he welcomed her with open arms. Kitty felt all the more shut out and excluded. Even her own house was not the same anymore. Since her marriage, Noni had taken up cooking, and now she produced huge meals that Dad loved. The pair of them would joke with each other throughout supper. Afterward they would go out together to the pub, leaving the washing-up for the morning.

The hopeless muddle that Noni created worried and upset Kitty. But the more she complained, the more Noni laughed at her. All the old hostility between them had returned. "Oh dear, hark at Lady Jane," Noni would say mockingly.

Kitty began to go out more during the week. She went to various clubs and dance halls and made new friends.

Sometimes Bertha would come up from Dorset to pay the rent on her flat, and then Kitty would stay the week with her. On Saturdays Kitty still spent ages getting ready for the evening. Her hair was now almost completely blond, and she wore dinky little hats and a tailored suit with padded shoulders that she had obtained on the black market, having run out of clothing coupons.

Noni squinted suspiciously at her sister's smart clothes one day. "What's all this poshing up for?" she demanded. "Trying to get off with the blokes, I'll bet."

"Don't be silly," Kitty answered. "And if you took

better care of yourself, you would feel better." It was a spiteful thing to say, as Noni was fat and sloppy in appearance.

"Get out of it!" said Noni, her big mouth wide in a grinning jeer. "I'm a married woman. Don't want no blokes after me."

"Oh, for God's sake don't be so bloody pious," declared Kitty impatiently as she marched out of the front door, slamming it behind her. She had completely forgotten how prudish she used to be herself.

Even the few letters from Bill had stopped coming, but so far this had not worried Kitty because she always thought that no news was good news. A letter did arrive from Bertha that was of great interest to Kitty. Her friend wrote to say that near the factory where she worked in Dorset, there was a camp full of the American soldiers who were arriving daily from the United States. Bertha had got herself one of these G.I.s and was going to bring him up to London with her on her next visit. She said he was very rich and spent money like water.

Kitty was eager to meet this marvelous American, and on the day they were arriving she rushed round to Bertha's flat. She was very disappointed. Sam was small, dark and wiry and, Kitty thought, full of hot air. He shouted and argued with everyone in the pub where they went, and he got very drunk. But Bertha was blooming; she was very proud of Sam, her soldier boy.

Kitty was not asked to stay for the weekend, and she took the hint.

"I'll bring up a mate for you, next time," Sam said as Kitty got up to leave.

"Don't bother," she snapped back bitterly. She did not like him one bit.

"You're a bitch, a bloody little bitch," Sam declared.

"Nuts," retorted Kitty, quite unashamed.

"If you were mine, I'd spank your fanny," cried Sam. Kitty was disgusted. She did not know that Ameri-

cans had a different meaning for the word. She
marched back home boiling with rage. What cheek, she
thought.

When Bertha next wrote to Kitty, she said she was
coming up to London again and bringing a friend for
her. At first, Kitty was not very keen on the idea of a
blind date, but for want of anything better to do, she
decided to go along with Bertha's plans.

On the day, Kitty went to Liverpool Street Station to
meet Bertha and her friends. When she arrived, they
were already there—Bertha, Sam and, to Kitty's astonishment, a big black man. Although Kitty had thought
Sam was dark-skinned, it had never occurred to her
that he might be in a black regiment. She gasped for
breath and turned around as if to run away. Sam
grabbed her arm. "Meet my friend," he said with an
oily smile of triumph. "His name's Jackie."

Bertha would not even look Kitty in the eye. She just
hustled them off down into the tube station. It seemed
the longest moment of Kitty's life as she went down the
escalator with Jackie holding her by the arm. Speechless with indignation, she saw the looks of the other
passengers going up in the other side and prayed she
would not be recognized.

Jackie tried to talk to her, and she realized that he
was very nice and polite. Kitty's conscience began to
prick her. "I'm sorry, Jackie, but I can't stay," she
murmured as they got on a train to Piccadilly. "Something has turned up, and I must leave you when we get
out at the West End."

Jackie smiled slightly. "It's okay, I understand. Bertha didn't tell me you were so sheep. I'm sorry, too."

Kitty had no idea of what he meant, but she felt
suddenly relieved. He was not going to try to hang onto
her. He was intelligent enough to know she had been
tricked.

Bertha suddenly realized what was happening.
"Don't be mean, Kitty. He's come all this way from
Dorset to meet you," she said.

Kitty wanted to weep. She felt she was being cruel to this young man, but nothing on earth could make her stay.

"Okay," said Sam, pushing in, "what's all the fuss? Let's at least get a meal, and then you can go where you like. Jackie will soon get shacked up with a Dilly; he's got plenty of dough," he said in his blunt way. Kitty seethed inside. How she hated this crude man, but she agreed to eat with them.

When they got to Piccadilly, they went into the nearest Chinese restaurant, which was known as Chop Suey. It was an enormous place and very popular with the Yanks. That evening it was full of them and all of them, except Sam and Jackie, were white. Chinese waiters rushed back and forth bringing bowls of this and bowls of that. Kitty did not know what any of the food was and became quite bewildered. Sam laughed loudly as usual and ordered wine while Jackie sat still and silent like a big, black statue.

Always sensitive to atmosphere, Kitty suddenly felt a strange tension in the air and noticed the way the rest of the customers stared in their direction. Suddenly one drunken soldier jumped to his feet. "I can't fucking stand it," he yelled at the top of his voice. "Two white birds with those black bastards."

The next moment the table had tipped over, all the little bowls of food had hit the deck and the floor was a mess of arms and legs as everyone started to fight. Bertha screamed and did her bit, lashing out with her handbag in all directions. Sam had disappeared under the pile of bodies.

Kitty stood staring in horror at this bunch of writhing, drunken men fighting each other rather than the common enemy. She was appalled. Suddenly someone took her arm gently. It was Jackie who guided her smartly to the door, shoving some money into her hand. "Go!" he said urgently. "Take a taxi. Don't get mixed up in a brawl." With that he turned and returned to the fight.

Feeling terribly ashamed, as though it had all been her fault, Kitty cried all the way home. She vowed that from now on she would stay out of the West End.

It was the end of her acquaintance with Bertha, who was apparently taken off in a black maria. She was warned for disturbing the peace, while her boyfriend was carted off by the military police. Kitty never heard what happened to kind, gentle Jackie.

CHAPTER THIRTEEN

Lover and Hero

It was 1942. The air raids continued, but the Londoners had got used to them and most folk went their own way.

Dad had recently started up his own business. He managed to obtain a contract from the council to pull up the old tram tracks that were now needed for making munitions, and then he replaced the road surfaces. Dad employed only Irishmen, many of whom were invalided from the army. Some of these young men came from very remote villages in Ireland and were quite green fellows. They never stayed long; they either went home or into the army. When Dad got them over to England, he found them lodgings and gave them wages in advance. Although he did occasionally invite them into his house for a beer and a game of cards, he did not encourage it often. He would watch like a hawk to ensure that no one got too familiar with his daughters.

Kitty trudged on through the year, very restless and unhappy. She still went out on Saturday nights, all dressed up and painted like a war chief. And Noni still voiced her disapproval whenever possible. "All dressed up like a tart, and out with blokes. It just ain't right," she would nag.

"Oh, well," Kitty would toss her head, "your man's still in the country, mine's a long way off."

"And I'm going to bleeding well keep him," threatened Noni, "so you can keep your paws off him."

Kitty sighed, sat down and wrote a long letter to Bill. Well, it won't come down so hard when it does come, she told herself, so convinced was she that things would never come right again.

In November, Danny came home on a weekend pass. He was a nice man, and Kitty was very fond of him. She often thought he was too good for her sister. Noni had met Danny on a blind date. It was the custom at that time for young women to put little love notes with their names and addresses into uniform packets. Noni worked in the tailoring of uniforms, and her own love note had brought her a date which had proved a winner. She and Danny were married three months later. An orphan, Danny had spent his early years in an army school and had naturally made a career for himself in the army. He was a smart, alert young man and very keen on reading, so Kitty and he had something in common. In his spare time he studied to train himself as a sports referee, which he wanted to be when the war was over.

On this visit Danny brought with him a brace of pheasants poached from the big estate where his regiment was stationed. They had a quiet party. Kitty cooked the Sunday dinner, and Danny showed her how to braise the birds with wine. It was quite a feast on wartime rations. Afterward, Noni did the washing-up while Dad snoozed in his armchair and Kitty and Danny sat together by the fire.

"We're off shortly, Kitty," Danny said. "I've been so happy here with you all that I don't want to go."

"Ah, well, you'll soon be back to annoy us," jeered Kitty affectionately.

He looked solemn. "It's a big do, Kitty. I might not."

"Oh, Danny, I never heard you talk like that before. I imagined that you were the real soldier, off to battle with banners flying."

"I still like the army, but I had no one before. I was an orphan, and now I have a lovely family. That makes a big difference." There were tears in his eyes.

Kitty snuggled up close to him on the settee. "Well, Danny," she said, "cheer up, it must come out right for us all in the end."

He cuddled her. "I know, Kitty, love, it's not been all roses for you, but you have tremendous courage. Look after Noni if I don't come back."

"I'll have no more talk like that," Kitty said as she tickled him. The two of them began larking. Suddenly Kitty was aware of Noni standing in the doorway, her face like thunder. "I've done all the washing-up, now you wipe them, Kitty, and put them away," she commanded, almost pushing Kitty off the settee.

For once, Kitty did what her sister wanted. She dried the dishes thoughtfully, and wondered if one could get a premonition of death.

On Christmas Day, Kitty set the table for dinner. She laid a place for Danny, knowing that he would escape home for Christmas if he could, whatever was on.

But it was only the usual three for dinner—Kitty, Dad and Noni. They ate their turkey in silence, each with an ear open, hoping to hear the doorbell ring. It was all in vain. After the meal the empty place stared up at them. Noni could not bear the tension any longer and burst into tears.

"He's been moved, I expect," said Dad, trying to console her.

"He might be overseas," said Kitty. "He did say

something about a big landing of the commandos somewhere."

"Oh, go on, rub it in," shouted Noni, "just because you ain't heard from Bill."

Noni's catty remark began to make Kitty worried. It was true; she had not even got a Christmas card from Bill this year. Last year he had sent her a lovely pair of high-heeled sandals. Perhaps the post was delayed, she thought optimistically, and it would all turn up together.

After Christmas, the atmosphere in the house became tense as everyone waited for news of the two young men.

Then, on January 5th, the telegram came for Noni: "YOUR HUSBAND MISSING STOP BELIEVED KILLED ON THE FIRST ARMY LANDING IN NORTH AFRICA STOP."

It came at midday, when Kitty had popped home from work to make a cup of tea and Noni was also home for lunch. She now worked in one of the factories nearby.

They read the telegram together, pale and trembling. Then they stood shocked and silent. After a minute of silence, Noni started to scream hysterically—long, piercing screams that could be heard down the street. Kitty tried to quiet her sister, but Noni backed away like a raging lioness. "Go away," she spat, "get away, you cow. Your man's all right, mine's gone. I've played the game. I've stayed at home, and this is what I get. You're a bloody whore, that's what you are!" She flattened herself against the wall, her head raised, her eyes shut, howling with misery.

Kitty was speechless with shock. She stood white-faced as she watched Noni, who was now banging her head and fists against the wall. She felt utterly helpless at the sight of this tirade. She wanted to help her sister but was afraid of being attacked again.

Fortunately, she was saved from the dilemma when the next-door neighbor came running in, having heard the commotion. The woman took charge of the situation immediately, pulling Noni firmly into her arms so that the girl stopped screaming and now sobbed loudly into her large bosom.

Still stunned, Kitty took this opportunity to leave the house. She could not face going back to work, so she went to the local where she stood with shaking hands, drinking one whiskey after another. Then she wandered the streets, trying to rid her mind of the image of Noni's hysteria. She ended up at the pictures, too unhappy to go home before Dad returned.

When she did go home that evening, she found that the doctor had been called and Noni was under sedation. She talked in hushed tones with Dad in the front room while Noni slept upstairs. But there was not much to say, and they went to bed early that night.

A few days later, the newspapers gave great publicity to Operation Torch, as the army called it, that courageous invasion of the beaches of Morocco where so many lives were lost.

The army sent home Danny's few belongings, along with a letter from the sergeant who saw him die. Apparently Danny had been refueling his tank a few days after landing when the Stucca planes dive-bombed the town. The British boys were leading the untrained Americans, who were on their first big mission. At least he died bravely, thought Kitty when she read this.

Noni eventually recovered from the shock and somehow came back to the living, but she was sullen and still very hostile toward Kitty. This caused Kitty to spend less time than ever at home, for she did not want to quarrel. Dad remained concerned about Noni and did not want her upset.

There had still been no letter from Bill. Had he forgotten her? Or was he lying dead in some foreign land? In desperation, she finally wrote to the War Office. To her surprise she received their reply almost immediately. It was a long apologetic letter stating that Bill had gone missing on a recent patrol and that so far no news had been heard of him. They added that they would notify her should the circumstances warrant it.

Kitty's tears dropped onto the letter. She had known it all along; her Bill had gone forever.

"Dear God," Dad said, holding her gently, "both our boys. Now there is only Bobby left." His face was white and drawn with anxiety for his only son and sorrow for his two fine sons-in-law.

The girls at work did their best to be optimistic. "I expect your Bill's a prisoner, Kitty. Lots of chaps have turned up in prison camps, it just takes ages to find out," one of her mates said.

"No, it's over," replied Kitty dejectedly. She had no hope left in her.

Kitty's sorrow brought about a sudden change in Noni. "I'm so sorry I was hateful, Kitty," she said. "We was also fond of Bill." So for a while, at least, the sisters' double sadness brought them a little closer.

During that spring, the heavy American bombers took off each day to give, as they said, the Germans a taste of their own medicine. The U.S. Air Force was now stationed in England, so London was full of G.I.s.

The blitz had died down, and many families were again reunited and much more life was now centered in the darkened city. There was plenty to do in the evenings. Kitty still went around with girls from work, but most of these new ones were a lot younger than the grass widows. They were youthful, unmarried, hard and very capable; they earned good money and liked a good time. "You should take your ring off, Kitty," advised one tough youngster. "No sense in letting them know you're married; they're more likely not to try to get around you."

Kitty remembered how Noni had accused her of being a whore. Her remark still rankled, for as much as she had often been tempted, so far no one had taken Bill's place. But she wondered how long it could go on like that.

Every day the wireless blared out the number of

enemy bombers that had been brought down and the number of bombs that had descended on German industries and various shipbuilding yards. Everyone cheered this news, cheered the King and Queen and Churchill. In fact, they cheered anyone they thought had anything to do with these victories.

Kitty, however, worked on silently. She wished she could feel such patriotism and hate the Germans, but in her mind she could hear the whistle and scream of bombs and the cries of small children. Then a picture of blond Danny lying in a desert grave would flash before her eyes. Her thoughts would turn to Bill—calm, placid Bill. If he was imprisoned, was he being treated right? Were they hurting him? Her heart would twist. Surely he must be dead. That she could face, but not the starving and haggard faces she had seen on the newsreels in the cinema. These thoughts worried her every day. She knew she had to drive them out of her mind—they were making her crazy.

Her journal was filled with her fears for the future. She still scribbled whenever she felt so blocked with emotions that she had to release them on paper. She had already filled up several notebooks and was well into another. Her handwriting was no better, but she was finding it easier to put her feelings into words. With no one else to confide in completely, Kitty's journal became her friend.

But even her writing would not purge her of all her worries, and Kitty began to drink more and dance more wildly. She flirted and cavorted and soon became the life and soul of every party.

Because the factory work they were engaged in was connected with the Air Force, a flying hero was occasionally brought in to give the workers a lunchtime pep talk. This was usually followed by an invitation to the squadron hop the next Saturday night.

Kitty had never been to one of these hops; those who went were mainly the girls who had friends in camp. One day Kitty was persuaded to join them. She hated

Saturdays when there was nothing doing, so she agreed to go.

Dressed in their party frocks and with war paint on their faces, a group of ten girls, including Kitty, got off the train at the country station. An Air Force truck was waiting to collect them and transport them out to the camp in the wilds of Essex. The lads were all outside the village hall anxious to get their pick of the London girls, and the village girls were already inside.

The minute she stepped into the hall, Kitty was glad she had come. The band was playing lively dance music and everyone was very merry even though only soft drinks were meant to be served. She was glad she had bought a new dress for the occasion, obtained without clothing coupons. It was full-skirted and made of a soft, navy blue transparent material that was interwoven with lots of silver threads. The silky underslip fitted close to her small bosom, and the deep neckline, which was also low at the back, showed plenty of her smooth white skin. Her hair was short and set in waves, and in her ears she wore silver earrings. To simulate silk stockings, Kitty had covered her legs with suntan lotion and then drawn a thin line down the backs of her legs with an eyebrow pencil. With her feet in high-heeled navy shoes, she felt in top form. She danced energetically with a young pilot officer who hummed softly to the tune of "Stardust," which the band was playing. As he twisted Kitty around the hall with lots of variations of dance steps, the eyes of the other servicemen standing about the edge of the dance floor watched her appreciatively.

"Stardust," said the pilot officer at the end of the dance, "that's just what you look like, and my word, you're a smashing dancer. Don't go away, I'll be back." He escorted Kitty back to her corner seat before retiring to his own place with his friends. When the band struck up another lively tune, the officer came over to her again and asked politely for the pleasure of her hand in the next dance.

All along one side of the hall sat a line of wounded young men in bathchairs. Many had badly scarred faces and brightly colored blankets on their laps to disguise the fact that there were limbs missing. They came from all ranks. As Kitty walked past them, one young officer hooked her leg with his stick. "Come here, dolly," he called. "Let's get a closer look at you."

Kitty's face flushed scarlet with embarrassment as she tried to pull away. Luckily she was saved by her friend the pilot officer, who stepped forward to rescue her. "Don't take too much notice of the old crocks," he said charmingly as he waltzed her around the floor. Kitty gazed up at this tall, curly-haired young man. He was at least six feet, with a wide smile which revealed lots of lovely white teeth. He told her that he was called Barry. "The old crocks are right, though, you're a cute dolly," he said. "It must be that dress you're wearing.

"Let's get out of here," he said suddenly in the middle of the waltz. "Let's get a breath of fresh air—I hate these squadron hops."

Kitty was glad to get away from the hot, heavy atmosphere. She had become uncomfortably self-conscious about all the eyes that looked at her so lewdly as the lads discussed her figure and her see-through frock.

"Fancy a drink?" Barry asked her as they got outside. "We can't get one here—let's get a lift down to the pub."

He hailed a passing jeep. "Going down to the pub?" he asked the two officers in it. "Come on, jump in, Stardust."

When they all reached the village pub, the beer and whiskey flowed freely. They sang songs and laughed at each other's jokes and stories. Barry held on to Kitty possessively. "Lay off," he told his pals when they tried to touch her. "I found her."

Kitty watched this young man with fascination. He was so different from the other men she knew—so boyish and spontaneous in his affection. And he was obviously very well bred. Every word he spoke was crisply and clearly pronounced. Having been pawed and petted by untold rough men since the war had begun, Barry the Spitfire pilot seemed unique.

When the pub closed she was undoubtedly tipsy, as was Barry.

"I know where we can get some more whiskey," said one of his pals. "You coming, Barry?"

"Jolly good show," said Barry, helping Kitty back into the jeep.

They sped through the country lanes, all singing and shouting. Now and again Barry and Kitty kissed and cuddled. His lips were soft, smooth and sweet. Kitty was really enjoying herself; all thoughts of getting back home had vanished.

At an isolated cottage they pulled up and got out of the jeep. Barry's chums rang the doorbell and knocked several times. After a few minutes a smart-looking blonde came out. She stared at Kitty with hostility in her eyes. "What do you want, Pete?" she asked one of Barry's mates. "You know I don't take women in. This isn't a knocking shop."

There was a lot of hurried whispering that Kitty could not understand and then a rustle of notes. Finally, the woman opened the door wide and they all passed into the neat cottage sitting room, with its chintz-covered chairs, vases of flowers and paintings hanging on the walls.

Barry flopped onto the settee, pulling Kitty down with him. Cora, the woman, went out into the kitchen and brought back a bottle of whiskey and several glasses.

From then on it was one glorious booze-up. They all sang rude camp songs and danced wildly. More whiskey bottles were produced as more notes were handed over to Cora.

Barry lay on the settee, bottle in hand as he swilled whiskey from it. Then suddenly he staggered to his feet and caught hold of Kitty as she danced with Pete. Barry held her with one hand and, with the bottle of drink in the other, guided her up the narrow stairs. Kitty made no protest.

In a tidy bedroom, Barry flopped onto the bed and pulled Kitty with him, kissing her and fondling her breasts. "Don't be annoyed if I don't make love to you, Stardust," he murmured. "I can't do it when I've been drinking."

"I wouldn't, anyway," protested Kitty weakly. "I never did yet, not since my husband went away years ago." Then suddenly tears rushed to her eyes and she sniveled. "And I don't know whether he's alive or dead, and I still can't do it," she cried.

"Oh, darling, don't cry," Barry returned as he dropped the bottle on the floor and swept her completely into his arms. Their lips locked and they clung to each other as they felt their passion stirring within them. Their drunkenness and Bill were forgotten in the blissful darkness.

"Kitty, Kitty, where did I find you?" Barry said gently when they lay still and relaxed. "Where did you come from—out of the stars?"

He rolled over and kissed her again. His hands felt the curves of her body. "Just once more," he whispered, "just for luck."

"Lucky for you or me?" muttered Kitty with a grin.

Suddenly Barry's pals charged into the room. "Get going, you bloody fool," they shouted, hauling him to his feet. "You know we've got a show on." They dragged him naked and protesting from the room, carrying his clothes with them.

"Don't go away, Kitty. Wait for me, Kitty," Barry called after him.

Kitty had no idea what a show was, but it had to be important, she decided. Exhausted, she dropped off into a deep, relaxed sleep.

When she came back to life the next morning she felt absolutely terrible. Her head throbbed and her vision was blurred. She stared about, looking for her clothes in the strange room. She climbed slowly out of bed and

went out to find the bathroom. There she looked at
herself in the mirror. Her hair was sticking up all over
the place and her face looked crumpled. She shuddered
at the sight. As she washed and tidied up her hair,
feelings of guilt welled up inside her. Dear God, what a
fool she had made of herself. Why did she drink all that
whiskey? Suddenly, with a breathless thrill she recalled
all that lovemaking with the beautiful curly-haired
Barry. What a wonderful, exciting experience sex had
been with him. But feeling that made her ashamed. She
thought of Bill, for whom sex had been something you
just did not get excited about. He often used to say he
did not feel like it even when she was keen, but her stiff
pride prevented her from letting him know that she was
disappointed.

But last night, here with a stranger, she had acted
like a whore. She shivered and smiled at the thought.
Oh, well, what's done is done, she said to herself; I
suppose I'll take the consequences. She began to cheer
up and started humming. Yes, he certainly was good-
looking and sexy, was Barry.

She dressed and came slowly downstairs. Cora was in
the kitchen pouring out coffee. "All right, duck?" she
asked, shooting a quick look at Kitty.

"Yes, thank you," said Kitty, sitting down to drink
the cup of coffee Cora pushed at her.

There was no womanly gossip or even small talk.
Cora just busied about, gathering cups and washing up
the glasses used the night before. When everything was
cleaned up she put on her hat and turned to Kitty. "I'll
walk you to the station. If you catch the ten-thirty train,
you'll get into London by midday."

As the two women walked to the station, Cora
showed no curiosity about Kitty at all.

Kitty felt prompted to say apologetically, "I hope I
didn't inconvenience you. I'm afraid I had too much to
drink."

Cora's eyes seemed to twinkle, but she said nothing.
As they stood on the platform, Kitty was impressed by

Cora's appearance. Her blond hair was set neatly with a felt hat perched expertly on top, and her tailored suit fitted her well. She was certainly a very smart woman, Kitty thought.

The train came roaring into the station, and Kitty turned to say goodbye. Over the noise of the train she shouted, "Once more, I hope I wasn't too much trouble."

"Don't worry so much, duck," said Cora brightly. "He paid me very well for you."

Despite the belching of the train, Kitty heard those words. If a bomb had exploded under her it could not have given her a greater shock. Her legs were trembling as she climbed into the carriage and turned to face Cora again. Rage made her chest feel tight. "You bitch! You filthy whore!" she screeched before slamming the door and escaping into the carriage.

Cora just shrugged her slim shoulders and walked daintily out of the station.

In the empty compartment Kitty wept. Tears of remorse trickled down her cheeks. How she wanted to be back home with Dad and her cats, knowing, perhaps, that Bill was coming home again.

As she thought of Bill she started to sob. She loved him so much and now she had betrayed him, whether he was dead or alive. She leaned her head miserably against the wall behind her. Her face was hot and damp, her eyelashes wet. The only reason she allowed herself to be unfaithful was that Bill did not give enough of himself to her when he did see her. He always held back from her when she wanted him totally. At times it did not seem that it was just the army or the war that made him like that. There seemed to be something more, some aloofness in his manner, something implied in his criticism of her appearance and his refusal to discuss the idea of having another baby.

She stared out of the window at the green fields racing past. She was just getting back at him, really, she thought. Oh, would this war never end? She realized that she was exhausted from lack of sleep. She closed her eyes and tried not to think about anything. Finally she slept.

When the train reached London, Kitty caught the bus back home from the station. As she jumped off the bus at Billington Road, a terrible sight of devastation met her eyes. The huge factory that faced the house was flattened. It was completely destroyed, and all the houses in the street were again shattered by the blast. Kitty's knees felt as though they would give way from under her as she started to run. "Oh, dear God, let them be safe," she gasped as she tore all the way down the battered street. Once more, windows had gone, doors were hanging off their hinges and pathetic ribbons that were once curtains flapped weakly in the wind. Like a lunatic, she burst into No. 8. There, to her immense relief, was Dad, sitting in his armchair, bottle beside him and Smithy Boy lying in his lap.

"Oh, thank God!" she cried. "I was so scared when I saw what had happened." She knelt beside him. He looked tired and very dirty, but he grinned casually at her.

"Oh, Daddy, I'm sorry I stopped out all night," she wept.

Dad patted her head. "It's all right, gel, I was also worrying about you. Thank God there were no casualties in the street, but a busload of people were killed on the main road, and I didn't know where you were."

"I'm sorry," she wept. "I promise I'll never stay out again. Where were you and Noni when it came down?"

"'Twas some kind of a new weapon," Dad said. "The blast spread. Noni and I had just popped out for a drink when it happened. She's up at the First Aid Post doing what she can. A good girl is Noni. I've been helping to get the passengers from out of the bus. It wasn't a nice sight." He sighed.

Kitty felt ashamed of herself but wanted to sound

cheerful. "Well, all's well that ends well. I'll make some tea," she said brightly.

That evening, when Dad and Noni went out to play cards with a neighbor, Kitty humped buckets of water upstairs into the bathroom. The hot water system had been destroyed by the bomb blast, the plaster from the ceiling littered the floor and the sink was cracked. She looked sadly about the nice bathroom that she and Bill had been so proud of and wondered what he would say if he saw this mess.

She climbed into the bath and scrubbed herself hard; she felt physically and mentally dirty. She lay down in the hot water and started thinking over the events of the night before. She had nothing but pleasant thoughts as she relived those moments. Barry had been lovely, so refined and well-spoken. He was obviously a gentleman. Unlike her, he had probably never known a moment's worry in all his pampered life. She knew she would never meet him again and wondered why she felt so strongly about him. He was so charming. Surprised and pleased that she did not feel guilty, she shivered with delight as she remembered his lovemaking.

After relaxing in the water for a long time, she climbed out of the bath, dried her body and wrapped herself in her warm dressing gown. She went downstairs and sat by the fire with Smithy Boy purring in her arms. In a strange sort of way she felt luxuriously happy. She turned on the wireless to listen to the news. The cultured voice of the BBC news reader was announcing that there had been a big air attack on Germany. All targets had been successfully hit. However, the voice continued, ten fighter pilots had been shot down on the return flight, including Barry MacFarlane, a top pilot in the Battle of Britain.

Kitty sat up straight in her chair. No, it could not be, she told herself; there must be lots of men called Barry in the Air Force. But there was a deep tug at her heart. She knew it was he.

On Monday morning, the newspapers printed Barry's photograph on the front page. The article beneath it gave some details about him. He was from a well-known, wealthy manufacturing family and was to be buried with full honors the following Friday. The service was being held in Westminster Cathedral.

For the first time in years, Kitty took the day off on Friday to attend Mass. She joined the end of the long queue of people going into the service at the Cathedral. She was struck by the large number of well-dressed men and women who arrived in big shiny cars.

All through that long memorial service Kitty sat at the back praying to God to help her to be a good wife, a good daughter and a good anything that she was likely to become.

Barry's coffin lay covered with a flag in front of the altar, surrounded by flowers and lighted candles.

The white-robed priest murmured the service and a feeling of peacefulness enveloped Kitty just as if she were taking Communion. I'm glad I made you happy for a short period, Barry, she thought. Then, thinking her words would surely reach him, she whispered, "Ask God to forgive me my sins."

Slowly the pallbearers carried the coffin down the aisle. Barry's broad-shouldered comrades bore him to his last home. Kitty, kneeling in the last seat, raised her eyes as they passed to meet those of Barry's pal, Pete. Both looked momentarily surprised, but he walked on.

Kitty put down her head and wept. She stayed in the peaceful cathedral for a long time, then said several Hail Marys and went home. She felt almost purged, happy, and certainly more at peace with the world.

CHAPTER FOURTEEN
The G.I.'s

Kitty frequently thought of Bill nowadays. Where was he? Lying in some remote desert grave or a prisoner in the hands of the cruel Nazis? Every possibility was unthinkable. She knew she had to pray and ask God to send him home safe. If He did, she would never be bad again, she promised. She really missed Bill, but at times when she tried to picture him in her mind, he seemed almost like an old photograph—dull and faded with time. She also often thought about Barry. She was not entirely sorry about her escapade with him, even if she had been bought and sold by that fast bitch Cora. In fact, she remained glad she had been able to make Barry happy on what had turned out to be his last night on earth.

These thoughts possessed her during the days and far into the nights, until one night, well after midnight, while Noni snored on the other side of the room, Kitty got up and began to write in her notebook. She had not written in it for months, but now she recorded all her feelings about that special night. Through her writing,

she relived her stirring sexual experience with Barry
MacFarlane. She recorded his tender words and gentle
movements. She described those moments of intense
passion in such detail that her heart beat faster and her
hand trembled. Would she ever experience such sensa-
tions again? Could Bill ever make her feel the way
Barry had? Even if such emotions were never roused in
her again, she thought, at least she would have this
record to remember them by.

It was past three o'clock before Kitty had finished
writing. She put the notebook back in the suitcase,
which she pushed back into its place under the bed.

In the morning Dad said, "Didn't you feel well last
night, gel? The light was on all the time."

"She was bleeding well scribbling," said Noni. "I saw
her."

"Mind your own business," flared up Kitty, furious
that Noni had been spying on her. After a short spell of
being nice to Kitty, Noni had reverted to her bitchy
ways. Kitty felt her sister now possessed Dad completely and, to Kitty, at least, she was as bad-tempered as
ever. Their arguments began to be more frequent and
violent, just as they used to be.

"Serve you right if you are left alone," Noni shouted
at her one day. "You don't deserve your Bill, he was
always too good for you."

"You dirty, untidy bitch," Kitty shouted back.
"You'll never get another man, no matter how hard you
try."

But Kitty knew it was useless to go on arguing like
this. Until Bill came home—if he did—the house would
never be the same. She began to think of ways of
getting out of it. As soon as she could she volunteered
to work on the land in Hampshire during July and
August in the voluntary movement that recruited
workers to help with the harvest. The workers lived
under canvas and got a small amount of money each
week. Most of them were students on vacation.

When Kitty told Dad about her decision, he was

encouraging. "I'll be all right, gel," he said. "I have Noni and the cats to look after me. But remember, this is your home and Bill's house, and I'll take care of it until he returns."

"If he ever does," said Kitty bitterly.

"Now, now, trust in God. They're still letting you draw his pay, and that's a good sign that they expect to find him," said Dad wisely.

Maybe Dad was right, Kitty thought, but she could not bear not knowing.

In July Kitty left her job at the radio factory and went off to stay at the camp. It was on land owned by a millionaire and it was well run, with good food and entertainment. Kitty loved the life. She was quite free from responsibilities as she hoed mangle wurzels, cut hay and picked up potatoes from behind a tractor. Her back ached and she got quite sunburned, but she was undoubtedly happier than she had been for a long time. There were no air raids out in the countryside, so it was easy to relax. She had plenty of good company and she loved the singsongs around the campfire.

When the harvest was finished, Kitty was sorry to leave the camp. The Hampshire landscape was so beautiful with its rolling hills and historic towns: Kitty had never seen the like. She told herself that she had to live in the country after the war and ride horses, grow flowers and do all those things she had been deprived of as a child. In the meantime, she thought, if there was still no news of Bill when she got home she would try to get into the Land Army.

Kitty stepped off the bus in Leabridge, well-tanned, a little fatter and much happier than before. She bounced down the street, pleased to be feeling excited at the thought of seeing her family again. The little house seemed quiet. Wooden boards had been nailed over the broken windows and, as usual, the street door stood open. "Hallo," she shouted as she entered the house. She stood there waiting. To her horror, Noni came out of the dining room, heavy-eyed and morose.

Behind her was Dad, shoulders bowed in grief and eyes red-rimmed from crying.

Kitty felt a nauseous feeling rising inside her. "You've heard about Bill!" she cried, her eyes wide with horror.

To her immense relief Noni shook her tousled head. "No," she said, "but our Bobby's been killed. We got the telegram yesterday."

Poor Bobby, their much-loved younger brother, was dead. Dad adored him more than anyone. What a blow. Kitty ran to Dad and held him close. "That's all our boys gone now, gel," he sighed. Noni came up and put her arms around them both and they all wept together.

The door of opportunity was once more slammed in Kitty's face. She had to forget about her plans for joining the Land Army. She could not leave now; Dad and Noni needed her so badly. Her own troubles were pushed aside. She did all the cooking and the house-work, and took them out on Saturday night sprees to an Irish pub where all Dad's compatriots gathered. There they sang Irish songs and danced Irish jigs and tried to forget about tomorrow. Kitty knew it would take Dad a long time to forget Bobby, but she did her best to help him.

Kitty had asked to go back to work at the factory, and they were pleased to have her. That great invention radar was now being used and the small radio sets, complete with radar systems, were being sped along the track. No one was allowed to talk about the work they did. Anyone caught chatting about this invention in the canteen was instantly dismissed. Kitty enjoyed the clandestine atmosphere and found it all rather exciting, so she was very happy at work there.

One day she received a letter from the War Office. It stated that Bill was in an Italian prisoner-of-war camp and Kitty could correspond with him through the Red Cross.

Kitty sat silently on the settee holding the letter in hand as she stared into the fireplace. So Bill was alive; thank God, she thought. Perhaps she had always known.

"Well, that's one bright spot in our miserable lives," commented Noni.

"Now it's come," Kitty said, "I can't believe it. I hope they're not unkind to him, not Bill. He's so gentle; he could not take cruelty."

"Kitty, dear," Dad said reassuringly, "they have to treat them reasonably well. It's required by the Geneva Convention."

Kitty sighed and sat down to write Bill a letter. She found it hard. Although she felt feelings of great warmth and love for him, she could not put them into words. She did not know what to say. It was as if Bill was now in some way a complete stranger. She knew her letter came out sounding flat and dull.

"The Italians might come out of the war—their heart was never in it," commented Dad optimistically. "Then they'll send Bill back."

By the next weekend, Kitty was very confused and extremely depressed. She felt like leaving them all to their own troubles. She was tired of trying to cheer them up all the time.

"I've got to get out, even for one night," she told Judy, one of her young workmates. "I need a bloody change and I'm going to get it."

"Come with us, up West," said Judy. "We go dancing, and it's great. All the G.I.'s are up there on leave. We have a good time."

"Oh, I've done all that," said Kitty, remembering her last experience of the West End in the company of G.I.'s, "and I'm still bloody bored. Anyway, I don't like Yanks. They keep popping into bed with this one and that, and you never know what you're going to get."

"That's up to you, Kitty, but we like the Rainbow Club," said Judy.

Despite her comments, Kitty went out that Saturday night with Judy and some other girls from work, none of whom were yet twenty. The bombs came down at intervals, but no one seemed unduly alarmed. They sat on the bus and giggled. Kitty's companions talked constantly about the Yanks that they were going to meet at the Rainbow Club. It was in a cellar deep down under Oxford Street and seemed to be alive with servicemen from virtually every country in the world. The first thing Kitty noticed was a big notice on the wall that read: NO JITTERBUGGING. NO ALCOHOL TO BE CONSUMED ON THE PREMISES.

After reading that, Kitty looked about her. People were rolling drunkenly on the floor, the music was loud and had a strange beat and couples were twisting and jiving and turning head over heels. Others lounged around the walls drinking bottles of cheap whiskey bought on the black market. From the moment Kitty entered, she knew she should not have come, and after several very fast hops about the crowded floor with fellows who slobbered all over her, she had had quite enough.

One youth went about the hall approaching all the women and asking pathetically, "Wanna shack, honey?" When he asked Kitty he got no answer at all and moved on to a crowd of girls who all went into hysterical laughter.

"Whatever does he mean?" Kitty asked Judy.

Judy leaned over and whispered a certain word. "That's what the Yanks call it," she said with a grin. Kitty was disgusted. She slid off to the side of the room to hide out until it was time to go home.

Standing idly by the wall, looking on, was a big husky chap. He had stripes and bars on his arm and seemed older than most of the other American servicemen there. Kitty sneaked behind him to stand by the radiator.

"Hell, ain't it?" the man said with a grin. He had a

nice smile that lit up a very ugly craggy face. His skin was tanned and rugged, his nose was flat and his lips very thick. He puffed on a small brown cigar and had a look of amusement in his eye as he surveyed the antics on the dance floor. "Come out for a beer," he said to Kitty. "It's stinking hot in here, and no bar."

Kitty agreed readily. She only needed an excuse to get out of that cellar. They left the club and crossed the road to a pub. The man said his name was Harry Cross. In spite of his ugly face, Kitty thought he had a lot of charm. He was very heftily built and joked about it. "I move like a tank on a dance floor; there never seems to be enough room for me," he said.

"Why go?" asked Kitty as she sipped the drink he had bought her.

"Well, some of my boys are there. They don't know this town, so I thought I'd better stay and keep an eye on them."

"As good an excuse as any," grinned Kitty, "but they all seem such kids. I must be getting old. I can't enjoy all that mad hopping around any more."

"You don't look very old." Harry looked down at her, scrutinizing her keenly.

"Well, what's the verdict?" she asked.

"Say twenty-five and you've lived a bit, but being so petite you would pass for much younger."

"I suppose I should be flattered. But I'm twenty-seven and I even feel it."

By now they were friends. They had a few more drinks and then went off for steak and chips.

Afterward Harry walked with her to the underground station. He made no advances. He talked mainly of himself and his life. He came from the town where Mark Twain was born and had been a newspaper man before he got called up.

"Is that a very interesting job?" asked Kitty.

"Well, you learn a lot about people. It's not easy to fool me, you know."

"Don't worry," said Kitty, "you're safe with me. I don't go around the town picking up G.I.'s and fleecing them of their money, like a lot of girls I know."

"Oh, my," said Harry, "on the ball, ain't we, honey?"

Kitty stared at him, not really understanding him. Suddenly they both began to laugh. As the tube train pulled in, Harry said, "What about meeting me tomorrow and showing me the sights?"

"I might," she said.

"Okay, in just this spot, midday. That all right?"

"Could be," said a noncommittal Kitty as she hopped aboard the train for home.

The next morning, Kitty put on her slacks and roll-necked jumper and kept the date with Harry Cross. The two of them walked down Petticoat Lane, visited the Tower of London and ended up at the London Zoo. They stood very close together, staring at poor old Winston Churchill, the Prime Minister's lion. The pathetic, mangy creature stared back disdainfully at them.

"How terrible to be shut up in a cage," said Kitty.

"He'd make short work of us if he weren't," jested Harry.

"I don't think so," said Kitty. "He looks so old and bored, he would probably ask to be let back in."

"You could be right, honey." Harry looked down at her, her hair wind blown, the blue jersey a little dusty, the slacks fitting trimly about the waist. "You are very cute," he said.

"Don't start," said Kitty. "I thought this was supposed to be a platonic friendship."

Harry laughed and put a comforting arm about her. She rather liked the firm warm feeling of his body next to hers. She allowed him to press her close.

"Next week, Kitty, I'm going on seven days' leave to Scotland. Want to come with me?"

"You got a cheek," retorted Kitty. "I don't hardly know you."

"Well, that's the best way to find out," said Harry.

They had tea and parted good friends at seven o'clock. He was due back at camp before ten.

"See you next Saturday, Kitty. Five o'clock by the notice board at Euston Station."

"You'll be lucky," said Kitty as they parted.

He pulled her back roughly and gave her a kiss. "Don't be silly, Kitty. It's fine up in Scotland, you'll love it. You might even like me a little," he said, suddenly wistful.

"I'll see," said Kitty, suddenly wanting to go home.

All that next week Kitty thought how lovely it would be to see Loch Lomond and Stirling, and the place where Robbie Burns was born. This is the chance of a lifetime, she thought. She was longing for Bill to return home from the war but she knew that once he did, she would no longer be able to have as much fun as she pleased. She certainly would never get the opportunity to go off to a strange place with a friendly stranger like Harry. There would be no need to get involved. Harry seemed sensible, and anyway, he was probably married out in the States. Yes, she thought, he was just a lonely soldier; she would chance it.

"I've got a week's holiday. Might go up to Scotland," said Kitty casually one night as the family ate supper.

"What, all alone?" exclaimed Noni, horrified at such an adventure.

"I like being alone," said Kitty unconvincingly. "I've been saving up. Might as well spend it."

Dad was not bothered. "Mind how you go, gel," was all he said.

On Saturday afternoon, feeling very guilty, Kitty sneaked out with her suitcase. She wore a navy suit, a white frilly blouse, straw hat, navy high-heeled shoes and sheer nylon stockings. She felt very smart.

At Euston Station, she spotted Harry lounging by the notice board looking as if he hadn't a care in the world. She smiled as she approached him.

"Good, you came," he said. "My, how fancy you

look. Any guy's gonna be proud to be seen out with you, honey."

"Flattery will get you nowhere," said Kitty, very chuffed.

They went into the buffet to get some traveling courage, as Harry called it. Then, after a good drink, they went aboard the eight o'clock train, the express to Scotland. It was packed with troops who stood or squatted on their kit bags in the corridor. Kitty and Harry could also find no seat and had to stand. Harry put a protective arm about her and said, "A lot of these will get off at the first stop, so we can bag some seats then."

Kitty was beginning to have doubts about being in the train with Harry. Had she been too hasty? What was she getting into? Maybe she should get out at the first stop, too, she thought.

When the train stopped for ten minutes and most of the troops departed, Harry got out onto the platform to get some coffee. Kitty did not run away but was sitting demurely in a seat when he returned. Soon the train was far from London. The hours passed and they settled down to doze. "Why choose Scotland for your leave?" Kitty asked sleepily.

"Two things," Harry replied. "One, the hotels are cleaner and cheaper, and two, my old mom is a MacGreggor and all for those clan laws. I promised her I'd visit Scotland whenever I got the opportunity, so I do when I can."

Kitty could not envisage this big man who had to be in his late thirties with a mother, and she said so.

"Well, of course I got a mom," he laughed. "Who do you think hatched me, some ape?"

Kitty laughed in return. She was enjoying Harry's company so much.

In the early morning, Kitty stared heavy-eyed out of the window of the speeding train. She had never seen such countryside—bleak hills with hardly any trees and miles and miles of flowering heather, which looked like a massive purple carpet.

"Oh, it's very nice," Kitty cried, leaning out of the window. The morning air on her face was cold and refreshing. "Look at the lake all shining in the sunlight."

"That lake is a loch," growled Harry tetchily. "Come in and shut that window, it's very drafty."

The train slowed down at Stirling. "We get out here," said Harry. "This is our first stop. Our train connection isn't until tomorrow."

Very stiff and travel weary, they climbed down onto the platform. As Kitty fumbled with her case on the platform, Harry became impatient with her. "Come on, for Christ's sake, let's get some sleep. I'm stiff all over; no comfort in those damn English trains."

They walked up the hill from the station carrying their own luggage. Kitty was silent, deep in thought, and Harry continued to be irritable. "This will do," he said, pointing to a hotel that had a big crown and a golden lion painted on its sign, which swung gently back and forth in the morning breeze.

They went in through the front door and Kitty put down her case in the foyer. "I'll book myself in," she said obstinately. Harry gave her a wide grin that revealed his large nicotine-stained teeth. "Got any money?" he asked. "You'll need it."

"That's all right," she replied haughtily. "I'm quite able to pay for myself."

"Well," Harry started to cackle, "this is going to be a damn fine leave, but come on, let's get some rest."

"I've only a single and a double vacant," said the receptionist, eyeing them curiously.

"Okay, I'll take the single. The double is yours, Kitty," said Harry, still smiling.

Acting as if she were well accustomed to booking into strange hotels, Kitty signed in and went up the stairs with the porter. "I'll be seeing you," she told Harry airily.

Harry lit a cigar and did not answer.

Kitty was thrilled with her room. There was a huge
bed covered by a bright blue coverlet. Matching blue
curtains hung in the window, and a pretty dressing
table and a large roomy wardrobe stood against the
wall. She lolled on the bed for awhile. This was the life,
she thought. How strange that some people lived like
this all the time. Kitty saw no reason why she should
not indulge in a little luxury even if it did cost her all
her pocket money. She took a bath, set her hair in clips
and then got into the big comfortable bed. No one, so
far, had disturbed her. She was surprised. She had been
sure Harry would craftily try it on and she was prepared to refuse him coolly. She smiled at the thought as
she drifted off to sleep.

When she awoke she was filled with apprehension.
She suddenly felt very guilty about what she was doing.
What should her next move be? she wondered. Better
pay for this splendid room and then go home. It was
going to make a big hole in the twenty pounds she had
brought, she was sure of that. She brushed her hair, put
on a smart brown, short-sleeved dress and went downstairs. Spying the bar, she decided a drink would give
her some Dutch courage before her departure. She sat
herself at a table and asked the lad serving for a
whiskey and soda. To her irritation, the boy gawped at
her and then hurried away. In a moment he was back.
His red face, topped with a shock of sandy hair, looked
embarrassed, but he opened his mouth wide and a
strange sound came out. "Arre ye in the hoose?" he
seemed to say to her.

Kitty stared haughtily at him. She puffed a cigarette.
She had not understood a word. "Whiskey and soda,"
she said angrily. "And hurry up."

Off the boy lolloped and in the space of a second, a
tall, angular woman arrived wearing a white apron.
"Arre ye in the hoose, madam?" she asked hoarsely,
hands on her hips.

"I'm being served," said Kitty, ignoring her.

The woman shrugged dramatically and went away muttering. Then there was a long wait until a big fat man in a striped apron boomed close to her ear, "D'ye bide in the hoose?"

Great guns, Kitty thought, what the devil were they all shouting at her for? She began to get alarmed, but then suddenly there was Harry, all smiles in a blue shirt and well-laundered trousers.

"Wake up, Kitty, they want to know if you're staying here before they serve you. Make it two," he told the man, who went off laughing.

Kitty's cheeks flamed red. She had made a good fool of herself this time.

Noticing the tears in her eyes, Harry put a big comforting hand over hers. "It's okay, honey. It's just that they don't serve unescorted women unless they are staying in the hotel."

"Stupid lot!" cried Kitty. "And what a terrible language. Don't think I'm going to like Scotland," she added petulantly.

"You will," said Harry, "but be my baby; let me look after you. I want to very much." His hand crept up her bare arm with a soft, smooth caress and then, when no one was looking, he bent forward and kissed her. His lips were sweet, dry and comforting. Kitty knew she was trapped, but suddenly she did not care.

They had dinner at the hotel and then went on a pub crawl down the seamy side of the town. Kitty had never seen so many drunk men so early in the evening. "It's only nine o'clock and they're lying down outside the pubs. Why, it's worse than London," she told Harry.

"Much worse," Harry replied. "Booze is stronger and cheaper here."

Certainly the booze the two of them drank put them both in good moods. That night Harry did not go up to his single room two floors up, and Kitty certainly did not mind.

In the morning, Harry said breezily, "Come on, honey, we're going traveling, away up to the beautiful highlands."

"Where exactly are we going?" she asked, feeling on top of the world that morning, and looking it. She was packing her suitcase once more.

"We're going to a place called Callendar. It's known as the gateway to the highlands and I have friends there. I stayed with them last year and I really like it."

It all sounded exciting and Kitty was thrilled at the idea.

They caught the local train connection and Kitty sat silently, staring at the scenery out of the window. She felt wonderfully serene and carefree.

"Kitty," Harry suddenly said rather quietly, "let me tell my friends we're married."

Kitty's peace of mind was shattered. "Why?" she demanded. Her lips tightened in a thin line.

"Kitty, where we're going, they are my friends and they accept me as one of their own. And I've opened my mouth about Mom being a MacGreggor."

"Why tell them lies?" she asked.

"They're maiden ladies and would be a little shocked at our behavior."

"Well, let's go somewhere else," Kitty said, quite unmoved.

"Kitty, my love, if we go there, we'll be well taken care of and it's only a week. I promised to return to see them. What have you to lose?" Harry's rugged face was very solemn and his brown eyes looked sincere.

"Oh, all right," Kitty said pettishly, "what do I care?"

The gateway to the somber highlands really impressed her. She loved the long, winding village streets and the old-fashioned gift shops. The shortages of war did not seem to have touched this place. Kitty was used to empty shops and broken windows, so it was fun to dawdle to look at hand-knitted shawls, crocheted tablecloths, leather handbags, tartan traveling bags and real kilts. It was a great treat.

"Oh," she cried excitedly, "I'll get that for Dad, and Noni would like that. . . ."

Harry looked at her in amazement. She was so juvenile in her ways, but perhaps that was part of her charm, he thought. They climbed the steep, hilly street. The mountain towered over them. Kitty was astonished by the colors—all different shades of brown, purple and green. It was breathtakingly beautiful. Halfway up the hill was the guesthouse. Built into the hillside, it had a staggering view of the loch below.

As they approached, a woman who must have been in her sixties came hurrying out, calling after her, "Annie, come oot, look who's here." A second later, another woman emerged from the house. She squealed with delight at the sight of Harry.

Kitty stood shyly to one side as they fussed over him, and he in turn hugged them and jested with them. Then he took Kitty's hand and said, "Told you I had a surprise for you. This is my wife Kitty. Kitty, meet Annie and her sister Jessie."

The women both kissed Kitty as warmly as they had kissed Harry, and Annie held her hand as they walked into the house.

The guesthouse was wonderfully clean. Kitty had never seen such polish on any furniture or such snow-white linen. They were given high tea with homemade cakes and bannocks, fruit and real cream. The sisters made them so welcome Kitty felt they were part of the family rather than paying guests.

There were two other guests: an old colonel and a major from the Scottish Highland regiment, the Black Watch. They argued constantly about the war but kept to themselves.

Annie and Jessie obviously adored Harry. It seemed that he and his mother had sent them several parcels from America. The sisters talked of his mother as though they knew her.

It surprised Kitty that Annie and Jessie did not probe into her background. They did not ask one question about how long she and Harry had been married or how long they had known each other. She took to them right away. They looked almost identical in their home-made tweed dresses, white hair, blue eyes and rosy cheeks. Kitty thought they looked like Tweedledum and Tweedledee.

Kitty and Harry roamed the moors, making love frequently in remote places. In the evenings they went to the village and chatted with the old folks. Harry was always very generous and plied all who needed it with free beer.

Kitty felt quite content in his company and in a strange way she had a feeling she had known Harry before, even though he was different in every respect from her kind of man. His body was hairy, his skin dark and he was heavily built. She would lie in bed and watch him shave with his army razor in front of a small mirror. She still thought he was ugly, but she also found him very attractive—his personality was so warm. She was also sure that he was married, but so far the subject had never been discussed between them.

At the end of the week they went to the pub for lunch. When they came out, Harry very happy after pints of strong ale and scotch chasers, a little lad in a ragged kilt came up to them. He wore a tam-o'-shanter on the back of his blond head. "D'ye want a guide? Tak' ye tae the meetin' o' the waters fur a pound." He held out a grubby hand.

"Okay," said Harry, "you do the job first, then get the pay."

The lad nodded. "Come wi' me," he said, and dashed off at a swift pace. Kitty found it quite difficult to keep up with him as he jumped over the stile and was off along the edge of the plowed field.

"Slow down, laddie," yelled Harry, waiting for Kitty. They laughed uproariously as they joined hands and galloped after him. They went down dales and along the riverside, past rocky caverns bordering hill-sides covered with green ferns and all kinds of wildflowers. It was remote and silent except for the sound of rushing water.

Then, in a clearing, the little boy stood still. "Look yon," he cried. "Here's the place. One pound if ye dinna mind." He put out his hand again.

There they saw it, a grand sight. Two great rivers met, frothed and boiled as they swept majestically toward the sea. The shining silver water contrasted with the deep green pine forest surrounding it. It was indeed an impressive sight.

Kitty stood very still. The view was so magnificent that she felt as though she were almost standing at the edge of the world. She was speechless.

Harry gave their guide his pound. He looked at the boy for a second and said, "Go get yourself a new skirt. And get your backside out of here very quickly, as fast as you can, and keep going."

With an impish grin the boy tucked the money into his kilt. "Yah, Yankee Doodle," he yelled, "find yer ain way back." With that he tore off as fast as his thin bare legs could carry him.

Kitty sat down by the river and Harry lounged down awkwardly beside her.

"Now you've done it; we don't know the way back," she said.

Harry put his arm around her. "We'll find it. Who wants an audience in a place like this and in such lovely weather?"

"Yes, isn't it beautiful? So still, so silent, and the smell of that pine forest is gorgeous," she replied.

"You appreciate nature a lot, Kitty," said Harry, "considering you were brought up in a big town."

"I've always longed to see places like this," she said. "When I was a kid I read all the travel books I could get my hands on, and I thought I would like to write books.

I never really wanted to get married. I used to dream I owned a gypsy caravan with an old gray horse to pull it and rambled along through green cool lanes. . . ."

Kitty stopped suddenly as she noticed that Harry had a faraway look in his eyes. He looked sad. "I remember all the bloody battles and the pals I saw slaughtered. . . ."

"Oh, Harry," exclaimed Kitty, "don't, not in this lovely spot. Let's forget the war," she begged.

Harry turned to her and gripped her shoulders as he looked deep into her eyes. Then he smiled as though he had only just returned to the present moment. He kissed her quickly on the cheek and leaped up, pulling her with him. They locked arms and laughed as a jay flew above them, screaming its mocking cry through the trees.

They walked along the riverbank until they came across a tiny brook that flowed down the mountain side, emptying its silvery beauty into the wide river. They took off their shoes and soaked their feet in the ice-cold water. Kitty looked up at the towering pines above them. "In a spot like this," she said, "I feel I want to pray. It's so quiet, like a church."

Harry threw a stick into the stream and watched the water jostle it down into the river, where it bobbed up and down helplessly as it disappeared from view. "Where's your husband, Kitty?" he asked quietly. "You never mention him."

Kitty looked at him sadly. "His name is Bill. He's just an ordinary chap. He's now a prisoner of war. We'd only been married two years when he went away."

"Well, that's okay, honey, he'll come back to you," said Harry, holding her tight. "Look at me. I've got a wife and two kids that I might never see again."

Kitty had thought as much, but what did it matter now? "Do you think we're very wicked, Harry?" she asked forlornly.

"No, honey, we just got to go on living. What else can we do?"

"Sometimes I get really worried about myself. I seem to have no conscience about things," said Kitty.

"Just as well, my love. It's a rough, tough, old world, and it's better not to let it beat us." Harry pulled her to her feet. "Last one stinks," he challenged and started to run.

Kitty laughed loudly as she ran after him. She forgot about Bill and her worries once again and felt like a young girl. They ran deeper into the pine forest and clouds of disturbed birds rose into the air squawking and flapping their wings.

"What are they?" Kitty asked when the two of them finally came to a halt.

"Rooks," he said. "Look up there."

In almost every tree there were big untidy nests and the shiny black, noisy birds swooped in and out of the tall branches. Down under the trees, the young ones that had not yet learned to fly floundered about, flapping in a confused manner over the skeletons of their unfortunate brothers and sisters who had not survived.

"Oh, poor little things," Kitty said and ran about gathering them up in her arms, stroking and fussing them and making little nests out of ferns to put them in. "Poor, poor little dears," she cried. "Oh, what a pity, why can't they fly?"

"Some will, and some won't," said Harry. "There are too many of them; they get pushed out of the nests."

"Oh, it's so sad. They will die tonight when it gets cold."

"Can't do much about it," Harry said, shrugging his shoulders. "You look like a born mother, Kitty. Why no children?"

"I lost mine," she said coldly, "but that's all."

"You wouldn't like one with me?" he jested.

"Give over, Harry, don't make jokes about things like that," she said, suddenly serious.

"Ah, well, let's go. I must say, you're a strange girl. I'm not sure I know you at all."

It took them a long time to find their way out of the forest, and it was dusk when they finally emerged. They found themselves on the grounds of a big hotel. In the fading light they could see grand sunken gardens, stone statues and all kinds of shrubs and trees.

"Good," said Harry as they neared the building, "now perhaps we can get some chow. I'm so dry I could drink a big pint."

"It's awful posh," said Kitty, hanging back a bit. She was very conscious of her untidy hair, her rumpled blouse and her skirt wet at the hem from when she had paddled in the stream.

"So what?" said Harry as he took her arm. "Come on, honey, I smell food."

The hotel was called the Roman Camp. They went to the dining room and ordered a scrumptious meal of fresh salmon, strawberries and cream. Kitty hid her feet under the table to hide the fact that she was wearing no stockings, for seated around her were what seemed to be all the society folk evacuated from London. Their jewelry flashed fire, and their conversation was low and modulated. They smiled with benign interest at Kitty and her friend, both of whom looked a little out of place.

Kitty suddenly felt awkward and embarrassed in Harry's company. He drank too much and drew too much attention to them.

"What's wrong, honey?" Harry asked, noticing her scowl. "Why are you so self-conscious? These guys ain't no one. We're fighting their war for them."

Kitty did not admire his arrogance and she did not like the Roman Camp. She did not belong there.

She was in a bad mood by the time they got back to the guesthouse.

"My, my," said Annie after they had told her where

they dined, "you were really living it up. All the aristocrats stay there. It must have cost a lot."

Harry roared. "No," he said, "I only paid for the booze. The bull-faced guy behind the bar told me that because I was one of Britain's staunchest allies the meal was on the house." He laughed with glee.

For some reason this made Kitty feel worse than ever.

That last night they talked a lot in bed. Kitty had calmed down and forgiven Harry. They talked about their dream for the future and what they were each going to do when the war was over.

"It's strange," Kitty said, "but I feel I could write. When I was very young and poor I used to invent a character and she would go with me everywhere. Each day, I'd make up a new adventure for her."

Harry grinned. "Well, go ahead, get it down, love, for that's the secret of creative art."

She thought he was mocking her. "Oh, nuts," she said, "can't you ever be serious?"

The next day, after an almost tearful goodbye from the two sisters, Kitty and Harry caught the train for London.

Kitty felt relaxed after all the fresh country air, but she was beginning to feel guilty about Bill. Again she had betrayed him, and again she had enjoyed herself. A part of her was glad for what she had done while another part was disapproving and scolding. The pleasures of the last few days were clouded by a sense of shame that made Kitty fall silent most of the train journey home.

The train pulled in at Euston Station. It was time to say goodbye.

"Kitty, my own true love," said Harry passionately. "I've got to keep hold of you. Say you love me." He kissed her hard on the lips.

Kitty drew away and shook her head. "Don't be so daft," she said indifferently. "Bye-bye, be seeing you." She jumped into a taxi and waved to him one more time. As the taxi pulled out she sat firmly in her seat and did not look back again.

When the taxi drew up outside her house her sense of guilt was almost overpowering. The windows were still boarded up and looked pathetic. She wondered if there was any news. As she opened the door Noni was coming downstairs in a grubby nightgown. "Oh, it's you?" she sniffed. "There's a letter for you. It came two days ago; I didn't know where you were." She went into the kitchen to make a cup of tea, her silence showing her disapproval.

"Is that you, gel?" Dad called from upstairs. "Had a good holiday?"

"Lovely, thanks, Dad," Kitty called back to him. She went into the dining room, and there on the mantelpiece was an envelope addressed to her in Bill's handwriting. She opened it up, trembling.

Dear Kitty,

   I don't doubt you were all getting worried about me, but I am all right. I have been in hospital. Was a prisoner, picked up by the Italians, but I am now back at last, having been in an exchange of prisoners.

                              Will be home soon.
                              My love to all, Bill.

"It's from Bill! He's safe!" cried Kitty.

She dashed up to Dad's room and jumped onto his bed. Dad smelled of rum and stale tobacco, but Kitty didn't care. She held on to him.

"Oh, Daddy, Bill's coming home! It's all over." She sobbed, quite unrestrained. Dad patted her back as though she were a baby. "Hush, hush, don't cry, my little wild goose," he murmured. "It will come out all right."

CHAPTER FIFTEEN

Bill's Return

Kitty had dried her tears and begun to look ahead. "Bill's coming home," she told Noni brightly, "very soon."

Noni was very sulky and stared at her with suspicion. "Have to mind your P's and Q's now your husband's coming back," she said sullenly.

"Exactly what are you trying to suggest?" demanded Kitty furiously.

"You know, you rotten cow," sneered Noni.

"Oh, shit," said Kitty impatiently.

Noni went on moaning. "I've stayed home and my Danny's dead and buried. It's not fair." Then she began what Dad called her Irish howl.

"Oh, Noni," cried Kitty, "don't cry. Try and be happy, just for me. Come on, let's go out. I'll treat you to a new dress."

She did not want to quarrel with Noni anymore. Bill would be back soon and then she would feel safe again. She sat down and wrote him a long letter, after which she began to put the house in order. Noni was still hopeless at cleaning.

That week, London was bombarded with another kind of enemy weapon—doodlebugs. They came over, night and day, long cigarlike objects traveling at a terrific speed across the sky. They made a deep droning sound which, to Kitty, seemed to say, "I'm coming, I'm coming." It always made her shiver, reminding her of the bogeyman tales she heard as a child. Whenever she heard the drone, she stood still, like everyone else, her tummy twisting in knots. She would listen for the engine to cut out and then dive for cover. The engine cut-out was the only warning of the bomb's progression as it sped down to the ground to take away complete streets of houses, great buildings and many lives.

Kitty knew she had to stay close to Dad and Noni, but she refused to go to the air-raid shelter. Despite her terror of the doodlebugs, she was not prepared to spend any time in that terrible place, whatever the danger. So she went to sleep in her own bed each night trying not to listen for the droning.

Each day she wrote to Bill and got airmail letters from him in return. There was still no definite date for his homecoming. She was lonely now that she waited for him. On Sunday mornings she walked down Petticoat Lane. She liked to rummage among the stalls looking for bargains. As she wandered she often thought about her adventures over the last few years. She thought of her holiday in Scotland and wondered if she would ever see Harry again. She now thought of him with fondness, even though the end of their relationship had been a little sour. Such is the way of the heart, she sighed.

On this particular morning she was looking over the dresses hanging on the secondhand stall. She glanced up at the buxom woman behind the stall who was shouting loudly to attract customers. She looked very familiar. Suddenly she looked at Kitty and exclaimed, "Cor blimey! If it ain't me old pal, Kitty Daly."

It was Bebe, Kitty's old friend who had taken her on
the prowl for boys and had shown her how to do herself
up. Her old companion who had rejected her so many
years ago when Kitty had tried to be philosophical
about Tommy Wright's consumption.

"Oh, Bebe, I hardly recognized you," cried Kitty,
suddenly delighted to see such a friendly face. "How
are you?"

"Well, I recognized you," replied Bebe, "with that
wide, cheery grin. Come and sit down here. We can
have a jaw."

Bebe had indeed changed a lot. She looked more
than her age with lines on her forehead and dark circles
under her big sad eyes. Her black shiny hair had an
auburn tinge and her face was rather pallid. But she did
look prosperous, with gold earrings, rings on her
fingers and a smart suit.

"What have you been doing?" Kitty asked affably.
"It must be more than five years since I saw you."

"That's right," said Bebe. "We got bombed out of
our flat." She looked mournfully at the ground.
"Tommy's dead," she said, "died just after the war
broke out. I've got a little girl. She's six next week."

"What are you doing with this stall?" asked Kitty.

"It's mine," said Bebe. "At least, I hire it. I'm a
wardrobe dealer. You know, Poppa left me quite a bit
of money, so I started my own business and I'm doing
fine. Secondhand clothes are all the go now; saves
coupons."

"Oh, I am pleased for you," said Kitty. "I've not got
any children. Lost my first one and my Bill's been a
prisoner of war for about a year."

"I'll pack up now," said Bebe. "Come home and
have a cup of tea. I only live around the corner. Got a
little house in Brentworth Street since I was bombed
out in Hoxton."

She began to take the dresses down off the rails and
put them in suitcases. Kitty helped her pile them into a
little wooden cart. Bebe called goodbye to her fellow

traders and the two of them set off for Brentworth Street. Bebe pushed her cart while Kitty walked beside her, chatting about old times.

Bebe's was a desolate little house and in a terrible pickle; cases and bundles were strewn everywhere and clothes were hanging on hangers all around the living room.

"It's a bleeding dump," said Bebe apologetically. "But it's me own home and I got a nice little business, so I'm not worried."

"Where's your little girl?" asked Kitty, assuming that someone was minding the child.

Bebe looked glum. "Evacuated. I couldn't help myself. Once the Blitz started, I dodged about. You see, I do different markets—Roman Road and Crisp Street—so I'm not often home. I let Melissa go to this school in the country where she's safe."

"Melissa—what a pretty name," said Kitty. "I'd love to meet her."

"Come with me next time I go to see her, Kitty," said Bebe. "It's not too far, down in Surrey. The school used to be in the East End but was moved out when the war started. I go Wednesdays because the markets close that day."

"I'll try to get a day off," said Kitty. "I'd love to come with you."

On Tuesday at work, Kitty pretended to have a sore throat so as to have an excuse for the next day off. On Wednesday she met Bebe at Aldgate, and from Victoria Station they caught the train to Surrey. On the journey down, Bebe gave Kitty the full story of Melissa.

"It's a school for disabled children. I don't like her being there, but what can I do? Tommy died of T.B. and it was in his family. Well, Melissa was born with a tubercular arm. In fact, she has no hand at all." Tears came to Bebe's eyes.

Kitty was shocked. "Oh, poor little darling," she cried.

Bebe continued. "That's why I'm working so hard. I don't want her to stay there. I'll get her good private treatment later on when the war is over. She's a pretty little thing, and my whole life. I don't know what I'd do without her."

They walked about half a mile from the station to the school, which was in a huge mansion. As they walked up the driveway Kitty marveled at the wonderful gardens and surrounding green woods. On the lawns the disabled children played. They had withered limbs, big heads or little humpty bodies, but they all seemed to be happy. Along the balcony were rows and rows of invalid chairs. "Oh, dear God," Kitty cried, "how awful."

"They're better off here," said Bebe gently. "If this was Germany, they would have been gassed. At least they stand some chance of a reasonable life."

As they approached the house, a nurse called out, "Melissa, Mummy's here." Out of the crowd of children a beautiful blond girl trotted shyly toward them. Her skin was the color of pale gold, and her eyes were large and black, just like Bebe's, but they stared a trifle vacantly. Her limbs were perfect except for that left arm. It dangled loosely and was without a hand. There was a bandage covering the end of it.

Bebe hugged and kissed her. Then she said, indicating Kitty, "This is Auntie Kitty."

Melissa acknowledged Kitty with a smile and then held out her good hand to lead them to play games with the other children.

That whole afternoon Kitty was ecstatic. She pushed swings, lifted children on and off ponies, pulled up knickers, wiped noses, hugged and kissed and comforted all these deprived little girls and boys. She had a marvelous time.

Later, as they traveled home on the train, Kitty said, "Melissa is a lovely child. I'd love to come with you to see her again, Bebe."

"We can go on Sunday afternoon after the market if

it's awkward for you to get time off in the week," said Bebe eagerly.

"Great. I'll come and meet you at the stall and we'll go then."

So for the next few weeks Kitty visited Melissa with Bebe and she loved every minute of it. She and Bebe became fast friends again.

"Why don't you look around for someone else? It must be lonely for you," Kitty said to Bebe one day.

Bebe looked at her sternly. "I've no time for blokes," she said. "Too busy making a living and looking after Melissa." Kitty felt very ashamed.

One day that summer Bill appeared. No one was expecting him; he had given them no warning at all. It was a Saturday and Kitty was slopping about the house in her dressing gown. Suddenly, there he was, standing in the doorway, thin and quiet. Kitty felt both joy and astonishment. She wanted to run to him, but the blank expression on his face prevented her. They stood staring at each other.

It was Dad who broke the silence when he came in that minute from the pub. "Billy boy!" he exclaimed, thumping Bill on the back, "I'm so glad you're home. The house is still intact and the rent paid regular. Now it's all yours, my boy."

Bill looked about the untidy room. He seemed confused and still had not spoken a word.

Kitty sensed what he was thinking. "It's not much good doing the housework, Bill," she said hurriedly. "As soon as we get straight we just get blitzed again."

Bill sat down in his old chair and began to take off his army boots. He looked so weary that Kitty wanted to cry. But she tried to be cheerful. "I'll make a cup of tea," she said brightly.

Bill sipped a big mug of tea, and over the rim his blue eyes surveyed Kitty. Finally, he said, "What have you done to your hair, Kitty?"

Her once chestnut hair was now bright blond with dark roots. "It's peroxided," replied Kitty. "Don't you like it? I thought gentlemen preferred blondes." She giggled to cover up her nervousness.

"Well, let it grow out," said Bill sharply. "You know I hate blonde: I've told you that before."

Feeling squashed, Kitty withdrew and made no more attempts to placate Bill. The harshness of his tone wounded her to the quick. For so long she had been anxious for Bill's return, and loving him all the while. Now he had returned and the only thing he could do was criticize her. He seemed so distant and cold. She wondered why he was so terse. Surely no one had informed on her.

Noni, who had been in curlers when Bill arrived, now came in, having made a big effort to look nice. She sat on the arm of Bill's chair. She fussed and kissed him and wept about her Danny. Bill responded to her kindly. He consoled and cuddled her. Kitty felt a little pushed out. That was Bill, she thought. He always had thought for others.

By the time they had finished supper the tension had eased, and all four—Kitty and Bill, Dad and Noni—went out to celebrate. After a few drinks Bill relaxed and held Kitty's hand. He kissed her and whispered, "It's great to be home. The old man looks just the same and Kitty, darling, you're still as young looking as when I left.

"I'll be stationed in England now, so we can have some good weekends together and get back to our way of living."

Kitty was content; his words were all that she had been waiting for. That night Bill was too drunk to do anything but sleep, but Kitty was glad to snuggle up close to his muscular back and feel warm, secure and happy once more. He was still her Bill, so clean-looking, so kind and gentle and precise. For all her adventures, no one had replaced him. She wished guiltily that she had waited for him, but it was too late for regrets now.

Slowly they built up their relationship once more. It

was not easy, for both Bill and Kitty had changed over
the years apart. Kitty still found him cool and detached
from her much of the time. She felt that she loved him
more than he loved her—that she gave him more than
he returned. But she put on a brave face and kept her
feelings to herself.

In no time at all Bill was in his shirt sleeves peeling
the wallpaper off the walls of the dining room. "Got to
get the house back in shape, Kitty. Might as well start
now."

"Yes, Bill," said Kitty with a keen sense of disappointment. "I'll start cleaning up." She hated housework and had become extremely lazy about it.

But soon the house took on a new look as Bill
repapered the walls and painted the woodwork. Kitty
did think it looked nice.

When they went out for a drink Kitty always asked
Bill to get her a whiskey and a beer to chase it down.
But he ignored her requests and she would get only the
beer. He did not comment on her drinking whiskey, but
Kitty knew that he knew she had not developed the
habit with him.

Some nights she was so anxious to make love that the
calm, cool Bill was a little embarrassed. "Oh, Bill," she
would say, "let's have that baby back, the one we lost."

"Now, Kitty," he would return, "the war is still on.
It's hard enough for us adults without bringing young
lives into the world."

So Bill continued to use a preventative and the
passionate hot nature in Kitty was never satisfied,
though she never said anything to Bill.

Kitty made every effort to please her husband. She
got her blond hair cut short and used a brown rinse to
cover the ugly line between dark and light. When she
wore her choker beads one day, Bill said, "For God's
sake, Kitty, you look like a Zulu." So she took them off
and did not wear them again.

She was very relieved when Bill was finally stationed
at the army camp. She went to visit Melissa with Bebe.

"Don't know what's wrong with me," she confided in Bebe. "I wasn't sorry to see the back of him."

"Well, Kitty," said Bebe, "I'd give almost all I've got to see my Tommy again. You should thank your lucky stars that Bill came home to you—so many boys haven't."

"I know you're right, but I wonder if I'll be able to settle down," pondered Kitty.

"You should have a baby; then you'll have something more than yourself to worry about," said Bebe.

"I wish I could, but Bill doesn't want me to, not until the war is over."

Kitty and Bebe spent another enjoyable afternoon playing with Melissa and her friends. It was a beautiful day, and Kitty felt relaxed and happy.

On the way home their train was delayed by an unexploded bomb on the line. The two women sat in the darkened carriage and talked about old times. They laughed uproariously at the memory of how they used to parade the main road looking for fellas, all dressed up in very cheap, flash-looking clothes. "Times have changed now, Kitty," said Bebe, suddenly saddened by their memories.

Kitty did not like to think about Hoxton. She was ashamed even to remember the squalor. "No good looking back, Bebe," she said. "I could never live like that again."

"I'm saving my money for Melissa. After the war I want to send her to a private school where they will train her to speak properly and fix her up with an artificial hand," said Bebe.

"She is such a darling. I really envy you, Bebe," replied Kitty.

For a while they were silent. Then Bebe said quietly, "Kitty, we have known each other for a long while. I've got no one who really cares about Melissa. My dad's dead, and my brother and sister-in-law have disowned me ever since I married Tommy. Even though Tommy's dead, they still won't talk to me. Kitty, will you promise that if anything should happen to me you'll take care of her?"

"Oh, don't be so morbid," exclaimed Kitty. "You have a good long life ahead of you."

"Well, promise me, just in case," Bebe said very abruptly, "that she will be well provided for. Can I rely on you, Kitty?"

"Of course you can," said Kitty, just to keep the peace.

CHAPTER SIXTEEN

Farewell to a Good Pal

The bombing of London went on day and night. There were doodlebugs, land mines, incendiary bombs and something known as a Molotov cocktail, a whole basket of incendiaries.

A surprisingly large portion of the population had become well seasoned to the hazards of wartime, and many came back from evacuation in the countryside and set up home again in the blitzed houses. No one was defeated. Hearts were broken, homes were broken but no one was beaten.

Kitty still worked hard at the factory. Many of the younger girls had been called up into the forces or onto the buses and railways, but those over twenty-five still held down skilled jobs.

For the last three months Bill had come home every weekend. He was cheerful and much like his bright, normal self. He was always busy with the garden or decorating the interior of the house.

So Kitty found herself tied to the gas stove at

weekends, cooking huge meals for the family, all of whom had excellent appetites.

Soon Bill obtained a good post in the army. It was the Quartermaster's Stores. He had two stripes and was corporal in charge of equipment. This meant he was to be posted up North, but he liked the job and was proud of the promotion.

In some ways Kitty was relieved when Bill went up North. She had begun to feel very depressed and was rather peeved because of Bill's attitude toward her desire to have a child.

"Why don't we try for a baby, Bill?" she had asked him again in desperation.

Bill had replied very quietly and firmly. "No, Kitty, I'm too fond of you to put you through all that again at the moment."

He still always insisted on using a preventative, and this made Kitty feel even more frustrated. The excitement had gone from her married life.

The first weekend after Bill had gone North, Kitty bought a very frilly dress, put on her war paint and went off to the Paramount. She jived and jitterbugged, got very tipsy, refused a male escort home and hopped on the last tube train all alone. She had a great time.

As usual, Noni showed her disapproval by not talking to Kitty, but Dad's eyes twinkled when she staggered in at midnight. He made no comment.

Later, Kitty was thankful to have got home safely because the rest of the night buzz bombs sailed overhead. Flames lit the sky and bomb after bomb fell on the city. By the morning it was a very sad sight— smoking ruins and devastated houses.

Kitty got up early to go down Petticoat Lane and meet Bebe. She was eager to tell her friend about her night out. When she got off the bus at Petticoat Lane she could see something amiss. A line of ambulances tore past and fire engines blocked the main road. Policemen were moving the bystanders on. Through the dust and rubble Kitty looked for Brentworth Street.

She was stunned. It was not there. It had completely disappeared. There were just piles and piles of smoking debris.

"What happened?" she asked the woman standing next to her.

"Buzz bombs," said the onlooker. "Direct hit on Brentworth Street. There are plenty of people buried— they're still digging them out."

Kitty's heart leaped in her chest. She pushed her way through the crowd. "Oh, I must get down there," she told a policeman as she tried to get past. But his strong arm prevented her. "No good you going there, madam," he said. "They're still taking out survivors. Go to the warden's post. If you got someone who's missing you'll get the news there."

At the warden's post they informed her that no one in number five had survived. "Took a woman out," she was told. "Do you wish to identify her?"

"No, no," cried Kitty, hoping against hope that Bebe had gone down the tube as she said she did on very bad nights. Kitty made her way to the local where she and Bebe used to have their lunchtime drinks. It was still open for trade even though the windows were broken and the ceilings were down.

"Sorry, duck," said the barman, recognizing Kitty as she ordered a drink. "It's sad your mate Bebe copped it." So Kitty knew for certain that Bebe was no more.

Hours later, still stunned, Kitty wandered down the blitzed street. It was desolate, and her nostrils curled at the acrid smell of burning. Bebe's house had completely vanished. It had been flattened by the blast and was now just a heap of rubble. Kitty picked her way over the bricks and plaster and gave a gasp when she suddenly saw a pile of the old dresses that Bebe used to collect for her stall. She put a finger out to touch some soft flowered voile that poked out from beneath the rubbish. She shuddered violently as a vivid image of the large, smiling Bebe came sweeping into her mind. She dashed back to the pub. Trembling, she ordered a

whiskey. She sat among the other sorrowful Petticoat
Lane traders who had lost their loved ones. She sat
drinking for many hours until her mind was numb and
her eyes were finally dry.

Bebe was buried the following week with all the
other casualties from Brentworth Street. The East-End
traders gave her a good send-off, but Kitty did not
attend. She could not face it; she was too haunted by
the memory of her friend.

A few weeks later a letter from an East-End solicitor
arrived for Kitty. She was a little nonplussed but went
to his office in Aldgate as he requested.

"My client left a letter in my charge that was only to
be given to you in event of her death," the solicitor said
when Kitty had sat down. He handed her an envelope.
With trembling hands Kitty read Bebe's bold handwriting.

> Don't forget, Kitty, you did promise me that day in
> the train to look after Melissa. She will be well
> provided for, and my friend Ike will assist you.
> Goodbye, old pal.
> Bebe.

"Oh, dear God, she must have known," cried Kitty.
"It's incredible."

"I have a copy of her will," the solicitor said. "She
made it a few weeks ago. There is four thousand
pounds to be spent on the education and welfare of her
young daughter. You and Mr. Ike Sneiderman are
assigned as trustees. She wanted the child to go to a
private school."

Kitty remembered Ike Sneiderman as a big jolly East
Ender who had always been popular with all the kids in
the neighborhood. At least she knew the other trustee,
she thought.

"Oh, poor little Melissa, what else can I do?" she
asked. "Perhaps after the war I can apply to adopt

Melissa. I will certainly visit and take care of her. She has no one."

When she got home, Kitty wrote to Bill. "Now I have my own little girl. I promised my friend I would care for her daughter and that's exactly what I am going to do."

Bill wrote back immediately, obviously alarmed by her decision. "Mind what you are getting into; you may regret it."

Fiercely Kitty screwed up Bill's letter and threw it into the fire. He would never understand her. She wanted a child desperately, and Bill had denied her that for so long. Now she did have someone to look after, a child who was virtually her own. Bill was not going to spoil anything, she vowed. Tears came to her eyes. She wished Bill understood how she felt. Only by having another child to look after—even someone else's—would Kitty fully get over the tragedy of having lost her first baby.

On her next visit to Melissa the child's dark eyes surveyed Kitty with concern. Kitty cuddled her close and in a choked voice said, "Mummy is busy. Auntie Kitty is here, and she loves you."

Melissa looked at her solemnly and then held up her arm. "Look," she said, "God did not finish me."

"Oh, darling," cried Kitty, pulling the child tighter. "You are my baby; I'll look after you."

Kitty visited Melissa every Sunday. The girl never once asked for Mummy, but one day she said, "Mummy's gone to heaven, the nurse said so." She did not cry, she never did. There was a strange, quiet seriousness about her.

Kitty spent all her spare money on toys, sweets and hair ribbons—anything that the child asked for. Melissa became the center of her life. One day Bill wrote to ask her to come up and visit him for the weekend.

Kitty wrote back immediately. "Sorry, Bill, but I must visit Melissa. She needs me."

This put Bill in a huff. He did not write to her for two

weeks, and when he finally wrote he said that all leave had been canceled for a while and that he was really busy with his new position.

Kitty was not unduly worried, especially as she was very preoccupied with her new charge. But one day she got an unexpected letter from Harry. He was somewhere in England. "Got a weekend pass," he wrote. "Will be in London. Want to hold you in my arms again, honey. Platform four, Euston Station, six o'clock, Saturday evening."

"Well, of all the bleeding cheek," cried Kitty when she had read the letter. But she knew she would be there.

She dressed very carefully for her Saturday date. Her thoughts were running wild. What the hell is wrong with me? Why am I going? Why can't I count my blessings and leave well alone? Then the mere thought of being wined, dined and admired increased her determination to go.

"I'm a bloody fraud," she told the mirror as she piled on the makeup. "I must be two people: one that's bad and one that's trying to be good. Bloody funny how the bad one always wins."

In this strange, undecided mood she went off to meet Harry. She wore a navy blue silk suit and a paler blue blouse with a silk tie and a little hat that leaned to one side and had a blue flower on the brim.

"Well, my, my," said Harry when he saw her, "you are a honey. Certainly a good sight for my tired eyes."

Harry was already a little drunk and in a very exuberant mood. He put an arm around Kitty and looked down from his great height. "You're prettier than ever, my pet, and I like your hair. That's your natural color, isn't it? Great balls of fire, you are a real honey," he repeated.

Kitty allowed him to cuddle her, pleased at this burst of admiration. "It's nice to see you again, Harry," she purred, "but I'm not staying. I only popped over to see you for old times' sake."

Harry gave her a wide, evil grin and his big hand held hers. "Let's get out of here, honey, and find a place to eat and drink."

In the taxi he started to fondle her, but she objected. "Give over, Harry, I told you I'm not stopping. My husband is home, and I only came to say hullo."

He leaned back and laughed uproariously. "Oh, Kitty, you kill me," he gasped. "Mean to say your old man's turned up after all?"

"There's no need to be disrespectful," said Kitty primly.

"Sorry, pet," Harry said, his eyes roving over her neat figure.

They went to the Blue Lagoon, a cozy restaurant in Kings Cross, and ate scallops cooked in their shells and creamed potatoes. They had lots of wine and finished with cheese and biscuits. Kitty began to enjoy herself.

"Here's to bonnie Scotland," Harry said, raising his glass. "Remember the Roman Camp, Kitty?"

Kitty became alarmed. "I mustn't be late," she said. "I'd like to get home before midnight."

"Okay, Cinderella," he grinned, "plenty of time."

They left the restaurant and visited many bars and clubs. Finally, they ended up in a hotel that was run especially for G.I.'s on leave. Kitty was strangely excited and, pushing aside any feelings of guilt, went to bed and made passionate love with Harry.

"If only you knew how I have longed for this moment, baby," Harry said afterward. "Give up that old Limey husband and come home with me after the war."

"When will that be?" asked Kitty bitterly, "and where will we all be by then? And anyway, you have a family in America."

Harry wasn't listening. He was looking distant, as he so often did. "You won't hear from me for awhile," he finally said.

"Why?" she asked. "Where are you going?"

"Hush," he said, "walls have ears. It's a big secret."

When they parted later that night, she clung to him. "I'm always happy with you, Harry, but it don't always mean a thing. I intend to be here when the war is over and start again from the beginning with Bill."

"I wish you joy, honey," said Harry fondly, "but I won't forget you."

All the next week Kitty was very quiet. Her sense of guilt was so strong that she could not even write to Bill.

CHAPTER SEVENTEEN
Demobbed

As the spring turned into summer that year, Bill's letters had dwindled down to just the occasional short epistle that asked after Dad's health and sent regards to Noni. There was never a lot in it for Kitty. His tone was cold and polite, and Kitty began to worry. Had Bill been sent a letter? "Dear John" letters, they called them; those evil anonymous letters that the soldierboys received telling them that their wives had been unfaithful to them. Many homes had disintegrated that way.

She thought of Noni but instantly dismissed the idea. They were sisters. They might be very different in temperament, but they had respect for each other and family understanding still held them close.

Noni had become a little subdued lately, and Kitty found it amusing to see her big bullying sister sitting knitting little gloves and socks for Melissa and the other children at the school in Surrey.

Kitty had taken Noni to meet Melissa one Sunday, and the sight of the disabled children had really disturbed her.

"Oh, Kitty, it's so sad," Noni had cried. "Both you and I with no children. How our dad would love to have been a grandfather."

"I know, dear," agreed Kitty, "but when Bill comes home I'll apply to adopt Melissa and you can share her with me."

Noni had wept and said, "You're such a sport, Kitty, and you are so generous."

The sisters had become very close, so Kitty had to put all thoughts of evil things from her mind. She might go up and visit Bill, she thought. With some proper time together they would no doubt soon patch things up between them. Perhaps she would settle down now and begin to make plans for after the war.

Dad seemed more relaxed lately. His business was going well, but he found it difficult to keep books and relied on Kitty to help him.

In his large, clumsy hand he would enter the names of his Irish lads in a book. Many names were spelled wrong, and Kitty was puzzled when she saw "Pat," "Mick" and "Hogie" and a "q" written next to them.

"Whatever is that?" she asked Dad.

"That means that they've been paid," replied Dad.

Kitty realized that he had turned the "p" back to front. "Well, well, if that ain't Irish, nothing is," she giggled.

Dad was offended. "Girly," he said, "value the fact that you got an education and make good use of it. In my country I got no chance to go to school. The Englishman forbade us even to speak our own language."

"Sorry, Dad," said Kitty, ashamed to have aroused his patriotic ire in such a way.

In the bars and the factories there was a lot of talk of a "second front." No one knew when or where it would be, but what they did know was that it was to be the last big push to try to end the war. Between May and June lots of leave was canceled, including Bill's. He wrote only to say that he was extremely busy.

There were huge transit camps on the outskirts of the city, and the military police came and chased the troops back to their camps before nine o'clock every night.

"Something's going on," said Kitty.

"They're getting them into camp before they have too much drink, in case someone lets the cat out of the bag," said Dad.

Then in the beginning of June the cultured voice of the BBC announcer said on the wireless, "The Allied troops have landed on the shores of France." D-day had begun.

The excitement was great, and many anxious wives thought of their husbands that day. And Kitty thought of Harry. This was the secret he had hinted about, and she wondered how he fared.

Later that day Winston Churchill gave a magnificent speech informing the population that the Allied troops were chasing the Germans back into Germany.

Everyone rejoiced. Dad was jubilant and wept tears about his lost son, Bobby, and Noni cried about her lost Danny.

Joe Fogerty, one of the Irish lads who worked for Dad and who was always around, wiped Noni's eyes with his handkerchief. "Be Jesus," he said, "what's all this weeping? We are winning the war at long last."

Kitty sat very silent through the excitement. She had an empty feeling inside her. She did not know why.

Then out of the blue came another letter from Harry. It was badly written, with no address. "I have been wounded," he wrote. "I'm back in England. If you go to the Red Cross they will give you money to travel up to visit me. I'd love to see you."

"Oh, poor old Harry," Kitty said out aloud, and went immediately uptown to the Red Cross offices.

A Red Cross officer examined the letter, asked for her own identity card and then went off, leaving Kitty waiting for quite a while. Finally an American officer returned to tell her that Harry had been sent home. Instinctively Kitty knew he was lying. It was all red tape. It was because she was a married woman and had no rights to visit another man. A melancholy feeling overwhelmed her. Maybe it was not a lie. Perhaps Harry had died. Why else would they send him back to America? She went back home very downhearted; she longed to see Harry one more time.

Kitty hoped that she might hear from Harry himself, but no more letters came. She was haunted by him; she heard his happy laughter and saw his ugly kind face before her. She could not bear it. It was not easy to forget him. She sought comfort in her journal, which she still scribbled in at night. He was a good man, Harry Cross, and she would remember him through her writing, she decided.

After the excitement of D-day had died down, the war still continued and a very nasty phase started. Troops poured out of England into France and Paris was freed. London had begun to calm down except for the rocket bombs that still came over at intervals when they were least expected. The weather became very cold that autumn and, before Christmas, Europe was snowed in. Gloom descended on London again.

At Christmas, Bill came home on leave. He seemed more like his old self, but, although he was very affectionate, Kitty still felt the barrier between them. He did not seem to be at all interested in Kitty's accounts of Melissa and actually avoided the subject as much as he could. He talked a lot about the small village up North where he was billeted. He was staying with a lady and her daughter who, he said, were very kind to him. Kitty felt very uncomfortable. She was annoyed at Bill's refusal even to talk seriously about her little ward, who was staying in Surrey over Christmas. But she also found that she was fiercely jealous of these two women Bill kept talking about. She did her best to hide her feelings, but it was hard. She longed for the war to be over so that she and Bill could build up their marriage again properly. Under the present conditions, it was impossible.

They had a real Irish Christmas at Billington Road that year. Joe Fogerty, who was now officially courting Noni, had asked his mother to send a food parcel from Ireland. She sent a big turkey, a ham and pounds of butter, which came in very handy.

Dad's Irish boys arrived after the dinner and everyone had to sing a song. In a high, nervous voice and after a few drinks, Kitty sang Dad's favorite, "Rose of Tralee." And in a deep sepulchral voice Noni sang of sweet Kate Farrel, that poor Irish colleen who got struck by lightning. Then the lads sang their pieces and they all shook hands and applauded at the end of each.

Finally it was Dad's turn. Everyone sat very quietly and listened to the tale of Bold Robert Emmet, the darling of Erin, who was hung, drawn and quartered and died with a smile on his face. They joined in the chorus, twisted their mouths into a grimace of a smile as they sang, miming the actions, holding their necks to indicate when he was hung, crossing their hands over their bodies to show where he was quartered. It was all good fun, and they washed it down with enough beer, as Kitty said, to float the bloody navy.

Kitty was happy with her family and enjoyed all the festivities. But after it was all over, she kept thinking about Bill, who had had to return to camp on Boxing Day. Quite apart from the gulf between them, he had seemed different in another way. She could not quite put her finger on it, but he had definitely changed. Kitty particularly noticed this in his lovemaking. Before now he had always been cool, calm and precise, just like Bill, but this time his style was different. In fact, Bill had been quite passionate, and he did things that she was sure she had never taught him. She was beginning to suspect that someone had, but she decided not to dwell on it too much. After all, she thought, it might only be her imagination.

A few weeks later, Noni said, "I've got something to tell you, Kitty. Don't think too badly of me, will you?"

Kitty was quite sure she knew what it was, but pretended to be surprised. "I'm getting married in three weeks," said Noni rather sheepishly, "to Joe."

"Oh, congratulations!" cried Kitty.

But Noni pulled a long face. "I'm not sure I want to, but I've got to—it was all that booze at Christmas."

Kitty laughed heartily and cuddled her awkward sister. "Oh, it'll be fine to have a baby in the house," she said.

"Yes, I expect I'll have to stay here for a time," said Noni. "Joe's lodgings are already overcrowded. Bill won't mind, will he, Kitty?"

"Why should he?" said Kitty. "It's Dad's house as much as Bill's; Dad has paid the mortgage all through the war. In any case, I'd like to go live in the country later on and adopt Melissa, so Dad would be happy here with you, especially if he has grandchildren. Don't worry, dear, it will all turn out fine."

Noni married in March, wearing a smart pleated skirt, a white blouse and a big white hat. She borrowed Kitty's fur cape and she looked super.

The wedding reception was held at Billington Road; the dining table was laid out in buffet style, and another grand booze-up was the order of the day. But Bill did not turn up. He just sent a congratulatory telegram saying he could not make it.

Kitty wrote to Bill after the wedding.

Dear Bill,

Sorry you never came up for the wedding. It was great and Noni seems very happy. One cannot live with the dead forever. Noni and Joe have moved in upstairs. So I was thinking, Bill, maybe we ought to start looking for somewhere else for us to settle

down when the war is over and let Dad stay with
Noni, as we will have Melissa to think about.

Love, Kitty

Very soon after Kitty had sent her letter, back came
a short, sharp reply from Bill.

Dear Kitty,
    The war is still on, and it is too soon to make
plans. I might still get sent abroad somewhere. So
content yourself with the family and give my
regards to Joe and Noni.

Love, Bill

Well, said Kitty to herself when she read this, *put that
in your pipe and smoke it.*

Kitty continued to visit Melissa on Sundays. The girl
was growing very tall and was still pretty. She was a
quiet child and took time to answer questions as if she
weighed every situation up carefully. It seemed unique
and rather attractive to Kitty. Melissa was not too
popular at the school because, as the headmistress
explained, she was subject to tantrums. Arrangements
were already being made for Melissa to go to a private
boarding school when the war was over.

At last the war did end. London went wild as it
celebrated VE-Day. There was a week of street
parties, dances, suppers and all the entertainment that
could be mustered. People could hardly believe that
peace had come at last.

On VE night Kitty was very tipsy. Dressed in a Black
Watch kilt that was much too big for her, she danced a
jig on the table of the local pub, while Joe Fogerty, who
had previously worn the kilt, marched up and down in
his short pants, blowing lustily on the bagpipes. Everyone was drunk and happy; the news was almost too
good to be true.

By the end of the week of celebrations, Kitty felt

exhausted. She wondered where Bill was. He had not written since the victory.

Kitty tried to organize the home so that the family could live fairly comfortably, and that was no easy task. She wrote to Bill telling him of her efforts and saying how she was so looking forward to them being together again.

But Bill's letter in return was short and to the point.

Dear Kitty,
    Getting demob leave in September. See you then.

                                                    Bill

It was September 1945. The war was officially over. The Japanese had at last surrendered, but not before that dreadful atom bomb had been dropped.

"Bloody Japs," people said. "Time they gave in."

One by one the factories closed down or were converted back to peacetime uses. Kitty was made redundant from her radio factory, but she had expected it. She was more horrified when she read of the many deaths that were caused by the atom bomb. It seemed such an inglorious way to end a war when so many heroes had given their lives, and so many women their children. But at least she still had her man, she consoled herself, and he was to be demobbed that coming weekend.

Bill's birthday was to be the following week, so Kitty decided to give him a party for that as well as his homecoming. It was almost impossible to buy luxuries like an iced cake, but a friend of hers, who was a cook, volunteered to bake a big cake with "Welcome Home Bill" in pink iced letters.

On the Friday when Bill was due home, Kitty went to collect the cake. She was not gone long, but she had a cup of tea with her friend. Then she very carefully and proudly carried the cake home. When she arrived at the

house, Noni stood in the dim lit passage looking like a
sick cow.

"Are you all right?" inquired Kitty, concerned because of Noni's condition.

"Your Bill's been home," blurted out Noni suddenly.

"Oh, great!" cried Kitty, looking around. "But
where is he?"

"He left you a note," said Noni glumly.

On the mantelpiece was a letter in Bill's handwriting.
Kitty grabbed it and tore open the envelope.

I am truly sorry, Kitty, but I cannot live with
you. We must take separate paths. I wish you well
and will send you money as soon as I have got a
job. Sorry, Kitty.

Love, Bill

Kitty let out a loud scream. "It's a joke," she cried,
"a dirty, bloody trick."

Noni stood looking at her woefully. "Oh, poor
Kitty," she whimpered. "Bill said he was going back up
North . . ."

"Don't you dare pity me!" screamed Kitty. "What
the bloody hell is going on here?"

She took the lovely birthday cake and threw it
violently against the wall. A shower of icing descended
on poor Noni, covering her tousled head. Noni just
stood there, shaking and shivering. At that moment Joe
arrived and looked in horror at what he saw. He took
hold of Noni. "Give over, Kitty," he hollered. "Noni's
in no condition for your bloody tantrums," and he
piloted his wife from the room.

Kitty sat and banged her fist on the table. In God's
name, what had she done? She thought of her past
escapades, but Bill did not know—how could he know?
Unless someone had informed on her. She thought of
Noni, then even of Dad, but they would not, she knew,
because they loved Bill and would not want her home

broken. She felt ashamed that she could suspect such a
thing of them. No, never again would she allow herself
to doubt their loyalty.

But Bill's behavior was a complete mystery and a
dreadful shock to her. He did not even want to give
their marriage a chance. She had waited for so long for
him to return to her properly when the war was over.
And now he did not even want to know her. She put
her head on her arms on the table and wept self-pitying
tears. Through her misery came a light. She lifted her
head and stared at the wall. She remembered that Bill
had changed lately. He had not come home so often
and his lovemaking had been different. It was something to do with that Godforsaken village in the North,
that cottage where he was billeted. She decided then
that she would find out his reason for deserting her,
even if it killed her.

Early the next morning she was on the train traveling
North. There was a cold mist on the hills and an east
wind blowing when she stood outside the small York-
shire station, wondering what direction to take, doubt-
ing whether she should have been so hasty.

She passed a line of small, gray-stone cottages as she
climbed up a steep hill. In front of her was an old inn
that looked warm and cozy in those bleak surroundings. She stood hesitantly, feeling the need of a drink
but not sure whether to go in.

A lone soldier wandered leisurely down the road.
She recognized the bomb flash on his arm and knew he
was from Bill's own unit.

"Excuse me," she said as he stared curiously at her.
"Do you know a chap in your outfit, a corporal called
Bill Ross?"

"Oh, the Corp. He's about. Seen him around,
though he was demobbed."

"You mean he's still here," she queried.

"Sure, over there in one of those cottages—the one
at the end, I think. That's where he's been billeted."

Hardly stopping to thank the soldier, Kitty stepped

briskly up the hill towards another line of dreary stone cottages. Her heart was beating fast as she stopped outside the last one. She knocked at the heavy street door. Nothing happened. She waited longer, and as she did so she felt sure that someone was scrutinizing her from behind the grubby lace curtains in the window. Finally, a slovenly-looking middle-aged woman came to the door. She peered at Kitty.

"Do you know Bill Ross? He was billeted up here," Kitty asked immediately.

She knew at once she had the right place, for the old lady seemed to try to back away from her. Kitty placed her foot firmly against the door to prevent her closing it.

"Ooo waants eem?" said the woman in an odd accent.

"His wife," said Kitty. "Where is he?"

"Ee bain't in, oot warkin' ee be." She stared at Kitty, and then, as if in a panic, she called out, "May, May, coom oot, somin's askin' fer Bill."

A tall dark girl appeared in the tiny hallway. She looked very young. She eyed Kitty coolly. "Better coom in," she said.

Kitty looked her over and saw that the old faded dress she wore was stretched tight over her stomach. She was obviously pregnant. Her feet were grubby and stuck into old lopsided slippers. Her dark hair hung down over her shoulders and was lank and greasy. Her mouth was full-lipped and very sullen. The only really appealing feature were her dark brown eyes.

"I am sorry to bother you," said Kitty curtly, "but I wish to contact my husband, Bill Ross. I know he has been billeted here."

The girl held her arms akimbo and looked very hostile. "He bain't a commin' back to yoo," she said slowly. "This be ees baaby an' ee be stickin' by me, bain't ee, Ma?"

The old lady nodded slowly and then asked Kitty, "Will ee no tak' a seat? Bill wi be in soon."

Kitty stared with repulsion about the untidy room. It was the squalor she remembered from her past, the product of soul-destroying poverty.

The daughter now looked aggressively at Kitty. The lump on her stomach made Kitty want to vomit. She turned on stiff legs. "I'll go," she said. "Tell Bill I'll wait for him down at the inn."

Then Kitty fled from the sight of that sluttish young girl and the tired old woman. She went down to the inn and booked a room for the night. She was taken up to a pleasant bright room with flowered curtains and a white bedspread. She looked at herself in the mirror and saw that her eyes were full of tears. She washed her face and tidied her hair and then went down to wait for Bill. She was sure that he would arrive eventually.

At eight o'clock he came in, looking pale and tired. He looked different in civvies—he wore an ill-fitting tweed suit and a cloth cap. He was dusty and slightly unkempt, which was unusual for the smart, clean Bill she had known. Kitty had never seen him in need of a shave or haircut. Now her Bill looked shabby and down-and-out. But a slow smile hung on his lips as he saw Kitty sitting forlornly at the bar.

Kitty gazed at him in silent reproach as he ordered two beers. "Come on, let's sit over there," Bill said, indicating a quiet corner. "Well, you now know the picture," he said calmly. "I hear you went to the house."

"What else did you expect me to do?" Kitty almost sneered. "Sit down and wonder why you left me?" More big tears welled up in her eyes.

Bill squeezed her hand gently. "Now, Kitty, don't be sad. It's just one of those things that happen in life."

"Oh, Bill, how can you be so casual about it?" she pleaded.

"I'm still as fond of you, Kitty, but she is young and I have ruined her life. This is a very narrow-minded village, and her mother is a widow and very poor."

His words cut like a knife through Kitty's heart. His

cold, calm, assured attitude shocked her. He did not seem to care about her.

"What about me, Bill? What about Melissa? How will we get by without you?" she asked.

Bill would not look her in the eyes. "I don't want to talk about Melissa," he said. "You got yourself involved in that business without consulting me." He began to fidget with his beer glass. "You have plenty of courage, Kitty. You'll survive, you always have."

"Thank you," said Kitty, swallowing down her drink. She could not believe he was saying these things.

Bill sighed. "Look," he said, "you've got Dad, and you didn't exactly live like a nun while I was abroad."

Oh, so that was it. He *had* been got at. Kitty's temper flared. "What the hell do you want of me? Must you also rub my nose in the dirt?"

He looked down rather miserably. "It's no good, Kitty. It's over as far as we're concerned."

"Oh, Bill, what will I do without you?" She could not stop the tears of despair raining down her cheeks. The little muscle in the side of his cheek twitched. Kitty knew he was trying not to show any emotion.

"Don't cry, Kitty," Bill said sharply. "It won't solve anything."

"But Bill, she's a slut and almost simple."

"It's not that way, Kitty; that's how these people are. I can assure you they are great folk and have been very good to me."

"I noticed that," said Kitty sarcastically.

"Oh, Kitty," he said in an exasperated tone, "why did you travel all that way up here, you silly girl? I intended to put matters right once I had got things settled."

"Bill," wept Kitty, "I simply can't believe it. I was so sure you loved only me."

"Kitty, darling," he said huskily, "in some ways no one will ever replace you, but we have outgrown each other. It might have been the war, I don't know. All I know is that I'm in a bloody mess. In all honor, what else can I do? I've got a job here in town. I'll send you a weekly allowance, and tell Dad to keep up the payments on the house. We'll talk about all that later."

"Oh, dear God, how can you be so casual about it?" cried Kitty.

"Kitty, my mind is made up, so stop crying. You'll find someone else, I don't doubt it. Now, get on the train back, there's a good girl."

He took her arm, but she wrenched it away. "No, you bloody don't," she said. "I'll make my own exit."

"Oh, well," he said, "I'm going home. Tell Dad and Noni I'm sorry."

Kitty sobbed hard dry sobs that wracked her frame. "Your home is with me down south, Bill," she said.

"Goodbye, Kitty," said Bill. "Get on the train and go home to Dad, promise me." Then swiftly he turned and the bar door banged. Her Bill had gone.

Kitty sat drinking in the bar until they called time. Then she crawled up to her lonely bed.

The next day Kitty arrived home. Her face was like marble—cold, white and very hard—but her step was brisk. She had already begun to cope. "What a bloody fool I was," she muttered to herself repeatedly. She was seething. Anger was her chief emotion. "Let him have his slut. I don't care; I'm free to pick and choose now."

Now there was no need to feel guilty about her past adventures. She would not sit and cry. She would hit Bill in his pocket, the place that would hurt him the most.

But for all her bravado, she was very hurt deep down inside. Bill's behavior was the last thing she had ever expected. She had been so sure of him. She really had loved him so much and had been convinced that everything would be all right after the war. Now he had deserted her. And it was all the more difficult to accept that she had lost him to a poverty-stricken creature much like the one she herself had once been.

Dad looked at Kitty with great concern but passed no

comment. He thought it was just a squabble and would soon blow over.

Noni had her baby the next day. The doctor and midwife were in and out of the house, and Joe was out all the time celebrating the birth of his bonny son. Dad assisted him, rejoicing in the birth of his grandson.

The fact that this was Bill's house still played on Dad's mind. "I said that I would keep a roof over your heads till Bill came home, and by Jesus I will," he said drunkenly later that evening.

"He's not coming home," Kitty said bitterly. "This is your house now."

"Nonsense, gel," Dad replied. "It will all blow over."

Kitty sighed, but she was glad of the warmth and comfort of her family. It helped to mend the deep wound that Bill's desertion had left in her heart.

Noni had given birth to a lovely red-headed boy who was named Cornelius after Dad. Very soon he was called Casey. Everyone from the street was in and out visiting Noni in the upstairs bedroom. And Noni sat like a queen, feeding the babe from her large breasts that overflowed with milk.

Dad was thrilled about his grandson but still very depressed about the fact that Bill had not come home. "It's Bill's house, I always said so. I'm willing to stand down when he returns to it. Meanwhile, I'll pay all the expenses while I've money to do it."

"It's over. Bill and I are finished," Kitty tried to make him understand.

"Don't talk nonsense," Dad said rather sharply. "You were wed in the eyes of God in a Catholic church. So it is till death you do part. It will all blow over," he added confidently.

Kitty was very irritated and refused to discuss the matter any further.

So life went on in number eight. Kitty applied to the court for maintenance from Bill and received an order for two pounds a week. Then she went out and got a job. It was a dull, boring filing job in a printer's office, but the good wages she received allowed her to bank all the money she got from Bill.

She had a dull, empty feeling inside her, as if there was little to look forward to. All she had, in fact, was Melissa, whom she still visited every week. The child was soon going to change schools. The arrangements were all being taken care of by Bebe's friend, Ike Sneiderman, so Kitty did not have to get involved in them.

CHAPTER EIGHTEEN
Alone

It was the summer of 1946. Casey now crawled around the house. He was a big, fat, lusty boy with a loose, wet nappy always dangling between his sturdy legs. Everyone fussed over him and fed him with sticky sweets and chocolate. Kitty was as bad as the rest of them.

8 Billington Road was very crowded nowadays, for there were three newcomers: a cousin of Dad's from Ireland and Joe's two brothers. There were beds everywhere, and it was chaotic. Kitty now occupied the downstairs front room. She slept and ate in it and tried to keep some law and order. Noni was pregnant once more and, apart from cooking, was as lazy as ever, so Kitty got no help with the housework from her.

Every morning Kitty would get up and feel nauseated by the mess that met her eyes—unwashed mugs with thick dregs of cocoa stuck at the bottom, empty beer bottles, greasy plates, filthy cutlery. She was always left with the clearing up.

Noni frequently cooked enormous Irish stews for supper, which Kitty could never touch. When Noni dumped the huge pot on the table, Kitty would sniff fastidiously. "Not for me, thanks, I'm eating out," she would announce.

"Oh, not good enough for Lady Jane," Noni would say in loud tones. "Chicken and turkey all the week, that's what she expects."

Dad and Joe and the lodgers would tuck in and enjoy the meal. Dad loved the Irish cooking, but he was worried about his eldest daughter. "Now, Kitty, try to eat a bit. You're very thin."

But Kitty would retire to her room and scribble in her journal, trying to forget the pangs of hunger.

Sometimes Casey got into her room and mischievously made a wreck of her makeup and costume jewelry. Kitty would get annoyed and complain to Noni, and then the two sisters would have a set-to.

"Do you good to have a few kids about your arse," Noni would always say vulgarly. Kitty would go into her room and dream she had her own little baby, pink and clean and cuddly. And she would care for it so well. Tears of mortification ran down her face. Never before had she felt so alone.

One day Kitty said to Dad, "Why don't you and I get a flat somewhere and let Noni and Joe take over here?"

Dad was well and truly shocked. "Can't do that, gel, this is Bill's house."

"Oh, don't be so foolish," she cried. "Bill has gone and he won't be coming back here anymore."

"No, Kitty, gel," persisted Dad, "I feel sure he will come back to you. Just be patient."

Then Kitty really lost her temper. "Oh, you stupid old sod!" she cried. "Don't you know that he lives with another woman and has a child?"

Dad flinched. "There's no need to be disrespectful, Kitty. If you learned to keep your temper, maybe your life would work out better than it has."

So a coolness rose between them. Dad seemed to blame Kitty rather than Bill. And that she could not accept.

Melissa had left the state school and was now at a
private boarding school in Suffolk. She was well cared
for and was now educated to a good standard. She had
an artificial hand that she used with great confidence
and skill. She had grown very tall, wore her blond hair
in two pigtails and spoke in a soft, well-modulated
tone.

Kitty was so proud of Melissa. She still visited on
Sundays to take the child out to tea. There was a lot of
affection between the two of them. Melissa would tell
Kitty of events that happened that week, of this girl or
that girl, of one who had befriended her or annoyed
her. She was evidently not an easy girl to get along
with.

There had been a bit of a problem with school
holidays. Kitty wanted so much to bring Melissa to her
home, but the house was so full of people and always so
untidy that Kitty felt the atmosphere would not be good
for the child. Therefore Melissa often spent the holidays with Ike Sneiderman's family in Barnet.

"I don't want to spend the holidays with them this
year," Melissa complained to Kitty. "I'd sooner stay at
school."

"But why, Melissa? They are very kind to you," said
Kitty.

"I don't like his children. They are all too Jewishy."

Kitty was astounded. She had been brought up in the
East End among the Jewish community, and most of
her dearest friends had been Jews. "But, darling," she
insisted "your mummy was Jewish."

"But not my father," replied Melissa haughtily.

This really worried Kitty. She wondered if the posh
school was really such a good idea. Kitty had learned
about life the hard way, out on the slum streets. She
had no hang-ups about race or religion and did not care
about politics, so Melissa's comments worried her. On
the way home it occurred to her that Melissa might one
day look down on her. She shuddered at the thought.

Apart from her weekly visits to Melissa, Kitty's life

was dull and empty. She needed a change. She decided to spend some of her savings on a holiday. She would take Melissa down to the seaside for the school holidays, and in that way they would remain closer to each other. Kitty was sure that Melissa had some kind of grand illusion about her father, and Kitty had known him as an out-of-work lad of the Depression who came from a consumptive family. Poor Tommy Wright—he never stood a dog's chance. However, Kitty would be the last one in the world to disillusion Melissa.

Noni had had her second child, a girl called Josephine. Dad adored his grandchildren and spent much of his spare time playing with them.

Kitty was well aware that she was gradually becoming the family spinster, a cold creature without a man of her own who hid in the background of this prolific family. She often thought about Bill. Her memory would fly back to the happy days when they were courting or first setting up house. Then Kitty would bring herself up sharp by suddenly remembering what he had done to her. She felt such bitterness and such pain and yet somewhere, deep down, she knew she retained feelings of love for him.

The idea of a summer holiday with Melissa gave Kitty a moral boost at a time when she was feeling particularly low. Melissa was delighted at the prospect of going to the seaside, so Kitty made all the arrangements. They went to stay at a neat guesthouse on the border of Norfolk and Suffolk in a place called Southminster.

Kitty had become so exasperated lately by aspects of her life that it was a very nice change to stay in this expensive place and be waited on, to have all day with nothing to do but amuse Melissa.

The other guests were very gracious to this young war widow and her lovely daughter. Kitty had seen no reason to tell anyone the truth. She reveled in the fact that for almost three weeks she was regarded as a real mother.

Southminster was a small naval town with its own lighthouse and a large maritime museum that Kitty loved to investigate with Melissa.

Melissa would play idly on the beach or sit in the garden of the boardinghouse lying in the sun. She was a quiet child and accepted the pleasures Kitty provided with a solemn expression in her dark eyes.

Melissa would never call Kitty "Mother" or "Auntie" but insisted on calling her Kitty.

"While we are staying here, pretend that I am your Mama," Kitty had requested of her. "It's better for all concerned." But Melissa had ignored her plea and continued to call her Kitty.

At night when Melissa was in bed asleep, Kitty would sit up and scribble away in the journal that now kept her company every day. It seemed like her only friend.

They had a marvelous holiday, and even though Melissa did not say much, it was clear that she had enjoyed herself. After the girl had returned to school, Kitty decided that she could not face going home. There was no reason to. The home no longer belonged to her; it had been taken over by Noni and her family and Dad and his Irish pals. Yes, she decided, she would stay up in Suffolk and get a job. That way she would be nearer to the school and could save on fares when visiting Melissa.

She traveled to Yarmouth, the nearest large town, and got a job as the barmaid of the Barking Smack, a little inn on the sea front. The work was hard, but it suited her. She liked the atmosphere, and the constant change of people as the holidaymakers came and went. It was a very busy season. Most families had not spent a seaside holiday together since before the war, but they came that year in droves. They sang, danced and spent their money freely and Kitty's small shape would dodge around the bar picking up empty glasses. She wore her hair neatly rolled up, and a black skirt and snow-white blouse completed the outfit. She always had a cold smile on her lips and remained aloof from the custom-

ers. In spite of her unsociability, she was popular.
" 'ave one on me, Kitty, darling," customers often said.

"No, thanks," Kitty would say, "I don't drink when
I'm working."

For quite suddenly she had an aversion to the smell
of alcohol. At the inn it was everywhere. It pervaded
the small room she slept in and contaminated her food
so much that she found it quite distasteful.

On her half days Kitty went to visit Melissa at the
school. She was developing very nicely; she played
tennis and, even with her impediment, managed to play
the triangle in the school orchestra. She obviously
enjoyed doing both and smiled more often now than
she used to. Kitty was both pleased and very proud.

The following Christmas the inn closed for the
holiday. After much thought Kitty took Melissa with
her to Billington Road. There they received a real Irish
welcome.

Noni was very tired and heavy carrying her third
child. But she was happy and as carefree as ever. Dad
seemed well, but to Kitty's alarm he was beginning to
age noticeably. There were silver streaks in his red hair
and his fine, strong shoulders were slightly bowed. He
had the patience of a saint with Noni's children and was
also very kind to Melissa.

It was a nice family holiday, that Christmas, with a
big Christmas tree, gifts, good food and Joe full of his
usual pranks. Melissa behaved herself and was very
popular. "I like your family, Kitty," said Melissa as
they sat on the train back to Suffolk. "I think they are
all so happy."

She paused and in her slow thoughtful manner
added, "Perhaps it's much better to be poor."

Kitty knew just what Melissa meant.

That winter at the inn, Kitty was very fed up. She
found it extremely difficult not to pack her bags and go
home. But she stuck it out, if only to be near Melissa.

Yarmouth was different in the winter. There were no holidaymakers from the big towns, and mostly young locals. These were of a new generation: gangs of tall, loud-mouthed lads from the cotton towns of Lancashire out on a weekend spree, sly boys from the fairgrounds, with not enough to do but hang about in the bars until spring came. Kitty did not like them or understand them and made it quite plain to them that she would stand no nonsense when they fooled about in her bar.

But one thin, nervous-looking boy called Leonard did get through to her. He was about twenty, having just finished his two years' National Service. He did not have a job or even any apparent intentions of getting one, but with his lank sandy hair and thick specs, he would lean on the bar the best part of the mornings and most of the evenings swilling down large, cold pints of ale. He was a reserved sort of lad and spoke with a good school accent.

"How about a date, Kitty?" he would often ask.

"No, thanks," Kitty would reply briskly. "I'm not a bloody cradle-snatcher."

"Have a drink with me then, Kitty," he would persist.

"I don't drink," Kitty would retort, "and you drink too much of that cold beer, sloshing it down night after night. Haven't got nothing else to do?"

Leonard would grin and say, "Why should you worry? I'm good for business."

"Fat lot I get out of it," Kitty would complain. But he made her smile, and their bantering built up a friendship between them. Kitty began to look forward to seeing his untidy sandy head and pale freckled face.

At night, when she was very lonely, Kitty would look out of the window of her attic room high up in the roof of the inn overlooking the sea. When the rain beat on the windows and the wind swept across the deserted sea front, she would think of home, of Dad sitting by the big coal fire, of Noni's children romping on the rug, of

Joe with his jokes and card-playing pals and of Noni
with that everlasting big tummy and her vivid, vulgar
humor.

When Kitty thought of her family like that, the
temptation to pack up and go was great, but she
resisted it every time.

One Sunday morning, Kitty got up early and went to
Mass. It was the first time in ten years. Amid the
candles and the incense she knelt, offering up her heart
to that unknown spirit she had ignored for so long.
"Dear God," she prayed, "please let me find peace of
mind. I am sorry I sinned. Tell me there is a place on
this earth for me, just a spot to live and love, that's all I
ask."

She came out of the church with a peaceful, happy
feeling and decided to go to Mass regularly.

A few weeks later, as she came down the steps of the
church, she noticed a young man sitting on the church
wall. He was shabbily dressed and his face looked
rather sad. His black hair blew about in the sea breeze.
As Kitty passed him, he rose. "Good morning,
madam," he said in a strange accent.

"Do I know you?" asked Kitty, slightly amazed.

"No, but I would very much like to get to know you.
I've watched you at Mass for several weeks." He
walked in step beside her. He was very tall and slightly
built. "One day I saw you in church. You were crying,
and I knew you were a lonely lady," he said. "So I got
my courage together today to introduce myself." He
smiled sweetly. Kitty noticed that his eyes were extraor-
dinarily dark.

"Well, yes," she said, "it can be very lonely in the
winter in a strange town. I suspect you're not English."

"No, I am Polish. I still live in the refugee camp on
the other side of this town."

Immediately, the stranger had won Kitty's sympathy.
She had heard of that dreary camp where people still
waited to be repatriated. "Oh, dear, it must be pretty
desolate out there," she said.

"It is not forever," the man replied. "Soon I will be going to West Germany to work in a factory."

"That will be nice," said Kitty sociably.

"No, it is not nice," the man said bitterly. "Poland is my homeland, and I would sooner return there."

"Why don't you?" Kitty asked.

"Because, madam, I am what is known as a stateless person. I fought for your country—I was in the Air Force—but now they do not want me and my own country is invaded by the Communists and will not admit me."

Kitty was puzzled; it was all very confusing to her. But the man seemed so unhappy that her heart went out to him. "Let's go and get some coffee," she said, indicating the café on the sea front.

Thus began another love affair for Kitty with Peter, the Polish refugee.

Peter was different from any other man in her life. He was moody, sentimental, jealous and very possessive. Kitty floated on the stormy surface of their relationship, loving Peter's caresses and ardent admiration of her. He was so good to look at with his jet-black hair and dark brown eyes. Even the shabby long trousers and faded pullovers gave her pleasure.

He would hardly discuss the war and was very bitter about England. "Next time, I fight for Russia," he said one day.

"But I thought you didn't like Communists," Kitty replied.

"Darling," he said dramatically in his strange lovely accent, "I will fight to free Russia and my own beloved country from its yoke of oppression."

"Oh, who cares?" Kitty cried impatiently as they strolled along the beach up into the sand dunes. They spent the afternoons lying in the sun, becoming hot and frustrated but knowing that they would wait until dark before making love.

Peter's stories of his homeland interested her, and he often sang Polish love songs in a sweet, melodious

voice. They made Kitty shiver with a passion that made
her want Peter all the more. Every day at five o'clock
Kitty had to return to work at the bar. She never
wanted to leave him, and their lips would cling passionately. Then Peter would arrive regularly at ten o'clock
and sit in the same spot, where he would watch her
possessively. Once the bar closed at midnight, Kitty
would sneak out and find Peter waiting in the shady
lane ready to sweep her into his arms. And Kitty was
always willing. She was never quite sure why, but she
felt as though she died each night and her soul soared
into eternity. If this was real love, she thought, then she
had found it.

But then in the daytime she would be filled with
doubt, and gradually she realized that she was being
owned, just like one of those small donkeys on the sea
front. She did not like it. In spite of his exciting
lovemaking, Peter was very cold, like that frozen
country he came from—Kitty thought of Poland as she
would the North Pole. She frequently found herself
wanting Bill, anxious for the warmth and security of the
old days, the laughter and tenderness she had shared
with him.

But then, she thought, what the hell did she want?
Bill had left her, and she was no spring chicken.
Perhaps she ought to think herself lucky that she could
still get a man at all. So through the spring and summer
of that year, Kitty went steady with Peter or "that
foreigner fellow," as some of the customers were heard
to refer to him.

Kitty began to sneak Peter upstairs into her little
room. This was particularly easy at weekends when the
guv'nor was off on his boat. In the kitchen Kitty would
cook Peter steak, eggs and mushrooms and then they
would have their midnight supper in bed before making
love. Peter would slip out every morning at daybreak
because he liked to go to morning Mass. Kitty, however, had again given up going to Mass; her conscience
would not allow her to attend.

Kitty went occasionally to visit Melissa, who had grown quite tall and very pretty. She was more outgoing than she used to be, and she had made friends at the school and talked and giggled a lot. Kitty enjoyed being with her and was extremely proud of her. But she did not let on to Melissa about Peter; for some reason she felt a little ashamed of her affair.

She received several long letters from Noni, most of them complaining about how hard she was finding it to make ends meet. She informed Kitty that Dad had been rather poorly recently and had not been to work for months. She said he was being very trying and got on her nerves being in the house all day.

Kitty sent Noni some money and wrote a long letter to Dad. She did consider that he might like to come up for a holiday, but she changed her mind about asking him. She was not sure of what Dad's attitude to Peter would be. The fact that Peter was a Catholic would not console him because he regarded Kitty as being married to Bill.

Kitty went on loving and fussing her new man, but his possessiveness disturbed her.

"I love you, darling," he would say. "I cannot live without you. I will strangle you with my own hands if you let me down."

Kitty would stare at him curiously, strangely afraid. I must be bloody mad, she would think. I could never get rid of him if I wanted to.

One night Peter said to her, "If you marry me, Kitty, I will be very happy."

Kitty looked worried. "Peter, you know I have a husband."

"But, Kitty, I never believed you. When you told me that, I thought you were pretending."

"Mind you, I don't even know where he is," Kitty said casually.

Peter looked very forlorn. "You do not love me as I love you," he said.

"Oh, of course I do," she said, cuddling him. He put

his head with its soft flowing hair on her shoulder and she ran her fingers through it.

"Soon I have to go," he said. "I cannot put it off any longer. There is a situation waiting for me in Germany. If you can't marry me, at least come with me, darling."

Kitty looked dismayed. Leave England with this stateless person who didn't even own a passport? How would they live? In a camp like that miserable old place down by the shore? She would never see Dad or Melissa. . . . No, she could never do that.

"I can't leave my job in the middle of the season," she said. "It wouldn't be fair. You go, dear. I'll come out to you in the autumn."

His dark eyes scrutinized her closely. "I would be so happy if I thought you meant it," he said quietly.

Peter left a few weeks later. There were many tears and sighs at their parting, and Peter went away promising to write once he was settled.

After saying goodbye, Kitty went back into the bar. She looked white and exhausted.

Leonard, who still lounged half tipsy by the bar, said, "Hullo, Kitty, where have you been? Out on the marshes all night?" He grinned.

Kitty gave him a shove. "Mind your own bloody business," she said.

"I've got a cold coming on," she told the boss. "I'm going up to bed."

"Christ," he said, "you look like death warmed up. Better get your head down; I'll manage."

Kitty crept up to her chilly attic and lay on the bed weeping. For what, she did not know. Because Peter had gone? Or was it happiness at the thought of being free again? She was too confused to care.

CHAPTER NINETEEN
A Change of Scene

The holiday season was in full swing and the bar was very busy. Kitty was glad because then she had no time to think about the past or the future.

Soon she was promoted. The boss had taken over another bar a little way out of town. "I'll put you in charge of the staff here and increase your pay," he told Kitty. "You are a hard-working girl and have stuck by me all this time, so now, dear, you can share in the perks."

Kitty ran the bar and organized the young staff, which consisted of girls who came up just to work for the summer season. It took all her energy to control them. They quarreled with each other, fiddled the till and got drunk on duty. But by sheer determination and scrupulous attention to detail, Kitty kept them on their toes.

Kitty was dismayed one day to hear one of the young girls remark, "Watch it, the old gel's coming along." She knew they were referring to her. She still looked quite good; her chestnut hair was full and neatly trimmed and she was very slim and dressed carefully. It had never occurred to her that other people thought she was getting old. She examined her face in the mirror. Although her small features were still very clear and her skin smooth, there were indeed faint lines showing now, lines that had been dimples not so long ago. Well, she was now thirty-three, so it was quite possible that to a young seventeen-year-old she seemed ancient. The old maid of Barking Smack. She smiled to herself.

Since Peter had sailed away she had not had one word from him. He had disappeared completely, as so many refugees did. But Kitty did not care. She thought of him with a kind of motherly feeling, but not much else. She thought of ugly old Harry Cross with fondness now, but no regret. And Bill. When she thought of Bill anger rose inside her, but there was also a tug at her heart, which she ignored as best she could. None of them was worth it.

Then out of the blue Kitty decided that she was finished with men. Never again would she allow herself to be used. She would save her wages and make a home for herself and Melissa somewhere, somehow.

Kitty just went on living, working hard during the week and visiting Melissa at school on Sunday afternoons and taking her out to tea.

Young Leonard still propped himself against the bar all evening. He was the first in and the last out. His freckled face was still thin and pale, and his lank hair hung over his specs. Some days his eyes would be bloodshot with alcohol.

It distressed Kitty to see him, always alone, staring mournfully at the line of bottles behind the bar. She would give him an encouraging grin. "Blimey, Leonard, you look terrible. Get a bloody pie or something; you'll rot your guts with all that beer."

"Who cares?" Leonard would announce and order another beer.

Kitty began to wonder about him. He always had money, so he must have a job now, she thought, particularly since he never came into the bar during the day anymore.

"Do me a favor," she said one day, "and have a pie on me. You look starved."

As Leonard munched his pie, he began to chat and tell her a few things about himself. He had recently got work in a council office in the town hall, and he lived some miles away in an old cottage that had belonged to his grandparents. Leonard had been brought up in London, but his parents had come up to Suffolk at the beginning of the war.

"My father copped it at Dunkirk, and Mum went off with a Yank."

"Well, well," said Kitty cheerfully, "that's one thing we have in common—both of us born in the smoke."

He leaned toward her. "You and I have got a lot in common, Kitty," he said eagerly.

"Such as?" Kitty said dryly.

"Well, you'd be better off going out with me than that rotten foreigner," he announced.

"Can it," said Kitty. "I ain't going out of the frying pan into the bleeding fire."

Leonard laughed, and from then on he became her pal and confidant.

As the season wore on and the bar became quieter, Kitty began to tell Leonard about her life. She told him about Bill and Melissa, and humorous stories about Dad and Noni. Her jokes about the Irish parties at Billington Road made him laugh heartily. Leonard helped her in the bar by collecting glasses, and he did not seem to get sloshed quite so often, though often enough.

His method of transport was an old bike. One night, Kitty watched him trying to get his lanky leg over the cross bar. He was so drunk that over and over again he missed.

"Good God," said Kitty the next day. "What are you trying to do? Commit suicide? If you get knocked off that bike in a dark lane the traffic will squash you flat."

Leonard looked at her seriously. "I know, Kitty. I've fallen off many nights. I was thinking that I might buy a car. I learned to drive in the army."

"Good idea," said Kitty, polishing up the glasses.

To her astonishment Leonard suddenly arrived one Sunday morning in a big old-fashioned car. He asked Kitty to go outside and see if she approved of it. Leonard was clearly proud of his new toy. "Do you like it?" he asked excitedly.

"Yes, I do," she told him, tooting the long brass horn.

"I'll take you for a ride this afternoon," he offered eagerly.

"Sorry, I'm going to see Melissa."

"I'll take you. Where is it?"

"Ipswich. It's quite a long way."

"That's all right. I'll call for you at two o'clock."

They took Melissa out to tea and stuffed her with cream buns and ice cream. The girl took to Leonard immediately and was very impressed by the car. She insisted that he drive past the school so that the other girls could see them. "Oh," she giggled, "this will kill them when they see me driving past in a car with a presentable young man."

The three of them had a marvelous time, and Kitty was pleased that Melissa liked Leonard so much.

After that first occasion, the Sunday trip became a regular event, and Kitty was delighted that Leonard was so happy to visit Melissa with her.

One Sunday as they were driving back, Leonard said, "Shall we go to my cottage, Kitty? Would you like to see it?"

"Very much," she replied. She had been hoping he would invite her.

They made a detour through the autumn countryside. The leaves on the beech trees had already turned a golden hue; the corn had been cut and the land was black in places where the stubble had been scorched. The air was fresh and crisp. It was a perfect day and Kitty felt fit, happy and relaxed.

When the car finally stopped outside a beautiful, isolated old cottage at the end of a long, shady lane, Kitty was remarkably impressed. "Is this it? Why, it's perfect," she cried ecstatically.

The setting sun made the bricks glow red and the tiny windows gleam silver. The front garden was a mass of multicolored dahlias. There was a lopsided stone chimney that stood out against the sky line. Kitty gasped at the sight of the miles of land behind the cottage. It was secluded and quiet apart from the singing of the birds in the trees and the lowing of the cows in the fields around.

"Would you like to come in for a cup of tea?" Leonard asked shyly.

"Try and stop me," said Kitty, clambering out of the car.

Kitty found the inside of the cottage as exquisite as the outside. Through a flagstoned hall they entered a tiny sitting room. All around there was old-fashioned bric-a-brac covered with a layer of dust, and Kitty noticed with amusement the cobwebs hanging from the beams.

The kitchen was also neglected, but it was spacious and furnished with a large wooden table and an oak dresser.

"Sorry, it's such a mess," apologized Leonard. "I don't seem to get the time to clean it up. It's a pity because Gran kept it immaculate."

Kitty looked around her. Her eye caught the narrow wooden staircase winding to the next floor, and suddenly she visualized the old couple who had spent all their lives here. She had a warm feeling inside her. "It's a fine place, Len," she said. "You say it belongs to you?"

"Yes, my grandparents left it to me. He was an old sea captain, my grandfather. You see those massive oak beams that support the porch? That was originally the mast of his old ship. He had them hauled up here, and he built this cottage for Gran when they married. They were together for fifty years."

They walked out onto the porch, where they stood silently watching the sun go down.

"If you did this up," said Kitty in a down-to-earth tone, "you could sell it for a lot of money."

"I'm not sure that I want to sell. I really like it here, though it is lonely sometimes and not easy to get into town."

Back in the kitchen they made tea. "Why haven't you got a girlfriend, Leonard?" asked Kitty suddenly as they sipped out of dainty china cups.

"I've got you," jested Leonard.

"Don't be silly. I'm nearly old enough to be your mother," Kitty said sharply.

Leonard looked down at the ground. "Girls my age terrify me. I get so nervous with them that they think I'm an imbecile," he said slowly.

Kitty sat back on the old sofa, ignoring his remark. "Oh, it is quiet up here," she said. "It really does one good."

Leonard slowly moved over and sat at her feet. He put his head on her lap and Kitty stroked his soft, fair hair.

"Kitty," he said, "why don't you come out here and live with me?"

She sat up quickly. "Don't spoil things," she said. "I've no intention of ever getting tied up with anyone again, and least of all with a young kid like you."

"It was just an idea," said Leonard quietly. "Never mind."

Kitty did not mind that he had made such a proposition. She regarded Leonard as a pal, and his foolhardy ideas would not spoil their friendship. After that first trip, the cottage became a place where the two of them went to every Sunday after visiting Melissa at school. As the air got colder and the evenings shorter, they would drive up to the cottage and immediately light a fire. Kitty would do some dusting and wash the china for Leonard, and then they would sit in the twilight talking of their youth and their parents.

"We are two odd bods, you and I, Len," Kitty said one day. "Perhaps we deserve each other."

Len hugged her warmly. He had not given up hope. Kitty's own feelings about Leonard were changing, but she did not say anything.

Just before Christmas, Kitty took a week's holiday and went up to London to see Dad. As she walked down Billington Road she thought of the day when she and Bill had chosen their little house. How proud they had been and so delighted to have a real bathroom and garden. Then it had all disappeared. Now the house looked battered and seemed to be crying out for a lick of paint. As she came to the door she noticed that the knocker was dull and unpolished. In the windows the net curtains looked grubby.

Casey, now a sturdy little boy, came dashing out to greet Kitty, followed by his dark toddler sister, Josephine. "Here's Auntie Kitty," the boy yelled.

Noni came slowly out of the front room to meet her. She had grown very stout and was untidier than ever. In her arms she carried a podgy baby. "Oh, this is the new one," cried Kitty. "She's lovely! You're so lucky, Noni, to have so many children."

"Dunno about that," grumbled Noni. "They keeps yer bloody poor. Joe got a job at last; he's been outta work for six months."

"I'm sorry to hear that," Kitty said. "If you need a loan, just let me know."

"No bloody good me borrowing money," complained Noni. "Can't afford to pay it back."

Kitty suddenly felt very depressed. She opened her purse and gave Noni a fiver. "Get something for lunch," she said.

After Kitty had given the children some sweets she had brought them, she looked for Dad. He was sleeping in his chair in the dining room. Kitty was a little shocked when she saw him. He was so much thinner and his hair was now nearly white.

"Dad doesn't look well," she whispered to Noni when she came back.

"Well enough to go out boozing with Joe," grunted Noni.

Kitty felt very disappointed. Something had gone from the old home. The happy family feeling of years gone by was no more. There was a sour atmosphere in the air.

She and Noni sat in the front room having a cup of tea and waiting for Dad to wake up. It was still the order of the day not to wake Dad when he had been drinking, to let him sleep it off.

"He wakes like a bear with a sore behind," commented Noni. "Dad heard from your Bill—I saw the letter," she said suddenly.

"What did he have to say?" asked Kitty as casually as possible, but her heart was thumping.

"I'm not sure. Crafty old sod wouldn't let me read it, but I know it came from Africa."

"What's he doing out there?" asked Kitty in astonishment.

"God knows," said Noni. "Joe said it was something to do with peanuts."

"Oh," said Kitty, "perhaps it's the ground nut project. I read about that in the paper." She suddenly realized that her throat was tight and the palms of her hands were damp. She wished Noni had not mentioned Bill. She had successfully managed to push him from her mind for such a long time, but now all those buried feelings were rushing to the surface.

"We pay the rent to an agent now," said Noni. "Don't know if he has sold the house."

"I might divorce him," said Kitty abruptly.

"You can't do that, Kitty!" said Noni, shocked. "You're a Catholic."

"Oh, don't spout religion at me, Noni," Kitty snapped.

"It's a dreadful sin. You'll be excommunicated," said Noni, very worried.

"So what?" said Kitty. "What am I supposed to do? Go into a nunnery?" She was angry at Noni's interference.

"That's it, Kitty," Noni snapped back, "mock. You always mocked, and that's why you have been punished."

The two sisters were on the verge of a vicious argument when Dad emerged bleary-eyed from the dining room. "Is that you, gel? Hello." He held out his arms and Kitty ran to kiss him. Her rage subsided as she buried her face in his chest just as she had done when she was a little girl. Dad hugged her tight.

The Christmas spent at home was grim. It was so unlike the ones the family had had in the past. Dad drank a lot and spent much of the time sleeping. Noni grumbled constantly and spouted at Joe and the children, who were badly behaved and noisy. Kitty was relieved when the week was over.

As she said goodbye to Dad, he took an extra puff at his pipe and said gently, "Why don't you come home, gel? What is there in that God-forsaken hole you're living in that you haven't got here?"

"I like it there," said Kitty defensively.

"Well, this is Bill's and yerself's home. While I live I'll keep it for him." It was the same old line.

"No, Dad, stop thinking that way. I'm going to divorce him." Kitty almost shouted this at him.

Dad took the old clay pipe from his mouth. "I hope you will do no such foolish thing," he said quietly. "Ye are married in the eyes of God, so pull up your socks, Kitty, and come home. Bill's in Africa and sends you love."

"Oh, damn and blast him!" she cried in frustration. "Why can't he leave me alone?" With that she marched out of the house.

CHAPTER TWENTY
The Other Man

Kitty lay awake in bed. She could not sleep. She felt uncomfortable and hot. Restlessly she lay listening to the sounds of gaiety still going on below. It was long after hours, but the guv'nor was having a party, as he often did for his friends, who all seemed to be male.

She got up and pulled out her suitcase from under the bed. Rummaging between all her journal notebooks, she found her post office book and a book of war saving certificates. She had not spent one penny of Bill's allowance, and from her own wages she had paid ten shillings a week into the war savings. Adding up the total, she realized that she had about five hundred pounds—an enormous amount. She was quite surprised.

In the dim light of the room, Kitty sat on the floor, her papers all around her, contemplating the bare walls with their faded wallpaper. She was gripped by a feeling of loneliness and despair. What the hell was she still saving for? she thought. She had nothing to look forward to, she would probably spend the rest of her life as a barmaid and get old and ugly with sallow skin and bags under her eyes from the hard work and late nights. Her future looked so dismal. She could feel tears rising inside her, and she sniffed unhappily as she recalled Leonard's frequent urging for them to live together. She found Leonard a bit of an ass sometimes, and he was so much younger than she.

Then she thought of Leonard's cottage and the serene feeling of peace that surrounded it. Perhaps she would find happiness living with him. Sex was not everything, and in many ways Leonard might be good for her. He would at least be someone to care for and laugh with and share Melissa with.

More doubt entered her mind. Would she be good for him? He was very young and did not get on with girls. Would the difference in age bother her? But yes, she decided she would chance it and look on it as a kind of business arrangement. That would be the best thing. She would offer him her savings to put the cottage into good shape: it would be well worth it.

Satisfied with her plan, she crept back to bed and slept peacefully until morning light.

The next day was Sunday, and as usual she and Leonard drove down to see Melissa in the afternoon. Melissa had grown even taller and wore her hair in two long braids. Her legs were well shaped and her short gym slip showed them off to perfection. They all went to the tea shop, then for a walk in the park. Melissa adored Leonard, and he was very happy to romp with her and talk about her schoolwork. While they chatted, Kitty sat feeling content and somehow supremely happy at having made her decision, but she had not yet said anything to Leonard.

Later, they sat in the cottage having a cup of tea. Kitty looked very thoughtfully into the big log fire, watching the smoke curl up the wide chimney.

"When I was a kid," she said, "I used to have to go every other day to get seven pounds of coal in a big shopping bag before I could light the fire. It must be nice living in the country, getting those big logs for a fire without a lot of trouble."

"Got a whole lot of them," said Leonard. "Up to the end of his life Grandad was out there sawing logs and stacking them for the winter. Then he sat down and went into his last sleep."

Kitty looked at the old chair with its well-cushioned seat and wooden arms. "Was that his chair?" she asked.

"The same one," Leonard answered a little sadly. "He never really got over losing Gran. I wish I had been here to look after him, but they called me into the bloody army." He sounded bitter.

Kitty held his hand. "They were a nice, peaceful old couple, weren't they? I get this feeling about things like that; it's as if I knew them."

"You are a fine person, Kitty," Leonard said. "I wish you could love me enough to stay here with me."

"Well, I'm going to really surprise you, Leonard. I've decided I will come and live with you anytime you say."

Leonard stared at her in astonishment. Then he pulled her into his arms. "Oh, Kitty, Kitty, you have made me so happy." He held tightly on to her and wept.

"Nothing to snivel about," Kitty said. "Open that whiskey and we'll have a good drink. I'll not go home till tomorrow."

Leonard dashed excitedly to the sideboard and poured out large drinks. Then they snuggled up beside the fire.

"One stipulation," Kitty said. "I keep my job and pay my corner. In fact, I'd like to invest a bit of money to make this place look good. It's really worth it."

"Do you want to, Kitty? It's all yours," said Leonard.

"Well, then, let's get on with it. Don't you want to make love to me?" She grinned. "Might as well start now."

On the sheepskin rug in front of the fire they made

love, but it was a little disappointing. Kitty was desperate to be loved, but Leonard was awkward and got excited too quickly.

"Sorry, Kitty," he said.

"Shut up," she replied. "Don't apologize; you'll probably do better next time." She was annoyed that it had not been successful, and that night she slept on the sofa by herself. Before she fell asleep, she remembered Harry's strong muscles and Peter's passionate skill at making a woman happy. *Oh, well,* she said to herself, *I'm not sorry. At least I now have a man of my own and a house to go with it.*

The guv'nor was very angry when Kitty confronted him. "I'll be living out from now on," she told him, "so you'd better put someone else in charge."

"You've made a big, bloody mistake there, Kitty," he said. "A warm little body like you tying yourself up with an immature boy. It won't last, and it's bloody kinky, that's what I think."

"It's not so bloody kinky as your goings-on down here on Saturday nights after time," she shouted back.

"Okay, Kitty," said the guv'nor, backing away at her rage. "No need to get nasty."

"Right," Kitty said, still bristling. "You live your life and allow me to live mine. If you don't want me to work here, I'll soon get another job."

An oily smile replaced his look of surprise. "Kitty, my darling," he oozed, "what would I do without you? You know I rely on you, Kitty."

"Too much, I reckon," she said dryly, "but nevertheless, I'll stay if you agree. I'll work some mornings, some afternoons—suit yourself. I'd like Sundays off to see Melissa."

"That's fine, Kitty. Maybe you can train a bright girl to be in charge. She can have your room. I might even do it up for her."

The guv'nor became almost humble, so Kitty gave him a charming smile. "Cheer up," she said, "I won't spoil your little pleasures." She was sure he was nervous because of his own sexual exploits.

"Great girl you are, Kitty. Pity you never got a good man."

"Don't start," she cried. "Hop it, off to your golf balls or whatever it is you get up to."

Having made her peace with the boss, Kitty began to settle down with Leonard. On the days she worked, he picked her up in the car at night and they would travel through the dark, silent countryside to the little cottage.

Their affair was a well-kept secret from both her family and Melissa. She wanted to see if it would work out before she said anything to anyone. If all went well, then she might let on that she was Leonard's mistress, though it was really in name only, for he was still very inadequate in bed.

After awhile, she repapered the spare room and bought herself a divan bed. Leonard helped her to bring up a heavy wooden bookcase from downstairs on which she arranged her books and small treasures. She spent much of her spare time in that room, reading or writing in her journal, lost to the outside world.

"You don't mind, do you, Len?" she asked. "There is very little room for both of us in that bed of yours."

"As long as you're happy, Kitty, I don't mind what you do," he said placidly. She was so determined that Leonard did not have much choice.

Leonard had recently taken up a course of architectural drawing at the Adult Education Center. "I'd like to try to get my finals," he said. "At the moment I'm just an office boy, but I would like to try for promotion. There's a lot of new building going on around here—council houses and all that."

Kitty was pleased. "Good," she said, "I knew you had it in you. While you're at it, you must apply to the planning office for permission to build an indoor toilet and bathroom. I've got five hundred pounds," she told him. "Might as well spend it on improvements since we both have jobs. There's no reason why we can't live comfortably."

As always, Leonard just gave in gracefully.

On days she was not working, and while Leonard was at his office, Kitty loved to polish the furniture and the little ornaments in the cottage. At the cottage, housework rarely seemed like a tedious chore. It gave her peace of mind when she was not reading or writing.

One morning, as she polished the horse brasses around the fireplace, her memory flew back to those dreary old rooms over the stable where it had all begun, where she used to get down on her knees blackleading the grate. She tried desperately to push it from her mind, but it remained like a heavy rock, until into her daydreaming came pretty Nelly Kelly dancing about, just home from boarding school. With joy, Kitty recalled the lovely dream world of those lonely days when Nelly was her companion and went everywhere with her in her mind, living the exciting life that Kitty herself missed.

Feeling an overwhelming passion to recapture her thoughts, she ran upstairs and began to write more about her childhood and those desperate fights for survival after her mother had died. Her memory was vivid and clear, and her energy seemed endless as she scribbled on and on for most of the day until finally, tired and cramped, she closed her book and came downstairs to cook the dinner. She felt wonderful, released of pent-up feelings after laying the ghosts of her past.

CHAPTER TWENTY-ONE

Home to Dad

At Easter Melissa came to the cottage for the first time. It was her school holiday. Kitty felt it was time to tell her about the situation. "You know, dear," she said, "Len and I are living together. The cottage was his home, but now we share it with him."

Melissa pushed the wide-brimmed school hat to the back of her blond head and her eyes scrutinized Kitty in disbelief. "Phew!" she said. "He's a bit young for you, isn't he?"

Kitty tried not to be hurt and laughed. "Well, I'm still young enough, Melissa, even if you don't seem to think so."

"That's your business," Melissa replied, "but I like this house. It's quaint and cozy."

Kitty showed her up to the small bedroom they had prepared for her. She and Leonard had decorated it with bright wallpaper, and pretty drawings hung over the bed and the small dressing table. Kitty had also placed her gramophone in the room for Melissa. It was an ancient wooden instrument that had to be wound up for each record. Kitty was very fond of it.

"What's that old crock?" asked Melissa when she saw it on the dresser.

"That's my old gramophone," said Kitty. "I've had it for years. I thought it would amuse you."

"It might," said Melissa flatly, "but I'll have to get some popular records." She picked up one of the records from the pile. "'Stardust'? Cripes! How corny can you get?"

Kitty snatched the record from Melissa's hand. "I'll take that, it's mine," she said angrily. "And the rest are Leonard's bloody brass bands."

Melissa shot her a smug look that made Kitty feel the girl was almost pleased to have got her into a temper. She was puzzled.

The rest of the day Melissa behaved like a cat showing her claws. Kitty tried to ignore her as best she could. She thought Melissa was perhaps still tense from school and in need of a rest. She was relieved when Leonard arrived home, for his presence dispelled the friction between her and Melissa. They ate dinner together and played cards and dominoes.

Melissa suddenly became as loving as she had always been and laughed a lot. She was now almost twelve years old, tall and well-built for her age. Her artificial hand was no longer a problem; she could do most things with it, but she simply hated any reference to it at all and wore a white glove over it most of the time.

When Kitty thought of herself at that age, as a little waif in that terrible school, she was amazed at Melissa's precocious behavior. But Kitty also found her demanding and very lazy, which she did not like. Melissa seemed to think that it was Kitty's duty to run around cleaning up after her. Kitty was not impressed by some of the attitudes the school had instilled in the girl.

On the whole, however, they got on fairly well together. They went to the local cinema and into town to do the shopping. The weather was still cold, but they sometimes strolled along the sea front. On one such day Melissa suddenly said, "I don't want to go back to the boarding school. I'd like to stay here; it must be very nice in the summer."

"I'm not sure about that, dear," said Kitty. "I'll have to discuss it with Mr. Sneiderman."

"What's it to do with him?" retorted Melissa rudely.

"You know perfectly well that he's your other guardian and the one in charge of your education," Kitty firmly informed her.

"Fat old fool. I don't like him," retorted Melissa sulkily, kicking a stone viciously across their path.

Kitty did not feel like arguing with her. "All right," she said, "I'll see what I can do. Go back this time, and before the next holiday perhaps we can arrange for you to go to a day school near here," she promised her.

After Easter, Melissa went back to school, and Leonard and Kitty settled back into their lives. They each had their own bedroom, but occasionally Leonard would pluck up courage by downing a few drinks and try to make love again. But it never worked out right. All Leonard's efforts did was add to his embarrassment and Kitty's frustration.

"Might as well give it up, Leonard," Kitty said one night after several unsuccessful and clumsy efforts on his part. "There are other things in life besides sex, and we're obviously incompatible."

"But I want so much to please you, Kitty." Leonard almost wept.

"I'm not worried. If men leave me alone, I can leave them alone. It won't bother me," she told him.

After that, Leonard did not try again, and they both diverted their energies into their work; he applied himself to his job and evening classes and Kitty to her work at the bar and her incessant scribbling.

Since she had been living in the cottage, Kitty's writing had begun to take shape. No longer did she just write descriptions of her feelings and dreams in the form of a journal. Now she found she was writing lots

of short stories and poems as well. But most important
of all was the life of Nelly Kelly, which Kitty had
recently started writing in the form of a long novel. She
knew it was ambitious and she doubted that anything
would come of it, or even that she would ever finish it,
but she got so much pleasure from writing it—nothing
made her happier.

Nelly Kelly was now the major character in Kitty's
fantasies. She had gone from the middle-class background into a wartime factory. In fact, Kitty had made
her one of the grass widows. Night after night Kitty
took her through the blitzed streets of London, through
traumatic affairs that finally left Nelly so disillusioned
that she became one of those young prostitutes hanging
about Piccadilly. The story began to get so exciting that
Kitty found she could not leave it alone. She felt driven
to write more and more. She always had a pad handy to
grab every spare moment for her scribblings.

Leonard treated her writing as a good joke. Whenever he came into her room she would hurriedly slip the
notebook under the cushion and sit on it.

"Gone broody again, Kitty?" Leonard would laugh.

Kitty hated any reference to her writing, and her
cheeks would flush angrily. She had no intention of
sharing this story with Leonard.

In July, Melissa arrived home once more. This time
she was loaded up with luggage, hockey sticks, tennis
rackets and all her belongings from school. "I've come
home," she announced. "I've left that silly school, and
I'm glad."

Ike Sneiderman and Kitty together had managed to
make arrangements for Melissa to attend a day school
in the nearest town, and a drama school two evenings a
week because she was very keen on acting.

Kitty had got the impression that Ike had been
pleased to be giving up some of his responsibilities with
Melissa. In a recent letter he had mentioned that he
was finding the girl a bit of a problem as he got older.
Kitty did not mind; she looked forward to having

Melissa living with her and Leonard and welcomed her warmly.

All through the summer holidays Melissa was extremely happy. In his spare time Leonard took her riding and swimming, and they played tennis together. They spent most of the time outside and looked fit and well. As long as they kept out of her way, Kitty was not bothered. She was busy with her job and the home, but most of all she was engrossed in her novel. She called it *The Grass Widows*, and was typing it up from the notebooks on an old typewriter she had bought in a junk shop. She was very pleased with her progress.

Kitty often felt a little guilty about Dad. She had not been to see him for a long time. She had once asked him up for a holiday, but he had flatly refused to come, even though he did not know about Leonard. Noni had become very silent lately and no longer wrote long letters of woe telling Kitty how poor she was. So Kitty slowly lost contact with her family in London, but as she became more and more involved with her writing she did not notice the months go by.

Nelly Kelly had now nearly completed her journey. Kitty was not sure where else to take her and decided to give her a rest. She stuck the book in her suitcase. She had recently joined a local creative writing group in the evenings. The other members of the group were mainly middle-class women who wrote as a hobby. At first Kitty had been tremendously shy of these clever people who had received the benefits of a good education. Writing was just another interest for them, but to Kitty it had become extremely important. It kept her going and helped her understand her life and her past a little better. When she read the first short story to the class, her voice was tense and she sounded very nervous. But as she became involved in her words she forgot about the audience and her reading came over well. When she finished there was a second's silence before she received a round of applause. Kitty was thrilled; she had never had such praise. After that, she felt she was right to make writing such a major part of her life. For the first time ever, she felt truly fulfilled.

Kitty had another success a few weeks later when the class was told to write a ghost story. The others were enthralled by her contribution and applauded her again. Afterward one of the women gave Kitty the address of a magazine to send it to because she thought the story was so good. Kitty did this, and to her complete astonishment she received a check and a letter saying that her story was to be published in the magazine. She could not believe her success.

She started to do research in the library for material to use in her next ghost stories. She was still bowled over by the fact that not only could she write stories but ones that other people listened to and enjoyed.

Neither Leonard nor Melissa took much interest in Kitty's achievements. Both seemed to be wrapped up in their own exploits. But Kitty did not mind; she loved every spare minute she spent writing or researching. She had never before been so enjoyably involved in anything that was quite so devoid of sex.

Leonard and Melissa kept each other company and were always dashing off somewhere. Melissa loved her acting, and now both she and Leonard had joined the local amateur drama group and spent many evenings rehearsing.

Leonard looked even younger these days and wore tee-shirts and tight corduroy slacks. He was always kind and courteous to Kitty but kept generally out of her way. He and Melissa often larked about in the bathroom and had pillow fights in the bedroom on Sunday mornings. "Crikey," Kitty would cry, "how many bloody kids have we got in this house?" But she rarely got annoyed by their antics, and the three of them remained on very amicable terms.

At the weekends, while the pop music and dancing went on downstairs, Kitty sat in her room and slogged away at her typewriter, slowly improving her writing skills as all her dreams and ideas came out on the paper. She was blissfully happy.

One day, out of the blue, Noni wrote to say that Dad was seriously ill. Kitty wept tears of dismay. She felt bad that she had not been in touch with her family for so long; it had been almost two years. She decided to go the next day and arranged time off from her job at the bar.

"You had better come with me, Melissa. You'll have to have some days off school. I can't have you gadding about up here all alone," Kitty said while they were eating supper.

"Why?" Melissa sneered. "Are you taking Len with you?"

"No, certainly not," said Kitty sharply.

"Don't worry, Kitty," Leonard said mildly. "I'll take care of things up here."

"I'm not going," said Melissa stubbornly. "I don't like London, or that smelly, vulgar house of Noni's. No, thanks."

"You will do as you're told," replied Kitty sharply. She was taken aback by Melissa's snobbish attitude. "You've changed your tune, since I seem to remember you enjoyed yourself there last time. And you're only fourteen and still at school. I am responsible for you."

"Too bad," replied Melissa. "I'm still not going." She flounced out of the room and locked herself away upstairs.

Kitty and Leonard finished eating in silence, and Leonard self-consciously got up to wash the dishes, a job he always insisted on doing.

Kitty sat with her elbows on the table thinking of Dad, wondering if he was being properly looked after. "Oh, well," she said suddenly, "you'll both have to take potluck because I'm off on my own in the morning."

Nervously Leonard rubbed the plates. His face looked hot and flushed. "We'll be all right, Kitty. I'll look after Melissa; she'll obey me," he muttered.

"See that Melissa gets to school on time," said Kitty as she said goodbye to Leonard at the station. "I'll try not to be too long."

For the first time in his life Dad was really ill. He had influenza so bad it had developed into acute bronchitis. He moved into the small box-room, where he sat up coughing and spluttering and drinking rum. The room was heated by an old oil stove, which gave the room a nauseating smell.

Kitty was appalled when she arrived to see this. "Why has Dad been moved from his bedroom?" she demanded.

"Oh, Kitty, don't start as soon as you come home," cried Noni, still stout and untidy. "I've had enough on me plate—three kids with the measles, then the old man got ill. He wanted to move in there, he said he didn't need so much room now. Besides, I had to have some place to put the kids."

"Oh, well," said Kitty impatiently, taking off her coat, "let's get him cleaned up. The smell's disgusting in there."

Tearfully, Noni went about the task of providing hot water and clean linen.

Dad complained bitterly as they washed and changed him.

"You've got to have the doctor to see you," said Kitty. "We're getting you spruced up for him."

"Nonsense, there's very little wrong with me," argued Dad. "It's only the old broncho. A tot of rum will clear my chest."

But Kitty was persistent and soon had him sitting up nice and clean, having taken away his pipe and bottle of rum.

"I'll give them back when the doctor has been," she told him. She went to find Noni. "I'll go up to see the doctor and ask him to come down," she said.

"He won't come," Noni said. "The last time Dad ordered him out."

"Well, I'll find another doctor," said Kitty.

"There's a new doctor down near the church. He's Irish. Someone at Mass told me about him."

"Well, that's where I'll go. It's better to pay privately than to put up with second-rate advice—didn't we have enough of that when we were young?"

Kitty went off up the road to visit Dr. Callahan. She found his surgery and sat in the waiting room for a long time. When she eventually went in to see him, she liked him immediately. He was tall with light-brown hair. He had a lovely, fresh Irish face. He reminded Kitty of Dad. "I'd like you to attend my father," she said. "He has a bad chill. I'll pay privately; he doesn't get on too well with his panel doctor."

"Can I have your father's name?" the doctor asked.

"Cornelius Erin Daly," said Kitty.

The doctor stopped writing and looked up with a grin. "No wonder; he's an Irishman."

"Yes," she replied. "He's been over here a long time." A smile lit up her face.

He took a good look at her. "What part of Ireland is your father from?"

"County Cork. A little village called Banteen."

"Well, I'll be jiggered!" Dr. Callahan exclaimed. "You are one of the Dalys of Banteen. It's incredible—that's my own home. My father farmed the land and your grandfather worked for him."

He got up and on the phone told his receptionist that he was going on a house call. Kitty stood up to go.

"Come on," Dr. Callahan said, "I'll take you in the car."

When Kitty arrived back home in a car driven by the good-looking doctor, Noni stared in disbelief. Kitty felt rather pleased.

"Where is old Con Daly?" Dr. Callahan asked cheerfully as he came into the hall.

Suddenly Dad's voice roared down from upstairs. "I'll see no doctor. Don't you send that old Scots fella up here."

The young doctor leaped up the stairs and stood in the doorway of Dad's room. "Well, now," he said, "you'll not throw out an Irishman and one of your own kin."

Dad looked at him in astonishment and then peered more closely. "Well, is it Mick Callahan or do me old eyes deceive me?"

"Indeed they do, Con Daly, you old rogue, because I'm his son fresh over from Banteen."

In spite of his shortness of breath, Dad grabbed the young doctor's hand. "Welcome, son. It's like looking at yer father."

The doctor laughed. "Now off with that shirt, we're going to overhaul you," he said.

Kitty watched him examining Dad. It was a liberty no one else had ever been able to take with him before. She was extremely impressed.

When he had finished examining Dad, Dr. Callahan sat on the bed. "You're to take it easy, Con, old man. Why don't you go home? The air is fresh and the beer cheaper." Dad laughed and the two of them chatted about their homeland. Kitty was delighted to see Dad so happy; he loved to talk about Ireland.

Dr. Callahan was a great success and a good doctor. Under his guidance, Kitty nursed Dad back to health. During those weeks, the one bright spot in her life was the visit of Patrick Callahan, who was related by marriage to the Irish Dalys of Banteen. He knew their history from beginning to end, and when he talked about it Kitty would look shyly at him and think how fine he was. Why wasn't she lucky enough to find a man like that? she wondered.

Soon Dad was back in good health and the doctor came no more. Kitty began to think about going home now that there was no reason for her to stay.

"Why don't you stay here, Kitty?" Noni said one day as they washed the breakfast dishes. "Dad likes you around, and there's nothing to keep you up in Suffolk, is there?"

Kitty shook her head. "No, Noni, I've made my own life. I'll never return to this."

"Well, I've got our name down for a council house, which might turn up any day. My Joe's fed up with all the traveling he has to do to and from work, so we may be moving soon." Joe had finally found a job in the car works at Dagenham, which Noni was pleased about.

The sisters had ended up as usual, drinking tea in the kitchen while the baby lay sleeping in the pram in the passage. The older children had gone to school. Kitty looked around at the old cream paint that Bill had put on the walls. No one seemed to be very interested in the house anymore. "But, Noni, you wouldn't leave Dad alone?" she asked anxiously.

"He can come with us if he wants, but you know he won't. It's time you did a bit, Kitty. I've done my share, and now I've got the kids to think of. It's nice and clean out in Dagenham and quite near to Fords. If Dad won't come with us he can stay here," she said. "I'm not going to let him stand in my way."

"I wonder if I could persuade Dad to give up this house and come and live with me," Kitty said thoughtfully.

"You'd be lucky," cried Noni. "He won't budge. He still goes on about it being Bill's house and he won't give it up till Bill comes home."

"Oh, dear," sighed Kitty, "but this house still belongs to Bill, I suppose. I could get a share of it, but I don't want it."

"Dad's a crafty old sod," whispered Noni. "He still gets letters from Bill—I've seen them. He's back from Africa; posted in London, the letters were."

Kitty did not want to hear.

"Oh, well, the sooner he comes and settles up his business," she said, trying to sound casual, "the sooner Dad will have a home with me. As for me, when I find Bill I'll try to divorce him."

"Oh, I don't like that idea at all, Kitty," said Noni. "I don't like it at all."

"Well, now that Dad's on his feet I'd better get back home and see what Melissa is up to."

"Who's looking after her?" Noni asked.

"Oh, she's staying with a friend," lied Kitty. Noni was such a prude and so behind the times in her own ways. She said no more and prepared to go.

Kitty was pleased to be going home after her visit. She did not like the hustle and bustle and dirt of the city or the noise of Noni's children. She would be glad to be back, enveloped by the peace of the country where the fresh air was like new life being forced into her lungs. How sweet it was, she thought. That was where Dad should be. She had to think of some way to get him there.

CHAPTER TWENTY-TWO
Something to Live For

No one was in when Kitty arrived back at the cottage in a taxi, but she knew where to find a key. Inside, she put on the kettle and went on a tour of the cottage. Everything seemed nice and tidy, except, of course, Melissa's room, which was always in a muddle.

Kitty cooked a nice meal and sat down to wait for them. She thought they were probably at a drama rehearsal. After awhile, she heard the car come up the lane. From the window she watched them get out of the car. They seemed to be arguing. Melissa was having one of her tantrums, Kitty decided. She knocked on the window and waved. "Hello, I'm home," she called.

They both turned startled faces toward her and immediately Kitty sensed that something was very wrong. Melissa dashed in through the front door without a greeting and ran upstairs to her room.

"Oh, dear," said Kitty to Leonard as he came in, "something has upset her apple cart. Not you, I hope, Len."

Leonard looked pale, but he gave Kitty a peck on the

cheek. "Had a good journey?" he asked. "How's your dad?"

Kitty thought he looked very nervous.

"He's fine," she said. "I thought you might have dropped me a line, and then I would have answered it and given you all the news.

"Come on, let's eat. Coming down, Melissa?" called Kitty.

There was no response from upstairs.

"No sense in wasting a good steak," said Kitty and served up the meal for Leonard and herself.

"Nothing special happened?" asked Kitty as they ate.

"Nothing important," Leonard answered without looking at her.

"I'll leave you to the washing up," said Kitty. "I'm tired from all the traveling. I might as well go to bed and get up early in the morning."

As Kitty lay in bed that night she was sure she could hear Melissa crying. But she was such an obstinate child that it would not do a bit of good to try and console her. Kitty felt a little hurt. They had made no effort to welcome her; it was as if they did not want to be bothered with her.

Next morning when Kitty rose, both Leonard and Melissa had departed; Melissa to school and Leonard to work. Kitty prowled about the house all day, tidying up and doing the washing and ironing. They did not come home until ten o'clock in the evening, by which time the dinner was spoiled. Kitty was furious. "Might have let me know," she grumbled when they finally appeared.

But Melissa seemed hot and angry. Her blouse was creased, and she stared at Kitty with malevolence. She looked from Kitty to Leonard and suddenly started screaming. "Tell her! Tell her! Because if you don't, I will."

"Tell me what?" asked Kitty, astonished by this outburst.

"Oh, it's nothing," said Leonard, trying to look calm. "It's just that Melissa's in a temper. You know what she's like."

Kitty shrugged and looked at Melissa, whose eyes were wide with rage. "What am I like?" Melissa shouted. "Go on, Len, tell her! What am I like?"

Leonard looked up as though appealing to Melissa. But she rushed at him, shouting and screeching, "You bastard! You slimy bastard you . . . you promised me . . ." She raised her artificial hand to strike him, but Kitty instinctively threw herself between them, receiving a sharp blow that slashed her cheek. Blood poured down her face, but she hardly noticed. "Don't, Melissa!" she yelled. "Whatever's wrong with you?"

"Wrong with me?" the girl shouted hysterically. "It's what's wrong with you. I'm young and you're old. Len belongs to me, not you—you're too low-class. And what's more, I'm not a bit sorry."

Kitty could not say anything; she did not understand.

"He had me, don't you understand?" screamed Melissa, almost beside herself with temper. "He fucked me, if you want it in plain English."

It was a vile word that brought Kitty to her senses. "Why, you little bitch, how dare you use such language." She reached out to slap Melissa for the first time, but Leonard moved between them.

"For goodness sake, don't make matters worse," he said brokenly, "because Kitty, it's the truth."

It was now Kitty's turn to go beserk. "Dear God," she screamed, "do you know what you are saying? She's under age, she's only fourteen. I'll have the bloody law on you."

Melissa just leaned against the wall with a sneer on her face, but she was quivering. Leonard moved over to her. "I'm sorry to let you down, Kitty, but we love each other." He put his arm around Melissa, who put her head on his shoulder and started to weep.

Kitty looked at them for a moment and then ran out into the darkness. She was confused, but what she did

understand she could not face. She sat on the garden
bench and put her head in her hands. It wasn't possible,
she thought. It was the last thing she ever dreamed of.
The blood from her cut cheek mingled with the salt of
her tears as she put her hands over her face to hide
from the world. She crouched down shivering, waiting
anxiously for one of them to come out to ask her
forgiveness, abuse her, anything but ignore her. Still no
one came. She was too chilled to stay out there any
longer and she rose on stiff legs. She decided to go in
and try to come to some terms with them.

As she walked across the grass toward the light of the
cottage, she heard the car doors slam. The engine
started up and the vehicle rushed down the lane past
her, headlights blazing. Kitty caught a glimpse of two
set faces as they left her. "Oh, don't go!" she cried,
trying to run after them. "Let's talk things over," she
shouted, but the mud and gravel from the lane sloshed
over her and they were gone.

"They've left me, they've left me all alone," she
wailed into the darkness as she wandered distractedly
back to the cottage.

For the rest of the night, before she went to bed, she
kept dashing to the window at the slightest sound, but
she knew they were not going to return. Finally, still
weeping, she went up to bed and instantly fell asleep,
blacking out the horror of the events that night.

The next morning she awoke, surprised that she was
very clear-headed about what had happened. As she
made herself breakfast, she thought carefully about the
situation.

It was her own fault, she decided. She should never
have left them alone together. Melissa's schooling had
turned her into a snob, and although it hurt Kitty that
the girl should look down on her and think of her as low
class, Kitty reasoned that she was too young to know
better. Melissa was at an impressionable age and she
had always been fond of Leonard. What was surprising
was that Leonard, who was so hopeless in bed, should

suddenly achieve what he did. Perhaps the whole situation was not so bad after all. Perhaps nothing had really happened; sometimes a teenage girl will lie to get what she wants.

Kitty decided she would wait awhile. They might repent, and, if they got in touch with her, she would try to explain to Melissa that there was a lot more in life for her than a man like Leonard. Maybe Melissa would come back to her without Leonard and they could start again somewhere. That would be even better. Yes, that was it, she would wait to see if they contacted her.

Kitty put a piece of sticking plaster over her cut cheek. Having decided what to do, she felt quite strong. With the faith that Melissa would need her and come back to her, she could get by. She smiled when she realized that she would have some peace and quiet in the cottage for her writing. At least there is a bright side, she thought.

Kitty went back to work in the bar. She was aware that money was going to get short, for Leonard had always given her his wages. But there was only herself to support now.

Each day she walked a mile down the lane to the main road to catch the town bus. Then every night when she came home she looked on the mat for that important letter. But there was no word, not even a sign. The couple had completely disappeared.

Kitty began to get used to the lonely life and kept on with her own writing. The writing group had disbanded for the winter because transport was difficult for most people. When she was not writing, Kitty now spent her spare time reading.

She could not pretend that she was not lonely, but she put on a cheerful face in the bar so no one would know or try to console her. The last thing she wanted was pity. Her pride would not let anyone else know that she lived alone out there in the isolated cottage.

In January a blanket of snow descended on the

countryside so she could not go to work. Every other day she trudged through the snow drifts to the nearest farm where she could buy bread, milk and eggs. So by hook or crook she survived.

She spent many hours during that time staring out of the window at the snow-blanketed fields and the dark, leaden sky. Sometimes she felt safe and secure snowed in like this; other times she had to fight back tears. Occasionally she played Melissa's pop records on the old gramophone, and one night she played "Stardust," humming the tune to cheer herself up. But she became so choked with tears she could not continue.

Each afternoon she settled down to write, determined to finish *The Grass Widows*. She sat up late into the nights, scribbling and typing, filled with a sense of excitement she had never felt before. Into the novel she incorporated the events of her own life as though they had been lived through by Nelly Kelly. She wrote of the sweatshops, and her workmates of so long ago. She wrote of Barry, the hero of the Battle of Britain, and that strange night of love, the sound of air raids, the laughter in the pubs, the battered bodies being dug from out of the debris. Kitty's experience came out fine and clear as never before, but now they were in the life of Nelly Kelly, the grass widow. And because Nelly Kelly was a grass widow whose husband was away throughout the war, Kitty managed to avoid dwelling too much on painful memories of Bill.

She worked solidly on the novel, day and night, for two weeks, until the sun began to shine and melt the snow. By the time the meadows were green again without a trace of snow, Kitty had finished. At last she had completed a real novel.

"Kitty, old gal," she said to herself, "I do believe you have found something that makes life worthwhile."

CHAPTER TWENTY-THREE

An Old Lover

Once the roads were clear again, Kitty returned to work. Every night she still looked for a letter on the mat, but there was nothing from either Leonard or Melissa. She still forced herself to believe that one day there would be. She had to.

She spent much time thinking about her novel. Was it good enough to publish? She did not even know where she might send it because she was not in contact with anyone in the writing group. She decided to ask at the library in the town. Someone was bound to have some addresses there, she thought.

On her next day off she prepared to go into town. She dressed very carefully in a pleated skirt and wool jumper. She pulled a little felt hat well down over her unmanageable chestnut curls and put on the fur jacket she had bought for herself last winter. The finished product looked like a neat suburban housewife off to town on a shopping spree. But Kitty had much greater things on her mind. Just supposing she did become famous? How surprised everyone would be.

Her dreams ran wild as she walked down to the main road. What if her book did get published? She would get some money and be quite independent of everybody. It would be her salvation. Then she would begin another book and write about all the grand folk she had met in her life. Wonderful people like old Nan, who lived sixty years in this lousy world without anyone knowing of her existence. Yes, she, Kitty Daly, would make her live forever. Then there was Dad, lovely old Dad. What a character he was. Oh, yes, she would let the world know that she was here and how she felt about it.

The librarian in town gave Kitty a book with the addresses of all the publishers in London. Sitting at a table, Kitty turned over the pages and felt in awe of this great publishing world. She felt so uneducated; would she be able to stand up to these literary people? She suddenly felt despondent but wrote down a few addresses and left.

She walked down the road roward the bus stop, passing the book shop on her way. A large sign hung in the window: "Signing today. Harold MacGreggor, author of *Blood on the Earth*. Get your personally signed copy."

Inside Kitty could see a queue of women surrounding the author, who sat at a table in the middle of the shop, looking very bored and wearing dark glasses. Kitty decided it would be fun to meet a published author even though she did not like war novels, which, from the look of the jacket, his was. It would be nice to have a signed book, anyway. She went in and bought a copy of *Blood on the Earth* and joined the queue.

As she stood in line she listened to the author chatting to his admirers as he signed their books. She recognized his accent as American, and somehow the man himself looked familiar; but she could not place him.

The queue moved along slowly until it was her turn.

A large brown hand, heavy with signet rings, reached out for her book. Kitty looked at this famous author and gasped. It was Harry Cross. Of course, MacGreggor was his mother's maiden name. There was now no mistaking that rugged exterior. A network of scars around one eye suggested that it had been injured, which was the reason for the dark glasses. Harry obviously recognized her. His hand grabbed hers tight. "My little Kitty Daly! Holy Moses, is it really you? Pru, Pru," he shouted, "come here and take over. I've met someone I know."

A smartly dressed woman who had been sitting at the back of the store came to his side. She looked frostily at Kitty.

"Sorry, ladies," Harry said to the women waiting behind Kitty. "I want a rest. No more signing for awhile." There were a few little murmurs of disappointment, but the queue dispersed.

Harry got up from the seat and lumbered from the table, pulling Kitty with him. They stood in the doorway looking at one another. He looked very much the same, with that big hefty shape, the kind smile and those brown stained teeth from his perpetual cigar smoking. It was indeed old Harry.

"What the hell are you doing up here in this Godforsaken hole?" he demanded. "I thought you lived in London."

"This place is my home now," Kitty replied quietly. "I heard you were injured and I was sure you didn't survive the war. It has given me a bit of a shock to see you alive and kicking."

"Only just, honey," Harry grinned, biting the end of a cigar. "And weren't you supposed to come and see me when I got croaked?" he demanded.

"I did try, but the army cold-shouldered me," she told him.

"Bloody red tape. Mean bastards," announced Harry, "they carved me up and sent me home."

The smart woman was looking very annoyed and started calling Harry, telling him to return to his post.

"That's Pru, my wife," Harry explained. "I'd better go. But Kitty, I'll find you tomorrow."

Kitty hesitated, but he put a pen and pad in her hand. "Go on, honey," he said in his old persuasive manner.

She wrote down her address. Harry grabbed it. "Great," he said. "See you tomorrow evening, honey. Bye-bye."

Kitty walked out holding the book, which had Harry's face grinning at her from the back cover. Tears filled her eyes as she noticed that it had not been signed.

That night Kitty felt lonelier than she had ever been before. She was convinced that Harry had not been sincere. She rose early the next morning and began to make the sitting room look nice. She put daffodils in a blue vase and relaid the log fire. She brought out the drinks tray and polished the glasses. God knows why I'm bothering, she said to herself; he won't come.

She took a bath and set her hair. She was overwhelmed by vivid memories of their week in Scotland when they had both been so carefree. Harry was middle-aged now and Kitty well into her thirties. Also, he had a wife and, by the looks of it, a very possessive one at that.

As much as it would have stimulated her to be wined, dined and made violent love to, her own senses told her she would only be used. Harry would go off back to America and forget her, and she was not going to allow a man to desert her again.

With mixed feelings she prayed that he would not come, but still she made preparations to entertain him. At six o'clock she put on a cocktail dress, brushed out her hair and waited nervously by the window. It was seven o'clock when Harry's big car slowed down at the end of the lane and stopped at her front gate. She watched him climb out of the car and noticed that he limped down the path. Something was wrong with his leg—how dreadful. Was this her big, husky American man? She took a deep breath and went out to meet him.

"I made it," he gasped. "Never thought I would. This must be the last place God made."

"Yes, it is a bit isolated," she smiled.

"Oh, honey," he said warmly, "it's great to see you. And you don't look any older. I can't believe it."

In the sitting room he immediately cuddled her close to him. Kitty was thrilled at his touch, and she liked the expensive smell of his aftershave and the aroma of Havana cigars. He was spontaneously warm, loving and gentle. He was the same old Harry.

"Sit down," she said. "I'll pour some drinks."

He looked about warily. "Where's the old man?" he asked.

"There isn't one," she replied flatly, without looking at him.

"You sure, Kitty? But you were married."

"That's right, but we never got back together after the war," she informed him.

"That might be just as well. But don't tell me no one took my place."

"No, I'm not a good liar." She grinned at him.

He pulled her down onto his lap. "Smart little dolly, pretty as a picture," he said, looking at her with admiration.

Kitty knew that he was hers if she wanted him, even though he had a wife. And so what? Someone had pinched her husband. She put her arms about his neck. "I'm still a free lance," she said. "Shall we go out and get drunk like we used to or stay here?"

He kissed her, but she was surprised that it was not with the old passion. After awhile he said, "Let's go out and find a pub. I still like your English beer."

Kitty felt a sense of disappointment. She got her coat and they went down to the local, where they drank whiskey and talked about old times. Then they talked about his first novel, which had been a great success.

"Couldn't have done it without Pru," he told her. "She was the one who egged me on. I was three years in some bloody disabled hospital. My first wife divorced me, and if it hadn't been for Pru—well, I'd never have survived. She was my support."

Kitty felt very jealous of Pru.

"Don't let me get too sloshed, Kitty," Harry suddenly said. "Pru doesn't like it when I've been drinking, especially over here where they drive on the wrong side of the road."

Kitty sipped her drink thoughtfully. "We'll go home and I'll make some coffee," she said.

Back at the cottage Harry sat by the fire while Kitty put on the coffee. She felt uncomfortable. They seemed to have said all that there was to be said and very little progress had been made.

On the table was Kitty's manuscript, ready to be packed and sent to whichever publisher she chose. Harry picked it up. "What's this, Kitty?" he called to her. "Do I detect a rival?" He began to turn over the pages and read.

"Leave it alone," Kitty called back. "You're not the only celebrity. I might be one next year."

But Harry had gone quiet, engrossed in her typewritten script. Suddenly Kitty heard him burst into roars of laughter. Her face flushed with embarrassment mixed with annoyance. He was laughing at it. She continued to pour out the coffee and put cheese and biscuits on a plate. He had gone silent again.

"Coffee," Kitty announced brightly as she carried the tray into the sitting room. "White or black?"

"Did you write this?" Harry asked, looking up at her.

"You know I did," she said defensively as she put down the tray.

"Kitty, in ten pages you made me laugh. I think it's great." He sounded completely sincere.

"Well, let's hope some publisher will think so, too," she said nonchalantly.

"Is this the first thing you've done?"

"Well, no, I've written short stories, and one of them was published in a magazine."

"Let me take this to read," Harry said excitedly. "If I can do something with it I will."

"No! I can't part with it, it's my baby." Kitty was panicked, and almost tearful.

"Well, I know how you feel, but honestly, I'm amazed. I remember how we used to discuss the fact that you wanted to write. I guess that was why we were so akin to each other. Kitty, that was the most wonderful affair of my life. I never ever forgot you. But now it's too late for us. I'm a bloody old crock, let's face it. See this?" He pulled up his trouser leg to display the artificial limb. "Cut my bloody leg off, they did."

"Oh, poor Harry." Kitty sat beside him and kissed him on the cheek.

"Kitty, darling, as much as I still want you, I can never make love to another woman. Pru understands me, looks after me. That's all I'm bloody fit for. All we have left, honey, is sweet memories. Do you remember the Roman Camp and Jessie and Annie?"

"Very well," she said, suddenly remembering the stupendous view of the loch from that little guesthouse.

"So, honey, that's how it is," he continued. "We must keep in touch; I'll write to you from the States." He cuddled her closer. "I'd better get on my way or Pru will get worried. Goodbye, darling." He picked up the manuscript again. "Let me read it, Kitty. I'll send it back, and if I can do anything with it, I will."

Kitty hesitated. "All right, then," she suddenly said,

surprised to find that she wanted him to read it. She helped him on with his coat. "Mind how you drive," she said softly.

Harry went out into the night and Kitty was left alone once more. She felt sorry for poor Harry. None of his fame would give him back his virility, and only Kitty knew about that.

CHAPTER TWENTY-FOUR

An Ultimate Decision

One Saturday morning Kitty awoke to the sound of tapping. She listened carefully. All the usual sounds were there: lowing cows, singing birds, rustling trees. This was an extra noise. She got out of bed and put on her dressing gown to go to the window to investigate, but before she got there, the sound of a human voice startled her. She peered out of the window into the front garden.

Two men were there erecting a notice board just inside the front gate. In large red letters it read: "For Sale. Apply to Pope & Son, Town Road, Yarmouth."

Kitty's mouth fell open in astonishment. They wouldn't, she thought, they simply couldn't sell the house over her head. It must be some kind of mistake. It had to be. Forgetting the cold, she went out to tackle the men.

"What's all this?" she said, marching up to them. "This place isn't for sale."

The men turned to look at her with placid expressions on their faces.

"You had better consult the estate agent," one of them said. "We're only doing a job that we get paid to do. He's the bloke who organized it."

Kitty was furious with indignation. "Take it down immediately!" she cried.

"Sorry, lady, we would only have to come back and put it back up. Do you have a phone?" he asked.

Kitty shook her head.

"Well, you'd better go into town and see the agent. We've done our part. Come on, Jim." Having secured the post, they both got into their van and drove away.

Kitty stood in her long red dressing gown looking at the board. It was horrible. Facts began to sink in. Leonard had actually put the cottage up for sale without even consulting her. The bastard, she thought. Well, he will never get away with it, she decided. She had invested more than five hundred pounds in modernizing the cottage, so she had a right to be consulted. No, he was not going to get away with that.

Rapidly, she dressed. She was due to work at the bar in the evening, but there was plenty of time to visit the estate agent.

As she sat in the slow country bus into town she had a heavy feeling in her heart. She could not believe that Leonard could try such a dirty trick on her.

The agent was extremely polite but not very cooperative. "All I can tell you is that our client lives in the southwest. He does own the property, we presume," he said to Kitty.

"Well, I suppose so," she said. "His grandfather left it to him."

"If you are his lawful wife you have every right to reside there, but you can't stop him selling it."

Kitty blushed. "We only lived together," she explained, "but I paid to have it modernized and shared the costs of running it."

The agent looked away as if embarrassed for her. "Well, madam, all I can advise you to do is to consult a solicitor, because unless you're a legal sitting tenant there is very little you can do."

"Where is he?" she demanded. "Give me his address."

"Sorry," he said coldly, "I cannot divulge a client's address if he does not want me to."

"Oh, blast him," she said and, picking up her coat, marched out.

She ate her lunch at a self-service restaurant, trying to pluck up enough courage to consult a lawyer or at least get some advice. But from whom? She was totally alone up there, and she had not one loyal friend. She had devoted most of her time and energy to the comfort and well-being of Leonard and Melissa. Now they had deserted her and did not even have enough courage to face her. She thought that perhaps Leonard would write and explain his reasons. If he did that, she decided, she would find herself a flat in town. And he could give her some compensation—after all, he would get a good price for the property. One thing she was sure of, and that was that no one was coming in to view it until Leonard came clean and brought Melissa home. She would get all the locks changed and bolt and bar the windows. She would stick to her guns and stay put until she got her way.

The news of Leonard's intentions with the cottage shocked Kitty quite considerably, despite her resolution not to give in. She found herself getting depressed very easily, particularly when she thought about Harry. She was now convinced that she should never have allowed him to take away the manuscript of her precious novel. She felt empty without it and could not begin writing anything else. She kept waiting to hear some news from him, but none came.

The local newspaper had printed a big picture of Harry with Pru beside him at the bookshop signing. The article stated that he was on his way back to the

States after a successful tour of Britain. Kitty's mouth
twisted as she thought how much more successful
Harry would have liked to have been, that big American G.I. with a taste for warm women. He might
remember her when he got home, but she was sure that
his smart woman would make sure it wasn't for long.

She plodded back and forth to work, hating it more
and more each time she went. There were constant
rows in the bar, and Kitty had taken a dislike to the new
manageress, a tall, long-nosed girl called Olga. She was
very bossy and reminded Kitty of her old enemy,
Sylvia, who had worked with her in one of the sweatshops. Kitty and Olga argued frequently and flung
abusive remarks at one another when they clashed, but
generally Kitty tried to stay out of Olga's way.

The holiday season had begun early that year because the weather was warm. The bar was extremely
busy as the day-trippers poured in; day trips and factory
outings were the order of the day. Sometimes the heat
and the noise of the bar were more than Kitty could
stand, and she lost her bright humor that had charmed
the customers in the past. She found the working-class
lads who were out on a spree the worst problem when
work was over, and she had to stand a long time on the
promenade waiting for that last bus home. The late
night revelers would push past her, off to the fun-fair
after the pubs had shut. They went along singing and
laughing, arms around their girlfriends. Kitty would
feel a strange detachment from them. Sometimes a lad
would stop and say, "Come on, pretty girl, come with
us." But a cold, haughty look was all he received,
though Kitty would have loved to go to those bright
lights, to ride on the merry-go-round. On these occasions she would recall her honeymoon night when Bill
and she got sufficient excitement from two beers and a
walk on the promenade. Those had been different
times, when they had had very little and did not even
worry about it.

When she got off the bus, Kitty would walk down the

lane to the cottage in darkness, her heart in her mouth. If someone attacked her, she thought, who would know? She always arrived at the front door breathless with fear and hurrying on legs that had ached even before she had started for home.

The cottage no longer seemed friendly to her. Kitty would lie awake at night thinking about how much she used to love the place and how it had inspired her writing. Now she did not even have the energy to write in her journal. She had lost all enthusiasm for life.

After several weeks of restless nights Kitty became very jaded, so she paid one of her very infrequent visits to the doctor. The doctor told her she was working too hard. "Take a holiday," he said.

"Can't afford it just yet," she informed him. "I might at the end of the season."

"Well, there's nothing else wrong with you. In fact, I find you extremely healthy. I'll give you some sleeping pills. Take one at night and stop taking them as soon as you feel you can sleep well without them."

Kitty took the pills home with her, but she did not take them; she did not like the idea of them. Instead she took a bottle of whiskey back with her one night and found that it did the trick. She went to bed tiddly with a feeling that nothing really mattered much anymore.

One day Kitty received one of Noni's morose letters in which she complained that Dad got on her nerves and that she was once more pregnant. She wrote that Joe was playing up and often missed the last train home and stayed out all night. She added that she would be very glad when she got that council house.

Reading this news, Kitty felt very little sympathy for her sister. She sighed and put the letter away. She was in no mind to answer it; she had enough troubles of her own at present.

A few days later there was a bad incident in the bar that upset her. A coachload of football fans had arrived very drunk. They were on their way home to the

Midlands after seeing a successful match. At first they were just a little rowdy and kept to their corner. Also in the bar was a party of young men on a day trip, most of them Irish. A lad played a guitar and sang their own songs. One of them had red hair, just like Dad's, and Kitty could not help admiring his fresh round face and wide smile.

Kitty stood behind the counter listening as he sang Irish songs in a strong, expressive voice. They soothed her and reminded her so much of her own old home and the Irish parties.

Suddenly the football fans interrupted the singing with their loud cries and rude songs. The Irish boys tried to ignore them and went on listening to their pal.

The guv'nor groused and grumbled. "There's going to be trouble, I can feel it in my bones. It's those bloody Irish boys. There's no stopping them once they start."

Kitty was vivid with rage at his comment. "Why are you so bigoted? Those boys are entitled to make as much noise as those bloody football fans."

"Oh, dear," sneered Olga, listening in, "forgot we have one here. If Kitty gets her Irish rage out you had better watch it, boss."

"You mind your own bloody business," retorted Kitty. "Ignorant bitch. I don't suppose you ever believed in anything."

"I can do without your insults," returned Olga. "You're getting like some crotchety old maid."

"Nuts," said Kitty and turned back to listen to the minstrel boy, who was now singing a rebel song in a defiant tone. It was the well-known ballad of Kevin Barrie. "Do not hang me like a dog," he sang. "What I did, I did for Ireland."

As she listened to the words of the song, Kitty was overcome with feelings of nostalgia for the past, not only her own but also of all the Irish. She could hear the cries from battles between the Irish and the British. She suddenly felt patriotic for Ireland, her family's land.

Her trance was broken by Olga's nasty, high-pitched

voice as she nagged away to a customer. "Bloody
sauce, singing that. They were never on our side. Me
sailor brother used to tell me how they sheltered the
U-boats in the Irish ports. Many of our lads went down
over that lot."

Kitty felt sick, but she had no time for anything as a
bottle was suddenly hurled across the room, striking
the singer on the head as he almost reached the last
note.

"Do the Irish bastards!" the football fans yelled a
familiar cry from Kitty's youth, and the two parties
plunged into battle.

Safe behind the counter, with tears in her eyes, Kitty
watched them all fighting. She had seen so many such
battles as a child in the back streets of Hoxton.

Soon the police were on the scene and the fight was
broken up. Some of the lads from both sides were
carted off in a black maria. Everybody left in the bar
chattered excitedly about the incident, but Kitty just
finished her chores, pale and silent. In her mind she
could still hear the boy singing, "Do not hang me like a
dog. What I did, I did for Ireland."

Never before had she realized how Irish she really
was and how close to her own kind. This world was a
lousy place, hardly worth struggling to survive in. Dad
had given her faith instilled with patriotism for a
country that was not really her own. She had thought
about it before. She recalled how she had knelt with
Noni and Bobby each evening while Dad said the
rosary beads. Then he would instruct them to pray for
the soul of Michael Collins or some other patriot about
to be hung. Were they all murderers? Kevin Barrie, in
that lonely prison cell—did he deserve his punishment?
Were they right, or had poor old Dad got his priorities
all mixed up?

As she sat on the late bus home that night she tried to
push the face and voice of that minstrel boy from her
mind, but she was not successful. When she reached
home, she took the rest of the bottle of whiskey up to

bed with her without troubling to light the boiler. She lay on her bed in her coat, pouring out one glass of whiskey after another. When the bottle was almost empty she laid down her head and tried to sleep, but she could not. Suddenly she remembered the sleeping pills in her handbag. She washed one down with the rest of the whiskey, and a haunting sadness welled up inside her. No one wanted her, no one really loved her. She had been deserted by both Bill and Melissa—the two people who had meant the most to her. She was thirty-eight years old and her life was practically over; she might as well hurry it on. She put a handful of pills into her palm and swallowed the lot.

Her mind became blank as dark despair took over. The room seemed to get very cold and dark. As she lay with her eyes open, unable to move, a vision appeared before her. It was of Leonard's grandparents standing over her, shaking their heads as if to say no. Never had she even imagined them so clearly; she could see the wrinkles on their faces and the veins in their hands. No, no, they seemed to say firmly, shaking their white-haired heads.

An atmosphere of the past enveloped Kitty as she hovered between two worlds, but an unconscious force within her suddenly shook her. She sat up, startled. Despite her drowsiness she was horrified at what she had done. She hurled herself out of bed onto the floor and tried to stumble to the door, but her legs crumpled beneath her. Oh, dear God, she thought, she had to get downstairs, get some salt water, make herself sick, keep moving. This was a mortal sin, against all Dad's teaching. Oh, what would it do to him if he found out? She crawled along out of the bedroom on her hands and knees, almost throwing herself down the stairs, and pulled herself into the kitchen.

Got to be sick. That would do the trick. She poured salt into a cup, held it under the running tap, threw back her head and gulped it down. Most of the liquid came back again, so once more she filled the cup with salt and water and swallowed it. Then she put her finger down her throat to make herself sick. Her stomach turned, she retched and vomited, hanging weakly onto the edge of the sink. Slowly she slid to the floor as faintness overcame her. Vomit and urine poured from her; she had no power to control herself.

"Oh, please, God, help, be merciful," she cried. She lapsed into unconsciousness, lying under the sink.

The morning sunlight lit up the room, streaming beams onto Kitty, who still lay prone on the kitchen floor. The warmth on her face made her stir. She came slowly back to consciousness. She felt cold and stiff and her lips were dry. Slowly she sat up and was filled with horror as she looked down at the vomit on her clothes. She realized that she had lain all night in this mess. She felt ashamed and degraded.

She tried to rise but felt too weak. She had to get up to the bathroom and clean herself. How disgusting; how could she get into such a low state? She had to get up, go on living, become a human being once more. She staggered toward the stairs, but on each step she felt the little energy she had leaving her. She grabbed the banister and prayed a little prayer that her father had taught her: "Hail Mary, full of grace." Slowly she heaved herself up one stair. Gradually she conquered the floating feeling. A little rest and another prayer: "Oh, dear God, I am sorry for my sins."

Halfway up. Would she make it or topple backward to the tiled floor below? She said the first prayer she had ever learned, concentrating on each word as her dry lips tried to form them. "Oh, sacred heart of Jesus, I implore daily, love me more and more."

Very gradually she got to the top landing and crawled into the bathroom, where she put her head under the cold tap. Gasping for breath, she silently repeated the prayer as a voice inside urged her not to give in.

It worked. Slowly her sanity returned to her. She felt

exhausted. Then she ran a hot bath, stripped off her
filthy clothes, poured lots of bath salts into the water
and sank into the perfumed warmth.

At midday she came down, clean and fresh but very
pallid. She made a cup of coffee and sat down to think.
She was very shaken by what she had done, but one
thing was certain: she had to get out of this sad place
with all its memories. Otherwise, there was no knowing
where she would end.

She looked out of the window at the grim "For Sale"
notice by the front gate. Let them sell it, she thought
angrily, and be damned. She was going home.

"Dad," she said out loud, "here I come. I'm coming
home. Not one more night will I spend here alone."

The door at 8 Billington Road was open when she
arrived. She stood in the doorway with her suitcases
and smiled. She was home. The house was strangely
quiet, and she wondered where everyone was. At that
moment Dad came pottering out of the front room. He
saw her immediately and, without saying a word, held
out his arms to her as though she were a little girl.

"Oh, Daddy, Daddy, I've come home." Kitty rushed
to him and wept on his shoulder, on his greasy cardigan
that still carried the familiar smells of rum and tobacco.
She felt safe for the first time in many days.

"Good, good gel," Dad muttered as he patted her
back. It was almost as though he had expected her.
"Now, what about a nice cup of tea?"

She sat in the kitchen while he filled a big mug with
weak tea. She began to take note of the surroundings.
The kitchen seemed clean and quite neat. The woodwork had been repainted and there was new wallpaper
of pink roses climbing up a green trellis. Where was
Noni? Where were the kids?

She walked into the dining room. It was quite bare,
but clean and neat. What was the difference about the
house? It was more like it used to be. Cups were

hanging in a tidy row, the fire was laid ready for the evening and there was no noise at all.

"Where's Noni?" she asked, wondering if something dreadful had happened.

"I was going to write and tell you," Dad replied. He suddenly became very fidgety.

"Dad, where is Noni? And who did all this redecorating?"

Dad still did not answer, but she noticed a twinkle in his eye and a smile on his lips. A shadow blocked the doorway. Kitty turned her head slowly. It was Bill, standing in his shirt sleeves and looking very much at home. "Welcome home, Kitty," he said gently.

Kitty was speechless for a second. She suddenly felt very alarmed and looked angrily at Dad. "Why didn't you warn me?" she demanded. "I suppose Noni got her council house." She was completely off her guard and hardly knew what to say or do.

"Yes," said Dad. "It's a fine house, and Bill and I get on well enough together here. Now you're home again, Kitty, things will all come right."

Kitty turned her back on Bill and glared at Dad, her eyes glistening with tears. "I'll stay tonight," she said, "but I'll look for somewhere else tomorrow."

"Indeed you won't," roared Dad. "Bill's your lawful husband. Now, gel, you be sensible and settle down." With that he stormed off into the garden.

Bill went over to her and put a gentle hand on Kitty's arm. "There's no need to decide now, Kitty," he said gently. "There's room for all. I've been getting the place straightened just in case it was necessary to sell it. Please stay awhile, just to give yourself time to think things over."

Kitty looked at him with soulful eyes. Bill's tall frame had filled out and matured since she last saw him. His blue eyes shone brightly from his open face and his whole presence suggested dependability and strength. Suddenly, she wanted him to hold her tight in his arms so that she would feel really secure. But, instead, he just said. "Come on, let's go and sit down. I've lit the fire."

At first Kitty thought Bill was being cool toward her, and she felt hostile and answered his questions stiffly. But he was very talkative and warm toward her. Before long, they were talking about the old times and Kitty began to relax.

"Do you remember when we moved here and lost the cats?" Bill said.

Kitty smiled and almost giggled. "Oh, yes, and that chap brought them all back in a big sack and then tipped them out onto the floor. They were so distressed; I called him every name under the sun."

They both started to laugh as they remembered the occasion. Kitty suddenly did feel at home. All those things had happened here in this house, so many years ago. As they relaxed by the fire, Dad crept back in, smoking his pipe and looking very pleased with himself.

"I'm doing the cooking tonight," said Bill brightly. "Coming to help me, Kitty?"

He cooked eggs and bacon and Kitty made a pot of tea and cut and buttered the bread.

"It's like old times," said Bill. "But don't let Dad rush you into any decision you might regret, Kitty. As far as I'm concerned all is forgiven and forgotten. Now it's up to you to decide if you can forgive me."

"Oh, Bill," said Kitty, "even though I was angry at first, you don't know how good it was to see you standing there. It was as if the last years were just a nightmare."

Bill put his arms around her and pressed a gentle kiss on her lips. "I hope we can start again, Kitty. In fact, I've always hoped so."

"I can if you can," she said more cheerfully. "Now, come on, let's get this supper on the table."

That first night, Kitty slept downstairs on the settee.

"Don't rush me, Bill," she had said. "Let me make up my own mind."

"Of course, darling. Isn't that what we both agreed?"

The next day she and Bill went for a long walk together. She felt very close to him but still was not quite sure about her decision. "Tell me, Bill," she asked at last. "why didn't you divorce me and marry that girl who had your child?"

Bill looked sad. "It's a long story, Kitty, but I was being taken for a ride. I discovered it wasn't my baby. Afterward, I went to Africa to work and lived like a monk there. I was so confused, it didn't matter. I couldn't divorce you because I loved you and I felt I had done you such a wrong I didn't dare approach you. Anyway, I heard you were doing all right. But I couldn't let you go. It was your dad who persuaded me to come back to the house.

"Even before I got involved with May—that girl—I didn't realize how much I was affected by the war and army life. I just found it impossible to talk to you when I was home on leave. I used to hate myself for criticizing you in the way I did, but I couldn't help myself. Somehow, seeing you coping with all the difficulties of life in London made me feel ashamed of my protected position in the army. Compared with what you were having to struggle with, I felt my life was so easy—I just did what I was told and was clothed, fed and housed in return.

"When I came home after being a prisoner, I still felt guilty, I still thought you had the worse lot. And I took my feelings out on you. I know I was selfish about your wanting a baby, and I refused to understand your feelings about Melissa. . . ."

Kitty was listening intently. She had never heard Bill talk so openly before.

"I could not bring myself to tell you how much I loved you," continued Bill. "Instead, I acted destructively by being cold toward you and, finally, getting mixed up with May and her scheming mother." He stopped short and sighed. "Even now I can't really explain why I behaved like that. I just know that I love you and that I have all these years."

Kitty stopped and took his hand. "It looks like we have both discovered what life's all about," she said softly.

"You are my girl, Kitty," said Bill, hugging her close, "and I can honestly say that no one ever replaced you."

The power of his body almost overwhelmed her. Inside, Kitty was singing. She was overcome with happiness. Bill was her man—she knew that now after all those years in between. The hard shell she had built around herself for so long was slowly cracking and crumbling away. Even if it had taken both of them all these years to realize that they were meant to be together, it did not matter. They were together now and she was content. "I'll stay with you tonight," she whispered.

CHAPTER TWENTY-FIVE
Just One Thing Missing

Kitty was very happy with Bill. They had both matured over the years. They were much more tolerant of each other and their relationship was full of affection. But despite this, a sense of dissatisfaction still nagged at Kitty. There was something else she felt she should be doing. What a waste, she thought, this overpowering desire to scribble, to write a great novel, to be known in the world for her own wonderful achievement. She had to conquer it, she felt, to avoid the big disappointments that a writing career was likely to bring. She remembered how excited she had been when she reached the end of her first full novel. She was bitter now that she had allowed Harry to take it away. He had never even bothered to return it or acknowledge her efforts. She went about her housework, simply refusing to allow herself to dream up stories as she used to do. But the boredom of routine domestic chores choked her and she could feel herself becoming very tense.

Bill was like a young husband again, bringing home little bits of china and furniture to brighten the home.

Every weekend he painted and plastered, sawed and sanded wood and made a dreadful mess for Kitty to clear up on Monday.

Dad seemed happy and went out to the pub only on Saturdays. He liked Kitty to sit with him in the afternoons and chat about the good old days.

Dutifully, Kitty complied with the requests of her men. She fed them, washed their clothes, cleaned and made the home comfortable. Dad puffed clouds of black shag smoke into the air and Kitty would sit facing him while they talked. To try to relieve her nervous tension she had taken up knitting, which she loathed and was not very good at, though she did manage to make a few badly shaped jumpers for Noni's kids. Often she thought of Leonard and Melissa and wondered if they ever thought of her.

The first Christmas after Kitty's return home they all went down to visit Noni, who was now well installed in the community in Dagenhan. Many Catholic families from Ireland had settled there so that the menfolk could work at the Ford car factory.

It was like the old days at Noni's. She had a nicely furnished front room and invited all her neighbors in for a drink. Joe played his bagpipes, Dad sang his rebel songs and they jigged, shouted and drank to their hearts' content. Everyone made a fuss of Bill and he reveled in it, but still Kitty felt a little lonely; she was not sure why.

She went up to the bedrooms to sit with the children. Noni's last child, a little girl, needed changing, and Kitty attended to her. The other three children sat on the bed talking excitedly as they examined their Christmas presents. Then she knew what was wrong. She knew it was the pleasure and comfort of children that she was missing. Casey was a big sturdy boy, Josie dark and petite with long plaits and bonny, lively Shaun was a real little demon. The baby was so sweet and tiny. She was just the kind of doll-like infant Kitty would have wanted herself. How she envied Noni.

Kitty tucked in the children and told them stories. She rocked the baby to sleep and then fell asleep herself beside them. That was how Bill found her in the morning. He had slept off his booze in an armchair and had had enough of festivities.

"It's a fine family Noni has," Dad said on the train home.

"Yes," replied Kitty, "that baby is beautiful. She reminds me of the fairies, small and sweet with a kind of mystery."

"Oh, Kitty, darling," said Bill, "you have a strange way of expressing yourself, but don't cry for the moon."

Dad retired from the conversation and Kitty felt glum and depressed.

Next day she said to Bill, "Do you think thirty-nine is too old to have a child?"

He looked at her with a slow smile. "Stop dreaming, Kitty, just get on with life. We only just got back together again, and it's probably too late for you. It would be dangerous now. But if you are to be childless, don't mope about it, darling. It's not the end of the world."

Kitty was annoyed by Bill's pessimism. "Bill, it's either now or never. Can't you understand how much a child would mean to me? I want one so much."

The defiance in Kitty's eyes made Bill hesitate. "All right, darling," he said gently. "We can try—but you must talk to a doctor first before we consider it seriously. I don't want you harmed."

Kitty jumped up and kissed Bill hard on the mouth. "Everything will be okay—you'll see."

Dr. Callahan came the next day to visit Dad. He often came in the afternoons to chat about Ireland. Kitty took him aside to ask his advice about the possibility of her having a baby.

"Well, Kitty," the doctor said, "I can't advise you professionally, not unless I give you an examination."

"Oh, no, I don't want that," Kitty exclaimed quickly.

Dr. Callahan smiled, for he knew how Kitty liked him. "I'll give you the address of a woman doctor if you like—she's a friend of mine. And, incidentally, I don't think thirty-nine is necessarily too old. Although there are more risks, I know of many women who have had healthy children at that age with no complications."

Dr. Callahan's friend was a small, lively Scot, an efficient and friendly woman who made Kitty relax immediately. Kitty was examined carefully by the doctor, and then she had further examinations at the hospital.

The doctor's final verdict was optimistic. "I think that you are quite healthy enough to bear children," she said, "but it seems that when you had your stillborn child the fallopian tubes became twisted. It is only a matter of adjustment and a minor operation if you decide to have it done."

"You mean I have to go into hospital?" asked Kitty nervously.

"It would only be a matter of a few days," the doctor reassured her.

"I'll have to think about it," said Kitty.

When Kitty consulted Bill about having an operation, he was definitely against it.

"No, Kitty, forget about children. If it means having an operation, it's not worth it. At your age an operation might be dangerous. I don't want you to risk it."

"Don't be such a coward," Kitty said miserably. "But if that's how you feel, Bill, it's not much good me bothering."

So the subject was dismissed and Kitty went on with her domestic chores. She got back to her reading habits and spent most afternoons lying on the settee reading the latest novels.

Bill went off to work each day at eight o'clock. After working for Lever Brothers on the ground-nut scheme in Africa, he had been promoted and now worked for them at the head office. He liked his work and was very careful with money. He had a box for rates, a box for holidays and another box for house repairs. He was in charge of all the finances, which frustrated Kitty. Apart from household goods, she had no idea of what anything cost.

Despite their little arguments about money, Kitty and Bill led a settled and happy life. The house was greatly improved, clean and freshly painted, and the furniture had been repaired and cleaned after the assault Noni's family had made upon it. Kitty had wanted to go out and buy bright, modern furniture; she hated drab-looking things around her. But Bill had been against it. "There's no point in it, Kitty. The money is better saved for a rainy day. All that modern furniture is rubbish; nothing like the good old stuff made when the workers put their minds to the job."

Kitty just sighed and continued to polish the old furniture and make bright covers for the three-piece suite, trying not to think about the shops full of very nice modern things.

Their neighbors were still mostly Jewish families who had lived there since before the war. They were friendly and gossipy. But Kitty often longed for some special companion of her own. The women went by in twos and threes, pushing prams or walking children. Their lives seemed so full and they were always laughing and joking with each other. She felt distant from them.

Kitty kept her nose to the grindstone in the way that Bill expected her to. She did the much-hated housework and tried to be careful when she shopped. She never indulged herself with afternoon pictures or stopped for a cup of tea as most young housewives did. Her life was dull but bearable.

Postwar London was changing. High-rise blocks were being rapidly built and many black immigrants came over from the Commonwealth countries to work on the buses and in the hospitals. Television, the new invention, was making its way into many homes, and

Kitty decided she wanted one, too. At first Bill insisted that they could not afford it, but Kitty was persistent.

"It will be so nice for Dad. It'll keep him company in the afternoons and evenings," she would declare.

"All right, Kitty," Bill finally said, "let's see how much money is in the box at Christmas."

Kitty was annoyed. "It seems that everything we acquire is done the hard way," she complained to Dad.

"Bill is a careful fellow, Kitty," Dad replied. "You should be very grateful. I'm happy because I know you'll never be in want."

"That's tomorrow," grumbled Kitty. "What about today?"

"I'll try to persuade Bill to get a television if it will please you, but I don't go much on these newfangled ideas. It will destroy me old eyes to sit peering at that thing all day. I likes me wireless."

After much debate the television arrived, and, regardless of his eyes, Dad sat watching it most of the time. With Dad occupied, Kitty had more time to herself during the day. Soon she began her writing again, hidden away in her bedroom. She wrote romance tales based on true stories she read about in the papers, and when she finished one she just stuck it in the suitcase and started another. She loved writing them and she found them easier and easier to do. As long as she had a few hours for writing each day, she could cope with the housework.

It was during that winter that Kitty began to feel very ill. She had lots of trouble with her periods; they were very heavy and extremely painful. Finally, she went to see her woman doctor again.

"You'll have to have a D and C, I'm afraid," the doctor said. "It's nothing serious, but if you want to have good health in middle age you'll have to go and have something done about it."

Kitty was alarmed, but she thought that if a D and C—whatever that was—would take away her pain, she was willing to go into hospital. So a few weeks before Christmas she spent two weeks in the local hospital. Bill came to see her every evening, bringing huge bunches of flowers, fruit and chocolates. Kitty actually loved all the attention; it had given her a new lease on life. To her delight, the surgeon had also managed to straighten out her fallopian tubes and he told her that there was now no reason why she should not become a mother. She kept this secret from Bill; she was so afraid that Bill might not want a family at all.

She decided to go regularly to church to light a candle to the Virgin and pray for a child. As soon as she could get out of bed, she was off to the hospital chapel offering up her prayers to God to make her a good wife, a good daughter and, most of all, a mother.

Two months later Kitty missed her period. She was overjoyed. After all this time, her dream had come true. She was to be a real mother again, at last.

She did not tell Bill the news until after she had been to the doctor. She was not sure of how he might react when she did tell him, but she was fairly confident that he would be pleased.

Bill was at first astonished when she revealed her secret. He looked half-awed. "But how's that possible?" he asked. "I thought the doctor said you wouldn't be able to get pregnant unless you had a special operation."

Kitty smiled knowingly at him. Her green eyes sparkled. Her face radiated happiness. "They fixed it when I had that D and C," she said.

Bill was silent for a second, then his face broke into a broad smile. "Really?" he asked incredulously.

As Kitty nodded, Bill swept up her small frame in his arms. "Oh, darling," he said between kisses. "I'm delighted for both of us. And I'm even glad that you didn't tell me until now—I don't know if I could have handled it." He nuzzled her hair. "I am happy, Kitty, but I'm still worried in case anything happens to you."

Kitty laughed. "Nothing is going to happen this time," she said firmly, looking him straight in the eye, "either to me or the baby."

Kitty decided early on to have the child at home, even though both Bill and the doctor were very against it.

"There may well be complications at your age," the doctor said. "But I can't force you to go into hospital, and you have a very determined little body."

Bill was still concerned for her life. "Oh, Kitty," he said, "I'm so worried. You're such a sprat, and they do say that small women have a terrible time. I'm so scared I'll lose you. I want nothing to change our life."

"Don't be silly," Kitty scoffed. "I know it won't be easy at my age, but I can assure you I'll know all about it this time. Before, I was like a babe in arms, absolutely bloody ignorant. Anyway, my mother had all her children at home, so why can't I?"

Kitty read all the books on childbirth, attended prenatal clinics regularly and told her doctor that she wanted her to preside at the birth of the child. She did not mind, she said, if she had to pay privately; she had no faith in that welfare clinic after the death of her first baby. For a fee the doctor agreed to attend and Kitty also provided for a state-registered midwife.

Once she had settled the details, Kitty went very happily into her pregnancy. She ate well and became very fat, particularly as Dad would insist on her drinking half a pint of Guinness each day. At first she rebelled at the idea, but she soon got used to that thick, sweet taste and began to enjoy it.

Bill was always worried. He did lots of overtime and started another savings box for the maternity expenses. Kitty, however, was placid and happy; she had not one ache or pain. The baby was due at the end of February, but Kitty was still waiting by the first week in March. Those last weeks seemed tedious, and she was determined not to get alarmed.

"Well, it will now be St. Patrick's Day, and that's for sure," said Dad. "It'll be a double celebration. We'll wet the baby's head and celebrate old St. Paddy at the same time."

Noni had kindly sent a whole lot of used baby clothes, but Kitty knew she would never use them for the baby. Her baby would wear only the best and finest—no secondhand gear for her or him.

It was March 10th and a Sunday morning when Kitty went into labor. For two days she was in agony. The doctor popped in and out of the house and Bill ran about nervously. The small house in Billington Road positively vibrated with excitement the day Kitty's and Bill's son was finally born. Dad stood at the gate giving a minute-by-minute account to the neighbors. Bill hid himself down at the bottom of the garden, unable to endure the loud yells that Kitty sent forth as the healthy ten-pound boy came slowly from her body.

Kitty ached inside. It was her greatest desire to have a lovely, healthy baby all of her own, and he looked as if he were already a month old.

"My, my," announced the doctor as she weighed him, "no wonder he was so difficult. Ten pounds, five ounces."

Kitty lay back, woozy with gas. She was only semi-conscious. Everything seemed too good to be true.

"What are you going to call him?" the kindly midwife asked.

Kitty's mind drifted to and fro. "I'd like to call him Kevin Barrie," she said dreamily, "but they say he was a murderer."

"Goodness gracious!" cried the doctor. "Don't name him after a murderer."

"But it's not true," muttered Kitty.

"Could be," said the doctor, going briskly about her tasks. "Still, Kevin seems all right to me. It has a Celtic flavor," she added with a smile.

Kitty slowly recalled Barry MacFarlane, the fighter pilot. No, this is Bill's child, she thought; she couldn't give him the name of Barry. "Well, Kevin Cornelius then, like me dad," said Kitty. "My mind is made up." She dropped off to that peaceful, contented sleep that follows childbirth.

A few minutes later Bill dashed in. When he saw Kitty lying so still, his knees went weak. He was sure she was dead.

"She's fine, just fallen asleep," said the doctor. "She was tired; it's been a long labor. Here's your son all clean and respectable." She handed him the little white bundle and Bill's blue eyes glowed with pride and happiness. "Look at him—he looks like a prize-fighter."

Dad crept up behind to view his grandson, hat in hand. "He's a fine big boy, be a six-footer when he's growed," he said jubilantly.

"Now, out you both go and let his mum sleep," said the doctor, taking the child.

Bill pressed a kiss onto Kitty's brow and crept out behind Dad.

Downstairs the whiskey bottle was opened and the neighbors took a drink while Dad told them of his fine big grandson. Bill sat dreaming of the great things he would do for his son.

When Kitty woke up Bill took her a cup of tea and sat on the bed. "Thank you for my son, darling. All those years I kept putting off us having a child, I didn't know what I was missing. It's all been worth it, but I could never go through all that again."

Kitty smiled sleepily. "The doctor says they've never lost a father yet."

CHAPTER TWENTY-SIX

A New Career

Kitty soon settled down with her new baby son and was very content. All thoughts and dreams took a back seat, and, for the time, she was completely taken up with Kevin, nicknamed Kiki by his proud granddad.

The summer passed and winter came once more. Fires were lit, and inside the house was cozy and warm. Kiki rolled about on the rug with Dad's watchful eye on him. Life for Kitty was wonderful; never had she been so conscious of her great attachment to her family. It matured her. She put on a little weight, but the dimples came back into her cheeks and she found herself smiling her way through life as she had done in her teens.

Bill was working long hours, saving up to buy a car. He now had another box marked S.F.C.

"What's that for?" Kitty asked when she first saw it.

"Saving for a car," Bill informed her.

"Who wants a car?" she demanded indignantly. "There's much more needed around here than a bloody car."

"Oh, don't grouse, Kitty," Bill pleaded. "I thought how nice it would be to take you all out for a ride on Sundays, seeing as you're always in the house now taking care of Dad and the baby."

"Sorry, darling," said Kitty, putting her arms around his neck. "I'm a vicious, unfeeling bitch, and I know you do everything for us."

Some weeks later a small Austin 7 arrived outside the house. Kitty stared at it in horror. It was at least ten years old and very battered looking.

"I'll work on it," said Bill. "Got it cheap. You won't know it when I've finished, Kitty."

"Well," she said diplomatically, "let's hope so."

Each day Kitty would bathe Kevin, brush his auburn curls and dress him in a snow-white woolly suit. Then she proudly wheeled him up and down the road shopping. The neighbors always stopped to chat with her and admire the baby. At last Kitty felt close to them and enjoyed the social gossip.

"How nice to see you settled down, Kitty," they would say, "and to have such a beautiful baby at your age, too."

Kitty took the sweet with the bitter, knowing that they referred to her past misdemeanors. She always smiled graciously at them.

One morning she was returning from the shops, pushing the pram, when she saw a large, gray shiny car next to Bill's old banger, which was propped up on three wheels waiting for another repair job at the weekend. A well-dressed young man stood at the gate talking to Dad. Who could it be? She hurried along. The man was dark with longish features, and Kitty thought there was something familiar about him.

"Here's my daughter coming down the road," she heard Dad say.

The young man turned to greet her. "I am Howard Sneiderman," he said. "I believe you knew my late father quite well."

Kitty was astonished. "Ike Sneiderman? Is he dead?

Oh, I am sorry. You're his son? I knew I'd seen you before—you were only a small boy then, and you look like your father."

"Can I talk with you in private, madam?" he asked. His voice was very serious.

"Yes, come in," said Kitty, taking him into the front room, which was reasonably tidy apart from the step-ladder and the box of tools that Bill had deposited in there. "Put the kettle on, Dad," called Kitty. "Well, Howard, what's all this about?" She knew it was about Melissa. She was going to hear news of her at last. Her heart pounded with excitement.

"Well, I'm a solicitor now. Dad died two years ago—it was a blessing really, because he suffered so."

"He was a fine man. I knew him well when he lived in the East End," Kitty said.

"Well, that's what we have to discuss. I took over my father's affairs, and he was custodian of your foster daughter's estate."

"You have heard from Melissa?" asked Kitty anxiously.

"Well, yes and no." Howard Sneiderman seemed hesitant. "She did contact me last year when she was eighteen and getting married. She received the residue of her money, which was not a lot. Most of it had gone into paying for school fees. But there is still some stock to be disposed of, so I tried to contact her and have only just been successful."

Kitty waited expectantly. Melissa had repented; she was sure she had asked to see her.

Howard went on. "It's not good news, I'm afraid. In fact, it's very bad. She was killed five months ago in a car crash on a south coast road. Both she and her husband died; only the child survived. Luckily the baby was on the back seat and was completely unharmed. But no one knew who the couple was until very recently, when the police managed to trace the owner of the car."

Kitty sat silently. She could not believe that they

could have met such a fate. She wondered what they had been doing all this time.

"Thank you for coming to tell me," she finally said in a low tone.

"I'm only glad to be able to help you," Howard replied gravely. "Is there anything you want me to do? Remember that there is a child, and, if no one claims her, she will end up in an orphanage. Here is my card, Kitty. Perhaps you could ring me when you've thought it over. On the back of the card I have written the address of South Down Hospital, where they still care for the baby. It's a little girl; I've seen her. Let me know if you need me."

Still in a daze, Kitty saw him to the door. The minute he was gone, tears flooded down her face as Dad came in to comfort her.

"It's God's will, gel," he said.

"I want her baby," said Kitty firmly. "I'll go and bring her home."

"Now, Kitty, be patient. Talk with Bill about it; don't be hasty," Dad warned.

That evening Kitty told Bill about Melissa's fate and her surviving infant. He listened with great sympathy. "Poor little kid; only eighteen and her life is thrown away. I wonder what happened?"

"I want her baby!" cried Kitty. "Let me have her, Bill."

He looked thoughtful. "They might not let you, Kitty. Your own baby is very young."

"Will you come with me, Bill, on Saturday? I'll ask Noni to come over and sit with Dad and Kevin."

"All right, darling," he promised.

Kitty dried her eyes. She could not save Melissa now, but her baby would be here and this time she would take no chances.

On Saturday morning they traveled on the train from Victoria Station. Bill wore his best suit and looked very sober and Kitty was as smart as always in a blue tailored suit that she had bought for herself when she

was in the money. Her rich chestnut hair was tied back
under a neat little hat and a bloom of excitement lit up
her fresh complexion.

"We came this way on our honeymoon," said Bill,
admiring Kitty's trim figure. "It doesn't seem so very
long ago."

"We've lived a lifetime since," said Kitty slowly,
looking straight at him. "Bill," she said, "tell me the
truth. Do you think I'm selfish trying to lumber you
with someone else's child when you work so hard to
keep us all and are so good to my old dad? I feel
terribly guilty."

Bill took her hand and looked at her with affection.
"Kitty, darling, don't jump ahead. It's possible that
they will not allow you to take the baby. You are not
actually related to it."

"Oh, Bill." Her lips trembled in disappointment. He
was going to back out, she thought, but his grip
tightened on her hands.

"Kitty, darling, I promise, on my honor, that if the
child is healthy—well, normal; you know what I mean
—that I will try my best for you. But I could not let you
involve yourself in bringing up a disabled child, however much you wanted to."

Kitty sat quiet. She still wondered what Leonard and
Melissa had been doing all this time. But now they were
gone and she would never know. Her thoughts turned
back to the child. Yes, it might not be normal. After all,
Melissa had suffered because of her father's illness, and
this baby's short life had already been very traumatic.
Trust Bill not to want to involve himself with something
like an abnormal child, but she did understand. She sat
silent and prayed: Poor little Melissa. Wherever you
are, help your baby to find its place in life. It's our fault,
mine and Bill's, that you didn't have a stable background.

Bill seemed to read her thoughts. He looked at her
very seriously. "I know it's partly my fault that you
didn't adopt Melissa in the first place when you wanted

to. For that I'm sorry, Kitty. I let you down, I know. But I won't this time. Provided the circumstances are right, you shall have this little one."

Kitty moved over to sit beside him. She kissed and hugged him. "Oh, Bill, darling, you'll never be sorry, I promise you by all that's holy. I swear I'll repay you if you let me have this child legally so that she is really mine."

The atmosphere of the hospital was kind and friendly. It was one of those small annexes attached to a big convent, with flowers and holy statues everywhere.

Sister Clare greeted them warmly in a soft Irish brogue. "I'm so pleased to see you. It was so sad that the child belonged to no one. By rights we should have parted with her to the council authorities, but I kept putting if off. I had faith that someday someone would want her."

A nurse brought in the baby. She was six months old, fair as a lily and sweet as a rose. She clasped Kitty's finger and cooed. Kitty knew everything would be all right.

In Sister Clare's sitting room they had tea while the sister took all their details. Consents were immediately set in action.

"Would you like to take her back tonight?" asked Sister Clare.

"Oh, please," cried Kitty.

"It's not usual, but the lady almoner who will settle the final details will visit you in London. The child is healthy and has been well cared for, so there is nothing to worry about. She has been baptized Catholic. I note you are also Catholic, and that was my final considera- tion. Believe me, it's not easy to part with her. She's named after me and I have a special interest in her."

That evening Kitty and Bill entered 8 Billington Road with a new member of the family. Noni was wild with joy and Dad was happy. "She's a fine child, and she'll have a good home here, thanks be to God."

"This is your little sister," Kitty informed Kevin, who was not sure what to make of the new baby.

Kitty went shopping every day with Kevin at one end of the pram and Clare at the other end. The neighbors were astonished. "Whose baby, Kitty? I didn't know you had twins."

At first Kitty would explain all about Clare, but she finally got fed up with their nosiness. One day she lost her patience completely and said loudly in the local shop for all to hear: "I got them from the milkman; one from the United Dairies and the other from the Co-op."

Everyone minded their own business after that.

Kitty was very busy with her babies. Bill worked long hours and money was scarce, but they were all happy. The house had a warm atmosphere of loving and giving, and Kitty felt that at last she had reached a safe harbor.

Of late, when the babies slept in the afternoon, she had returned to her reading. She did not write much these days, but she often got out her own manuscripts from the battered suitcase under the bed and read them through. She would sigh and stuff them all back. Well, it was only a dream, she thought—one can't have everything in this world, I suppose.

The letter was addressed to her and stamped with an American postmark. It had to be from Harry, but Kitty could not believe it. She just stood looking at the envelope, hardly daring to open it.

"Any post?" asked Bill as he put on his coat to go to work.

"No," she lied, hiding the letter behind her back.

As soon as Bill had closed the front door, Kitty tore open the envelope with trembling hands and there, in Harry's big scrawl, was a letter for her.

Dear Kitty,
    I hope that at last I have found you. I lost your

address in Suffolk and I could not find your London address until recently when I found it amongst my old papers after Pru left me. Yes, I am now a middle-aged, two-time divorcé. How are you faring, dear little Kitty?

I did not forget you, how could I? I have at last found someone who is interested in your novel, *The Grass Widows*. He is a young English publisher who has your manuscript at the moment. When you have a moment after reading this, please contact him. His office is in London. It will be to your advantage. He is wild about your work and considers it a real work of art.

I don't do much now, just living it up on past proceeds. Would love to see you anytime you might visit the States.

       Your friend and admirer, Harry Cross

At the bottom he had written a name and telephone number.

Kitty blushed scarlet and her hands trembled. It was a joke; it could not possibly be happening. What should she do? Bill would not like the idea of Harry writing to her. She could not possibly afford to destroy her happy home now.

She pushed the letter into her apron pocket and went about her chores in a daze. That afternoon when she went out to shop, she parked the pram outside a telephone kiosk and rang the number. She asked for a man called Ronald Mansford, who was on the line within a second. He spoke as if his mouth were full of peas.

"Good show," he said. "Tell me where you live and I'll come right over to see you."

"Oh, no," cried Kitty nervously, "not today. Don't come today."

"But when? Make a date, I must talk to you. It's such good stuff you've written. Don't you want it published?"

Kitty hesitated. "All right," she said. "Come tomorrow in the afternoon."

After lunch the next day, Kitty took the babies into the dining room.

"Look after them, Dad," she said. She felt very much on edge. "I'm having a visitor. They will sleep, I hope, so don't you wake them."

"Who's coming?" asked Dad. He liked to know all that went on.

"It's the insurance man," lied Kitty. "Got to talk about insuring the house."

"All right, gel, the babies will be safe with me," he said, satisfied with her answer.

She went to watch for the young man from the front room window, waiting for the arrival of this strange publisher. She saw him walking down the road. He carried a briefcase and was dressed very simply in a pair of worn jeans and a gray roll-necked jumper.

She greeted him at the door. His thin face broke into a radiant smile, and right away Kitty was attracted by his youth and his mild manners. She knew they would tick over from the start. They sat on the settee and she dug out a hidden bottle of whiskey.

"You look exactly as I knew you would," said Ronald Mansford. "When Harry talked about you, I had a picture of you in my mind."

She grimaced and looked down at her red work-worn hands. "I look a bit different now," she said. "How's Harry?" she asked abruptly.

"He's well, but a bit lonely at times, I think. I was staying at his house in the States and he showed me your manuscript, which I think is great. Don't tell me you have stopped writing. I'll be disappointed."

"With two babies and a husband, what do you expect?" Kitty replied a little bitterly.

"Well," he said as he opened his briefcase, "I've got very good news for you. I should like to make you an offer for *The Grass Widows*. I believe that it is not only a fascinating and original piece of writing, but also a book with considerable commercial appeal."

Kitty did not reply. She was not sure what he meant by any of that.

"Come on, Kitty," Ronald Mansford cajoled her, "we will have the book published in six months. And, of course, I'm going to offer you a good advance."

Kitty did not know what an advance was, but she did not like to say so.

"How much?" she queried.

"Two hundred pounds," he said.

"Two hundred pounds! You think it's worth it?" Kitty was astonished.

"Of course I do! Your book is new and fresh, and it's authentic. I've such hopes for it," he cried enthusiastically. "You have nothing to worry over; I will do all the donkey work. Come on, Kitty, take a chance." From his briefcase, Ronald Mansford pulled out a long agreement and laid it out on the table.

"Oh, well, what can I lose?" cried Kitty, signing in the place he indicated.

"I'll send you a check next week," Ronald Mansford said as he got up to go. He bent and kissed her cheek. "Here's my card, so you know where we are, and ring me whenever you like. It's been lovely meeting you after reading your work. I knew you could only be your own sweet self. I know your book is fiction, but surely it's based on some fact."

"Oh, everything in the book really happened," she said, "but not to the same person. I collected the material from different sources, mostly from people I met."

"Well, you go on, Kitty, because you're a born storyteller. Don't stop now," he said as he left.

Kitty sat down to regain her composure. She could not believe this was happening. Her two life's ambitions—to have children and to be a writer—had at last come true. *The Grass Widows* was to be published. She was indeed a writer now—this was one in the eye for her old headmistress, Miss Victoria.

She smiled as she remembered that last day at school when, as a scrawny waif of a girl, she had announced that she wanted to write. She had come so far since then, despite the hardships—or perhaps because of them.

She felt a wave of happiness rush through her. Nelly Kelly, the grass widow, she thought, was like another child she had given birth to years before when her life had been so tough. At last they were all together now. She did love Bill, she was sure of that, and she always had done, but she also had her babies to enrich her life more than ever before.

She knew then that she would go on writing as well as being a good wife and a loving mother. And a daughter, too, she thought, as she watched Dad through the window, shuffling about in the front garden. Everything was happening at once, but her life was all working out. She was fulfilled at last.